Heartspeed

Daniel J. Stutzman

For Pam. My Ride or Die, The Love of My Life, and the one who always believed in me, even when the months turned into years. I could never have written this book without your unwavering support.

Prologue

The memories haunt me. We didn't have to lose him. I could have stopped it, but I just didn't know before she took him...there.

My name is Leigh Shires. I don't know where I'll be when you read this, and I don't know where you are or what year you are reading, but my story started on Earth, on a Pennsylvania farm about forty miles north of Pittsburgh, in the USA. The year was 2225. I was eighteen.

Telling stories isn't my forte, but he told me I should write everything down, from start to finish, as if it'll be therapeutic or something. I keep telling him I'll be fine, I'll work through it in my own way, but he says that I still whimper in my sleep.

Chapter One

The Garden

Joe still hasn't liked my post from last night. It's a super cute picture of us from the Memorial Day fairgrounds last week. The Ferris wheel is the perfect background with all of its lights and riders. Now there are 43 likes, and not one of them is from him.

I return my phone to my pocket and grip the wooden fence surrounding the herb garden. This is usually my peaceful place, but there is no peace for me this morning. Joe's been distant lately, and I can't figure out why. We haven't even had sex in probably two weeks now.

It's not like I don't already have a reason to be nervous, with my final dance competition happening later today. I try not to grind my teeth.

The sound of the mailman rolling up the road pulls me out of my thoughts. Thankful for the distraction, I make my way down to the mailbox.

His smile is visible from three telephone poles away. Old Hank is probably eighty years old, and proposes to me at least once a month. It's funny, and I can't help but return the smile as he approaches.

"Speedy delivery," he says with a wink while handing the mail to me.

I wink back. "How are ya today, Hank?"

"They gave me a stack of these flyers to deliver to every single mailbox. Saturdays are usually my easy day. What a pain in the tookus."

I shuffle through my mail to see if I got one. Yep, here it is. They're looking for volunteers for that colonization thing I keep hearing about on the radio. It looks like they'll be screening potential colonists today at the abandoned clothing store in the same plaza as my dance studio. It's going to be a crowded mess. I roll my eyes and hold it up to him. "What do you think of this?"

"Beats me, Ms. Shires. I'm far too old for those shenanigans. Besides, all that fine print is too small for these old eyes. Well, I best get goin' if I want to make it home for Jeopardy. See you again soon, I hope."

He steps on the accelerator and is on his way with a lurch. And now I know those old eyes are why my neighbor's mail winds up in my mailbox occasionally.

Once back in my house, I throw the mail in the trash. It's all junk.

My cap and gown from last night's high school graduation lie in a heap on the kitchen table, just where I left them. We barely got home last night, and Mom left for work. She said she had to pull strings to even make it to graduation, and was sorry she couldn't make it to my competition today. *Break a leg,* she said. She's in Puerto Rico this morning; she's a flight attendant.

My favorite thing about Saturdays this time of year is that they've been dance competition days for as long as I can remember. I won't know what to do with myself during the weekends next season. After today, I will have aged out of the league. I still can't believe it's the end. I've been dancing there since I was three years old.

There's a thump from the second floor as my dog Baxter jumps from my bed and lopes down the stairs to greet me. I pat his head, then fill his food dish.

I push my graduation stuff aside and sit down with a bowl of cereal. While Bax crunches his food, I try to time my crunches with his. He looks at me for a second, then gets back to business.

He's a Sheltie/shepherd mix. We found him at an animal rescue, and they told us that people kept bringing him back because he escaped from crates and chewed everything in sight when left home alone. That's not an issue for us because we have a veterinarian-grade crate for him. A local clinic closed its doors and sold it to us cheap.

Now that I think about it, I need to ask Joe to swing by and let Baxter out later. I type a text to him in between cereal bites.

Maybe when he responds, I'll tell him to look at that picture I posted.

This whole dance thing really has me in a contemplative mood. I wander to the kitchen window that looks out on our big oak tree, the one I've climbed a thousand times, the one I fell out of when I was ten and broke my arm. Birds jockey for seed at the feeder that hangs from one of the branches.

This old farmhouse sits on fifty-seven acres of rolling

Pennsylvanian foothills. The tractor sits by the barn and reminds me of old times with Dad when we went for rides through the woods. I still think about him at times like this when it's quiet, before the day starts. I should give him a call soon.

We used to have animals, but Mom sold them off to other farmers when money got tight. We tried to keep up with the cornfields for a while, but the combine stopped working and the repair bill was about ten thousand dollars. It's still out there somewhere, rusting where it died. Nowadays, we just tend the herb garden. We sell some cilantro and basil, but our money mostly comes from Mom's job.

My phone vibrates.

JOE

Sorry, you know I'll be busy later with the party. I'm dating you, not your dog.

I stare at my phone for several seconds in disbelief. Did he really just type that to me? I stand up, take what's left of my cereal, and dump it in the sink.

"Well Bax, looks like you're staying with me, at least for a while."

I grab the leash and he does a spinning leap into the air because, to him, the leash means it's time to jog. I've always been a runner, and I ran on the high school track team. I like to stay in shape for dance, but Mom says I'm just addicted to the endorphins. Either way, I need all the endorphins I can get because it's time to drop in on Joe and see what the hell his problem is. I don't deserve this kind of treatment.

I inhale deeply and bound back out into the cool, spring air, Baxter loping alongside me.

Chapter Two

Infidelity

The ground glides under my feet, and Baxter follows along at an easy pace. Walk, run, he doesn't care, as long as he gets to join me.

Joe doesn't live too far, and Baxter especially likes to join me on trips to his house because Joe gives him hot dog chunks. Going to Joe's house is a big deal for Bax.

It takes about twenty minutes and I work up a light sweat. He lives just outside of the plan near the fairgrounds where I took that selfie last week.

It looks like they already got started with the decorations last night. A big HAPPY 25th ANNIVERSARY banner stretches across the rain gutter on the house, and the tent is already erected over the picnic table.

A Toyota Corolla sits in the driveway. It looks oddly familiar. Where have I seen it before?

Baxter looks up at me, confused at why we aren't moving. I take a few tentative steps toward the car and wipe the morning dew off of the window. A pair of pink sunglasses sits on the console and several fast food wrappers litter the passenger seat and floor. It's a slob's car. A girl slob.

Whose car is this? I'm wracking my brain. A relative who's here for the anniversary party? My intuition says no. There's a green vest in the back seat, the kind workers wear in the service sector. I open the back door as quietly as possible. Baxter tries to jump in, but I pull him back by the collar. "No, Bax." He sits and cocks his head at me.

I reach inside and take the vest. I know that perfume. I turn the vest over and see the name tag over the burger iron-on and my blood turns to ice.

Erica.

Erica who works at Last Burger.

Erica from my dance team.

There's only one reason she'd be here at this hour. She's always been friendly with Joe, but I never saw this coming. I toss the vest back inside and slam the door.

I stomp up his porch stairs and lean on the doorbell.

After a minute of my door-belling, he yanks the door open and stands before me in his boxers, his face flushed with annoyance. As soon as he sees me, his mouth drops open. Behind him are two suitcases.

I scowl at the suitcases and then at him. "Really, Joe?"

He's still reeling. "Wait—"

My voice is ice. "You thought I wouldn't find out."

There's a voice from farther inside. "Joe, what—"

It's Erica. She turns the corner and sees me. She pulls a bathrobe closed.

I try to keep my voice as steady as iron. I stare at Erica. By the look on her face, I'm guessing Joe assured her I wouldn't catch them. "How could you?"

She waves her hands in front of her. "I can explain. I'm going away. We're friends."

Joe moves to block my view. "Please, it didn't mean anything. It was just goodbye sex."

I feel like he just punched me in the gut. "Goodbye sex? Fine. It's goodbye sex, all right." I slap him in the face.

Baxter interrupts us with a sharp bark, and Joe looks down at him with what has to be the saddest expression I've ever seen. Now that he has Joe's attention, he waits for his treat, mouth hanging open.

I return my attention to Erica. "I thought you were leaving. So, leave."

She runs a hand through her greasy hair. "I'm sorry, I—"

Joe rubs his temples. "Leigh, please stop. My parents are going to come out." He sees that I'm drawing a big breath, and he tries to shut the door, but my foot is in the jamb.

My voice rises. "Good, let them know their son is a cheater. Maybe they can teach you the secret of 25 years since you can't even manage 25 months."

As if on queue, his mother's voice comes from another room, "Joe? What's going on?"

Erica turns around and runs back to the bedroom.

"Don't even think about showing your traitorous face at competition," I yell at her back, then pull my foot from the door and slam it myself.

I stare at the closed door, the door I walked through so many times. That was *my* bathrobe. Baxter seems confused and jumps up on the door and licks the glass. He gives another hopeful yelp for a hot dog.

And that's it. Eventually, Baxter settles back down from the glass and relaxes. I turn away without another word and walk down past the car. I take one last look at the burger wrappers inside and hope that she won't be able to fit into her costume next year.

Maybe getting cheated on feels different for different people. Right now, Joe feels like a colossal waste of time and emotional investment. Why can't men ever be satisfied? To think that I was giving 100% and he was giving me 50%. It's betrayal, and it sucks.

This is how Dad must have felt when he saw that text on Mom's phone. When it happened, Mom admitted to joining the mile-high club with some guy in a bathroom above Detroit. She crushed Dad's heart, and all she kept saying was that she didn't know how that guy got her number. Ever since, I don't really talk much with her. Could we be close again? I don't know.

Cheating. It's how relationships end in my world.

I break into a jog to leave them behind, at least physically. Mentally, the image of Erica in my bathrobe is all I see.

Dammit. *Why?*

My hand still bristles from the slap, and wetness finally springs to my eyes.

Chapter Three

A Fateful Breakfast

Runner's high. It's hard to feel "high" when your emotions are running *low*, but in a few minutes, Baxter and I are back into the rhythm of the run and the trees drift by as my steady footfalls add to the music of the morning—the birds, the rustling of leaves in the breeze, and the occasional jealous dog barking as Baxter and I pass by. My mood improves by the inch.

I think I'll just run to the dance studio and get a shower there. If I get there early enough, I can beat the crowd of people for that colony thing. Not to mention I don't want to go home; I'd just have to run past Joe's house again.

The dance studio is a renovated old movie theater and has been my second home for almost my entire life. It has a musty smell and could use a paint job, but the classes have always been affordable, and I like the teachers and my teammates (except for one) on the dance team.

It's still early and nobody is there when I arrive, so I unlock the door and head in. They have complementary snacks for the dancers, so I grab a water and a granola bar out of the basket. I get some cheese out of the fridge for Baxter.

They kept some of the original movie seats and installed them at the entrance. I find the least-lumpy one and lean my head back, breathing the dusty air, trying to process everything. I'll need to get Joe out of my head if I'm going to perform well today. After a few minutes, I stand and let Baxter off his leash, telling him to be a good boy. He knows to stay when I say that, but he follows me anyway as I walk to the washroom.

There's a single shower in there with a frosted window up high to let some light in. I always thought that it was weird that they have a window in the shower, but Miss Tracy told me it was because it was there before they put a washroom in, and it would have cost more to have it sealed-up, so they stuck the film on it and called it done.

It occurs to me I don't have a change of clothes, so this running outfit will have to do for now. I won't be putting the leotard on until we get to the competition. I'll be pretty ripe by the end of the day, but I'll deal.

The shower doesn't have much pressure, so it takes longer. I'm about halfway through when I hear the dull roar of many voices outside. I need to get dressed before some yahoo wanders in looking for a toilet. I rip the shower curtain open and grab the towel. I get myself mostly dry and then bound across the room to my clothes and whip them on.

I open the door to the studio and peer out. There are hundreds out there, but the bulk of them is a little farther away, near the strip mall.

Baxter and I leave the studio and get back into the morning sunshine. My hair is soaking wet, and I probably didn't get all the shampoo out. This isn't my best morning ever.

The throng of people mill about. It's as if they're waiting for the stores to open for a holiday sale. A line forms at an old clothing store that's been closed and boarded-up for the last couple of years. Nearby, three white vans stand in a neat row. On the side of each there is a red "G" logo made from what looks like a twisted DNA strand. Underneath the logo is the word GENOMICA.

None of the stores are open yet except for the diner, and it is busy. I wander over to enjoy the smells. The outdoor seating is full, and judging by what I can see through the windows, the inside is just as bad. The wait staff run between the outside tables. A guy in uniform is sitting by himself at one. He catches me staring, and I look away, pretending to look at the menu posted in the diner's window.

When I think it's safe, I let my gaze drift back to him. Now he's staring at his phone, clearly confused by what he's seeing. He looks maybe a little older than me, and probably a little taller. His uniform is stark black with a silver aircraft pin on the left breast. He has a bouquet of pink carnations and red roses sitting across the table while he feasts on a huge garden salad with extra cherry tomatoes and black olives. I didn't even know you could order a salad for breakfast.

He glances at me again and I look away again, my stare boring a hole into the breakfast menu. Breakfast muffins are $10.00. I can see out of the corner of my eye that he's still looking at me. French Toast is $20.00. I'm really studying this thing.

"Hey," he calls out.

He's not talking to me. Why would he be talking to me?

"You with the dog. Hey, do you have a second?"

Yep, he's talking to me. I look over and he's staring at me over his coffee cup while he takes a steaming sip. His eyes are very clear and intense. I take a step toward him and stop. He has a piece of lettuce on his chin. He's a little less intimidating that way, actually. I'm not sure what to say, so I stand there, eyebrows raised in anticipation.

He swallows and puts his mug down. "Hi. Are you from around here?"

"Hi. Yes."

"The signal here is crap and my phone maps aren't loading. Can you give me directions?"

I don't feel like dealing with people right now, but there's something about him I like and I want to keep talking. And he's right, the cell signal here *is* crap. Welcome to backwoods Pennsylvania. "Where are you trying to go?"

"My parents moved here a couple of years ago and I'm trying to find their new place. They live in Fox Chapel."

"Fox Chapel? That's in Pittsburgh, almost an hour away."

"It is? Oh." He nods at the bouquet sitting across from him. "They're supposed to be for my mother, but it doesn't look like I have enough time."

I absently stroke Baxter between the ears. He nestles close to me and does his happy pant. "What kind of work do you do?"

"I'm a pilot."

"Oh, I was wondering about the uniform. What airline are you with?"

"No airline. I'm with Genomica."

I never heard of Genomica, but I don't want to sound ignorant, so I change tack. "How's the salad?"

He seems surprised for a second. Maybe he expected a different reaction. "Um, good. It's great, actually."

"For breakfast though?"

"On the station, we have loads of veggies, but not like these. Nothing tastes like home, ya know?"

My hand comes to a rest on Baxter. "Station?"

He looks askance at me and motions to the throng of people in the strip mall. "Yeah, the space station, you know, over New Mesopotamia. Aren't you with this crowd?"

"No, I'm just here by coincidence."

"Really? Wow. Well, are you hungry at all? I wouldn't mind a little company." He reaches across the table and moves the bouquet away from the place setting, then motions to the chair.

I sit, and Baxter curls up at my feet under the table, just like I trained him to do. The server comes over and asks me what I want. I tell her I'll have the salad, too. Not to be outdone, Baxter munches on a nearby clump of dandelions. He loves the things. After she leaves, I ask my pilot friend his name.

"Oh, it's Celeres. I'm sorry I didn't introduce myself earlier. What's yours?"

"Leigh."

"Hi Leigh, it's a pleasure to meet you." He extends his hand, and we give a slight shake.

"You too, Celeres. You have lettuce on your chin."

His hand snaps self-consciously to his face. "Oh, thanks." He picks it off, then gives a crooked grin. "Well, your shirt is on backwards."

"*What?*" But I see that he's right; the tag is sticking out at my neck. I wasn't exactly paying attention to detail when I jumped into my clothes.

There is a pause, and then we both start talking, then

stop. Another pause. There is an old beat-up speaker above our table playing a piano melody, and I bob my head in time with the music to make the moment a little less awkward.

He clears his throat. "Sorry, what were you saying?"

I take a moment to tuck a napkin into my neckline to hide my tag. "What's New Mesopotamia?"

He laughs. "You know the space colony thing? That's where it is: New Mesopotamia. It's a planet several light years away."

I raise my eyebrows. "Why here?"

He shrugs. "You mean for colonists? Why not here?"

He's interrupted by our server as she brings my salad. She bustles off to wipe a table down before I can even thank her. There's quite a line of people now waiting to be seated. It looks like I got the same extra portion of tomatoes and olives that he did. He notices my expression and offers to help, and I let him steal some tomatoes from my plate.

He pops three cherry tomatoes into his mouth, closes his eyes, and sighs, as if they're the best things he's ever eaten.

He finally opens his eyes and realizes I'm watching him with amusement. "Sorry, I just haven't had them in some time. So what do you do?"

"I just graduated from high school, and I work on a farm."

He nods. "College?"

"Maybe. I have a friend at Ohio State. I was thinking about that."

"Good choice. Hey, if you work on a farm, you must know something about growing vegetables, right?"

Now I've met a lot of guys, and not one has ever asked me anything like that in the first fifteen minutes, let alone one who claims to come from outer space. For my part, this is the first time I met a guy with my hair soaking wet, wearing no makeup, and my shirt on backwards. Under normal circumstances, I'd be intrigued, but after Joe this morning, I just don't have an appetite for chemistry.

When I say nothing, he continues. "I do a little farming myself. Well, maybe just gardening. Here, look at this."

He digs around in one of his zipper pockets and produces a little baggie. He appears to consider or even reconsider for a moment, then shrugs and gives it a little toss across the table. It lands beside my plate and a few seeds roll around inside. They almost look like a mini version of the candy corn you get at Halloween. They're barely bigger than grains of rice.

I lean in to get a better look. "Where did you get these? I've never seen seeds like this before, and I've seen a lot of seeds."

"From work. I don't think they have a name yet. They're sort of like carrots, though. I can't get them to grow for me."

I pick up the baggie and hold it up to get a good look inside. "Well, they don't *look* like carrot seeds, but if they are anything like carrots, just sow them shallowly and keep the earth moist. They should germinate for you in two to three weeks."

I hand the bag back to him, and we eat in silence for a while.

Across the parking lot, people file into that boarded-up old clothing store. I lean to get a better look. "Are you going to take all these people to the planet?"

He shakes his head no. "Only a few will make the cut. There's a psychological evaluation they have to do, and we do a DNA test."

"Why a DNA test?"

"I don't exactly know. I think it has something to do with staying healthy on the planet."

"So what's the catch?"

"Well, you leave your life behind while you're gone. There are no special trips home because the transport costs are so high."

"Is it safe?"

He takes a furtive look around and leans forward. "What do *you* think?"

I lower my voice. "So it's not?"

"I'll put it to you this way. I live in the station. That's what I trust. I have a garden on the planet, yes, and I sometimes go camping, but I spend as little time down there as possible. Would I want a friend or family member to join that colony? Hell no. There are way too many unknowns."

I nod slowly.

He looks over my shoulder and squints. "Uh oh, this can't be good." He dabs his mouth with his napkin.

I turn around to see what's going on. A guy dressed just like him approaches. "Sorry for interrupting," he says.

"No problem, what's up, Brisk?"

"It's go time."

Celeres pops another three tomatoes in his mouth. "Already? I'm busy."

"I know. Sorry, Captain," the stranger says, and then seems to notice me again. "Excuse me, ma'am." He turns and leaves before I can respond.

The server must have been waiting for a good time to pounce because she brings a to-go box for me and slaps the check down in front of Celeres.

He grabs the check. "I guess they want to turn this table. I have to get going, anyway."

"Everything okay?"

"Yeah, I think so. There are some protesters giving us trouble. You know, the anti-col crowd."

"Huh?"

"Sorry, anti-colonist. I need to fly some VIPs out as a precaution."

When we stand, he is indeed taller than me; the top of his shoulder is at my eye level. He stoops to pet Baxter, who licks him all over the face.

Celeres wipes the dog slobber off with his sleeve. "Friendly dog."

I give an apologetic grin and hand him a napkin. "Maybe a little too friendly."

He gathers up his belongings and the bouquet. "So, what are you doing the rest of the day?"

"I have to dance today."

"Oh, you're a dancer? What kind?"

I lean back and give him a cautious look. "What kind? I hope you're not expecting a lap dance."

"No."

I raise an eyebrow. "Pole dance?"

He smiles, and his teeth are white and perfect. "No... yes? I mean, you could be. You're in amazing shape."

"Alright, alright, I'll cut you some slack. It's nothing like that. I'm on a competitive dance team, that's all. I should head back to the studio. My teammates will show up soon."

He smiles. "It was nice meeting you, Leigh. Good luck with your competition."

"Thanks. I hope you're still able to see your Mom. Good luck with your carrots."

He pats his zipper pocket where he keeps the seeds. "I think I can handle it. Hey—"

"Yes?"

"If they don't germinate in three weeks, who do I call?" He holds his phone out with a questioning expression.

"Thanks for lunch, but I just got out of a relationship. I don't think I'm ready. I'm sorry."

"No problem, I'm sort of in the same boat. Hey if you let me call, it'll be strictly carrot business, I swear."

Like I said, this guy is completely original. What the hell, I'll give it to him but I'm not going to ask him for his. I shrug and take his phone and put my number into it.

He looks at it for a moment. "Thanks, Leigh Shires."

"What's *your* last name, Celeres?"

"Nightingale."

"Ok then, you're welcome, Captain Nightingale."

I turn and walk back to the dance studio with Baxter's leash in one hand and the to-go box in the other. Interesting guy, that Celeres. I feel like he's watching me go, but I don't turn around. If there's ever a next time, maybe I'll fix my hair first.

Chapter Four

Dance Team

Soon, I'm just another lost soul in the crowd, surrounded by people from all walks of life. There are teenagers, people in their twenties, thirties, men, women. There's even an old guy with white hair in a suit that looks like he bought it for his first job interview out of high school. Baxter lopes along beside me, oblivious to the lot of them. I feel like several people are giving me sidelong glances, thinking that I'm cutting in front of them or something. As more people file into the old store, I keep my course straight to the studio, but then I stop short and look down at Baxter.

"Hey Bax, we have some time. Let's take a break from this madness and get you that hot dog."

Oh, he knows what a hot dog is. He jumps about three feet into the air with excitement. "Come on, buddy," I say, and we make our way to the Wiener Wagon on the far side of the shopping center.

The vendor sees me coming. "They aren't hot yet. I just put them on."

"It's ok, it's for my dog. One hot dog without the bun, please."

He chuckles and pulls a fresh one out of the pack, spilling hot dog juice on the ground. "Here, it's on the house."

"Thank you, kind sir." I hand it down to Baxter, who gives it a sniff, and then wolfs it down in about two seconds. "See Bax, you can still have hot dogs. Who needs Joe, any—"

"Are you with this crazy crowd?" the hot dog guy asks.

"Me? No, I didn't even know this was happening until five minutes ago. I go to the dance studio over there." I nod in its direction. It occurs to me that once I go to the studio, we'll drive straight to the competition. I have to get Baxter home. I wasn't thinking clearly when I left Joe's.

"How would you like to sell hot dogs?" His voice penetrates my foggy brain.

"What? Are you offering me a job or something?"

"Maybe. I might even sell you the wagon." He hands me a brochure. "Look at this. It looks like a pretty sweet gig."

It's the same brochure that everyone's been getting in the mail. It shows a green planet against a starry background with the words, "Fresh Start" along the top.

Get a fresh start!
Be one of the first to travel to New Mesopotamia
Free transport
Free lodging
Free meals
Low Risk
Modest Pay
Accepting colonist applications
June 1st - 3rd only

Under that, in fine print: *All Life insurance voided*

upon acceptance into the program. Interstellar travel carries risks, including loss of life. Return to or communication with Earth is not guaranteed. New planet carries undiscovered mutagens and pathogens. Possible encounters with intelligent indigenous life are likely.

I hand it back to him. "You're doing it?"

"I think so. It looks like today's crowd is already pretty high, though. Was the same as this yesterday. Tomorrow's the last day, so I'm gonna sleep on it."

"Well, good luck. Thanks for the hot dog." I thread my way back through the crowd to the studio.

New Mesopotamia. Wouldn't that be something? I look up into the sky and wonder what it could be like to fly in a spaceship or go for a jog on an entirely different planet. All of this hoopla will be gone in a couple of days, and my little town will be back to normal. A small part of me is sad that I'll probably never see Celeres again.

God, why is he in my head? Celeres, Joe...men are making me crazy. I need to take a serious vacation with my dog and nobody else. Preferably on Earth.

I lean down and hug Bax's neck. "What do you think, Bax? Does true love really exist?"

He licks my cheek in response, and I let out a giggle. "I mean besides you. Come on, let's get going."

Bax and I approach the studio, and there's Megan, who I haven't seen in a year, standing outside and talking to some of our team members. She sees me and waves wildly. Bax lurches forward when he sees her, almost pulling my arm out of its socket. I'm just as excited to see her, and we both run forward. I release the leash so he can give her a proper greeting.

She's still weathering Bax's tongue onslaught when I get there. "Hi Meg!"

"Hi Leigh. I was in the neighborhood, so…"

"You coming to the competition?"

"Yeah! I miss this team like crazy."

"How's college?"

"Oh, you know. Study, party, teach spin classes, dance at the basketball games. I'm keeping busy."

I give her a hug.

She looks through the open door to the studio where my coach is, staring me down. "I think you're late."

"I am. Hey Meg, can you please do me a favor before you drive to the competition?"

"Once a best friend, always a best friend. What can I help you with, Leigh?"

"Can you please take Bax and my to-go box to my house?"

"Absolutely. Now get in there, and have a cracking great dance today."

As soon as I walk into the studio, Miss Tracy sees me and her mouth drops open. "What happened to you? You look like you wrestled a swarm of bees and the bees won."

When my hair dries on its own with no product, it poofs out and I look like a wild woman. I don't know if it's the auburn, the curls, or what, but before I can count to three, my friends are hustling me over to a seat where they can fix me and pummel me with questions.

"You know your shirt is on backwards, right?"

"What are we going to do with that hair? We have to leave in fifteen minutes."

"Did I just see your dog?"

"Where's your makeup? Here we'll use mine."

But I stay quiet, and they stay amazing, like they always are. After the fifteen minutes, I have my costume on and I look pretty good.

"Erica isn't here yet," says Miss Tracy.

"I don't think she's coming," I say, patting down my costume. "I just caught her with Joe at his house."

"Caught her?" asks my friend Terrie.

"Caught her. Caught them. In the act."

They all freeze, and it feels like forever until it sinks in for everyone. Terrie is the first to talk: "Oh no, I'm so sorry." She puts her arms around me.

Everyone is sad, but not surprised about the whole thing, considering how well the two of them got along. They do their best to comfort me. Miss Tracy has us wait an extra ten minutes anyway, just in case Erica comes, but she doesn't. It's going to be harder to win today without her being there, but I can't compete with her beside me. Not today. Not after what she did.

I push myself away and let out a deep breath. "The show must go on. Let's change the subject and get out of here before I ruin my mascara."

We pile into cars and head to the competition. Joe tries to call me twice while we're en route, but I block his number.

The competition goes well, and we're able to dance in a closer formation to make up for our missing person. There's a part of our dance where we're supposed to look sad. All I have to do is think of Joe, and I'm able to manage a couple of tears for it.

They read the scores at the end of the night, and we win by two-tenths of a point. Our team is strong—nobody is head and shoulders above the others. In competition, we are greater than the sum of our parts, and we get it done. I'm tired, though. Dancing always takes a lot out of me. That, combined with the emotional drain of the day, leaves me exhausted.

Afterward, we're clearing out of the gym, and one of the organizers approaches my teammates and I. She seems rushed. "Is one of you Leigh Shires?"

My first thought is that something happened with Mom's flight. "Yes, what's wrong?"

"Oh, nothing. I'm sorry, I didn't mean to scare you. There's something for you at the concession stand."

I'm way too jumpy right now. I do some breathing exercises on my way over. I'm guessing Mom called in a candy-gram for me, which sounds amazing right now. I haven't eaten since that salad earlier.

When I get there, I tell the concession lady who I am, and she reaches under the counter for a grocery bag and hands it to me. I look inside. It's the bouquet from this morning, the roses and carnations. Celeres. Wow. Was he here? Did he see my performance? I look around, but don't see him. It's all just a bunch of dancers and their parents heading home after a long day. How did this get here? I ask the lady, but she says that one of the younger dancers gave it to her. She doesn't remember which. She thinks we all look the same. Truth be told, we kind of do in our costumes.

I should be charmed, but in reality, I can't help but feel weird holding the bouquet that he bought for his mom. I guess it's the thought that counts, plus the flowers bring back memories of the pleasant meal we had earlier. My teammates assume they're from Joe, and they curse his name. When I correct them and let them know they're from Celeres, they seemed shocked.

Terrie guides me to her car as we walk out of the gym. "Wow, you move fast."

A couple of others join us and hop in the back seat.

Soon, we're on our way to Miss Tracy's pool. We don't wash our costumes during the season, and our tradition is to go swimming in them at the end. I'm the only one "aging out" of the team this year, so this is my last dip.

The whole car wants to know who Celeres is, and what's going on with him. I try to explain what happened—how he finessed my number, and how he's a pilot for Genomica. Judging by the flowers, he must be at least a little interested, but he'll be gone, probably forever, after tomorrow.

Of course, they all want to know if he's good looking. He is, I guess. I tell them he looked like he kept himself in good shape, and had a mop of dark hair, square features, maybe of Italian descent. He looked sharp in that uniform, and the more I talk about him, the better-looking I remember him.

They can't believe I didn't snap a lunch photo for Insta-gram. Riiiiight, that would not have been awkward at all.

After that conversation, my mind wanders as we travel. "What did he mean about goodbye sex? Where's she going?"

Terrie looks at me for a second, then looks back at the

road. Her eyes seem sad. She slows the car down and parks at the side of the road. "Leigh, I have to tell you something." The girls in the back seat were looking at their phones, but now they give Terrie and me their full attention.

I have a feeling this is about to suck. "What?"

"We knew about Erica and Joe. We tried to keep it a secret until after the season. They've been messing around for a couple of months now."

"*You knew and didn't tell me?*"

"We just wanted to keep the team in one piece. Erica felt so guilty all the time. Last night, she said she was going to end it with Joe and leave town after the competition."

"You put the team above our friendship," I say, hurling words like rocks. "What if it were the other way around? What if *I* knew your boyfriend was banging Erica, and I kept it from you?"

"It was wrong, Leigh. We just thought it would go away when she left."

"When she left? I can't believe this. Where the hell is she going, anyway?"

One girl in the backseat digs a piece of paper out of her purse. It's the New Mesopotamia brochure.

I snatch it from her. "Seriously?"

I whip the car door open and jump out. Terrie leans across the seat. "Please come back, Leigh. At least let me drive you home."

"No thanks. Have fun at the pool."

I whip my flowers at her windshield so hard that several petals fly off in a red and pink flurry. I climb the embankment beside the road and march away. I'm not too far from home, especially if I cut through a couple of cornfields. At least this way, they can't drive alongside me and make this any more pathetic than it already is.

By the time I get to my house, it's after midnight. Baxter barks a few times, but stops when he sees that it's me. I've never seen a tail wag so fast. He's so happy. I let him out to do his business, and I fill his food bowl.

When it comes back in, he goes straight to his food. I sit at the table and devour a bowl of Cheerios.

My mind wanders, and I think about the poor bouquet that I whipped at Terrie's car. Why did Celeres send it to me? Does he have intentions or just doesn't want the flowers to go to waste? Either way, I smile for Celeres's mom. She has a pretty wonderful son, even if he wasn't able to get those flowers to her. I pull my phone out and check it to see if there were any calls or texts. Nothing.

I finish the cereal and do my dishes along with what remains in the sink from today. A couple splashes of water hit my dance costume and I think about everyone at the pool party. I can't believe they kept Joe and Erica a secret from me. They all knew. It makes me look like such a fool.

I head upstairs and jump in the shower. As I scrub the day's grime off, I blast some loud electronic dance music from my phone. Once I'm clean, I brush my teeth and straighten my hair.

Celeres has been on my mind during all of this, and I decide that there is something I have to do. I find some yoga pants in my dresser, and a long sleeve T-shirt. I pull on a fresh pair of running shoes and head downstairs. I grab my backpack from the entryway and jam a small blanket from the couch into it.

I should be back tomorrow morning before Mom gets home, but just in case, I dash off a quick note for her.

I kneel to pet Baxter. "Tonight's going to be different, little buddy. Go sleep by yourself. You be good."

He's just a dog, I know, but he's a stickler for routine and he knows that tonight isn't going according to plan. He licks my face, and I scruff his head. I stand, keeping eye contact.

"Go up to bed now. I left my bedroom door open."

I turn to leave, and he follows me anyway. I have to shove his nose back into the house just so I can close the door.

Right before I make it to the end of the driveway, I hear the pitter-patter of paws, and there's Baxter right beside me, leash in mouth. How...

Then I look back and see a jagged hole in the kitchen window screen where he jumped through. "*Baxter!*"

He looks at me as if to say that he is coming, whether I like it or not. And he's doing the happy pant that I can never resist.

"Suit yourself." I know I could go back into the house and shut all the windows to keep him from following, but it's true—tonight isn't going according to plan, and I have a feeling that I may need him for whatever is in store.

I hook him up to the leash, and we walk into the dark together.

Chapter Five

No Dogs Allowed

After a few blocks, we turn a corner, and there is Joe's house up ahead. Erica's Corolla is gone. There are a few lights on inside, and I take a peek through the gaps in the curtains. Inside, he crosses the living room into the kitchen. I'm tempted to linger, but we continue past. Baxter tugs in that direction, but I pull him back.

I wonder if he saw us? A small part of me wants to give him another piece of my mind, because I can't believe that he thought he'd just stay with me and never tell me what he and Erica did. But I keep going and don't look back.

Soon, we're past the house, walking deeper into the night. "We're going back to the strip mall, Bax." My voice is a little shaky. *I'm* a little shaky. Seeing Joe affected me more than I expected.

It's a beautiful night, if a little on the balmy side. Thoughts of the day continue to swirl in my head until the lights of the strip mall come into sight. All the people here the last couple of days have filled the parking lot with litter. I pass a parked car with Texas plates and a sleeping couple inside. A flickering collection of weathered street lamps light the area.

Bax and I wander over to the diner. I find the table where Celeres and I had lunch. I pause for a moment, remembering the strange seeds, the huge salads, me giving him my number. For a second, I think of how funny it would be if he showed up here right now, reminiscing about the same things. Stuff like that doesn't happen in real life, though.

Next, we go to the Wiener Wagon. The guy covered it with a patchy vinyl tarp. I shouldn't be doing this, and I feel a little dirty, but I lift the cover a few inches, and then a little more.

I take a deep breath, look around to make sure I'm still alone, and yank the tarp off of the wagon. It falls into a heap on the asphalt, and Baxter goes over to sniff it. I hope there aren't hidden cameras around, but I need to search this thing.

Like a librarian looking for a book on the stacks, my fingers sweep the contents of the cart: salt, pepper, pickles... There it is: the brochure. He has it tucked between the ketchup and mustard bottles. I unfold it and look at it again. Maybe I do want a fresh start. Maybe a new life wouldn't be so bad on New Mesopotamia. What would it be like to help colonize a new planet? Plus, Celeres will be there.

Parts of me are still at war—the part that hates men right now, and the part that wants to see him again. It might also be a good idea for *me* to go somewhere, away from Joe, away from my so-called dance friends. There's nothing left for me here.

The dance studio stands across the way, empty. Like my heart. I still remember walking through those doors for the first time, making Mom and Dad stay until my lesson was over. So many memories: good, and now bad. Baxter sits and leans against me. He always seems to sense my mood. I scratch him under his collar. My eyes glass over at the thought of leaving him behind, but I put it out of my mind. They won't pick me, anyway. What are my chances? One in three thousand?

I keep the brochure, but put the cover back onto the Wiener Wagon. I wander over to a park bench and lie down. Baxter cuddles next to me, and I put my arm around him and cover us both with my blanket. It isn't long before I succumb to my exhaustion and drift off to sleep.

I'm awakened by the sound of voices, and for a moment I forgot where I am. The sun isn't even visible over the eastern hills yet, and there are at least a dozen people here, already forming a line at the clothing store.

I'm still blinking the sleep from my eyes as I guide Baxter to the end of the line and take our place. The people in front of us sip delicious-smelling coffee and chatter away to each other.

"They're gone already. They loaded 'em onto a bus last night and took 'em away."

"How many did they take?"

"Not that many. Maybe a dozen?"

"How can you colonize a planet when you're only taking a dozen people a day?"

"I don't know, maybe that's all the space ship will hold."

Three of them look nervously at each other. "Don't forget the deal," one of them says. "If they don't take all three of us, then none of us go."

"Right."

"Right."

I look at my phone. Still no missed calls, but I see that it's 6:00 AM. The reflection of my face on the screen tells me I must have been sleeping with my cheek between two slats on the bench. I look marvelous.

By 6:30, there are probably three-hundred people behind me when a guy in a bright yellow mesh vest opens the door to the building and talks into a megaphone.

"Listen up, everyone. We'll do our best to interview all of you, but to do it, we're asking for your full cooperation as the day unfolds. If you get hungry, there are some boxed lunches on that picnic table over there from the sandwich shop next door. For now, we're going to let a group in at a time."

How hard can this interview be? If Erica can get through, I can. I can't wait to see her face when she sees me again.

He puts the megaphone on the ground and walks over to where I stand. He gives a questioning look at Baxter, but then grunts when I say that he's my service animal. He ushers about twenty of us into the building before he shuts the door again and stands there with his arms crossed and his legs spread wide.

I look around. I used to go school shopping in this store back before it went bankrupt. There are different service desks throughout the floor plan, repurposed to be interview stations for us. The individuals, couples, and then the three-some in front of me take their turns to talk to a guy at the first desk. After about five minutes each, the interviewer thanks them and another lady ushers them out the door, past the guy in the yellow vest, back to their normal lives. I'm next.

I walk over to the desk and take a seat. The man ignores

me while he taps something into his laptop. He looks up. "No dogs allowed. They were supposed to put up a sign."

"He's my service dog," I say. Who knows, it worked for the guy at the door. It might work again.

"Look Lady—"

"Leigh."

"Look *Leigh*, you can't take a dog. It—"

"He."

"Are you serious? Listen, you can't take your *dog* to an alien planet. Do you know what might happen if he introduces some foreign animal disease? It could disrupt, even destroy, an entire ecosystem."

I lean forward. "I slept on a park bench last night. Aren't you even going to ask me anything?"

"I don't think so. This is a quick-screen, and I'm afraid we are not a good fit for you. Thank you and have a nice day. You can grab a free boxed lunch outside."

I stand up and hold my chin high, just like my dad taught me. "Come on, Bax, I'll get you another hot dog."

We're halfway to the exit when I hear a whistle. I turn around to see a woman sitting at a different service desk motioning to me. "You with the dog! Come here."

I glance at the guy who just dismissed us, but he ignores me just like he did when I first walked in. As I cross the floor, past what used to be the jeans department, I get a better look at the woman. She has brown eyes and blond hair, but with brown roots showing. She looks to be about twenty years old. There's a smoky, smoldering beauty about her. She stands with a smile and extends her hand. "Hi, I'm Doctor Krysta Collins, Chief Geneticist on the project."

"Leigh Shires." I take her hand and give a slight shake, smiling myself.

"Have a seat, Leigh," she says while returning to her

own. She has a presence about her I can't quite explain, except that I feel comfortable and at ease almost instantly.

She continues, "We have some time before McClure sends the next candidate to me for the blood test. He's in a foul mood. What did he ask you?"

"Nothing."

She nods. "Because of your dog, right? You'd be surprised...or maybe I guess you wouldn't, but we had three dogs in here yesterday. We don't take pets up, but people still try. I guess it's the closest thing to taking your best friend."

I beam at Bax. "He *is* my best friend." His ears don't even twitch when I speak. In fact, he is 100% focused on Krysta.

She stands again and walks around the desk to get a better look at him. As she approaches, his tail wags, and just before she extends her hand, he jumps up on her.

"Baxter! We don't jump on people!"

Krysta laughs and lowers him back to the ground by the paws. "It's okay, I have a way with dogs."

"You certainly do. He never jumps."

She tries to pet his head, but he keeps lifting it to lick her hand.

"*Baxter*," I say, and then look over at Krysta. "Sorry."

She eases herself into the chair beside me, and Bax gets as close to her as possible without jumping again. She chuckles. "Aren't you cute?"

I hold up my end of the leash. "Let me know when you tire of him and I'll pull him away."

"Don't worry."

She stops petting him and leans back in her chair. A few moments pass, and I feel like I should say something. "So what is this blood test all about, anyway?"

"Standard stuff," she says as Baxter curls up at her feet. "New Meso has a plethora of alien flora and fauna. We are experimenting with the effects of intermingling humankind with them, among other things."

"How is the colony doing?"

"It's coming along, but not as fast as we'd like. It's because we're picky, you know? We want smart, healthy people who seem to be easygoing. Picky or not, there will always be a segment of rotten apples who slip through."

"Tough problem."

"Indeed, but what can you do?" She scratches Baxter behind the ears. "And then you have to worry about natural resistance to disease and overall vitality. It's expensive to transport someone. You don't want to take someone who gets sick a lot."

"Oh, I never get sick. I guess that's one thing I have going for me."

"You don't?" Krysta looks skeptical but maybe a little amused, too. "I have some extra immunity tests and it looks like we have time." Krysta nods over to McClure's desk where a middle-aged guy stands up and heads outside where the boxed lunch table awaits. "Another one bites the dust," Krysta mutters.

She looks back at me with a mischievous look in her eyes. "There's something about you. I want to test you if you don't mind. Maybe see if you're eligible?"

"McClure said I can't come."

"So what? I want to see what you're made of." That mischievous look is still there. I'm feeling like a co-conspirator. I'm not one to break the rules, but she's in charge...

"I guess so. What do I have to do?"

"Just give me your arm. Yep, like that." She takes my outstretched arm and stabs me with a gigantic needle that looks much bigger than it needs to be. She fills a vial in a few seconds and then it's over. A bruise appears almost instantly, and she covers it with an adhesive bandage with a cartoon beach scene. Baxter follows the action with a low growl.

I rest my hand on his head. "It's okay, Bax."

"Sorry about that," says Krysta. "Some people bruise easier than others. Let's see how your blood looks."

She puts one vial into a strange machine on the desk and pushes a button. "What's it doing?" I ask.

"Checking your antibodies and immune system markers against common pathogens. We're going to see how tough you really are." She smiles, but it almost feels like a challenge. I picture my blood in some gladiatorial arena somewhere deep in that machine, fighting off germ monsters.

The machine continues to churn, and in that time, McClure dismisses two more hopeful candidates. This last woman walks away from him backwards, flipping him off with both hands. At least he's an equal opportunity jerk. Krysta rolls her eyes and shakes her head.

"Let's try something else while we wait," she says, holding up a card with a painting of a carnation on it. It makes me think of the flowers that Celeres had for his mother. "How does this make you feel?" she asks.

"Happy."

She raises her eyebrows, but says nothing. She holds up another card with a picture of a submarine submerged in a dark place.

"Thrilling."

A tree.

"My childhood."

A dog.

I smile at my furry friend. "Bax."

An ocean.

"My mom."

She cocks her head. "How about this one?" It's a picture of a shiny black wasp.

I recoil. "Ew."

"Why?"

"Because...wasp?"

She holds up a picture of a clown.

"Double ew."

"Which one is worse?"

"What do *you* think?"

She smiles and puts the cards down.

I crack my knuckles. "Did I pass?"

"It's not a pass/fail thing. I'm just—"

She's interrupted by the whirring of her machine as it prints out a report. She looks at it for a minute and then gives a low whistle. "Jackpot. You *are* a hearty one, aren't you?"

I shrug. "I guess so. What do you mean, *jackpot*?"

Her brow furrows, and she seems lost in thought. "I'd like to test this blood against some pathogens from New Meso too, but I'll have to do it from the ship. I'm not allowed to bring them to Earth." She bites her lower lip. "Do you think...Can you leave your dog behind?"

I never counted on bringing Baxter along to begin with. He sort of came along on his own accord, but now that they keep bringing it up, I want him to come. "I'd rather not leave him. How long would I be gone?"

"Well, it's like the brochure says, it's a new life. It's possible you'll visit Earth once in a while when we screen for new colonists, but there's no guarantee." She pauses for a moment, tapping her fingers on her laptop before continuing, "It's not for everyone."

I decide to play a little hardball; she wants me. "If there's a chance that I'll never return, then Baxter and I are a package deal."

She grimaces and stands up. "Excuse me for a moment."

She walks over to McClure, drops my test results onto his desk, and leans forward. I can't hear what she's saying, but he scowls in response and shakes his head. "No dogs."

She points to some results on the paper. She mutters something else in what sounds like an even, almost threatening tone.

"Do what you have to do, but it's your ass." He's talking loud on purpose so that I'll hear.

She returns to me. "I know you heard him. He isn't on board, but I'm going to pull some strings." This time, Krysta talks loud enough for McClure to overhear, but he's doing his ignore trick again.

I shake my head. "Isn't there more to it than a blood test? Didn't you say something about...Aren't you guys going to screen me to make sure I'm not a psychopath or something?"

"I think you're okay. I have a pretty good sense for people, and my gut is hardly ever wrong."

This is all going so fast. It's almost surreal. It sounds like they might shoot me into space after nothing but a blood test and a gut check, here in the old store where I bought my blue jeans in tenth grade. What can I say? I go with, "What's next?"

She answers me by handing me a stack of paper. "Sign these."

When someone tells me to sign something, I usually just sign it. Doesn't everyone? Especially when there are pages and pages to read. But this is different. "What is all of this?"

"Pretty much what you'd expect. This one is your release for research experiments, and that you agree to do what we ask. Here is a liability waiver in case you get hurt. And this is where you list your next of kin. Finally, here is where you answer questions about basic medical history, if you're on any medications or anything else you might miss if you were a million miles away from home."

"So I'm signing my life away? There's no cooling-off period?"

"You sign up, you go up. In return, we give you an opportunity of a lifetime." She looks and sounds like a woman in a recruitment commercial. She leans back in her chair, looking at me. She has such a penetrating stare, and I can't look away. The moment breaks when McClure calls, "Next!"

She leans forward so that McClure can't hear, "He's right about Baxter, though. If you bring him, he must stay at the station. He can't go planetside. Ever."

"But how will I see him if I'm at the colony?"

"Ships go back and forth every day. You can visit him all you want."

I nod. It's a reasonable compromise.

What's left for me here? Why not start over in the grandest way possible—a once-in-a-lifetime experience? My stomach does a flip-flop because I know what I want, but I'm scared to death: I'm going for it. "As long as Baxter can come."

"I'll handle it."

I look over at McClure, and then back to the stack of papers. I guess this is real, this is happening. Krysta gives me a pen and I sign my name on all the dotted lines.

Chapter Six

Phoenix

For better or worse, I finish signing the papers and hand the stack back to Krysta. She takes them and nods as she looks through them, signature after signature. This "fresh start" had better be the right thing to do. I smile as I picture another lunch with Celeres. I wonder what kind of food they have there. I probably won't order the salad next time.

"You have a pleasant smile," Krysta says, interrupting my reverie. "It'll help with your reproductive efforts in the colony."

"My *what?*" I stand bolt-upright.

"Relax," she says, as she doubles over with laughter. "Sorry about that." She takes a moment to compose herself. "It's just a joke. Your reaction was priceless. Most women act surprised when I say that, but one lady actually looked pretty excited, a lot like the college guys do."

I sit back down. She continues to chuckle. I continue to scowl.

She clears her throat and tries to look serious. "Okay,

the first thing we need to do is get you registered. What's your phone number?" I give it to her, and she taps a few keys on her laptop but stops dead after a few moments, and bites her bottom lip again. "This is strange."

I can't imagine what she could be talking about. "What is?"

"You're blocked. McClure must really not want you to take this trip. Let me see if I can remove it." After a few moments, she looks over her screen to where McClure sits. He appears to be having a verbal sparring match with a woman who brought her three young children with her. He points over at Baxter and then at her children while shaking his head no.

"Hold on," Krysta says in a voice edged with frustration. She picks up her phone and rants to the person on the other side. "Yes, McClure is back at it. He is killing me. Can you help me remove a block? Yes. Leigh Shires in Rochester, Pennsylvania. Okay, yes. I'll wait."

This is uncomfortable. She's going to an awful lot of trouble to get me included in this study. I've never felt this important before, that I was worth causing a fuss. After a minute, she speaks again. "Thank you. One other thing: I'm bringing someone up with their dog. Yes, I know. I'm overriding that. I think we're done here. Send the others up. We're heading to Arizona now." She stabs the disconnect button and glares over at McClure. "There's always that one person at work." She shakes her head and returns her attention to me. "Let's try this again."

This time when she taps a few more keys, the laptop gives a pleasant tone, and she exhales. "It didn't have to be that hard." She raises her voice for McClure to hear, "That's a wrap. Lock the doors."

He looks surprised. "Really? Already? What do we do with all those people out there?"

She's already on her feet and gathering up her stuff. "I don't know, just give them a lunch and tell them to try again next time."

McClure shrugs, walks to the doors, and turns the lock. "Tell 'em yourself. I'm sneaking out the back to find me a nice Bloody Mary."

I watch him disappear through the old clothes racks and then turn back to Krysta. "Wait a minute."

She puts her phone in her pocket. "Yes?"

"Could any of you block a person from the program?"

"Yes, why?"

I reach over and take the stack of papers that I signed and put them on my lap.

She looks confused. "What are you doing?"

"There's someone I want you to block. It's either her or me."

"I'm already bringing your dog. Isn't that enough?"

"You block her, you get Baxter to come, and I promise I won't ask for anything else."

She stares at me for a while, then looks back down at my blood test results. "What's her name?"

"Erica Shumaker."

Krysta taps a few keys on her keyboard. "She interviewed two days ago. I remember her—nice girl—she's already in."

"Can you get her out?"

"Why?"

"She's my worst enemy."

Krysta pauses for a moment like she wants to know more, but then shrugs. "We can't have that." She taps on her computer. "Erica's on a flight to Phoenix as we speak. She won't be happy when they put her on a plane back to Pittsburgh as soon as she lands."

"Phoenix?"

"It's where we launch from. It's our only approved airspace," she says, holding her hand out as she looks at the papers on my lap. I hand them over and she sets them back down a little farther away this time. "Okay, Leigh Shires, let's finish getting you processed."

Processed? It makes me feel like fresh meat headed to the factory instead of a volunteer to go into space. She strides in the same direction that McClure went. "Wish I had time for a Bloody Mary. Let's get out of here."

Krysta takes me to her rental car. Baxter piles into the back seat and in a few moments we're heading to Pittsburgh International Airport.

She claps me on the shoulder. "Thanks. You got me out of a grueling day of work. Now I just have to get you to Arizona and into space."

"So fast? All I have is this backpack."

"The station has clothing. What else would you bring?"

I think about it for a moment. "I guess nothing. All the pictures I care about are on my phone."

"You can call someone."

I think about who I'd call. Not my (ex)boyfriend. Not a friend...they were all on the dance team. I already left a note for Mom. I lift my phone and punch my dad's number. It rings a few times and then goes to voicemail.

"Hi Dad, it's Leigh. Call me if you get this. Love you."

When we arrive at the pet check-in counter at the airport, they inform us we have to have Baxter crated and provide food and water dishes inside the crate. Krysta comes to the rescue again and makes another phone call. When she gets off, she laughs. "You will not believe this. They're making McClure buy protective booties for Bax, and a crate for travel. They told me it'll have to be an air-conditioned one, too."

McClure arrives in a rented pickup truck with a big box and a bag of dog food in back. A couple of nearby baggage handlers help him unload everything. He doesn't make eye contact with me, but when Krysta thanks him, he tosses a pet store bag to her and grunts. As soon as the stuff is off the truck, he leaves. The airport guys set Baxter up in the crate and cart him off to our plane.

Krysta hands the bag to me. "Baxter's booties for Phoenix. Now let's go grab a seat on the plane where McClure won't be able to sit near us."

"He's coming?"

She gives me a sidelong look. "Unfortunately."

Once we're on the plane and comfortable, I look at my phone one last time to see if Celeres tried to contact me, but there's nothing. I lock it and stash it into the handy pocket in my yoga pants. Krysta watches me for a second and then tries to stir up the conversation. "So why do you want to leave Earth?"

"You know...a fresh start."

"Why? Work? Family? A guy?"

"Some of it's family. Some of it is just for me to make something of myself. I told myself that I would at least try to get into this program. I knew the odds were against it, but I figured if it worked out, I'd go. If it didn't, I wouldn't. Plus, yeah, there's a guy."

"What did the bastard do?"

"Oh, not *that* guy. Yes, I mean, I did just get out of a relationship, but there is someone else. I met someone who works at the station."

"You *did?*" She seems very curious and very shocked. "How? Who? Tell me!" She takes a sip of coffee and sits on the edge of her seat, leaning in.

"Do you know a guy named Celeres? He said he's a pilot."

Krysta spits her coffee back into her cup, then turns to gape at me.

My eyes go wide. "Am I...in trouble?"

Still on the edge of her seat, "How do you know Celeres?"

"I don't. Not well, anyway. We met yesterday while he was off duty. He was going to visit his mother, and he asked me for directions."

"That's it?"

"We had breakfast. We talked about gardening. Small talk, you know."

Slowly, Krysta leans back in her seat, then takes another sip of her coffee and stares out the window at the people moving around on the tarmac. "Yes, I know him. We were close once."

"You dated Celeres?" I'm remembering my conversation with him yesterday. He said that he was just getting out of a relationship, too. There is no way that it could have been with Krysta. That would just be too crazy.

"It's complicated."

Great. How do I get myself into situations like this? "Do you want to talk about it?"

"Not much to talk about. Things just...we had some conflicts."

She's obviously uncomfortable, so I lean back in my seat and close my eyes. It's been a doozy of a day, for sure.

I open my eyes again when the plane pushes back from the gate. I look over at Krysta, who quietly sips her coffee. "So, what kind of job can I get in this new life?"

She shrugs. "It depends on a lot of things. You might work as much as me, you might even work *with* me. Which won't be so bad. I like you. I think we could have a good time on *Sumerian*."

"*Sumerian?*"

"Oh, yes. That's the name of our space station in New Mesopotamia's orbit."

"Wait. I'm not going to the colony?"

"We'll figure it out. If you stay, I can keep you plenty busy."

"Oh." I pause for a moment. "At least I'd see Baxter more. What will he do if I'm so busy?"

"You don't have to worry about that. He'll have more friends up there than you can count. Like I said, there are no dogs on the station, and plenty of folks can use some dog therapy."

Therapy? Did McClure tell her I said Baxter was a service dog? Maybe if I come clean, she'll think I'm dishonest enough and I can get out of this fix before we even get off the ground. Besides, maybe it'd be better just to forget about Celeres if I'm going to get in the middle of something. "He's not really a service animal."

She smiles. "I figured. Service animals don't jump up on people's knees."

"So, about Celeres. Should I try to see him? Do you mind?" It might be my imagination, but I feel like she's regretting bringing me.

She shrugs. "He's just as busy as I am. It's tough up there. Maybe you can get it to work."

"He seems important."

"How do you mean?"

"Some other guy in uniform interrupted our breakfast, and he had to go transport some VIPs or something."

She nods. "You could say he's sort of a big deal."

She warms up a little after an hour or two from take-off and unwraps a new pair of ear buds she picked up at the airport. "Here. We can share. I'll show you my favorite old movie." She pulls a tablet from her bag and we watch *The Shawshank Redemption* together for the rest of the flight. It's such a fantastic movie, even today.

She turns it off as soon as the ending credits roll. She rests her head back in her seat with a contented grin. "So satisfying. It has a double happy ending. You never see that anymore."

I nod. "The way Andy escaped—"

"And Red got parole and found him? It gives you hope happy endings are still out there, ya know?"

"I hope so."

She looks out the window and adds, "I gift this movie a

lot. I even gave it to Celeres on his birthday, but I don't think he watched it."

The captain's voice cuts through the cabin, telling us we'll be landing at Phoenix Sky Harbor International Airport in about twenty minutes, and that the temperature on the ground is 102°F! I've never been to Arizona, but I've heard that there is no humidity like what we have in Pennsylvania. Your moisture evaporates almost as fast as you can sweat it out, and it's easy to get dehydrated if you aren't careful. I'll have to be careful with Baxter.

After landing, we stop at Taco Tuesday in the terminal for tacos and I get a container of pulled pork for Baxter. The bag smells delicious, and all I want to do is rip into it as we walk.

When we approach the doors to the outside, I brace myself for the heat as they slide open and let us out into the bright day. My caution for Baxter is confirmed when we step outside and head to our rental car. I feel like I just stepped into a blast furnace. We get our Subaru Outback and turn the air conditioning on as far as it can go. We have a little map of the airport, and after a short drive, we find the cargo facility where they have Baxter. Once we get him to the car, he jumps right onto the floor of the back seat where the A/C vent blasts him with cool air. I give him his container of pork, and he dives in.

Soon, we are on our way down Route 10. We feast on our Taco Tuesday food while we play the local hit radio station, singing along with the music in between bites. Krysta has a pretty singing voice, hitting all the highs. I'm more of an alto, so we sound good together. We touch heads a few times while we belt out the lyrics, but after she swerves off of the road once or twice and I spill my soda, we tone it down a little. It occurs to me that Baxter might want to have his head out the window, not just because he likes to sniff the air, but because of our singing. He'll have to grin and bear it; this is an A/C kind of day. For now, everything seems great, and I feel like I'm a million miles away from my life, but mostly Joe. Soon, I guess I will be.

Chapter Seven

Ice Arrow

After a half hour, we're still having a pleasant drive, enjoying the vibe, when we see a column of white smoke rising from the ground from somewhere far up ahead. Up, up, it goes, through the clouds and even higher yet. I creep down in the front seat just to see it as it gets too small to see.

I squint. "What the heck was that?"

"That was the rocket. The one you blocked your friend Erica from boarding."

"Why aren't we on it?"

"No dogs, remember?"

I freeze. Did she betray me? I look straight ahead and say nothing.

She pats my knee. "I've arranged different transport. Something a little more...pet friendly."

After another hour of desert driving, Krysta turns the music down and announces that we're almost there. We're stopping at North Maricopa Mountain Wilderness Area in the Sonoran Desert. "It's where the launchpad is."

As we approach a parking area, we have to slow down because there are hundreds of people here. Some of them hold up large signs with photos of various faces on them. They look like they are protesting, but I can't imagine what they would be protesting against out here in the middle of the desert. In my confusion, I ask, "Are these people going to be joining us?"

Krysta looks very distracted and maybe she didn't hear me, but after a few seconds, she shakes her head no. She slows the car to a stop right there in the middle of the road and seems lost.

Baxter decides this is a good time to bark at some people, and they look over at us. They hear him even though all the windows are shut. A group of ten breaks off from the main crowd and walks over to the car.

Before the group can get any closer, she hits the gas and drives *around* the parking area, and into the desert, kicking up sand and dust. "McClure will be here soon."

"Where are we going?" I try to ask while we bounce along.

"I'm just trying to get away from these people so that I can call him."

Luckily, none of them follow us, so we're able to stop after a couple of minutes. Krysta pulls out her phone and stabs a number in the address book with her finger. Someone answers almost immediately.

"McClure! The place is overrun with protesters. What am I supposed to do?"

I can hear his voice through her phone: "I'll be there in fifteen."

Krysta disconnects the call with an even bigger finger-stab than she used when she called him. "Change of plans."

Suddenly the tacos aren't sitting so well with me. Heartburn claws its way up my throat, and I have to chase it back down with a sip of soda. "What's going on?"

"Let's see if we can wait at the launchpad," is her only reply as she drives us deeper off-road into the desert. Our mood is somber, and the only noise in the car is the rush of the A/C.

We approach a tall chain-link fence. The closer we get, the more we see of debris all over the ground; it reminds me of the plaza back home where the colony interviews took place. People can be such pigs.

The fenced-in area has a gate large enough to drive through with a little booth beside the opening where there might be an attendant or guard. The booth is empty and the gate hangs open. Krysta drives through and then comes to a stop, but leaves the engine running. "This is it."

A large cement slab dominates the ground. The mess from outside seems to have found its way in here as well. There are a lot of cups and food bags. Baxter noses around in them, but I pull him away. He's been known to eat Styrofoam.

One of those picket signs we saw earlier lies face-down nearby. I kick it over to see what's on the front. There's a face, a photo of a pretty woman. She's in her early twenties, has a full smile, yellow hair, and bright eyes full of hope. There's nothing written on the sign, though. It's just her face. I point at it. "What is this?"

"I might as well tell you. You're going to find out, anyway. Some don't agree with our program or our research. The faces on these signs are of people who have already left Earth with us. Communication is limited, even nonexistent sometimes between the station and Earth. If you join the planet colony, there is no communication at all. It's part of the acclimation phase of beginning a new life."

"So, these people, the ones outside with the signs—"

"Are protesting because they haven't heard from their loved ones, yes."

This is a little unsettling to me. My mom and I aren't on the best of terms, but it might be nice to check in on her once in a while.

Krysta seems to read my expression. "Having second thoughts?"

"No. Yes. I don't know. Is it dangerous? I mean, *is* there a reason to be concerned? Do these people have a legitimate worry?"

"No Leigh, it's just like I said. There will be periods of time where there is no communication between the station and Earth. Anything could happen, of course. We're talking about space travel, life aboard a space station, and life on a foreign planet. I mean, you could fall out of a tree on Earth and break your neck, you know? Anything could happen while you're out there."

I look back at the sign on the ground, at the girl on it. "I wonder if I'll meet this person, or if I'll get a chance to tell her that someone back home misses her."

Krysta shrugs. I wait for a few more moments to see if she'll offer any more explanation, but she doesn't.

A metallic dot on the horizon catches my eye. Krysta sees it too. "That's him."

She turns off the car and puts the keys in the visor. "They'll have to return the car for us. Let's go."

It looks like a stealth bomber or something similar is coming straight for us. It's triangular and dark. Once it gets to us, it stops in midair and settles straight down to the pad.

Besides the dark body paint, a large painting of a hunting arrow spans the entire raised section of fuselage. It's blue and covered with horizontal icicles to give the impression of an arrow in flight.

There are a lot of things swirling through my head, but the only thing that comes out of my mouth is, "They're going to let Baxter in, right?"

For a second, it looks like I took her by surprise with that question, but she composes herself. "It—he should be fine." She bites her lip. She does that a lot, and I'm wondering if that's a good sign or a bad one.

By now, the ship sits on the pad and has already lowered a boarding ramp. Up close, it's even bigger than I originally thought. It's the size of *two* bombers. It is dull black, but has a series of lights along each side. Right now, the starboard lights are all green, and the port lights are red. The lights blink in a chaser pattern as the ship sits.

We walk over to the ramp, and McClure appears at the top. "Get moving ladies. There was a problem at the hangar and I need to get back." He's changed clothes since the last time we saw him, and he now wears a kilt. Plaid. Besides that, he wears a dark green tank top and work boots.

A smell wafts out of the ship. It's like when you walk past a scented candle store. Besides that, there are also odorous undertones that remind me of farm animals. Weird. He holds a beer can, which he spits into before his impatient grimace showcases his stained teeth. Good old McClure.

Chapter Eight

Space

Baxter isn't interested, and I have to I tug him toward the ramp. "I don't like the smells either, buddy."

Krysta shakes her head and travels up the ramp in five fast strides. She's already jabbering to McClure, and they both disappear around a corner at the top.

I look down at my pup. "Well, this is it, Bax." I give him a scratch under the collar and a kiss on the forehead. "Let's get this over with." He licks my cheek.

Krysta and McClure reappear at the top of the ramp. "What are you waiting for?" Krysta calls. McClure spits into his can and glares down at us.

I dry my sweaty palms on my legs. "Coming."

Baxter decides this is a good time to be stubborn, and lies down, refusing to budge. I'm forced to carry him to the top.

Once we're in, McClure hits a button beside the door, and the ramp folds back into the ship and the door closes. We're immediately surrounded by very cool air conditioning.

I set Baxter down and look around. It's roomy in here. It almost reminds me of the inside of a nice-sized camper, the kind you see towed with fifth wheels on pickup trucks. There's a small kitchen, a dining room table, a video panel, and even an electric fireplace. Each room has at least two different scented candles sitting around. None are lit at the moment. "You have it all. Where are the beds?"

I go to the fireplace and hit the "On" button. It springs to life, but sputters back to darkness as McClure slaps the button, almost whacking my hand in the process. "Ask first."

He spins to point toward the rear of the ship. "Bed's in back, Darlin'." His kilt flares into the air and I can't help but to risk a quick glimpse. It doesn't go high enough for me to see anything, but out of the corner of my eye, I catch Krysta watching me.

"What?" I mouth, shrugging my shoulders.

She snorts and beckons me to where McClure pointed. She opens a door to a tiny room with a queen size bed and about a foot of clearance on all sides. Krysta points to a door on the wall across from us. "Bathroom."

McClure calls from the main room, "You like it back there? Party in the back, business in the front, you know."

Krysta closes the door behind us. "Ignore him."

"Don't worry, I am. Is there another bedroom?"

"No. McClure has his own room, but we'll be bunking together in here. Come on, I'll show you the rest."

We return to the main part of the ship, and I point to a door that has an old-fashioned deadbolt lock on it. "What's in there?"

McClure answers, "Cargo. You don't want to go in there, trust me."

"He's right," says Krysta, looking at her watch. "We good to go, Jimmy?"

"Yeah, we're green for liftoff. Let's rock." He goes to the front and straps in. He hits a few buttons and the dash lights up in a captivating display. A small pyramid of empty beer cans decorates the flight console. "Think I can lift off without tipping my pyramid over?"

I look at Krysta and she shrugs. I follow her to the table and grab one of the bench seats. She takes the one across from me, and Baxter curls up underneath. I look around for seat belts, but Krysta stops me. "We won't need them."

I'm feeling the beginnings of a panic attack. "Aren't we going to shoot up into, you know, space? What's keeping us from flying into that electric fireplace or the kitchen sink? What about Baxter?"

"Oh, right. You're new to all of this. There are gravity controls on the ship. We won't pull any G's in here."

"G's?"

"Right. We won't feel turbulence or gravity, and besides, how many times have you needed a seatbelt on a plane?"

Come to think of it, never. I shift my attention to the window beside the table and look out over the landing area. I wait. The vibrations of the ship increase in strength and a low hum fills the cabin. I grip the table in front of me and clench my teeth. Krysta smiles reassuringly. "It's fine, you'll see."

"Why did we have to fly to Phoenix for this? Couldn't we have just taken off from Pittsburgh?"

Krysta shakes her head no. "Airspace is restricted to spacecraft; they say it's too close to D.C. and the eastern seaboard."

Suddenly, but slowly, we rise into the air. Our Subaru shrinks as we go higher, as do all the little protesters. Some of them point at us and I try to imagine what they may be saying.

I jump when something buzzes in my pocket. My phone! Now? Celeres? I rip it out of my pants and I'm astounded to discover that I still have a bar of reception.

It's not Celeres, but Dad, returning my call.

Krysta leans forward. Maybe she's wondering if it's him, too.

"Leigh, where are you?" asks Dad.

"I'm on a plane, Dad. I have Baxter with me."

Krysta settles back into her chair, pretending like she hasn't been paying attention. "I have to put it on airplane mode soon." How do I tell him I'll be in space within the next few minutes?

"With Baxter? Is he okay?"

"Yeah Dad, we both are. Listen, I might not be able to call for a while. But I'm okay. Can you check in on Mom from time to time?"

"Yes, but—"

But that's all there is. My single bar of reception is gone, and we're almost through the first layer of clouds. We're still going straight up. I feel terrible that I couldn't explain more, but I'm happy that I at least got to talk to him once before I left.

Krysta's attention is out the window and I decide to take a good look, myself. It's not every day that you get a front-row seat when leaving your planet. The clouds are way below us and McClure speaks from the cockpit.

"Changing pitch. We'll be flying straight out of the atmosphere from here out. Your best view will be out the front."

I shift my attention to the front of the ship as he pulls back on the stick, and now we're going nose-first, straight up. The azure sky darkens, and a few stars become visible. Then more. The sky darkens further and I see even more yet. I look out my window and see the curvature of Earth. I believe we're in space. Baxter gives a little snore from under the table and I burst out laughing with nervous energy. Krysta laughs too. After a moment, she exhales a giant breath. She taps the glass. "That never gets old."

Up in the cockpit, McClure whistles and taps his leg while he flies the ship, his pyramid of cans still intact. He still holds his spit can and I can't help but wonder if he ever accidentally took a swig of tobacco juice. I shiver to think about it before my focus returns to my present situation. I have so many thoughts and emotions going through my head that my focus right now is to just hold myself together. Earth drifts outside of the window. I try to find home from here.

McClure gets up from the pilot's seat and comes back to join us. "What did you think of that?"

I'm still full of nervous energy and I just sort of chuckle. "Your pyramid survived."

"Impressive, yeah. Hey, how about you and I go break that bed in? Party in the back? It's the least you could do for making me go shopping for your dog."

Krysta and I both give him a flat stare.

He snorts. "No? Well, if he shits on my ship, you owe me. Anyway, there's ISS VI right outside the window."

The idea of punching him in his stained teeth crosses my mind, but my attention is quickly stolen by the expanding gray dot outside. The sixth generation International Space Station. It looks like a giant building block project. It's all boxy, with a lot of windows, lights, and antennas and stuff jutting in every direction.

"We could dock with it if we wanted," Krysta says.

"But we don't," he retorts, heading back to his seat in the cockpit. Krysta stares at his back with a face that looks like she just bit into a Madagascar cockroach.

He sits and puts on a headset. Now his voice sounds over the cabin speakers. "Get comfortable. No cryo-sleep on this ship, but it's only a few days to Pluto. Help yourselves to the fridge and cupboards. I think there are a few games back there somewhere. Look around. Here we go. Next stop, Sol jump gate."

I nudge Krysta. "Why couldn't he have just said that while he was standing right here?"

"McClure is...McClure. I'm sorry about him. He takes a lot of getting-used to, but he's mostly harmless, if you can believe it."

Now the earth is sliding by like a rock on the side of the road. "Will we see any other of the solar system planets as we leave?"

"Probably. If we do, McClure will point them out. He has his rare useful moments."

"What is a jump gate?"

"Oh. I keep forgetting that this is *all* new to you. Think of it as an instantaneous teleporter to somewhere else."

"Can't we just fly to where we're going? You said this ship was fast."

"It *is* fast, Sweet Cheeks," McClure interrupts from the cockpit, "but we built the jump gates because of the time dilation of FTL travel. If it weren't for jump gates, you'd go to *Sumerian,* then back to Earth, and everyone there is dead or old."

I pull Krysta off to the side. "What about that rocket launch we saw earlier, the one you said we should have been on? How will those people get there?"

"Same as us. Their trip to Pluto will take longer because they have a slower ship. We'll still have a delightful ride and have time to get to know each other better."

I grin. "I'd like that."

"I would too."

Chapter Nine

Bed of Blood

As Earth fades into the background and we go deeper into space, an excitement wells from deep within. A smile creeps onto my face, and an incredible rush flows through my body. My heartbeat picks up in response to the thrill. In some ways, I feel like I'm free, as if my "fresh start" has already begun. On the other hand, out here in the blackness of space, maybe I'm going into some deep danger, like a sea explorer delving into the darkest watery caverns with her submarine. There are a million ways to die, yet she plunges farther into the unknown...and she brought her dog.

I look under the table, and Baxter continues to snore. I poke him with my foot, but he doesn't even crack an eyelid. I'm pretty tired myself after this unusual day. Now that we're off the ground and the scenery is nothing but blackness and stars, it feels like night. A quick glance at my phone shows it's 10:00 PM. Right above the time are the words, "No Service."

"Krysta?"

She's across from me with droopy eyelids of her own. "Hmm?"

"I think I'll hit the hay."

"Good idea. You'll find some clothes in the drawers. They're just standard Genomica issue, nothing fancy." She pulls her laptop out of its bag and I head toward the bedroom.

I find an XL T-shirt to sleep in. It's got a Genomica logo on the breast. In fact, every shirt in these drawers is the same, except the sizes. For pants, there's an assortment of black leggings.

I have trouble falling asleep, and I'm still awake when the bedroom door slides open and Krysta's silhouette stands in the doorway. McClure's voice carries after her: "Come on, Krys, what do you say? I'll open a bottle of wine."

She turns and says in an even tone, "Keep your kilt on, big boy. Just get us to *Sumerian*."

"I'll even pop a breath mint."

She hits the button to close the door and creeps around our bed to disappear into the bathroom. Fifteen minutes later, she reappears amid a cloud of steam. She sees I have my eyes open.

She waves her hands through the cloud. "That fan is useless. I already told him to replace it."

I raise my eyebrows. "It's none of my business, but are you and McClure..."

She laughs. "You're kidding, right? I mean, he already came onto you. You can have him."

"No, thanks."

She crawls into bed and is snoring almost instantly. I stare at the ceiling.

~

I don't remember drifting off myself, but I awaken in the middle of the night to both Krysta's and Baxter's snores. I can actually *feel* Krysta's soft snores. My back is to her, and her breath tickles the back of my neck. She's so close that I can smell her shampoo and toothpaste.

The bed isn't that big, and she hasn't left me much room, but I don't mind the human closeness right now. There's a sense of comfort. I'm asleep again before I know it.

~

Coffee. I smell it. My eyes snap open and I look around. Is it morning now? The little porthole in the bedroom shows darkness and stars, just like it did when I went to bed. How long will it take for me to get used to this endless night? I hadn't expected it, and I don't think I like it. It's almost... depressing? What will the sunrises will be like on New Mesopotamia?

Baxter must have jumped up in the middle of the night. He's curled up on the foot of the bed on Krysta's side. She's already up and out. Usually when Bax sleeps on the bed, he sleeps between my legs, but Krysta smells better than me, I guess. I reach at him under the covers with my toe to prod him. After a couple of pokes, he lets out a broken snore and cracks his eyelids. I hoist myself into a sitting position and blink the sleep from my eyes. "Come on, Bax. Let's go see what that coffee is all about." He follows me out of the room and stays close at my heels as I head back to the dining area.

Krysta and McClure sit at the table, both with their laptops. McClure's looks like he dropped it on the road and it skidded about twenty feet. He also has a sticker of a football on the lid. "What are you guys doing?" I ask.

McClure ignores me. Krysta looks up. "E-Mail. How'd you sleep?"

I help myself to a cup of coffee. "Okay, I guess. How can you send E-Mail from space?"

Krysta lifts an eyebrow. "That's a vital question. We have a subspace radio." She rises to her feet and closes her laptop lid. "Look over here."

I follow her to the cockpit, and when we're inside, she points to the ceiling at a greenish gold device that sort of looks like a starfish surrounded by a glowing purple nimbus. It's a little bigger than my hand and it's attached to a scratched and dented black metal box. I'd say the box could probably hold a basketball if it were empty, and two leather straps lash the box itself to the ship. "Ta-da. It's genuine alien technology, and the only one in the fleet. McClure gets it in his ship because he does all the Earth back-and-forth."

I squint at the box. There's a red crusty substance in the seam between the box and starfish on one side. "Why is it so banged up?"

"I don't know the details, but someone tried to steal it, and by the time we recovered it, it was in this condition."

"And you can send E-Mail with it?"

"E-Mail, voice comms, video, you name it."

"But isn't the planet a million miles away?"

McClure approaches to stand directly behind Krysta.

She touches the device with reverence. "A lot more than that."

McClure gets closer and sniffs her hair so nonchalantly that she doesn't notice.

Ew. I give McClure the same look I'd give a week-old tuna casserole, and he backs off a step.

This radio gives me an idea. "Do you think...if it's not too much trouble...do you think I could send Celeres an E-Mail?"

McClure rolls his eyes and returns to his seat.

"Oh," Krysta says. She starts to say something else, but then stops, dropping her hand from her starfish gizmo.

"If it's too much trouble, I understand."

"It's just, well, the radios rely on an alien power source, and we're running low."

"Oh, I'm sorry."

"Don't be. Once we get back to the station, you'll learn all about it." She offers nothing else.

Baxter paces around the room, and I realize he's looking for a place to relieve himself. "Guys, Baxter has to go to the bathroom."

McClure snarls and walks to the locked deadbolt door. When he throws the deadbolt free and pulls the door, a foul air pours out. It smells like a barn, and trust me, I know what a barn smells like. I half expect to see a cat dart out.

Inside are a dozen stalls, each large enough for a horse. Straw covers the floor.

McClure gags. "Get in there so I can close the door. I'm a little behind on mucking these out. I told you that you wouldn't want to go in here."

He shuts us inside and I hold my breath. "Make it quick, Bax."

Thankfully he does, and soon we're back with the other two. McClure lights a few of the scented candles.

~

The hours pass, and I spend some of them looking through the window. I can't believe how many stars are out there. I feel like I'm a character in a snow globe except that instead of snow, I'm surrounded by beautiful stars. McClure plays some game on his laptop and Krysta must be in the bedroom. She closed the door.

"McClure, if you're here, who is flying the ship?"

He dodges from side to side in his chair while he plays. "Autopilot."

I walk over to the cockpit and settle myself into the copilot seat for an even better view. The spectacular vista of the Milky Way galaxy stretches before me. I've seen pictures of it taken from Earth, but they don't even come close to this. I get lost in its beauty and I'm struck with an odd feeling—of how insignificant I am. Compared to the vastness of space, I'm less than a microscopic speck. How much of what I do really matters in the cosmic balance of it all? And if my life is just a flash in the pan, my time in this universe is a simple instant in the grand scheme of things. Maybe it's a good thing that I broke out of my old life and went on this trip. Life is too short to get stuck in a rut.

I look at the galaxy, and my mind wanders. Is the autopilot smart enough to dodge comets and meteor showers and stuff like that? It has to be, right? But I guess if you have to die eventually, plowing into a comet would be one heck of an exit.

I sit in that seat for most of the day pondering and stargazing, only getting up long enough to use the restroom and microwave a frozen turkey dinner. As evening approaches and my butt is numb, I push myself away from the console and walk back toward McClure. He's still playing his games. I head into the bedroom, where I expect to find Krysta. She's there all right, but she's not taking a nap; she has beige canvas tarp covering the bed, with several stainless steel gadgets and an assortment of glass flasks spread out. Her laptop is open with a spreadsheet on the display. There are three racks in the center of the bed containing rows of blood vials.

She's in the middle of writing on labels and looks up. "I thought I locked it."

Chapter Ten

Love Letters From Space

Krysta stares back at me with one hand still on her laptop. I purse my lips while I assess the situation. "What are you doing?"

She motions to the rack of blood vials. "DNA testing on this round of colonists. Standard stuff. Hey, you have remarkable genes. Do you know that?"

"Um, thanks?" I survey all the equipment on the bed, the vials, and a few other flasks filled with strange, bubbling liquids. "Is that sanitary? That's our bed, you know." As if on cue, Baxter jumps up onto the canvas, almost knocking everything over. I push him back down. "Sorry."

She doesn't answer right away. I think she's recovering from the mini heart attack Baxter just gave her, so I continue. "Krysta, do you have any idea how weird this is to me? What's so important about my blood and DNA? I thought you were just trying to check my resistance to disease and what-not."

She lets out a deep breath. "I'm a geneticist, and part of my work is to speed up our habitation of the planet by identifying the most compatible genomic models. There is something about your...composition that gives you a robust immune system. I say robust because of your cytotoxic CD4 T-cell concentration—it's almost *twice* that of any colonist on New Mesopotamia. Over here, I have the machine that we used back on Earth during our first blood test with you. With a little blood, it can replicate your immune system and we can observe behaviors. I just introduced synthesized samples of the COVID-19 virus from the 2020 outbreak on Earth, and then one of the 1918 Swine Flu pandemic. Your system neutralized each in what would be the equivalent of three days. Any normal immune system would take much longer to do the same thing. Are your parents superheroes?"

I'm in awe of what I'm hearing. "My dad is to me."

"Well, if he isn't, you certainly are."

My superpower is that I'm great at not getting sick? Why couldn't I get flying, or heat vision, or amazing à la seconde turns? For a moment, I imagine myself doing flawless turns at a competition, but then I return to reality. "What other kinds of things am I immune to? If I go to live on the planet's colony, I wonder if I'd be immune to whatever viruses they have."

Krysta's hands stop their rapid workings of the machine, but she doesn't look up. "I'm wondering that, too."

Suddenly, I feel a little less insignificant in the universe, like there might be something special about me.

Krysta turns a few more dials on the machine and several lights flash on its face. I imagine the little anti-germs in my blood blasting viruses in the face with each flash. Even if I can't take credit for my superpower, I feel kind of good about myself right now.

She pats the machine in much the same way that I pat Baxter. "That'll take about fifteen minutes. I'm going to grab a snack. Please be careful around this stuff. We don't want any spills."

I step back, my hands in the air, eyebrows raised. "No, we don't." I mean it, too. That's my blood, and this is where I sleep. I try not to mix the two. Krysta gives me a look that reminds me of the look we got from our junior high teachers back when they needed to step out for a moment. I give *her* the same innocent look I gave my teachers in return. Seemingly satisfied, she heads out of the bedroom. She's out there telling McClure to "Turn off that damn game and fly the ship." He says something in return, but the door slides shut before I can make it out, and now I'm in here alone with Baxter and all this blood.

And Krysta's laptop.

This is my chance. Krysta won't like it, but all is fair in love and war, right? I'm not very computery, but I know how to do E-Mail. I bring up her mail program. I might not have much time, but all I have to do is find Celeres's address and send something quick. They used to date, right? It's fair to assume that she might have some old messages in her "sent" folder to him, so that's where I look first. I scroll through the items as fast as I can. There's a lot of stuff here about DNA and tests and the recent trip to Pennsylvania. I scroll faster. I have to go back about a month, but I find a message with his address. Bingo. I hit the "new" button and put his address into the "To:" field.

Celeres,

Hi, remember me? This is Leigh Shires from Earth. Your friend Krysta promised to get this to you. I wanted to thank you for the flowers, and to ask you how your carrots are doing?

I hit the send button and switch the computer back to the spreadsheet that Krysta was working on. I don't want Celeres to know that I'm on my way. I think a surprise would be fun. I wonder if he'll write back, and if he does, will Krysta let me know? Will she be angry? By the sounds of it, she will want to stay on good terms with me (and my blood), so I think this is one of those times that I can say that it's easier to be forgiven than it is to get permission.

My hands are a little sweaty, so I try to dry them off on my leggings. Baxter senses my nervous energy and comes over to check on me. I pet him for a few minutes while my heart rate comes back down. When I think I'm ready, I check myself in the mirror and head back out into the main room. McClure is up in the cockpit, and Krysta is bent over a noodle bowl at the table.

She looks up at me in between slurps. "You know, Leigh, I've been thinking. Remember how we talked earlier about you possibly working with me in the lab? The more I think about it, the more I like it."

"Do I have any choice? I thought I was going to live in the colony."

"Why? Are you that excited to test your immunities?"

"Maybe, I mean, it's nice to know that I have an excellent shot at staying healthy, but I've only been in space for less than a day, and I feel like it's night all the time."

"Oh, yes, I know what you mean. It's one drawback of space living. I'd like to say that you get used to it, but I never have. On Earth, we take sunrises and sunsets for granted."

"Sometimes."

"True...Well, we do have a retreat on New Meso that

we use as a sort of vacation destination. Some sunrises there are just gorgeous. Not just that, but there's a zoo and everything."

"A zoo? What animals are in it?"

"It changes all the time. It's filled with animals indigenous to the planet."

That might not be too bad, especially since Baxter has to stay at the station. If I could live and work there, but visit the planet from time to time, it could be the best of both worlds. Not only that, but Celeres probably lives on the station, too, since he's a pilot.

"Well, let's get back to work," says Krysta. She cleans up her snack and we return to the bedroom. "Look, the machine is done already!" She walks over and examines the screens. "Remarkable. Leigh, can I ask you for a big favor?"

"What's up?"

"Can I take some more blood? I'd like to get a pint, if you don't mind." She smiles sweetly. I can tell that she practices that smile, and that she probably gets her way with it more often than not. It makes me *want* to please her.

The next thing I know, I'm sitting on the bed with a needle in my arm. She sets up the blood bag beside me and allows it to fill while she runs a few more tests. After that, she disappears into the main room and then returns with a plastic cup. "Here, it's apple juice."

I take it with my "good" hand while she pulls out the needle and covers the wound with a bandage. After that, she peels a sticker from a nearby pad and slaps it on the blood bag.

She takes the blood bag out of the room while I sit and wait. I drink the juice and put the cup on a small shelf built into the wall. Soon, she's back and chats with me while she stores her makeshift lab into several hard cases. "We'll be at the station tomorrow. The lab there is fully equipped. All of this portable stuff is nice to have in a pinch, but you'll like it better there."

I get off of the bed so that she can fold the tarp. I try to help, but she shoos me away, telling me to relax.

Once she packs everything away, she rejoins me in the bedroom with a bag of caramel corn. "There's not much to do on these flights besides eat and sleep. True, we did a little work this time, but I couldn't help myself. You are just so darn interesting." She shakes the bag in my direction. "Want some?"

I take a handful. "Don't mind if I do. I haven't had this in forever."

"I always pick some up when I visit Earth, and I always get tacos, too. It's like going to Grandma's house for some old-fashioned home cooking."

"Your Grandma worked at Taco Tuesday?"

She pops another piece of popcorn into her mouth and laughs. "You know what I mean." And then she tries to toss one into my mouth, but it bounces off of my nose.

I smile a little, but I feel exhausted, and I let my eyes close. She lets a few seconds pass. "Surely, you're exhausted. Giving blood always does that to people. Lift your head."

I do, and she shoves a pillow behind it. I close my eyes again and I feel sleep closing in just as a soft little dinging sound comes from her laptop. In that one fateful moment, I go from almost-dreaming to adrenaline overload. My entire body tenses as the mattress shakes while she drags herself across the bed to reach the laptop. That might be Celeres. I might be in trouble.

After a few moments, my worries are confirmed. "Leigh, were you using this?"

I open my eyes slightly and look over at her. She looks perturbed. My heart pounds because I know that I'm caught.

"Yes, I looked at it while you were eating noodles earlier."

"And what did you do?"

She knows what I did. Time to face the music. "I just wanted to check in on him. I'm sorry, I should have asked you first."

She's quiet for several moments. "He wrote back. Do you want to know what it says?"

I reach for the laptop, but she pulls it away. After a moment, she turns it to face me so that I can read it from where I'm sitting.

Leigh,

Hi, I am surprised to hear from you. Why are you writing from Krysta's computer? She let you use it at the event? So you tried to apply even though I warned you against it? It's not a simple life in the colony, so don't feel bad about not getting in. Few do. You probably met McClure. Nice guy, huh? You were wondering about my carrots? They're doing the same as they were before I left—not good. I'm glad you liked the flowers. I didn't have time to get them to my mom, and I wanted to give you something to remember me by. I enjoyed the lunch. I'll try to call next time I'm in town and we can go to that great breakfast place again. I'd love to see you again.

Best,
Celeres

Chapter Eleven

Surprising Celeres

Krysta sits cross-legged before me with her laptop balanced on her knees. She looks at me over the top of the lid. I'm not sure what to say, and she must feel the same because the silence envelops us completely. Finally, she breaks the silence. "Look Leigh, what you do with Celeres is your business. I just wish you wouldn't do your business with my laptop, okay?"

"Okay."

"Good. Tomorrow is the big day. You'll see him. You should get some sleep so you can recover from blood loss. You don't want to faint in front of him tomorrow and give him the idea that it was because of his smolder."

I give a quick grin, but she doesn't seem ready to smile again. She folds the laptop and tucks it under her arm. "I'll be out in the main room for a while." She strides away and pointedly shuts the door behind her. I feel like I'm supposed to stay in here as if I'm grounded, forced to think about what I've done. For now, she's not kidding about my needing some sleep, so I curl up on the bed.

A few hours pass and I awaken because I'm cold from sleeping on top of the bed. To my surprise, Krysta's in bed beside me, facing my direction. I lift the covers and crawl in, facing her. The clean scent of a fresh shower fills the air. I examine her face in repose and wonder what happened between her and Celeres. They seem compatible, looks-wise. Her little nose and mouth are perfect complements to her sparkling dark eyes. Her still-damp luxurious brown/blond hair spills across her shoulders. Whatever happened between them, I doubt she'd tell me.

Now that we're both under the covers, I feel her body heat. With no warning, her eyes flick open and she catches me looking. "Hi."

My heart rate picks up, and I swallow hard. "Hi."

She winks. "Having trouble sleeping?"

"A little. I was cold."

She closes her eyes and sighs. "It's warm under here. Here, this might help." She wiggles a little closer.

She doesn't open her eyes again, and is soon back asleep. I can't believe she caught me looking at her like that. How embarrassing. I roll over so that my back is toward her and I stare into the darkness, doing breathing exercises until I return to dreamland.

~

Eventually, McClure's voice in the cabin's speaker breaks me out of my sleep. Of course, the room is still dark, like it's the middle of the night. There has to be a sun around here some-where. "Attention passengers and crew, this is your captain speaking. We are on course to dock with *Sumerian* in thirty minutes. As always, thank you for flying with us. I know you had a choice, even if I didn't, but trust me, this is much better than the tin can that the other fools rode. Please pack up your belongings and prepare to land. Oh, and if you glance out the port side of the ship, you will see...absolutely nothing." He laughs, but turns the microphone off in the middle of it.

Krysta is already bustling about the room, gathering up the few belongings she had strewn about. I bolt upright. "What about Pluto? What about the jump gate?"

She throws items into a duffel bag. "I'm afraid we slept through it."

"Oh." Maybe it's not a big deal to them, but I wanted to see it, to see what it looked like, felt like. I sigh and look around the room. I don't have any packing to do at all. I grab my backpack, and I think I'll just wear this Genomica outfit for now.

"Sorry," she says. "Let's join McClure, and I promise you'll see some equally amazing sights."

My excitement returns and I let out a little squeal.

She recoils. "What was *that*?"

I cover my mouth with both hands. "Sorry, it slipped out. I can't believe this is real."

She chuckles. "I hope you like it. I remember when I first got here. The first two weeks were so surreal that I got no work done. I spent most days looking out of windows and sampling the food from New Meso. I got used to it, though."

I follow her out of the bedroom to see what's going on with McClure in the cockpit.

He's up there, engrossed in what he's doing. I expected him to be lurching back and forth in his seat like when he plays video games on his computer, but he's remarkably composed.

I look past him through the cockpit glass and I gasp. The stars here aren't like the ones on Earth. Don't get me wrong—most of the stars are just like I remember in a night sky, but there are also several large stars of brilliant colors: blue, yellow, orange, and red.

Krysta spreads her arms at the stars. "It's the first thing everyone notices. The stars in this part of space have a lot of colored giants a lot closer than anything Earth has."

McClure looks nonplussed and, after Krysta finishes talking, he spits in his can and squints up at me. "What do you want?"

Krysta shakes her head and sighs. "She's sad because we slept through the jump gate. You should have gotten us up."

He spits in his can again.

She walks to the copilot seat and beckons me to sit down. "Come on, Leigh. McClure is going to make it up to you."

He sneers at me as I sit down. "What? I'm not turning around for another jump. Sorry."

Krysta reaches around me and straps me into my seat. "No, McClure, you're going to give her a landing lesson."

He snorts. "Are you serious?"

"Yeah, McClure, let her have a little fun."

He shakes his head and flips a few switches. "This will be a great laugh. Just watch and mimic what I do. I have your side turned off, so you won't be able to kill us. When I push a button, you push the same one on your side. When I pull the stick, you pull the stick."

Krysta pats McClure's shoulder. "That's a good boy. Be nice to her. I'll be sitting back at the table." She turns and leaves.

I never would have dreamed I'd have an opportunity like this. "Okay."

He points. "Look, there it is up ahead. Welcome to New Mesopotamia."

I squint. "It looks like a tennis ball."

"Just wait."

The tennis ball grows in size. After about a minute, it looks like a honeydew melon. "How fast are we going?"

"Oh, we've slowed down to three thousand miles per hour."

This trip continues to blow my mind. I can't decide what's harder for me to grasp—that we "slowed down" to three thousand miles per hour or that we were moving faster than that to begin with. I nod as wisely as I can so that I don't look like a bumpkin who lived on a farm until a few days ago. He returns his attention to the controls, and New Meso gets closer and closer. What would happen if we crashed into it going this fast? Would we just vaporize? Would we make an enormous crater? Come to think of it, we'd vaporize either way.

"How's it going up there?" Krysta calls from the dining room table. Baxter is in his normal spot, curled-up underneath it, on top of Krysta's feet. She likes to use him as her foot warmer, and I don't think he minds. He's grown so close to her in this short time. I admit I'm a little jealous, but happy that he's able to make new friends. I hope he likes this fresh start as much as I'm planning to.

McClure glances back at Krysta and grunts.

He pulls back on the throttle, and one gauge drops. Ah ha! That must be the speedometer. It drops from 3 to 2.5, and then to 2. The planet gets bigger and bigger. A nearby screen fills with glowing white dots.

McClure leans over. "Looks like you aren't the only one

getting a lesson today. That's pilot school, but let's steer clear of these idiots. One of them dumb shits clipped the side of a hangar entrance during a botched landing while we were gone, and now the door won't shut. It's why I need to get back."

When I look from the screen and out the cockpit glass, I think I see them. I wouldn't have noticed them without the radar because they're no bigger than little dark gray gnats right now. They sit motionless, all pointed in the same direction, as if they're in some sort of spaceship classroom and they're all taking notes.

McClure points in a different direction. "There it is. *Sumerian*. Home. Whatever you want to call it."

When we get close enough to read the numbers painted on the outside of what looks like giant garage doors, my first observation is how much bigger the station is than ISS. There's no comparison. This thing is gigantic, as long as a skyscraper from New York City is tall, and twice as wide. I see the damaged door McClure mentioned. There's quite a gash in the side, with an occasional shower of sparks.

McClure flips a switch on the console. "Going open-mic."

I flip the corresponding switch on my side.

"*Sumerian*, this is USS *Ice Arrow* requesting permission to dock," McClure says into the air.

A voice responds from throughout the ship's cabin speakers. "Roger *Ice Arrow,* please transmit authentication."

McClure looks over at me. "Go for it. Blue button." He points to the button on his side, and I find its match on mine.

I hesitate. "Will it work?"

"It will work."

I push down on the button and a series of beeping sounds fill the cabin.

I smile and he smirks.

While we wait, I notice that our speedometer reads 0. That's strange. We were going three thousand miles per hour five minutes ago, and now we're going zero. I would have expected to feel some sort of braking action, but I didn't. Wouldn't such a deceleration be pretty violent? I guess I have a lot to learn about spaceships.

"Looking good, *Ice Arrow*. Welcome back, Jimbo. How was your trip?" asks a friendly voice.

"Same as always, *Sumerian*."

"Looks like you have to do a shipment tomorrow. We'll brief you when you land. Hey, we're detecting four life forms on your ship. Who do you have with you?"

"Krysta is here, along with a test subject and a dog."

Test subject?

"Really? A dog? How did you get clearance for that?"

"Krysta arranged it. Where should I park this pig?"

"Oh, right. Please proceed to landing bay 11."

"Roger, on approach vector to 11."

Now I'm hoping for McClure to reach up and push a garage door opener, but he doesn't. Instead, the bay door with the huge "11" painted on it lifts on its own.

He repositions the ship with deft movements on the controls, and we move toward the bay. A strange grinding sound reverberates through the ship and McClure looks over at me in surprise. "What did you do? What the hell was that?"

Oh, my God. "I didn't do anything! What's going on?" I wail.

Krysta punches him in the shoulder. "Knock it off, McClure. Look at her!"

I feel faint. If I don't pass out from blood loss, I'm going to pass out from the stress.

McClure cackles. "That was just the landing gear. It could use a little grease."

I glare at him with my most withering stare, and he giggles like a tenth grader.

Now that the big hangar door is open, I get a good first look at the inside of the station. It's well-lit for one thing, and very white. Tracer lights along the floor of the landing bay guide us in. Inside, several other ships line the walls. This bay is about as big as a football field. There is a thin, blue film across the entrance, and it pulses. "Is that a shield or something?" I ask after an unusually bright pulse.

"Sort of," McClure says. "It just keeps the air and gravity in. It wouldn't stop a projectile or anything. Hold your breath, here we go."

We glide closer and closer and soon pierce the blue veil. As we transition from outer space to inside the station, I'm aware of a thousand distinct sounds coming from outside of the ship. Mechanics with power tools work on some of the docked fighters. Some of them holler over the noise. Our own engines seem much louder as the sounds echo off of the walls of the bay. We're jarred as McClure brings the ship down.

He cuts the engines and now the loudest sound of all is the huge bay door grinding shut. It stops with a resounding bang. "Home again, home again," Krysta says from behind me. I hadn't even heard her approach.

"Home again, indeed," McClure says. "Let's stretch our legs." He pushes another button on the console and our door slides open while the ramp lowers. "Stick with Krysta. I need to do the post-flight stuff." He lowers himself to the floor to gather up all of his empty cans.

Krysta nods toward the ramp, and we walk in that direction. Baxter prances around, barking at the occasional mechanic below who gets too close to the ramp. I attach his leash. "Ready," I announce.

"Hey Krysta!" comes a male voice from below. He sounds a little out of breath. Baxter tugs forward, but I hold him back.

Krysta glances at me, and while still facing me, she answers in a loud voice, "Hey what?"

"You met Leigh? On Earth? Why was she on your laptop?"

It's Celeres. Goosebumps cover my arms. He's at the bottom of the ramp, on his way up.

Krysta motions to where I stand behind her. "Ask her yourself."

Celeres gets about halfway up the ramp and sees me. He freezes. Baxter barks. I give him a sheepish smile. "Surprise."

His eyes widen, and he takes a step back. Is that worry on his face? Concern? Could it be anger?

I feel my cheeks growing scarlet, and I turn to Krysta. "What's happening right now?"

By the look of her, she is just as confused as me. "Yeah, Celeres, is something wrong?"

"You tell me," he says and turns right around. His footsteps echo through the hangar as he stalks away. Several other men in uniform scramble to steer clear of him. I suddenly feel very foolish. Foolish for being here, for thinking those flowers meant anything, and for looking at my phone every five minutes back home. I've been dreaming of how fun this moment would have been, should have been.

Krysta raises her hands in the air. "He drives me crazy."

I'm so stunned that I barely register what she said. Does he have a new girlfriend? My thoughts race back to seeing Erica in Joe's house. I think of my mom and her secret lover. There's always someone else. I should have known better than to come here. Did Krysta bring me only to use my blood for her experiments? Am I the prisoner of a modern-day vampire? I still have goosebumps, but for an entirely different reason.

Chapter Twelve

Beastarium

Celeres has barely left, and now several folks dressed in overalls stand at the foot of *Ice Arrow's* ramp, with more joining by the second. Not knowing what they expect, I'll follow Krysta's lead. This feels like some sort of standoff.

I look over at her. "What are all these people doing here?"

So far, this whole *Sumerian* welcome is going sideways. To my surprise, smiles creep onto their faces. One guy—he's as big as a bear with a bushy brown beard—steps onto the ramp with one arm outstretched. He walks toward us, bouncing the ramp with each step. I realize he's heading toward Baxter, offering his palm for a sniff.

Krysta puts a reassuring hand on my shoulder. "I guess word got out. Some of these folks haven't seen a dog in a long time."

By now, the big guy is close enough that Baxter gets a good whiff of him and decides that he's okay. Bax licks his hand and the guy pets him vigorously. "Welcome to *Sumerian!*" the guy says to Bax. And then, as if he just realized he's forgetting himself, he addresses me. "What's his name?"

"Um, it's Baxter."

Krysta cuts in. "Brose, this is Leigh Shires. She's from Pittsburgh, Pennsylvania."

Brose laughs a deep guffaw and ruffles Baxter's head before standing up. "Hello. I'm Rusty Brose. You just call me Brose." He extends the same hand that Baxter just enthusiastically licked. Ah, what the hell. I steel myself and shake his sticky hand.

"Brose is the Chief Engineer on *Sumerian*," says Krysta.

"Nah, shucks. Only by rank—all these folks are a lot better than me." He motions to everyone standing at the bottom of the ramp.

Krysta rolls her eyes. "You're too modest, Brose. How about you let us off the ship so we can stretch our legs?"

Brose claps himself on the forehead, and then he retreats to the bottom of the ramp. "Sorry about that! Of course. Welcome, welcome." He gives a sweeping bow as we descend.

Once we reach the bottom of the ramp, several other people come over to pet Bax. It looks like he's going to be popular here. "Where are you going to keep him?" asks some woman covered in grease.

"Beastarium," says Krysta.

"Wait," I say. "You mean he won't be staying with me? And what's this *Beastarium*? He's not a beast, he's my pet."

"Don't worry, Leigh. They'll take care of him there. That's where all the station pets live. We have people who feed them and clean up after them. Plus, you'll be able to see him all you want. You'll thank me. In fact, let's head over there now."

On cue, the workers divide and make a path for us. As

we walk through the throng, most of them pat Baxter. By the look of his wagging tail, I'd say he enjoys this new home already. We leave the hangar, winding our way through white-painted metal hallways. The air smells antiseptic, sort of like when you visit a hospital.

Krysta looks at her watch. "We'll drop Baxter off at Beastarium and get you to your quarters. You can get situated and then we'll meet back up for dinner tonight. Sound good?"

"Thank you."

The door to Beastarium differs from any other door or fixture so far on *Sumerian*. It consists of a half dozen bark-covered logs lashed together with yellow rope. Above the door is a sign with the silhouette of what looks like a wolf painted on it.

Krysta bends down to say goodbye to Baxter. He licks her nose, and she yanks the door open by a rope handle. "Doctor Carter's expecting you. I'll see you after you drop him off."

"You aren't coming?"

"No, I have to do something. Maybe next time."

"Okay." I pull Baxter away from her into a small room beyond. The log theme continues in here as I now feel like I'm in a small log cabin about ten feet on each side. Krysta closes the door, and my first feeling is that I'm trapped. Before I can try to push the door back open, another door swings open on the opposite wall. Fresh air rushes into the space, and when I turn around to look beyond the new door, my jaw drops open in amazement.

The first thing I notice is that Beastarium looks and

feels like the surface of a planet. There's a lot of grassy space for running and playing (and in some cases, grazing), there's a lake, and a lot of trees. Some look familiar, and some don't. My favorite part is that there's a sun in the blue "sky" of the place.

The second thing I notice are the creatures. I was never much of an animal expert, so even if some of them are alien, I wouldn't be able to tell them apart from actual Earth animals. They all seem pretty basic to me. There's a herd of sheep on one hill, and colorful birds fly about. It looks like a rabbit just jumped into a bush not too far from here.

"Wow!" I say to Baxter. "Can I live in here, too?"

A female voice chuckles. "You aren't the first one to ask, not by a long shot. In fact, people love this so much that they want us to terraform the next station completely, including villages, hiking trails, and all the amenities, even weather."

The owner of the voice appears around a nearby tree as she walks along a worn dirt path, her tawny ponytail swinging. She wears a pair of sunglasses on her head, khaki shorts, and a green "Beastarium" polo shirt. I'd say she looks prim. You'd think someone who works "outside" and with animals all day would be a little more disheveled, but not Dr. Carter. Not even a hair is out of place. Her simple uniform is becoming on her. On her hip is a long-barreled pistol in a leather holster. She kneels to pet Baxter. "What do we have here?" He looks straight into her blue eyes and bends his head to the side so that she can scratch under his collar.

"Hi are you Dr. Carter?" I ask.

"Sure am, but call me Ashlan."

"It's nice to meet you. My name is Leigh Shires, and this is my dog, Baxter. Do you have room for another mouth to feed?"

Ashlan continues to pet Baxter's head and neck. "Of course. I think we're going to get along just fine, aren't we, Baxter?" She pats his head and rises to shake my hand.

"I feel like I'm outside," I say.

"Isn't it great? Baxter will love it here."

"Where will he be staying?"

"I'll show you." She leads us around a copse of fir trees to what looks like an immense house. The windows have decorative shutters and flower boxes outside of each over-flow with Wave Petunias. She opens the door to let us in, and at first I can't believe they keep animals in an actual house. Once inside, however, I see that it's a cross between a kennel and pet hotel; a long hallway runs down the length of the building with doors on both sides. We stop at door 3, and she opens it wide. Inside, it's a nice little room, about ten square feet. There's a soft pillow on the floor, some food bowls, and a pet door on the far wall so that Bax can go outside. "This is it," she says as she slides her sunglasses to the top of her head. "What do you think?"

"This is it? Now I just leave him?" I kneel to give him a hug.

"Don't worry. He might even make a friend or two."

"This is so hard. I don't have kids, but this must be what it's like to drop them off at daycare for the first time."

Ashlan hands him a treat. "I'll spoil him."

"And I can come see him anytime I want?"

"Absolutely. Just wait outside, and I'll join you in a minute."

It's better than the straw-covered cargo hold aboard *Ice Arrow*. I hand her the leash. Baxter tries to follow me as I turn to go, but Ashlan distracts him with another treat. You can tell when someone loves their work.

It isn't long before she rejoins me with a spring in her

step. She clenches her fists in excitement. "I'm so thrilled to have a dog here."

"Me too. McClure was being mean about it, and for a minute there, I didn't think I'd be able to bring him. I told Krysta that Bax and I are a package deal, so she pulled some strings."

Ashlan nods. "That sounds about right. Krysta gets what Krysta wants."

"I'm getting that impression. So, where do you live?"

She motions to a brick structure with several windows. "See that other building? That's my office, quarters, vet clinic, and animal intake station."

"You live at work."

Ashlan takes a large whiff of the fresh Beastarium air. "I love it."

I look around, admiring the breathtaking scenery. "I'm sure you do."

"You're always welcome to stop by for a visit."

"Thank you, Ashlan," I say, and shake her hand before leaving.

Chapter Thirteen

Traitor

Krysta is just outside. "What'd you think of Ashlan?"

"She seems nice, but what's with the gun? I haven't seen anyone with a gun so far, not even Celeres."

"The pilots have blasters, but they're small and concealed. Ashlan's is a tranquilizer, you know, in case an animal gets out of hand."

"I guess that makes sense. At least it's not a real gun."

"She has one of those, too."

I nod. "I guess you can't be too careful. What's next?"

She taps her watch twice and then leans against the wall. "Now we show you your place."

In a minute or so, what looks like a little golf cart rides into view. "We call these moon buggies," she says.

I look at it with a skeptical smile. "You *drive* in the station? It's not *that* big."

She shrugs. "Hop in."

We drive through a commercial area where there's a fitness center, a coffee shop, and several restaurants. Every area teems with people. The way everything is confined inside the station, it kind of reminds me of the cruise ship we took before my parents split up, back when we toured the southern Caribbean.

She turns off the main thoroughfare and we travel into a residential section where the corridors resemble hallways in a hotel. Up ahead, men carry boxes out of one door and load them onto carts. When they see us coming, they stop talking and keep their heads down.

"What's going on up there?" I ask.

Krysta looks over at me with a big grin. "Welcome home, Leigh. This is you."

I squint at the men. "It looks like they're moving someone *out*."

Just then, one of them pointedly drops a box onto the cart with a dull, heavy thud. Krysta looks annoyed.

Once we park, a guy with an electric tablet approaches us. "All done, Dr. Collins. What do you want us to do with all this stuff?"

She looks at the carts for a second. "Incinerate it."

He shrugs and taps on his tablet. "Suit yourself. Let's take it away, guys."

Krysta takes me by the wrist and guides me to the door of my new place. She points to a chest-height metal pad on the wall. "This is a palm reader. We program them so that they only open for the people who live here and the people they grant access. We'll skip that for you because since you work for me, you have a universal clearance, meaning you can open any door on the station already."

I put my hand on the pad, and its border turns green. The door slides shut. I try again and it slides open. "So it's official then? We're coworkers?"

"Yes, you're my assistant."

Something isn't adding up. "So then, what did McClure mean when he called me a test subject on the radio?"

"He doesn't know what he's talking about. Come on, let's get inside."

Krysta walks through the door, and I take one last look at the carts rolling down the corridor before I enter.

It looks like a hotel room. There's a queen-size bed with a display panel on the opposite wall, a dresser with a speakerphone on top, a bathroom, microwave, and mini refrigerator. Pretty standard stuff, but the crown jewel of the room is a window wall with a magnificent view of New Mesopotamia outside. I gasp when I see it. The multicolored stars in this system frame the planet, and I stare at a brilliant green one until my eyes water.

Krysta walks to the dresser and opens a couple of drawers. "There are some standard issue clothes in here. I guessed at your size when I called ahead." She bites her inner bottom lip as she looks me up and down. "Most should fit you."

"Thank you."

"But as far as your needs go, you should find just about everything. If not, start a list. Make yourself at home, get a shower, rest, enjoy the view. I'm going to go freshen up myself and I'll swing by later this afternoon. We'll grab some dinner."

"Thanks Krysta. I'll see you in a little while."

She turns around when she gets to my door and points at a button with a red light in the door frame. "This locks the door. When it's green, it's unlocked; anyone can come in. When it's red, you have to get up and answer the door."

I give her a thumbs up. "Leave it unlocked for now."

"You got it. See you soon."

And just like that, I'm alone at last. I toss my backpack into a closet and look out of my window and I'm struck at how spectacular the view is. I can make out some bodies of water on the surface of the planet, some mountains, and there are even some lights down there in small clusters. Not a lot, mind you, but enough to make me wonder how established the colony or colonies are. Patches of clouds hide secrets below.

Was my last shower on Earth before the competition? I think it was. I hop in for a quick dip, then wrap one towel around myself and one around my hair.

I have to cross the big window to get to my dresser. As I pass, I pause for a moment, shrug, and smirk as I open my towel. I'm flashing an entire planet right now. I give a small curtsy before closing the towel again.

I get to the dresser in two more steps and pull the drawers open. Inside, I find bundles of black leggings and black, long-sleeved T-shirts with the red Genomica "G" on the left breast, just like the clothes we had on *Ice Arrow*.

I'm a little irked that these leggings don't have pockets, so now I don't have anywhere to put my phone. I mean, it's not like it matters—it doesn't work on the station, anyway. But I still feel naked without it; I don't remember any moment in my life when I didn't have my phone on me.

I take a little time to fix my hair, and then I do as she suggested: I rest and enjoy the view. I'm just beginning to feel bored when the sound of an approaching moon buggy is outside of my room. The door hasn't even slid all the way open before Krysta pushes her head in and has a big cheesy grin. "Hi! Hungry?"

"Very. What's for dinner?"

"Let's go to Solar. They source all their food straight from the planet."

"Alien food?"

"It's not *alien* food. It's bounty from the planet. It isn't bad."

I give her a questioning look. "Will it fill me up? I'm a jogger, you know."

"Trust me."

We hop on the moon buggy, and as she drives us to the restaurant, I feel as if I'm on some attraction at a theme park. I can almost hear a prerecorded tour guide explaining what our future may look like when we live in space and colonize new planets. The future is now, but you wouldn't know it from the news on Earth. They say that most of what happens in *Sumerian* and on New Mesopotamia is classified. "What happens on *Sumerian* stays on *Sumerian*." I wonder if this is why Krysta told me I may never return to Earth.

We stop outside of the restaurant in a row with other buggies. An open archway stands at the entrance with a wooden sign with "Solar Snax" carved into it. Below the letters is an intricate painting of a backyard grill in the middle of a forest. Rays of light emit from the cooking surface, illuminating the leafy canopy above. Krysta swings herself out of the buggy and points inside. "Let's do this."

We hustle in and get the last table. It's a mahogany booth with one of those fake flickering candles in the middle. Just as the sign outside suggested, there is a forest theme here. The floors and furniture are all of a dark, polished wood. Support beams dot the room, all resembling polished tree trunks, and the ceiling is a canopy of leaves. The scent of a wood-fired grill fills the air, causing my mouth to water. Vast windows dominate the outer walls, revealing massive solar arrays just outside of the restaurant.

Krysta motions at a nearby server, and he nods at her as if in recognition. Instead of coming our way, though, he goes straight to the bar. "I'm a regular here," she explains.

After a minute, he comes to our table with a pitcher of

pale blue liquid with lots of ice cubes floating around, some mugs, and a couple of menus. After he leaves, Krysta pours a drink for each of us. "Your first IridiDew Brew. It's *my* favorite."

"What is it?"

"It's from a fern that grows down there. Our olericulturist calls it Iridilume."

"It makes you drunk?"

"Not *exactly*, but it has a similar effect. It's not fermented, like alcohol. It's actually a tea. Still, you don't want to have too much. Shall we?" she says, holding her up glass for a toast.

I swirl the liquid like it's a fine Cabernet, wondering what I'm getting myself into. When in Rome...

I clink my glass against hers, and we drink. I'm surprised at how refreshing it is. It's like iced tea, but with a hint of citrus. It goes down smoothly and leaves a delicious aftertaste.

"That's good."

"Right?"

I look at my menu, but it's pictures-only, and nothing looks familiar. I put it down and give a helpless look to Krysta.

She smiles. "How about I order for you?"

I'm not a picky eater, so I agree, and soon we're waiting for our food and half-way through the pitcher of Brew.

"So how do you like your room?" asks Krysta.

"I love it. The view is spectacular."

"I know. Between the planet and the colored stars, I don't know how it could be any better."

Krysta narrows her eyes, but she's not looking at me; her gaze fixates on something over my shoulder. "Don't look now, but he's here."

"McClure? Can we hide—"

"No, Celeres. He and Brose just wandered in. I don't think he saw us. Maybe they'll see there are no seats and leave."

A sudden rush of adrenaline floods my body, and my grip whitens on my mug. I'm not ready to see him yet, not after his little tantrum in the hangar this afternoon. My back is to him, and I don't look back. "What are they doing now?"

Krysta grabs her menu and peeks over the top, but then ducks behind it.

There's a sound of chairs scraping behind us, and then Celeres's voice. "No guys, don't get up."

"It's fine, Cel, we're just about done. You look like you could use a good meal after your trip," comes another voice.

"No, no, I couldn't. Finish your dessert. In fact—"

The server across the room looks behind me and hustles over to where Celeres and Brose are.

"A round of Brew for my friends," says Celeres, and a cheer rises from the table.

"You are a leader of men," one of them says.

Celeres gives a good-natured laugh. "Enjoy, boys. See you tomorrow."

After a minute, Krysta peeks over the menu again. "They're gone."

The tension melts from my shoulders, but I'm still frozen, my hand gripping my mug.

Oblivious to my nerves, that same server appears and sets two identical plates of food before us. "Two chef's specials."

He walks away and we both finish our glass of Brew. She pours a couple more, and I look down at my plate. The meal looks pretty normal: It could pass for a pile of peas, maybe a chicken breast, and a baked potato with yellowish flesh. I take a bite of the meat. The seasoning tastes familiar, and Krysta confirms they use Earth spices with the New Meso food "to help us with the transition."

I relax and enjoy my meal. We're quiet while we eat, and it doesn't take me long to clean my plate.

Krysta nods to my empty plate. Hers is still half-full. "Glad you like it. Want more?"

I'm still chewing my last bite, so I hold my hand in front of my mouth. "Maybe some dessert?"

She calls the server over, and after she sends him off, rests her elbows on the table and folds her hands to rest her chin. "So, questions so far?"

That's funny. I only have about a million, but there is something I really want to know. "Yes. Celeres."

"What about him?"

"I want to know what just happened. How is it he can be 'a leader of men' and a pretty good breakfast date, I might add, and then turn around and be a total jerk?"

She sighs. "I think I might have something to do with it. We've been friends for a long time, but something happened one night about a month ago."

The dessert comes. It's some sort of pudding. It looks like vanilla. The server drops it in front of us and leaves. I don't try it yet.

"What happened?"

She grimaces. "He wanted it to be more. I didn't."

I take a bite of pudding, and she follows my motion. Yep, it's vanilla. "Why not?" I ask after I swallow.

She pauses. "I don't know. He was always sort of like a brother. It's hard to explain...I just didn't have those feelings."

"You were good friends."

She nods. "We were. Now he won't speak to me. Be careful, Leigh. Trust me when I say that if things go south with you two... Well, this is a small space station. It'll be awkward, and you don't want that."

I don't? Maybe it's worth the risk. I wait for her to continue.

"I just hope he comes around and we can be friends again."

"It looks like he's friends with everyone else."

"He has that way with people. I get along with just about everyone on the station, too. We're just two people who shouldn't have gotten too close."

I sigh. This complicates things. A part of me was hoping to have a semi-normal life up here, and maybe even a semi-normal relationship for a change. There has to be more to my future than doing research, or worse, being researched-upon. It doesn't help that my one friend here has history with the one guy who I met. This sucks.

"Are you okay?" she asks.

I know I look pretty pathetic with my spoon hanging from my grasp while I stare into space. I shake my head. "I guess so. I don't know. I don't want to make anything worse for you."

"Don't worry about it."

We say little on the ride back to my quarters. When we get there, I drag myself out of the buggy and shuffle to the door.

"Leigh," Krysta says as I push my way into my room.

"Yeah?"

"Do you have a little more time? There's something I need to tell you."

Ugh, I'm so tired. Why couldn't she have just told me at dinner? All I want to do is curl up on my bed and be miserable. With Baxter. I want to see him tomorrow.

I step aside so she can walk past me into my quarters. I brace myself for whatever she might have to say and follow her in.

She sits on the bed and takes a deep breath. "You don't want to hear this right now, but I didn't want to ruin dinner."

I sit across from her on the mattress. She'd better not need another pint of blood in the morning. "Go ahead."

"Do you remember back on Earth, when I was fighting with my computer to get you into the program?"

"Yeah, when McClure blocked me."

"What if it wasn't McClure?"

"Who else could it have been? I had met no one else before you two."

"You met one other person."

Who? Wait a minute... "*Celeres?*" I ask, incredulous. "How could he? How did he?" This can't be true.

"When you met him, did you give your last name? Your phone number?"

"Yes. Both. But McClure—"

"McClure told me he didn't do it..."

She closes her eyes and draws a breath before she finishes.

"...I believe him."

Realization seeps through my cloudy head. It was Celeres? I feel a little lightheaded and I fall back onto my pillow. Not only am I not supposed to be here, I'm not even wanted. What have I done?

Chapter Fourteen

Temptation

Krysta tries to hug me, but I shrink back. "I shouldn't be here. What are my options?"

"Yes, you *should* be here. It's in your DNA...literally. You have so much to offer. Forget the stupid block. It doesn't matter. You're here, and *that* matters."

"You thought it was McClure, now you don't."

"It's true. I thought it was him, but he denies it. Why would he lie about this? He has nothing to lose or gain."

Maybe.

I'm going to pry this out of Celeres, but I don't know how. He doesn't even want to talk to me.

"Please, just sleep on it, Leigh. Tomorrow, we'll visit Baxter and take a tour of the lab. You can see what we do here, and maybe you'll find something you like. I'll introduce you to some more people. You could make a life here."

I turn to face her. She seems sincere. This is so much to process. I look up at the ceiling and think. After a long silence, I look back at her and nod my assent. "I'll try, but I don't know how I can sleep on that, or anything. I won't get a wink tonight."

"You will. And tomorrow night you'll get a little more."

"I'm so alone."

"Do you want company?"

"What do you mean?"

"Do you want me to stay?"

I smirk. "I don't know. Didn't we just sleep together on *Ice Arrow* last night? It's getting to be a thing."

She blushes a little.

Is it weird? Do I care? If she stays, I can get her up early so we can see Bax and maybe some new faces. "Why not?"

She touches her watch, causing the moon buggy outside to make a few noises and motor away. After it's gone, the only other sound is the slight hum from the lights.

"It's so quiet," I say.

"Yeah, it's late. Mind if I use your shower?"

"Go ahead."

Tiredness descends on me. Or is it the Brew? Whatever it is...

I don't think it's morning when I open my eyes, but there's no way to tell. Back home, I had an alarm clock that projected the time onto the ceiling, and right now I feel lost without it. I hear Krysta's soft snores beside me. My head hurts and I have to pee. I creep out of bed, careful not to awaken her. Guided only by the starlight filtering through my window, I shuffle across the floor to the bathroom.

She didn't clean up after herself. The bathmat is still on the floor, as are the crumpled up towels she used. My toothbrush lies on the vanity instead of in my water glass where I always keep it. Please tell me she didn't use it.

When I return, my foot brushes against a pile of

clothing on the floor. Krysta's complete outfit lies there in a heap.

She stirs, but her breathing stays regular. I return to my side and lower myself back onto the mattress, being sure to stay on top of the covers like I was before.

She's facing me, her torso rising and falling with her gentle breathing. The sheet is loose around her naked shoulders. Is she really nude in my bed right now? Curiosity almost gets the better of me as I lift the sheet to see, but I stop myself after only lifting it a couple inches. As the sheet drops back down, her scent wafts up and out of the covers. I'll give her one thing—she might be a little strange, but she sure smells good.

She has some small red dots on the back of her neck. They're hard to see in this dim light, but there must be a half dozen of them. Allergies? Bug bites? I never noticed before because she wears her hair down.

What is it about her that is so...captivating? She's attractive. Nobody can deny that, but there's something else I can't put my finger on. I can't explain this fascination, but I'm just going to play it cool.

Those eyelids, those parted lips, the hollow of her neck, the way her necklace disappears beneath the sheet... Wait, what am I doing? I need a distraction. Maybe my window. I roll back over.

The planet floats outside. What is it like down there? I want to see what that retreat is like, and maybe visit the zoo Krysta talked about. What animals might be down there? The same as in Beastarium?

Thoughts of Beastarium make me think of Baxter, and I wonder how his first night is going. Did he get enough food? Did he make any friends?

Then I think about home. What are my parents up to?

What about Joe? Are he and Erica all cozied up in his living room right now? Is she sitting in my spot, resting her head on my ex-favorite shoulder?

But I can't worry about Joe, my folks, or anyone else on Earth, at least for the foreseeable future. I need to focus on myself.

Thoughts of Celeres jump to my mind even though I've been trying to block them out. He has a lot of nerve flirting with me, sending me flowers, and then acting like a big jerk when I show up here. I will not let him snub me like this. If nothing else, I want an explanation, and I'm going to get it.

Chapter Fifteen

Teaching Celeres a Lesson

So much for pinning Krysta down this morning. When I awaken, she's gone without a trace. I'm not going to just wait around in my room. Maybe I can find someone to get me to Beastarium. While they're at it, maybe they can give me a bagel or something.

A veil of clouds mask much of New Meso's surface today. I wonder what the temperature is down there, if they ever have snow or hailstones or tornadoes? How heavy are the rains? Are there floods?

A knock at the door pulls me from my reverie. I assume it's Krysta.

"Welcome back," I call.

But when the door slides open, it isn't Krysta. It's Celeres, and he's alone. We're alone. He walks into my room, but stops just inside. When the door slides shut, he leans back into it and crosses his arms. This is the first I've seen him out of uniform. He's wearing a gray sweat suit. My breath catches in my throat. He makes that sweatshirt look amazing. I'm still wearing my black leggings and Genomica T-shirt that I slept in.

"What do you want?" I ask in shock.

"Welcome to *Sumerian*," he says. His tone is pretty flat, not too excited or too contrite. It's like he's waiting to see how I react.

As far as reactions go, I'm still picking my jaw up off the floor. I'm itching to confront him about his rude conduct in the hangar and dig into his past with Krysta. Unfortunately, all I can manage is "Thanks."

"How do you like it?"

"Krysta was supposed to give me a tour this morning, but she was already gone when I woke up. Excuse me a minute."

My hair must be a disaster. I disappear into the bathroom and close the door to make some adjustments. It's as bad as I feared.

"Are you okay?" comes his muffled voice from the other side.

"Yeah, I just need a minute."

There is no way I can make this red mop look good quickly, so I put it in a tight bun and apply a light layer of makeup. This will have to do. I step back out of the bathroom and find him in the same place I left him, leaning with his back against the wall. His eyes drop to my shirt, which happens all the time with guys, but when he smiles, I look down myself. It's a wrinkled mess. I didn't even notice it in my rush to fix my face.

"Turn around," I say, grabbing him by the hips and facing him toward the door. I go over to my dresser and put on a fresh Genomica shirt. I take a deep breath. I think I'm presentable now. "It's safe."

He turns around. "You said Krysta was here?"

"Yeah."

He pauses for a moment and inhales through his nose.

"I thought I smelled her perfume or deodorant—whatever it is."

Um.

I roll my eyes. "Can you believe she used my toothbrush last night?"

He looks over at the bathroom. "You're kidding."

He seems to notice my annoyed expression and attempts to change the subject. "I like what you've done with the place."

I look around and roll my eyes. This room is as spartan as it gets, without a decoration in sight. "Yeah, I know. Unfortunately, I didn't bring any knick-knacks from home. I got nothin'."

"I'm only kidding. I was the same way at first. Hey, I brought a ride." He points his thumb over his shoulder toward the hallway outside.

"A ride?"

"My moon buggy. Do you want to go grab something to eat?"

I almost ask if he wants to get another whiff of Krysta before we leave, but I let it drop for now. I do want to get out of this room. "Does it have to be a breakfast salad?"

He laughs, I smirk. I extend my arm toward the door. "After you."

He leads me out of the room, where his moon buggy sits in the hallway. This isn't like any moon buggy that I've seen so far, though. This looks like one of those electric cars that toddlers drive, except it's a grown-up version. It's bright red with dual chrome exhaust pipes, painted yellow flames along its body, and a number 7 painted on each door.

"This is yours?" I ask. I'm not sure if I should get in or just walk beside him like a mom while he rides. He answers my silent question by opening the passenger door and patting the seat.

"Oh yes. If you like this, you should see my ship." He helps me in, and once I'm situated, he climbs aboard himself.

I run my hand along the dashboard. "I can't wait."

He steps on the pedal, and the buggy responds with a quiet hum and fast acceleration. As my back presses into the back of the seat, I discreetly find something to hold on to.

We stop at Solar Snax and park his fancy buggy in one of the little parking spaces. It's early enough that there are only a few other buggies here already.

We get the same server who I had last night. "Back for more?" he asks me with a smile once we're seated.

I give him a you-caught-me expression. "Can't get enough." He bows and promises to come back in a few minutes.

I prop my elbows on the table and cup my chin. "So what's with the race car theme on your buggy? Do you just like to be different?"

"I'm a NASCAR fan. You met Brose when you first landed...the big hairy guy who first walked up your ship's ramp. Yeah, so anyway, he knows how much I like race cars, so when I asked for my very own buggy, he added the paint and effects. It was sort of a gift."

"Interesting. If you like cars so much, why are you flying spaceships? Aren't they sort of like opposites?"

"I don't know. I guess so. There are no race tracks on New Mesopotamia, though."

"Not yet, at least."

"You're right, not yet. I'll have to look into that." He

takes a sip of ice water and stares blankly at the ceiling. I picture a little thought bubble over his head with race cars zipping around a track.

"Those flowers you sent to me at my dance competition were a pleasant surprise. Thank you, but I have to ask, why did you send them to me if you were just planning to disappear forever?"

"Well, you know. Like I said in my E-Mail, I didn't think I'd have time to visit my mom. I knew you would take care of them."

"Oh, I took good care of them."

"Good."

The server returns to our table with a plate of warm cinnamon rolls and a pitcher of coffee. He takes out his notepad and looks at me.

I grab a roll from the plate. "I can just eat this."

Celeres shakes his head. "Nonsense. We'll both have my regular, please."

"Absolutely," says the server. He pours a steaming cup of coffee for each of us and then hurries off toward the kitchen.

"What's your regular?" I ask with my mouth full. This is no time for perfect manners. I'm starving.

He raises a cinnamon roll like he's toasting. "You'll see. Cheers."

It turns out his regular is a skillet meal that appears to be eggs, potatoes, sausage, and some kind of savory gravy that tastes like a cross between beef and pork. There is a lot there, and since I don't like to stuff myself, I give about a third of it to him. By the time we are ready to go, the restaurant is full and there's a wait.

"I was planning to hit the gym this morning," he says. "Do you want to join me?"

Now I'm glad that I didn't eat all of that food. "Sure, I have nothing else to do." I'm still leery about him and how he could forget me so easily, and there is something he needs to explain.

He snorts and leads me out to the buggy. Soon, we're cruising down the walkways. Several people wave as we pass. He reminds me of one of those people who knows everyone.

"Were you surprised to see me this morning?" he asks as we bump along.

"Yes, especially considering your cold welcome yesterday."

He grunts and continues to look ahead while he drives.

He's not getting off the hook. "What was that all about?"

He shrugs. I wait for him to explain, but he offers nothing.

I continue. "When Krysta signed me up for the program, she ran into some sort of block on the computer. As if that wasn't bad enough, you treated me like your worst enemy when I arrived. You know, if you didn't want to see me again, why did you take my phone number? I don't get it. There was chemistry between us when we first met. I felt it, and I know you had to have felt it, too. Let's be honest right now. I took a big chance coming up here, and I thought that maybe I'd at least have one friend up here."

"We *are* friends."

I study the ceiling as we ride down the corridor of this strange place. "Great."

He looks over at me a couple of times. "Sorry."

I keep silent.

"What's wrong?"

"Nothing."

~

When we arrive at the gym, the morning crowd is still here, and most of the equipment is in use. Some people arrive in swimsuits and disappear into a door on the other side of the room. Before it closes, I glimpse a large swimming pool, something I never expected to see on a space station. A sign above the door says, "Natatorium."

A giant display on the wall shows the setting of every piece of equipment, the workout lengths, calories burned, and other data.

Celeres and I are each able to find treadmills, but they aren't close together. We can see each other across the room, but we won't be able to talk, which suits me fine. Walkers occupy the treads to my left and right. The guy on my left has his set at a 10 percent incline, and the woman on my right has hers set at some negative slope.

I locate both Celeres's treadmill and mine on the giant display, and give a little snicker. I start my workout with no angle and speed it up to a jog.

Across the way, Celeres speeds up as well, and we're both jogging. While I run, my mind wanders, and I replay the conversation in my mind. *We are friends. Sorry.* That's all he has to say about the whole thing. I speed my treadmill up to 7 mph and my body responds. My lungs fill and my heart settles into a steady rhythm. Endorphins work their magic and my mood lifts. Across the room, Celeres runs at the same speed as me. Maybe it's time to teach him a little lesson.

I increase my speed to 8 mph and now I'm taking long powerful strides. He matches me again. I can't run much faster than this, so at this point it's going to be an endurance contest. Let's see what you've got, fly boy.

Sweat forms on my brow. I'm glad for the carbs I ate, but something feels off. I feel a touch of nausea. It's got to be that pint of blood that I just donated to Krysta. I dig deep and press on.

Celeres is sucking wind over there, and I know he doesn't have much left in him. I don't either, but I'm not stopping first. Drops of my sweat cover the tread's belt and my feet slap as I pound out another mile.

Now he's over there trying to slow down without being obvious, but the display panel gives him away. A smile creeps onto my face and I run another minute before hitting the cool down button. I want this win to be decisive. The belt slows to 4 mph and my breathing stabilizes. I try to catch his eye, but he won't look. That's fine. He knows I beat his ass.

We meet at the water cooler. I'm feeling a little smug, but I say nothing. We each chug a few cups of water before heading back out to the buggy. He's the first to break the silence. "Nice run."

"Thanks, you too."

"You left me in your dust."

"I am competitive."

"Is that why you and your ex broke up?"

Wow. "Why didn't you and Krysta work out?" I counter.

"I asked you first."

"Fine." I finish my cup of water in one gulp. "His name

was Joe. I caught him messing around with another girl." I crush the paper cup and slam it into the waste bin for emphasis.

"Ouch."

"Yeah, and not just any girl—she was on my dance team."

"Double ouch."

"That's what I said. So, how about you?"

"Krysta?"

"Yeah. What happened?"

"What did she tell you?"

"I want to hear your side."

"You know McClure?"

"The guy who flew me here?"

"That's him. Anyway, he flies her everywhere now, and I barely see her. She used to go with me to the surface all the time. I would go down to gather plants and tend my garden. She'd have personal business and wander off. Sometimes we'd grab dinner afterwards."

"And?"

"This is embarrassing."

"Just be honest. I need that right now."

"She sort of grew on me."

"But you didn't grow on her?"

"No."

I nod.

Sweat drips down his face. He rips a paper towel from the dispenser and rubs it all over his head. "I felt like she led me on, but I was *so* wrong. Anyway, it all blew up one day. I'd rather not get into the details."

His face still glistens with sweat, and his eyes sparkle with intensity. His hair is so messed up that he rivals me on a bad hair day. How could Krysta not fall for this man?

I force myself to stop admiring him long enough to say, "It's okay. I get it." I won't tell him how much McClure hovered over her during our *Ice Arrow* voyage.

"Love sucks sometimes," he says, watching me intently.

"I know. My mom cheated on my dad, too. Can you believe that?"

"No. I'm sorry."

"My life would have turned out differently had they stayed together. Now I have serious trust issues."

He nods. "I guess everyone is damaged in their own way."

There's an awkward silence.

"Are you over her?" I ask.

"I think so."

But he doesn't *know*.

"What about you? You over Joe?" he asks.

"I got even with them. You know his new girlfriend? She was going to join this program. I got Krysta to kick her out just before she boarded the rocket. She had to turn around and fly back to Pittsburgh."

"Whoa. Now I know not to piss you off."

"That's right."

A little more silence, and I feel like I should go for now. "I want to take a walk. Clear my mind."

"I could come along."

I shake my head and turn around.

"So where are you going?" he says to my back.

I don't answer. I barely know where I am to begin with, much less where I'm going.

At least he's smart enough to let me go. He scores a point for that.

After I turn a corner, I lean with my back against the wall. I feel woozy. I slide down and sit with my arms on my knees, my head resting on them. Moon buggies whir by and people go about their business as I sit.

"Hey Miss, do you need any help?" It's a man's voice. I look up to find a gray-haired guy in oily overalls looking at me with concern. His grease-smeared buggy is nearby. He offers his hand and pulls me to my feet. When he does, I realize his hands are just as greasy as the rest of him. I don't want to slip, so I hold on to his hand a little tighter than I normally would. He grins so much that his eyes almost close.

I extract my hand from his. "Do you know how to get to Beastarium? I want to see my dog."

"Your dog? There are no dogs here, but yeah, I know the way. Hop in."

Besides the grease and filth, his buggy looks a lot like Krysta's—standard issue, basic golf cart design. He has a little pennant flag on top of an antenna.

"You sure you're okay?" he asks. His buggy has a whining noise and doesn't seem to have the same amount of power as Celeres's. I could run faster than this. I did just run faster than this.

"Yeah, I'll be fine. Thank you."

That's the end of the conversation until he drops me off three minutes later. He waves goodbye, and I let myself into Beastarium.

I haven't even taken three steps before a woman's voice rings out, "Leigh Shires!" It's Ashlan. She still wears her khaki shorts and that green polo shirt outfit. She's wearing her sunglasses today instead of propping them on top of her head. She walks straight to me with a big smile.

"Nervous or something?" she asks.

"What?"

She points at me, up and down. "You're all sweaty."

"Yeah. Hey, do you have somewhere I can sit down?"

"Of course. You okay?"

"I overdid it on my workout. I wasn't thinking about all the blood I lost yesterday."

"Oh. You're doing Genomica experiments already?" She leads me by the elbow to a nearby bench.

"I guess. It was on the *Ice Arrow* on the way here."

She brushes some matted hair from my forehead. "I'll get you some ginger ale...and I'll see if I can find your furry friend."

I smile despite how I feel. "Thank you."

It doesn't take long before Baxter's pants fill the air, and then his form bursts around the corner. When he sees me, he picks up speed and barrels into me. Ashlan is right behind him with a can of soda with a drinking straw poking out of it. She hangs back while Baxter jumps all over me. "He missed you."

"I should have told you. He has separation anxiety," I say as he licks my face. I push him down and Ashlan hands the can of soda to me. I take a quick sip and I feel a little better almost at once. "Thank you. It helps."

"You're welcome. Yeah, Baxter has eaten nothing since you dropped him off, but I'm sure he'll come around."

"He will. The kennel at home used to give him canned food when he went on a hunger strike."

"I've decided to give him steak tonight."

"He'll love that. Thank you again."

I visit with Baxter for a while, but after a few minutes, Ashlan stands up. "I have to get going so I can prep some animals for later."

"Prep?"

"The animals come and go. We don't keep them on the station for long, except for the ones at the pet house, of course. They are only here for a couple of days and then we replace them with new ones from the planet. We don't want to stress them by keeping them out of their natural habitat."

I kiss Baxter on top of his head. "Oh. Okay. See you again soon, Bax."

She leads Bax away, and I head back to my quarters for a shower.

Chapter Sixteen

Apocrita

I feel a little better after the shower. I'm a little less woozy (I might have drunk some water out of one of the shower nozzles), and even a bit hungry. My mom would tell you that one of my favorite pastimes is checking the refrigerator. I do it all the time, and not always when I'm hungry. It drives her crazy. It's not like the contents change every 45 minutes. I look across the room at my little fridge and before you know it, I'm digging around inside. There are a few microwave meatloaf meals in there and some orange energy drinks. Yuck. I'm not a meatloaf fan. I grab a bottle of the orange stuff and sip on it while I head to the dresser for a fresh change of clothes.

While I pull out another boring T-shirt and pair of leggings, a small blinking light on top of the dresser catches my eye. It's on the speakerphone. There's a button beside the light, so I press it. A recording plays.

"Leigh, it's Krysta. Sorry I missed you this morning! I'll try back in an hour. I'll give you the grand tour of the lab, and we'll set you up on a bench where you can do your work."

Work? What work? I know how to farm and that's about it. I hope that my "job" is more than just being the resident blood bag. I tremble at the thought that my arm may soon resemble that of a drug addict. The bruise on my inner elbow hasn't even faded yet.

I gaze out at New Mesopotamia. Lazy clouds drift in its atmosphere. It's relaxing in its own way. When I go on vacation to the beach or the mountains, it's always nice to take a chair and a book while I immerse myself in the scenery. But from here, I can see it all—mountains, beaches, you name it. The clusters of light from the colonies twinkle, and I think of what life might be like down there. What do people do for work? What do they do for fun?

My display screen piques my curiosity. I don't see a remote control for it anywhere, so I thumb the power button on the front. After a couple of seconds, the screen shows the hallway outside of my room. That's interesting. I didn't notice a camera out there. Are there any other channels on this thing? I look around the bezel for any other buttons, but there's nothing besides the power button. I turn it off. Since I have nothing better to do, I lie down for a nap.

...But I can't sleep. I keep replaying my morning with Celeres. How much of an obstacle will Krysta be? And what's this business about him and me being friends? I don't care what he says; I know there was something there. Women's intuition. Something isn't adding up, and speaking of Krysta, maybe she was right about one thing— he can drive you crazy sometimes.

I'm still looking up at my ceiling when there's a knock at my door.

"It's open," I say.

And there she is. Krysta. She's dressed in a white lab

coat with a "Collins" name tag on her chest. She wears a pair of black frame glasses. "Ready?"

"Sure, let's go."

Her moon buggy is just outside the room. While we climb in, I ask about the remote for my display panel and she tells me there should be a keyboard in one of my drawers. I guess that'll give me something to experiment with later. The buggy makes a few clicks and we haul off to work.

Speaking of experiment, I'd better find out what she expects of me. "About this lab. You realize that I'm a farmer, right? What will I be doing here?"

"I'll train you. We'll start with some data entry and you can assist with some experiment set up and clean up."

That sounds super boring.

As we chug along, I lean forward, eyes scanning the twisting corridors, trying to memorize each turn and landmark. It would be fantastic if I learned to navigate to a few locations on this station by myself.

We wind our way through the rest of the residential section. The sweet smell of freshly baked cake fills the air, and I inhale deeply. Do some people have ovens? All I have is that microwave. How many people call *Sumerian* home? Which one of these doors leads into Celeres's quarters?

I return my attention to the passing scenery. We pass through the commercial area with the restaurants, fitness center, and shopping. Once through there, instead of turning toward Beastarium, we go the other way, and now everything is new. In this section of the station, the hallways are very wide, with metal doors on each side. Most doors have windows where it's easy to see what's going on in the rooms. In the first section, we pass what I'd call Engineering —each room full of heavy machinery and people wearing greasy coveralls. Once again, I compare the station to a cruise ship, where in old movies they sometimes show the bellies of the vessels. At least here, they aren't shoveling coal into furnaces. I smile at the mental image while we pass by. Krysta explains that if Chief Engineer Brose is not in the hangar, he spends his time here. Next, we pass several rooms full of cubicles with people hunched over computer terminals. Now, I think we're getting close to the lab because the rooms *are* resembling labs more and more, and the people inside dress similarly to Krysta. They occasionally look up from their work and wave as we pass.

Krysta waves back. "They all work for Genomica like us, but just the general stuff. You and I will work on the *actual* stuff."

"They seem friendly."

"Every single one of them wishes they were you right now, but they won't show it. What goes on in my lab is a topic of great discussion and debate on *Sumerian*."

"And nobody knows what it is?"

"Nope. All they know is that I'm the exclusive supplier of special resources. Also, I get the most funding. I get more than the pilots and engineering."

"Science gets more money than military? That's different."

"We don't have anyone to fight, and our advanced research will do a lot for humanity. I'll explain more when we get there."

We stop at a solid door. Instead of a window, it has a red, backlit Genomica logo in its center. She gets out and puts her palm on a copper plate that looks like the one on my door. The DNA strands that make up the letter "G" in the Genomica logo turn green in a glittering pattern until the entire "G" is green. The door slides open and we drive through. We're barely on the other side before it closes behind us. On this side, another hand plate shows a Genomica logo that changes back to red.

We're in a room that has some couches, a vending machine full of snacks, and a water fountain. Round windows so large that their tops touch the ceiling and their bottoms touch the floor, dominate most of the wall space. Across from us is a heavy airlock door with a wheel attached to allow manual opening and closing.

"That's a dock we use to embark on research missions," she says.

"What is this place?"

"Classified section. Whatever you see or hear on this side of that door stays on this side. You can bring no one in here. Understand?"

"Don't I need a clearance or something?"

"I've already cleared you."

"All by yourself?"

"I'm in charge of the project. Plus, you swore secrecy on one form you signed back on Earth."

Maybe I should have read those forms better. There'd better not be too many more surprises. I walk over to the vending machine to see what snacks they have in space. Surprisingly, it's the same stuff we have on Earth.

"Hungry?" she asks.

I shake my head and survey the rest of the room. This "classified section" is a glorified lounge. I flop down on a couch and wait for whatever is next. Krysta grabs a chair and drags it across the room to sit across from me.

"You need to know a few things before we go any farther." Her knee bounces for a few seconds with nervous energy. "*Sumerian* has a dual purpose. Everyone knows the first one: it exists to support and facilitate the colony below through science."

"What's that mean to me?"

"It means that instead of a colonist, you're a scientist."

A scientist? I only got B's in Chemistry, but I'll keep that to myself. I let out a deep breath. "And the second?"

She rubs her hands together. "Before I tell you the second purpose, I need to know if you're in or out. You're free to choose. If you're out, we'll send you to the colony to live your life."

I want to see Celeres again, and if that means I work for Genomica, then so be it. I've come this far, and we have unfinished business. "I'm in."

"Good." She stands up and walks to one of the huge circular windows with her hands behind her back. She nods at the floating planet below. "Genomica doesn't refer to it as New Mesopotamia. We call it Apocrita. Have you ever heard of the word?"

"No." I walk over to join her. The planet is so large below us, the colorful stars...it's all so breathtaking. "What's it mean?"

She purses her lips for a moment. "I'll show you. Follow me."

She stands on her tiptoes and reaches to the top of the round window, feeling around for something. There's a click and the window pops open, like a door. I step back in awe when she grabs the edge and swings the window open wider.

Now that I'm a scientist, I hypothesize this entire room will get sucked out into space (starting with me), but that doesn't happen. Krysta walks right out the window and then turns around to face me. She taps her foot on what seems to be an invisible floor beyond the window. "It's glass. Invisible. I told you this section is classified. Come on, and shut the door behind you."

She turns away from me again and disappears around the corner, walking down a set of invisible stairs.

"An invisible stairway?" I ask.

"Yeah, except I call it a starway. Seems more appropriate, don't you think?"

I'm terrified as I pass the threshold into the strange walkway. Krysta drifts downward ahead, walking with her arms outstretched as she touches the invisible walls on both sides. I do the same...it helps me keep my balance. My heart thuds in my chest first because of how exposed I feel, but then because of the colorful, starry beauty surrounding me.

Once at the bottom of the stairs, we stop at another window/door that leads back into the station. We pass through into the room beyond, leaving the space tunnel behind.

"What do you think?" she asks.

I look back through that window. "Words can't describe it. It's a little scary."

"They tell me it's unbreakable, so don't worry."

I turn back to her, and I take in a view of the room. It's about as large as the whole first floor of my house, but I can't see many details because it's only lit by the reflected light of New Mes—Aprocrita and the stars. There are stainless steel tables everywhere, surrounded by stools. Some tables have computers and some have strange machines that remind me of some of the equipment she had on McClure's ship. A strange bubbling sound comes from the opposite end of the room.

"What's that sound?" I ask.

"My aquarium. Want to see?"

She grabs me by the wrist and leads me through the lab until we get to a shelf holding a nice-sized aquarium. She turns on its interior light and picks up a plastic container of fish food while I push my face close. Inside are a half dozen black and yellow striped fish.

"They're tiger botia loaches, but most people call them clown loaches. These are from home. Earth-home. I brought them with me on my first trip."

The clown loaches chase the food flakes drifting to the bottom of the tank. They are fast swimmers and dart everywhere, even swimming in loops. They're fun to watch.

She traces one loop with her fingertip on the glass. "Aren't they great?"

I nod.

She walks to another dark section of the room. "Okay, come over here."

I follow her into the shadows. "Can't we turn a light on?"

"Sure, after this. Look."

I follow her to a window where a tall telescope stands, pointed at the planet. She puts her eye on the eyepiece and makes some small sweeps. After a minute or so, she steps away and motions for me to look.

I put my eye on it, and I'm treated to a close-up view of a grassy field beside a tree line, but I see little else, so I pull myself away and look over at Krysta, who seems to watch me with major anticipation. I ask, "Is it okay if I move this? There's not much to see right here."

She lets out the breath she's been holding. "Look a little closer, a little longer."

I hold my own breath and move so close that my eye almost touches. There's high grass, just like on Earth. Trees. Rocks. If I didn't know I was orbiting a different planet, I wouldn't be able to distinguish this scene from Earth at all. A slight breeze causes the grass to ripple and roll. As the breeze blows some of the grass sideways, I notice something dark and shiny on the ground. It's an insect, a large one. It could be a beetle, but not quite. I strain my eye. The wind blows again, and it flies into the air. It looks like a huge wasp. It fights the wind for a moment, and then goes straight into the tree line and disappears into the forest. I jump back from the telescope, my heart thumping.

She stops me from tripping backwards. "So you saw one."

"Yes! How big is that thing? It looked bigger than me."

"It's possible. Some of them are pretty good size."

"The colonists know about those? What if one gets into their house? How many cans of bug spray would it take?"

She snorts a laugh. "They learn about them in orientation."

I look in the telescope again to get another look at that nightmarish creature, but it's gone. I turn back to Krysta. "You showed me a flashcard with one of those on it."

"I did."

"Do they sting?"

She turns from me to look at the planet through the window. "Apocrita."

"Right. You call the planet Apocrita. I still don't know what it means."

"Apocrita is a suborder of insects that includes wasps, bees, and ants. I named the planet after them. Plus, it sounds a lot better than New Mesopotamia."

"You named the planet after the scariest thing on it?"

"They are the apex predator in this world. They are intelligent. You could say they are Apocrita's counterpart to Earth's Humans."

"Have we contacted them?"

"Oh, yes."

"Do we, you know, get along?"

"Mostly. This is the perfect segue to our second purpose. We have a sort of research alliance. We trade technology and science. You remember that starfish device on McClure's ship that allowed instant communication? It's Apocritan tech."

I sit down on a nearby stool and plant my elbows on the stainless steel table so I can cup my chin in my hands. "We trade—"

"Technology and science, yes."

I look around this classified area. "You mean *we* trade," I say, pointing my index finger back and forth between the two of us.

She nods.

"Just us?"

"Us and McClure. Nobody else is involved. Well, nobody here. Of course, we have a headquarters back home."

"Celeres—"

"Celeres doesn't know specifics. He helped with a trade run once when McClure was sick, but never again after that. Everyone knows there's a joint research agreement, but the details are classified."

"So now what?"

"Now, we get to work." Krysta hits a nearby switch to turn on the lights. Now that I can see the room better, I see there are no other obvious exits. In fact, with the window/door closed, we seem to be completely enclosed. She walks over to a table by a window and pulls out a stool with a backrest on it. "This is you."

A white lab coat sits folded on the corner of the table.

She hands it to me and turns to open some drawers. The coat smells of stale perfume with a trace of cigarette smoke and has some minor stains, maybe from grease or chemicals, on the sleeves and front. I hold it at arm's length. "Is this one of yours?"

"No." She offers no more explanation, but pulls some shiny metal gadgets from the drawers and sets them on the worktable.

The coat doesn't have a name tag like hers, but it did; a couple of holes in the breast area betray that a name tag was pinned there once. I don't like the smell. "You wouldn't have a clean one by chance?"

She stops and gives it a critical look over the rims of her glasses. "I see what you mean." She takes it from me and stuffs it into her laptop case. "I'll get it washed tonight. Sorry about that."

Next, she hands me a pair of goggles. "You won't need 'em, but here you go." I put them down beside the other stuff and stand back to watch. She opens a large drawer and pulls out a greenish gold device that looks a little like a pistol, except instead of a barrel, it has curved golden calipers that look like they could grip a softball. Down at the inside base of the calipers is a needle made of what looks like solid gold. It tapers to a hollow open point, like a hypodermic.

"Speaking of McClure's starfish, this metal looks just like it," I say.

"It's made of the same stuff, yeah."

She makes a display of turning the device to give me a good look at it from every angle and then flips it upside down so the trigger points up. Through a small glass window about the size of my pinkie nail, a dim purple glow emanates from the grip of the device.

I recoil. "What should I do?"

"We need you to help us solve a big problem."

I take a seat on the stool, squinting at the strange device. "Uh...okay."

She presses something on the grip and a glass cylinder pops out of the butt of the handle, sort of like a magazine ejecting from a semi-automatic pistol. Inside the glass is a swirling, smoky cloud of purple light. "This is the battery."

I reach for it, but she pulls it away. "Not so fast. First, you need to know that this battery is one of the most valuable things on the station. Remember how you wanted to use the subspace radio on McClure's ship, and I told you the power source was low?" She sets it before me on a small round tray with raised edges so it can't roll off. "We need to find a way to synthesize our own. The Apocritans demand too high a price for these, and we can't keep paying it. Not at the rate we need."

"How's it going so far?"

"Nothing works, so we keep going back to the drawing board. That's where you come in." She slides the battery back into the device and pulls a little black box with a pair of probes attached from a drawer. "This is a voltmeter." She waves the probes and crosses their tips, looking down at the digital display on the meter. As the probes touch, the display shows a zero. "I need you to probe every little part of this artifact, record the voltages, the times, and locations of each reading." She pushes a notepad to me and pulls a pen from behind her ear. "We'll get you a laptop soon. Our old one broke. And one more thing...don't touch that needle at the base of the calipers with your skin. Only use your probes."

I take another look at the needle and wonder if I'm

probing the thing that the aliens probe people with. I'll be sure to keep my fingers and every other body part clear of it.

~

Over the next several hours, I poke at that device and write numbers down until my shoulders and neck ache. Krysta sits at a different table, working on something with blood. It might be mine. I don't know, and I don't feel like asking. The pages of my notebook fill with my recordings. I only look up once in a while to see what Krysta is doing, and to look out the window at the spectacular view of the planet and stars.

Just when it seems like my eyes are crossing from all of this focus, I feel a presence at my side, a white lab coat, and then she leans into me as she looks over everything I wrote. The entire side of her body presses into mine.

She runs her fingers down the column of numbers. "This looks good. Ready for a break?"

She's so close that when she exhales, her breath tickles my neck and shoulder. It always smells so fresh.

I give her a sidelong glance and a mischievous grin. "Did you just brush your teeth? Planning to kiss someone?"

She looks down, and her cheeks turn a slight pink. "I brush my teeth a lot. It's a little OCD, I admit."

She steps away to show me where all the equipment goes. "Next time, you can set this stuff up yourself. Once we figure out how to power this thing, I'll give you more interesting work, I promise."

We pack everything up and I follow her out of the lab and up the invisible staircase. After a long day like this, my fur baby always perks me up. "Can we go see Baxter?"

"Sure, then I'll drop you off at your place."

A few minutes later, we're strapped into her moon buggy, and we're on our way.

~

When we approach Beastarium, a parked moon buggy with chrome exhaust pipes and yellow flames comes into view. Celeres. Celeres? Krysta and I look at each other with puzzled expressions.

"What's he doing here?" she asks.

I shrug. Once we climb out, she opens the Beastarium door for me but doesn't follow me in. "I'll be out here."

It appears to be "daytime" in Beastarium; the sun is high in the sky and the fresh air fills my nostrils as a slight breeze blows. Don't get me wrong—the air in the station is perfectly breathable, but this feels like real fresh air. If they can make this kind of air for Beastarium, why don't they just do it for the entire station? I'll just add that to my list of questions for later.

I see Celeres right away—he plays fetch with Baxter in a nearby grassy area. I approach, but don't get very far before Baxter sees me and runs in my direction, his tongue flapping out the side of his mouth. Celeres looks over and sees that it's me and walks over as well. He's going at a pretty slow pace, almost like he's not real excited to see me.

Baxter, on the other hand, is as excited as ever and is already jumping at me and licking my hands as I try to keep him from knocking me over.

When Celeres gets within earshot, I call out. "What are you doing here, and why are you playing with my dog?"

"Oh." He stops. "I miss my own dog. I hope you don't mind."

I stare back, not sure if I'm ready to talk to him again so

soon. He didn't do much earlier to reassure me that he was over Krysta, and that's obviously a sore spot of mine.

"Are we good?" he asks.

Now that I'm over my initial shock at seeing him, I take a few steps closer. "I'm good. Are you?"

"I just feel bad about how we left things this morning."

"Look, forget it."

"I know trust has to be earned." He looks at me with even better puppy dog eyes than Baxter does.

"Maybe I'll cut you a little slack."

"Hey, listen. Can we go for a ride and talk a little? I could show you around some more."

Getting to learn a little more of the station layout could be useful. "I don't know. I guess, but only if we talk about our happy memories this time."

Baxter follows us to the exit, but I tell him to stay. His tail droops, but I do my best to cheer him up with a little scratch on the rump. He likes that.

Krysta stands against her buggy, not looking surprised at all when she sees us. She purses her lips, but says nothing.

"Hi Krysta," says Celeres.

"Hi."

This isn't awkward at all.

I break the silence. "Celeres wants to show me around."

"You don't need to go back and grab a quick bite or anything?"

"I'll get her something," says Celeres.

"Okay, I'll see you tomorrow then," she says, climbing into her buggy and driving away. We both watch until she disappears. I hope she isn't too weird about this next time I see her.

Celeres breaks me out of my thoughts. "So, how was your first day at work?"

"Simply amazing."

"Sounds sarcastic."

"It is."

He helps me into the buggy and we set off on our way.

Chapter Seventeen

First Kiss

As he drives, Celeres furrows his brow, appearing to be lost in thought. He's clearly not thinking about his driving, however; he drifts and corrects as we move along.

I look over. "Penny for your thoughts?"

He blinks a few times. "I'm trying to decide something."

"Oh?"

He doesn't answer, so I sit back and let my mind wander. Now that I've been here for a solid day, some of the awe is wearing off, and I feel like I'm noticing some of the more mundane (for a space station) things now. For example, while Celeres and I leave Beastarium behind, the hallways don't seem so gleaming white and clean as they did when I arrived. Scuffs cover the floors and the occasional light fixture might be a little dimmer or brighter than the others. The people mill about just like they would at a mall back home. Some go to jobs, some go to the stores, and some spend their evening in the bars, only to get up the next day, go to work, then head back the next night. I guess we humans still act like humans, whether we're on Earth, or if we're far, far away.

It also makes me wonder what it's like in the colonies. What is A Day in the Life like down there? Is it just more of the same? Some people on Earth worry about dangerous neighborhoods. Do they have that here? It's a new world; maybe there are pockets like the Wild West. I picture outlaws on wanted posters and sheriffs with six-guns. A change of scenery doesn't change evil men. Or women.

Now he's the one breaking me out of a trance. "Okay, I've decided. Do you want to go for a ride?"

"Isn't that what we're doing?"

"I mean in my ship."

"Your ship? Like your space ship? Tonight?"

"Yeah, right now."

I barely know this guy, except that he tried to block me from getting here in the first place. How much do I trust him? Maybe I can stall. "I don't know. I have to work in the morning. I have to eat dinner. Couldn't we go on, like, Saturday or something?"

"You get the weekends off?"

I didn't expect that answer. "Uh, I hope so." I'd *better* get weekends off. I never thought about the possibility that I might have to work in the lab every single day.

He looks over at me for a second. "You said something about dinner. How about I cook for us?"

He's a nice enough guy, and Baxter seems to like him. Maybe that's all I need to take a first step. At least for now. I lift my hands like I'm giving up. "I guess so." This should be interesting.

He makes a quick left turn. As we move along, it's easy to tell when we leave the residential/civilian parts of the station because people's clothing changes. Instead of casual and typical work attire, more and more people wear military fatigues and uniforms. We get to a point where Celeres trades salutes with nearly everyone we pass. Almost everyone stares at me.

I feel out of place. "Should I have a flight suit or something?"

"No, you're fine."

We soon arrive at the hangar and he parks his moon buggy in a nearby parking row.

"Celeres!" comes a cheerful voice from several yards away. I recognize it instantly. It's Brose, Chief Engineer.

Celeres waves. "You on deck instead of McClure today, buddy?"

Brose looks over his shoulder and back. "Yeah, it's Jerk-wad's day off."

"I like you better. We want to take *Big Seven* out for a ride. She gassed up?"

"Always. The boys take good care of her," says Brose with a huge grin. I can barely see his teeth through that unruly beard of his. I bet some of my hair products could help that monstrosity. "Hi Leigh, how's your dog doing?" he asks me.

"Good. We were just visiting him. Looks like he's been making friends." I point at Celeres with my thumb.

He lifts his chin at the moon buggy behind us. "How's *Little Seven* treating you, Cel?"

"Much better turns since you replaced the steering rack," Celeres says.

Brose gives a devilish smile. "This one's titanium. I know how much you appreciate a good rack."

Oh, brother. I slap my palm to my forehead and shake my head.

Celeres sees my expression and laughs. "That's enough vulgarity out of you, Brose."

Brose laughs in kind. "Okay, man. *Big Seven* is in her normal spot. Be careful out there."

"We will."

~

After a short walk, we get to his ship, *Big Seven*. Its paint job is like a big version of *Little Seven*, with flames along the side, and a 7 painted in the middle.

He opens the hatch, and a ladder extends to the ground. "Up you go. There's plenty of room."

I take a quick look around to say goodbye to Brose, but he's gone. His voice carries throughout the hangar, though. It sounds like he's ordering someone around. After that, his booming laughter echoes. I grab the sides of the ladder and hoist myself into Celeres's ship.

It has a leathery smell, which is much more preferable to the oily undertones of the hangar. It's a lot roomier than I expected, too. Of course, it's not as roomy as *Ice Arrow*, but it has pilot and copilot seats, and a bench seat behind those.

"It folds back," he explains, appearing through the hatch. "It has a mattress—"

I give him a look. My eyebrows arched.

"—You know, for sleeping."

I give a teasing smile and head to the copilot seat. "Can I sit up here?"

"Uh, yeah. Of course," he says while he takes a seat himself and punches a few buttons.

The ladder retracts, and the hatch closes behind us with a soft sliding sound. There's a subtle chime, and we're surrounded by hissing as air from the life support system circulates in the cabin. It smells the same as the recycled air in *Ice Arrow*.

Once we're buckled in, he puts his hand on a palm pad, and it turns green. He then pushes a few buttons, and we rise straight up into the air. My stomach does a flip. "Whoa. A little warning next time."

He laughs. "We're only leaving our berth."

He pushes the throttle forward and moves the flight stick so that we point toward a giant opening into star-filled space. "One student clipped the side of the hangar while practicing landing a few days ago. Let's see how the repairs are going."

"Yeah, I heard about that. Did they get in trouble?"

He shakes his head. "No. When the poor kid hit the side of the door, he did a flat spin, coming in like a Frisbee. Just about gave Brose a heart attack. Good thing the arrester cables caught him before he crashed into something more expensive than a space-sized garage door. He'll have to take some safety classes and spend more time in the simulator before they let him back out. Plus, he'll have to get back on Brose's good side."

We float toward the door as if we're on a cloud. There's a slight vibration in the ship, but nothing more. The sound of the thrusters is barely perceptible. This feels exactly like flying in *Ice Arrow*.

As we approach the hangar door, I scrutinize the opening to find the damaged area. A second later, a shower of welding sparks gives it away. As we approach, the cockpit glass in our ship darkens to protect our eyes from the bright light of the welds. I was expecting to see men in space suits working on the repair. Instead, it looks like a giant spider, big as an SUV, is doing all the work.

I'm throughly creeped out. "What is that?"

"That's Max. I'm told he started off as a medical robot, but being a car-sized spider, I think he scared more patients than he healed. Anyway, due to popular demand, we taught him how to fix mechanical things instead. He's so good at it that now he gets all the big jobs. He can even work outside in zero-grav. His feet are like big electromagnets."

"Where'd he come from?"

"Krysta traded some tech for him."

"He's an alien robot?"

"Yep."

Now that we're closer, the details of his body are easier to see. At a distance, I doubt anyone could tell him apart from a giant living spider, but up-close, his entire body is of a burnished green-gold metal. A purple glow emits from the sockets where his eight legs attach.

I shiver. It figures a race of wasplike aliens would make a robot that looks like another bug. "I wouldn't want him touching me, either."

We float by, and Max gives us a wave with one of his appendages. I wave back with a sickened expression, and Celeres laughs. "The thing learns behavior from us. He can wave and...watch this." He salutes, and Max salutes back. "See?"

I salute, and he repeats the gesture back to me, too.

"Get back to work, Max. No breaks for robots," says Celeres.

I don't think Max heard him, but he returns to his welding job, anyway. When I turn and look back through the cockpit glass, we're in space. It's easier to see now that the auto-darkening in the glass fades.

A male voice fills the cabin, "Authenticate for departure."

"Big Seven," says Celeres.

"Roger, be careful."

"You can just leave anytime you want to?" I ask.

"I can. There are no restrictions on the fighters."

"What do you guys fight, anyway?"

"Nothing, but every station has defense, security, police, all of it."

I nod like it makes perfect sense. "Because you never know."

"You got it. Suppose some other corporation or government on Earth wanted *Sumerian*. We'd have to stand our ground."

"Makes sense."

I settle back in my seat to enjoy the ride. One major difference between this and *Ice Arrow* is that the cockpit has a much larger view of the outside. There's like four times the glass in *Big Seven*.

Once we are far enough from *Sumerian*, Celeres turns his ship until we face Apocrita. This is even a nicer view than what I'm used to in my room. As I watch, the planet gets closer and closer.

"Celeres, are we—"

"—going to the planet," he says. "I told you I'd cook dinner, didn't I?"

"Down there? Do you have a house or something?"

"Nah."

"Restaurant?"

"Nope. We'll build a fire. When was the last time you had a good fire-cooked meal?"

We used to have campfires all the time when my dad was around. That's where Baxter got his love of hot dogs. "It's been a long time."

"Well, it's perfect timing. The sun will set soon."

As we approach, he picks a spot that's several miles away from the lights of the colonies. I spot a campfire ring near the tree line. "Privacy," he explains.

The trip takes only about five minutes, and before I know it, we touch down. "This is my spot," he says. "We'll gather wood in the forest and have our fire right here by the ship."

I can't believe I'm on a completely new planet. I pop my harness and go straight to the door.

"You're excited? Good," Celeres says as he gets out of his own seat. The interior lights dim to a very low level and the engine vibrations become so soft that I have to strain to know that they are still there.

I reach up to the button on the side of the door. "Can I open it?"

"Be my guest."

The door slides open, and the ladder lowers itself to the soft turf of the new world. Fresh air rushes in. It was just a few days ago when I thought that stepping out into the heat of Arizona was the biggest transition I'd ever experience. But wow, how about this?

I leer into the world beyond. "It's safe?"

"It is. See for yourself."

Ten seconds later, I stand in the grass up to my knees and wait for him to join me. Everything about this is like the synthetic world in Beastarium on *Sumerian*. Even the fresh air smells the same.

Celeres catches me inhaling deeply. "Nice, isn't it? You know the air in Beastarium is actually *from* here. We take it up in large cannisters at least once a day."

"That explains it. I was wondering about that."

"Yep."

He pops a compartment open on the fuselage and pulls a couple of camp chairs out. He unfolds both of them and sits them together near the fire ring. "I'm going to gather some firewood."

I'm not real keen on him disappearing off into the woods and leaving me here by myself. "Wait, I'm coming with you."

"Sure, come on."

We cross the tree line and walk into the forest. It's quite dark, but light enough to see sticks on the ground. We hunt around and collect the easy pieces. The wood has a very pleasant smell that is unlike anything I've smelled before. All I can say is that it's pleasant in much the same way that birch and sassafras are.

"Is this your get-away spot?" I ask as we work.

"It's so much more."

"Oh?" I'm wondering if this is where he brings all his women.

"Whenever I feel like I need to get off the station, which happens quite a lot, I come here. My garden is nearby. You know, the one with the carrots?"

"It is? The very garden we talked about on Earth?"

"The same. It's getting too dark to appreciate it, though. Come on, let's finish with the wood and I'll get the fire started. Then you can try my famous kabobs."

"Sounds good to me."

So far, Apocrita has reminded me of Earth. What's different so far are the sounds, particularly the crickets. I mean, maybe they aren't crickets at all, but that's what I'm going to call them for now. On Earth, they have their chirping sound and soothing night chorus. Here, they all sort of have their own tone. If I were to compare it to anything, I'd say it's like the sound when you walk into a casino and even though all the slot machines are making their own bleeps and bloops, they all sound pleasant together. It's kind of like that, but not exactly. These are the musical crickets of Apocrita, and their symphony surrounds us.

Without realizing it, I let Celeres get ahead of me, and it's not until he calls out for me from deeper inside the forest that I realize that I've been standing amid the sounds in a daze. He waves his hand in the deepening darkness to get my attention and I head in his direction.

"I call it nightsong," he says.

"It's beautiful."

"I knew you'd like it here."

I point to a bluish glow a short distance away, deeper into the forest. "What's that over there?"

"Oh, that's a patch of Iridilume. Come on, I'll show you."

We hike over that way, and it turns out the source of the glow is a patch of ferns, glowing with an iridescent blue light.

He picks one and hands it to me. "Meet the Iridilume fern. It collects light during the day and glows at night, just like a lot of plants here. It makes a great tea."

"Oh, I know. I had some with Krysta."

He gives me a knowing smile. "Okay then, so you know all about it already. Let's finish getting that wood."

Soon, our arms are full, and we head back to the campsite. Celeres has a baby flame going in no time. The nightsong fades into the background, just behind the crackling of the flames. Smoke winds its way into the air and I get a whiff of it—it's just like how Dad's fires smelled, but with the undertones of the alien wood I smelled before. A goofy grin forms on my face as I lean backward with my eyes closed. Celeres is right; I do like it here.

He pulls a cooler from the same compartment where the chairs came from and sets it down below the hatch with a grunt, and then he opens the lid. "I got some meat from Brose earlier. He sometimes comes down with me to hunt." He digs around inside and pulls out a plastic bag of meat chunks in some kind of marinade.

I try to look at the meat through the bag. "What kind of meat is that?"

"Matlurf."

"Meatloaf?"

He smiles and shakes his head at the ground. "Good one Leigh. They're a grazing animal that you find all over the place down here. They're shaped like buffalo, except they don't have horns and maybe only twice the size of your dog. Instead of hair, they're armored with bony plates. Brose likes to hunt them for the meat and thrill."

"Thrill?"

"Oh yeah. You have to hit them in one of their few soft spots, or get ready to dodge a ricocheting bullet."

I sigh. "Men."

"We're incorrigible, I know."

"Do the Matlurf have beards like buffalo?"

"No, but Brose does."

I snort. "He's closer to buffalo than they are."

Celeres points at me. "I've seen him without a shirt. You're more right than you think."

Once he spears about twenty pieces of meat, he puts the bag away and pulls his camp chair closer to mine. He looks at the fire for a good cooking spot and holds the stick over it. I look up at his face, at the firelight reflecting in his eyes.

"What are you looking at?" he asks, still focused on his cooking.

"You. You're so serious."

"I know. This is serious business. Wait until you try it."

I lean back and enjoy the moment. He turns the sizzling

meat within the flames. I catch a whiff of the aroma and my mouth waters.

"Celeres?"

"Yeah?" he replies, never taking his eyes off of his kabob.

"How old are you?"

"I'm twenty-four. How about you?"

"Eighteen."

He nods and continues to cook. We're both quiet for a little while. Eventually, he speaks in a low voice, "When I first came here, I used to build these fires and look up at the stars. Wouldn't it be nice if we could see the ones we remembered from Earth? You know, the Big Dipper, stuff like that. I guess we're too far away, or maybe we're just pointed different or something. That connection would have been cool, you know?"

"Maybe there's no Earth-star connection, but I'm the same Leigh you remember from Earth, you know."

"I like that connection."

"I'm glad."

He looks at me again, and we lock eyes for a few moments. This is it. He leans into me with a little smile, and I part my lips ever so slightly, but a sizzling sound from the fire interrupts him.

He turns the stick to cook the other side. "I think of other things, too—"

I close my mouth and sigh through my nose.

"—like the colony. Do you wonder if it's possible that the humans on Earth started like this? Just a bunch of colonists from another planet somewhere? You know, Mesopotamia—the original one—is known as the cradle of civilization on Earth. Who knows? Maybe a previous expeditionary ship left them behind and forgot about them.

"Are you saying that humans were alien invaders on Earth?"

"Maybe, I guess so. But if you think about it, humans are aliens without doubt. Even the Matlurf here would call you and I alien, wouldn't they?"

"These are some deep thoughts, Celeres."

He pulls the stick out of the fire and balances it on a log. "Just look at these babies." The skewered meat sizzles and pops. It smells amazing.

He gets up and tosses more wood onto the fire before heading to the ship's compartment for a couple of plates. Like a proper host, he fixes a plate for me and offers it with a bow.

I accept it graciously. He makes a plate for himself and sits down.

The meat's still too hot to handle, so I blow on it for a second, and then look into his eyes. "Now that I have you cornered, I have a question for you."

He was just getting ready to pop a bite into his mouth, but puts it back on his plate while his mouth slowly closes.

"Should I be worried?"

"Just tell me the truth. Admit it was you who blocked me from coming."

He puts his plate down and stares into the fire. "Yes, it was me."

"Why would you do that? I've been trying to figure it out. Even if you weren't interested, even after sending me the flowers and everything, why go to the trouble to single me out and block me from coming to *Sumerian?*"

Now he does get a bite and chews while he forms a reply. I will not let him off the hook, not this time. I can outwait him just as well as outrun him.

"Because, Leigh. There's something going on with

Genomica. I don't know what it is, but I don't think it's honest or good. I blocked you to protect you, because I liked you."

"Liked me?"

"Like you."

I take a breath to talk, but he continues instead. "I don't know what it is, but I have a feeling. Why can't colonists contact their Earth families? We have the technology. That's what all those protests are about. Those people are literally disappearing off the face of Earth, never to be heard from again."

"Krysta said communications were prohibitive because of a battery shortage and—"

"I know. It's what they signed up for, but I just don't like it. Not only that, I don't know if I trust Krysta."

"Don't let your emotions carry you away, Celeres."

"This isn't about me. I'm over her. I feel there's something going on with Genomica and she's in the middle of it."

I look up through the trees where the colored stars beam down on us. "I don't know. She hasn't said anything suspicious to me."

"Hmm."

I snap my attention back to him. "What? You're giving me butterflies, and not the good kind."

He purses his lips. "Have you heard of Sharon Hone?"

"Doesn't sound familiar. What does she look like?"

"Middle aged, short brown hair, normal size, about your height, never smiles. She was one of the lab workers. She spent a lot of time with Krysta."

"I haven't met any of them yet. Next time I walk past the labs, I'll look."

"You won't find her."

We're quiet for a minute. I poke at the embers with a long stick. "So, do you think Krysta did something to her?"

His face looks so sad. "I do."

"You talk about her as if she's dead," I say with more than a little trepidation.

He stares at me, his eyes full of concern. "You know your new quarters on Sumerian, your new home? Those were Sharon's."

Now it's my turn to put my plate down. "What?"

He nods. "Yes. As I said, I don't like it."

I gulp. "Can we change the subject for now?"

He pushes his food around with his fork. "I'm sorry. I just didn't know how to tell you. But now you know."

A small flame appears at the end of the stick I had in the fire. I pull it out and slowly trace my name in the air with fiery letters.

The firelight reflects in his eyes as he considers me. "You're quite the firebug."

I allow a slight smile to creep onto my lips. "My dad always called me that."

"So you've done a lot of campfires, then?"

"Yeah, camping with my family, parties with my friends. I lived in the country, you know. We like to burn. Sometimes we'd clear some land for a new field, and there'd be all this wood."

"How big was your farm?"

"Fifty-seven acres."

He gives a low whistle and nods.

"That's right. I'm quite the country bumpkin. I'm still looking forward to checking in on your carrots, you know."

"Yes! That's right. We'll pick some veggies next time and take them back. I'll cook a proper meal for you."

Hmm, is this his way of getting me to his place? That could be interesting.

"I don't know. I'm picky, you know."

"Picky?" He looks worried.

"Yeah, picky eater. Sometimes." I smile.

He takes a bite of kabob. "You're teasing me."

"Maybe a little. Well, maybe we should get back before it gets dark. I have another exciting day in the lab tomorrow."

"You forgot to tell me about your day."

"I don't want to talk about the lab anymore. Maybe some other time. Besides, I have a feeling that most of my work days are going to be exactly the same."

"That's depressing."

While we talk, he packs up the campsite and tucks everything back into the fuselage compartment. I glimpse some canvas, blankets, and pillows in there while he arranges everything to fit. Maybe camping under the stars sometime would be nice.

Just as he's shutting the compartment, there's a faint buzzing sound, like when you trap a bee in a blanket. He must hear it too, because he fully opens the hatch and cocks an ear into the storage space. I hold my breath.

"It's not coming from in there," he says, shutting the hatch in one quick motion.

We stand still and listen. The buzzing gets louder, but only a little. Off in the distance, over the treetops, a shifting cloud of insects rises into the night. It's almost impossible to see them in the deepening darkness, but it's a clear night and the stars provide enough light to see it.

"What is that?" I whisper.

"I think it's *them*."

"Them? The aliens?" I shiver. "What are they doing?"

He shakes his head. "Looks like they're swarming."

They rise higher and higher, up into the sky until they are out of sight.

"Where are they going?" I ask.

"Who knows? There's a lot to learn about our new neighbors."

"I'm ready to go."

"Yeah, me too."

~

Our trip back to *Sumerian* is just as quick as our trip down to Apocrita, and before I know it we're on his moon buggy, heading back to my place. Minutes later, we're at my quarters. I lean over and bump shoulders with him. "Thank you for today. I'm looking forward to next time."

"Me too."

He leans over for a kiss, and I wrap my arms around his neck because this is going to take a while.

Both of us blush when we part.

He reaches into a pocket. "Before I forget, I made something for you."

"No one has ever made me anything. What is it?"

He pulls out a wooden figurine carved into the shape of a dog. "It's Baxter." He hands it to me.

It really does resemble Baxter. My eyes feel glassy. "Thank you, it's beautiful. How long did it take—"

"Not long. It's a hobby of mine."

"I love it."

"I'm glad. I wanted this to be the first knick-knack for your quarters."

I smile and kiss him again. When we part, I rest my head on his shoulder.

He runs his fingers through my hair. "I'll see you tomorrow?"

"Absolutely."

He whispers into my ear, "Remember what I told you about Krysta. Please be careful."

I nod, then let myself out of *Little Seven* and into my quarters. I walk over to my dresser and set my little Bax down.

"He's one of the good ones," I say to myself as I change into bed clothes and climb into the covers. Fifteen minutes later, I'm fast asleep.

Chapter Eighteen

A Deal in the Dark

I awaken some hours later to the speakerphone ringing on top of my dresser. I jump out of bed and hit the button. "Uhh, hello?"

"Hi, it's Krysta. I have something fun for us today. A field trip."

A field trip? Is this a dream? Did I oversleep? I need a shower because my hair still smells like campfire smoke. My eyes are itchy and watery from it too. "A field trip? To where?" I don't want to go on a field trip. I want to see Celeres.

"The zoo I was telling you about. You'll see new animals. It'll be fun."

I put the phone on mute and groan. I need to get a clock in here. I couldn't have gotten any more than a few hours of sleep.

"Leigh? Are you still there?"

I blink a few times and hit the button to talk. "Is it safe? Do any of the monsters spit acid or anything?"

"Animals. No. Trust me."

Trust isn't really in my vocabulary, but I'm here, so...
"When?"

"Fifteen minutes?"

Oh, man. "Okay, see you in fifteen." I slam the button down on the phone and run to the bathroom to take the universe's fastest shower.

When she knocks on my door, I'm wrestling with a piece of floss stuck between two molars. I swear that was only ten minutes. "Just a second," I yell. I dash to my dresser and find a fresh Genomica uniform. I take a quick look in the mirror. Yep, same look as always: Little Miss Genomica. We'll go with the wet hair look today. I work the floss loose and throw on a pair of shoes.

When I walk outside, I'm immediately jealous; Krysta wears a nice pair of white shorts and a pink tube top. Not cool. "When do I get some casual clothes?"

"I'll take you shopping as soon as you get paid."

"Am I getting paid for this field trip because—"

"Yes, you're getting paid. Hey, what's the hurry? You look nice in company gear."

I look myself over and then back to her. "Spare me."

We cruise down the hall, and I'm still amazed at how quiet these buggies are. There are still no signs of neighbors, and I don't see another living, breathing person until we're on the main thoroughfare. The good news is that I'm getting familiar with some twists and turns, and it won't be much longer before I could jog to work, breakfast, Beastarium, and the hangar. I wonder what else this station has to do and see.

"You're going to love Apocrita, Leigh. I've been looking forward to showing you around."

She doesn't know I was on the planet last night with Celeres. Glad I washed the smoke out of my hair. I don't want to dampen her excitement, so I play along. "Sounds exciting. I haven't been to a zoo since I was in fourth grade. Come to think of it, that was also during a field trip."

She laughs and gives me a playful punch on the shoulder. "You've come full circle."

Soon, the hangar entrance comes into view and we park about two spots away from *Little Seven*. Of course I glance around for Celeres, but don't see him.

We step out of Krysta's moon buggy amid a handful of technicians and mechanics. They stumble around, tired, like this is the start of their shift or the end.

She pulls three backpacks from the buggy and shoulders them. "Let's go. I'll show you Celeres's ship."

"Can I help you with those?"

She turns and walks toward *Big Seven*. "No, let's go."

Soon, I see it, just like I left it last night. Celeres stands on a wing with some sort of meter as he paces back and forth with a look of concentration. He seems very intent on what he's doing. When we approach, he looks up and breaks into a wide grin. His entire face smiles: his lips, his teeth, his ears, and his eyes, those beautiful eyes, sparkle as the smile lines at their corners reveal themselves. "Hey, it's my two favorite ladies," he calls.

I break my gaze from those eyes and look at Krysta. She smiles back at him. "Hi Cel."

Is she blushing? I feel my face flush and I look away.

He hops from the wing and puts his tools away. With his back to us, he continues, "I hear we're going on a zoo adventure today? Climb aboard."

We climb in, and I'm more than a little annoyed that Krysta takes my seat in the front, but this gives me a chance to test out the rear bench. It's comfortable, but I still scowl when I see them up there. I feel like I'm sitting in the back seat of the family car while Mom and Dad have their own conversation up front.

We proceed out of the hangar, and it looks like Max finished the repairs because the hangar door looks whole again, and I don't see him anywhere.

Five minutes later, we're floating over the surface of the planet. Celeres flies over the campsite and tips the wing so that I get a good view. Krysta doesn't give any reaction. Maybe he never took her there? I have little time to think about it because in just a minute later, we land. He looks across at Krysta. "I need to run a couple of errands. Pick you up at 17:00 then?"

"You aren't coming?" I ask, but he doesn't hear me because Krysta talks over me.

"That's perfect," she says with her trademark smile, and touches his arm.

I bite my tongue and head over to the hatch. She joins me and ushers me out of the aircraft, into what feels like the tropics. Heat washes over me, and the humidity is high. The air feels thick to breathe. It wasn't like this last night. Before I know it, *Big Seven* lifts back off and I barely get a glimpse of Celeres in the cockpit. I wave, and he salutes me. Cute.

Krysta takes a deep breath. "I just love this fresh air."

I look down at the sweat stains already beginning to appear on my black outfit. "Yeah."

We're left standing in the center of a big concrete slab. Next to the slab is an asphalt parking lot, and it's filled with all-terrain vehicles like the Quad my uncle used to have before he flipped it over while cutting grass.

Vehicles continue to arrive, and people file through the parking lot to a nearby moving walkway. Only a handful of couples push babies in strollers. I squint, trying to see if I'm missing any. "I'd expect to see more children."

Krysta nods. "Very observant. We only colonize adults. These things take time."

"I don't think I've ever seen so many grownups at the zoo without kids."

She shrugs. "There's not a lot to do down here. We're working on adding more, but in the meantime, they can entertain themselves by having more babies."

Forest surrounds this entire property. It's like we're in the middle of nowhere. I look past the treetops. "Where's the colony from here? I expected to see buildings or something."

She points. "Far. Since the zoo is also a scientific lab for the Apocritans, they wanted some distance from the colony. It takes about thirty minutes by road."

"I'd like to visit the colony sometime."

"We will. So what did you and Celeres do last night?"

"Went for a ride, talked, just hung out."

"You think there's something brewing there?"

"I hope so. He can be hard to read."

"You know you can talk to me if you ever need a shoulder to cry on."

"I hope I don't need that anytime soon. I'm still stinging from my last relationship."

"I hope you don't need it, either."

There's a scent in the air. I don't recognize it, but I think I know what it is: pollen. There's so much vegetation here. It's like my farm, except here I don't have my allergy pills.

She looks at me like she expects an answer, and I snap out of my thoughts. "What? Oh, right. Thank you. Sorry, I'm just taking this all in. Should we just follow all these people?"

"No. I'm going to leave you here for about twenty

minutes. There's something I need to do, and I have to do it myself."

"With your three backpacks?"

"Yes. Just wait for me here, and I'll be back in a jiffy and we'll go in."

She turns and walks straight for the woods, disappearing down a dark path in the trees, and now I'm by myself on this cement slab that's radiating heat from the relentless sun. I'm getting cooked out here, and those arriving zoo visitors are staring at me like I'm lost or something. It couldn't hurt if I just wandered to that tree line just to get a little shade and be out of plain sight.

I meander to the trees like I'm out for a leisurely stroll and know where I'm going. I don't look back, and nobody calls out to me.

Once I get there, I'm greeted by the dark path Krysta took. It winds into the woods, beckoning me to enter. The forest is thick here, in a primordial way. I take a few steps in and look around, thinking about how Celeres and I collected wood last night for our fire.

I take several more steps and glimpse Iridilume ferns off to my left. They aren't glowing at the moment because they're collecting light.

Now that I've gone this far, why stop? There's no harm in a leisurely hike while I wait. If I come to a fork, then I'll just turn around.

Suddenly, Krysta appears ahead, coming this way. "What are you doing?"

I squeak in surprise.

"Quiet! I already heard you from way up ahead. I told you to stay back at the landing pad."

"Sorry. I just wanted to get some shade, and then I saw these ferns, and then..."

"Listen, if I tell you to stay back, it's for your own good, so will you please go back to the landing pad until I'm done here?"

I just look at her. I'm not going back there to stand by myself, not in the blazing sun.

She clicks her tongue. "Fine. We have to meet someone. When we do, keep a fair distance and don't talk, okay?"

"Okay."

She walks back down the path and looks back at me. "This leads to the backside of one of the buildings."

I want to ask her why we just don't go to the front, but she's already moving at a brisk pace, her three backpacks thumping against her body with each step. She brushes broad leaves and branches aside as she goes, and I have to bob and weave to miss them. I keep my mouth shut so I don't eat a branch.

"Here it is," she says between huffs and puffs. Up ahead, about twenty feet, is a squat, cinderblock building. A dumpster sits beside it, with dual PVC pipes protruding up and out, higher than the roof of the building.

I look at it for a second, curious. "Why are they venting a dumpster?"

She follows my stare. "Oh, it's not. It's for zoo compost. The pipes vent it for better decomposition and less stench. I helped them set it up."

We approach the building, and she heads toward the building's only feature—a greenish-gold metal door. I want to have a better look at the dumpster, so I walk over and lift the lid.

Krysta sees what I'm doing. "Leigh? Come on."

I stand on my tiptoes and look inside. It's not only empty, but it's squeaky clean, as if compost never touched the inside. It appears to have a drain of some sort on the bottom.

Krysta continues to stare at me, with one hand on her hip. I go to rejoin her at the door before she actually taps her foot.

Stenciled onto it are a few dark glyphs in a jagged alien alphabet. She pulls the handle, almost tentatively. When it opens, she closes her eyes and lets out a long breath in the middle of her already-labored breathing. "I didn't think we'd make it in time."

I look behind, moving my head from side to side, trying to see around all the vegetation. I listen for anything unusual. Nothing. She pulls the door open an inch, and air conditioning rushes out of the crack.

She slips inside. "Okay, come on. Remember to stand back."

I follow her after a last furtive glance behind.

When the door closes, we're in near-total darkness. The only light in this room comes from blinking instrument panels, and there aren't many at that. She told me to stay back, and that sounds good to me. I keep one hand on the door handle and squint at Krysta's shape in the gloom.

She takes about a dozen steps into the room and stops. Every nerve in my body tenses and I wish I had just stayed back at the tree line like I was supposed to. I trust her, though. She wouldn't knowingly put me in danger, at least I don't think so. I'm just getting myself worked up for no reason. I regulate my breathing to calm down.

She stands there, still. What is she waiting for?

Then, out of the eerie silence, there are scraping foot-steps approaching us from deeper in the room. They stop in front of Krysta.

Darker than the darkness itself, the silhouette of a wasp,

maybe four feet tall, materializes in front of her. Without a word, Krysta removes her backpacks and drops them to the floor at its feet.

It makes some clicking sounds, and something attached to Krysta's waist translates in a metallic voice, "How many?"

Krysta unclips the device from her belt. It's a black plastic sphere, the size of a baseball, with lights and buttons. She speaks into it, "Same as always—thirty, and no more."

The device clicks several times and then makes a disgusting slurping sound.

The wasp walks past her and approaches me. Its eyes fill me with dread. I freeze.

Krysta sighs and approaches as well. "Dammit, no."

It leans closer so that it's only a foot away and its antennas reach toward my face. Any closer, and they'd be tickling my cheeks. I am paralyzed with fear.

Then it turns toward Krysta and issues a rapid series of clicks. Her translator crackles to life again. "I will take—"

She turns it off, causing him to look back and forth between her and I. She points at the backpacks while putting herself between us.

It makes a few more short, loud clicks, and then picks up the backpacks before melting back into the darkness.

"What are we doing here?" I ask Krysta in slow, even tones.

"I'll tell you in a minute. Let's go." She puts her translator away and walks in almost the same direction the wasp went, further into the darkness. My heartbeat thrums in my chest as I rest one hand on her shoulder so that I don't get lost.

We shuffle along for a few seconds. From the darkness beside me, cold metal brushes against my little finger and I jerk my hand away from it.

A few more steps and the air fills with a subtle hum and the sounds of bubbles, like we're in a giant tropical fish store. My hand covers Krysta's shoulder in sweat. I wish I could see...anything.

My fingers brush against metal once again, and then someone presses something, possibly the same thing, into the palm of my hand. It feels like a cold pencil.

"Krysta? What's this for?"

She pauses for a moment. "I'll tell you when we get out of here."

I slip the object into my pocket.

"How much farther? I'm having a panic attack."

"We're almost there. It will be okay."

I gulp. "Please hurry."

She grabs my sweaty hand from her shoulder and pulls it down. With a firm, warm grip, she picks up the pace.

She stops and taps a wall near us. "There we go."

A vertical slice of light pierces the darkness and widens quickly. A door to outside. She slips through and I follow on her heels.

"Shut it," she hisses. "Quick."

I steal a glance behind while the door closes. Light pours in, revealing a cavernous room, full of large vertical cylinders connected to both floor and ceiling. Each cylinder is glass, full of liquid, containing...specimens? The door clicks in the jamb and I let out a shuddering breath.

Chapter Nineteen

Contraband

With my back against the door, I slide down and hug my knees. We appear to be right smack in the middle of the zoo. People walk by with popcorn and cotton candy. An overhead water mister sprays a cloud a few feet above, and the water particles rain down on me. It helps, some. People amble by, paying no attention while I sit on the ground, waiting for my anxiety to ebb. Krysta stands in front of me, blocking me from view as best she can. I take a few minutes to collect myself.

I'm still a little shaky, but I rise to my feet. Krysta hears the motion and looks over her shoulder at me. "You okay?"

My mouth is completely dry. "Water."

"Come on," she says. While we walk, I try to take in my surroundings. This is a lot like an Earth zoo. She's taking me to the water station up ahead, but I can still catch glimpses of some exhibits and exotic animals around us.

We walk past a fenced-in area with a pond, lots of grass, and about a dozen furry gray-brown balls rolling around. Every now and again, one will stop and its eyes pop open to look at the crowd. The women visitors give a collective

"Awwww." I roll my eyes, but I have to admit, they *are* awfully cute.

We get to the water station and I grab a plastic cup and fill it. I drink one, two, then three cups.

Krysta holds out her hand, palm outstretched. "Careful, there. You'll float away."

I crush the cup and toss it into the bin. "You said you'd tell me when we got out. We're out. Explain."

"It's their research facility."

"Yeah, but what did you han—"

She makes a lower-your-voice gesture and looks around. "Hand it? It was blood, Leigh."

I was going to ask her what she handed me in the darkness, but now I'm wondering if it was Krysta who handed it to me at all. Whatever is in my pocket is going to stay a secret for now, and I'll let this conversation flow.

I take a step back. "Krysta, did you...give them my blood?"

She shakes her head. "I would never do that, Leigh."

A few people gather close to us and I realize that I'm blocking the water station. I pull Krysta over to some nearby shrubs and lower my voice so she can barely hear. "Why are you giving them human blood?"

"Our form fascinates them. They are trying to create human clones within their own society."

"Why would they do that?"

"I don't know all of their intentions, but it's part of our trade agreement."

If this isn't creepy and sketchy, I don't know what is. I make a gun gesture with my hand. "They traded us that caliper gun device we have up in our lab. The thing I'm taking readings from?"

"Yes."

"Tell me more about it."

She gets very close to me now and lifts her mouth so her lips brush my ear as she whispers. "Be quiet about that. I'll tell you more later, but this isn't the place." While she talks, she inches even closer, until we're touching. Her breath, clean and fresh against my neck, is a sudden reminder of her allure. If the circumstances were different, I might feel tempted to kiss her. She wants me to. I can tell.

But I can't. I really want to see where things go with Celeres. I force myself to take a step back, and we lock eyes. She smiles a crooked smile and backs off a step, too. I blink a few times and sigh. This is new. Part of me wants to run away from her as fast as I can. The other part of me...I don't know.

She looks at her watch. "We have one more errand to do."

"You are changing the subject."

"I know. It's a conversation we should have later."

I take a deep breath. "Fine. What errand?"

"Don't worry, this will be easy. Enough zoo for one day?"

"But we just got here."

"I know, but there's something I need in the forest. If we have time to spare, we'll come back and I'll show you how a drossler drinks. You have to see it."

I shake my head and follow her. There's a couple walking in our general direction, hand in hand. The woman is rapt at the sight of the strange animals, but the guy seems a lot more interested in Krysta and me. As we get close, he smiles and says hello. The woman casts a sidelong glance at us and drags him along.

～

By now, the parking lot is full of vehicles, and the people are all inside the zoo. The landing pad where Celeres dropped us off is still empty. There's not a soul out here. She heads straight into the trees again, but this time to a different spot. I follow for now, but I'm absolutely not going to walk into any more cinder block buildings.

I look at the small spherical device clipped to her belt. "Where did you get the translator?"

She looks down at the device. "We made it. Certain labs on *Sumerian* work on stuff like this."

I stop and cross my arms. "And...why did you turn it off?"

She turns to face me, impatience obvious in her eyes. "Because the wasp was going to say it wanted you, and I didn't want you to come unhinged in there, at least any more than you already were."

"Wanted me? For what?"

"Research? Who knows? They have a thing for people... like you."

I envision some sticky probe, and my stomach flips. "Research?"

"That's why I didn't want you to come."

"You could have told me."

She grabs my wrist, urging me to continue. "You could have listened."

We get to the tree line and I venture one more question. "What were those big cylinders in there?"

"Cloning chambers."

"That's where they clone *people*?"

She lets out a sigh. "It's animals, mostly. It's a zoo, you know. Speaking of animals, can you please keep an eye out as we walk? I'll do my best to keep us downwind from anything."

I look left and right. "Should I be worried?"

"The wildlife here isn't as skittish as on Earth. Sometimes they get a lot closer than you'd want them to."

Krysta pushes into the trees. I pick up a sturdy stick and follow. Soon, we're deep in the forest, surrounded by alien vegetation. She appears to be searching for something on the ground. I feel like we go in big circles and figure-8s. Sometimes we're so deep in the forest and I'm so turned around that I wonder how we're ever going to find our way back to the landing pad. I'm thirsty again, despite all the water I drank back at the zoo.

"Isn't it getting close to the meeting time?" I ask.

"Yes. Let's head back." Her tone betrays disappointment, but I'm more than ready to get back up to *Sumerian*, back to Celeres.

I put my faith in Krysta's sense of direction, following her twists and turns through the unfamiliar terrain. After about a half hour, she stops and drops to her knees. "This is it!"

She produces a small gardening shovel and digs a plant from the forest floor. Its leaves are green with red dots, and slightly triangular. There are no flowers or buds as far as I can see.

I lean in to get a good look. "What is that?"

"A popular herb with the Apocritans. That's why it's so hard to find."

"Is it a drug? Like pot?"

She stores it away in a belt pouch. "You don't smoke this, it's decorative."

"How much farther until we get back to the zoo?"

She zips the pouch. "Not much farther."

I follow her in my nasty, sweaty black outfit. The only

benefit I have over her and her cool clothing is that she has several bug bites around her tube top and I do not.

We soon emerge from the forest and back into the vast open parking area. *Big Seven* sits on the landing pad, engines idling and steam coming out in random jets around the ship. When we get a little closer, Celeres climbs down the ladder to meet us. He has a weird expression on his face, something between puzzlement and annoyance, as he gazes back toward the forest where we emerged. He looks from Krysta to me, and his gaze softens. "Hello again! How was your day at...the zoo?"

I look at Krysta and let her answer. Going into the forest wasn't my idea.

She gives a thumbs up. "Mission accomplished. We dropped off some lab work, Leigh got to see an exhibit or two, and we managed a hike in the woods, all with time to spare."

Celeres inhales as if he's going to say something, but then he just looks at his watch and nods for a few moments. "Okay, well, are we ready, then?"

We follow him into *Big Seven* and I suddenly feel like I'm back in the forest because I'm surrounded by plants—inside the ship. Every available surface has several bundles of vegetation piled with their roots wrapped in damp rags. Not just that, but he has about a dozen baskets of different fruits scattered around. He stacked several piles of plants high, bound them together, and latched them to anchor loops in the cabin with bungee cords. The copilot seat has a box full of produce on it.

"Where are we supposed to sit?" snaps Krysta as she looks around with her nose crinkled up.

"Oh yeah, sorry about that," says Celeres as he hustles to the back of the cabin where the bench seat is. A pile of bamboo-like stalks takes up the whole seat. With a sweep of his arm, like he's brushing crumbs from a table, he clears the bench, sending the stalks to the floor. One snaps in half and he grimaces. "There," he says, clapping his hands together, letting dirt fly in different directions.

Krysta and I look at each other as if to say, *seriously?* Celeres misses the sarcasm though and turns away to approach the pilot seat. He's not getting off that easy. "Celeres, what is all of this?"

He holds his hands out wide to encompass the contents of the ship. "I mentioned I had errands. I transport the plants, and McClure taxis the creatures."

I look around at the dirty mess. "So you're a gatherer?"

"Some stuff for Beastarium, some stuff for the Solar Snax. It's a few extra credits."

I give him a flat look, then brush some dirt from the bench seat and sit down with Krysta. Celeres seats himself up front.

I'm glad the trip to *Sumerian* is only about five minutes, because I'm already feeling claustrophobic. Up front, Celeres apologizes about the smell of such-and-such plant and promises to get us there even faster than normal.

We shoot up into the air without another word. Krysta and I sit so close that we're touching. Our thighs press together, and when she reaches down to scratch a bug bite, she leaves her hand there, sandwiched between us. It's a mere inch away from the object in my pocket. I put my head back and look up at the ceiling for the rest of the trip.

Chapter Twenty

Casa Celeres

Celeres makes good on his promise. We're back at *Sumerian* in record time, and before I know it, a team of people are on board with us, extracting the bundles of plants. One worker attempts to take the box of vegetables in the copilot seat, but Celeres shoos him away. "This is mine."

The worker grabs an octopus-looking rhizome from the floor instead. "You got it, Boss."

The cabin remains filled with debris after the workers unload all the vegetation. I stoop down to pick up a couple handfuls of leaves, and when I look up, Celeres stares at me with a very amused expression. "I'm honored, Leigh—"

"Happy to help."

"—but we pay people to do that."

I drop the leaves to the ground.

Celeres turns and heads for the ladder. Krysta falls in right behind him, looking back at me with the same amused expression that he had. I'm so glad that I can give everyone a chuckle today.

Once we get back to the moon buggies, Celeres hands

me his box of produce. "Would you mind holding this for me?"

The box is heavier than it looks, and dirt falls through some slits on the bottom. I know I grew up on a farm, but sometimes a girl wants to be clean. I try my best to position the box so I get the least amount of crud on myself.

He mounts his buggy and waits until I board with his box before he starts it. Meanwhile, Krysta looks back and forth between him and me with a raised eyebrow.

Celeres says, "I could use her help to keep the box steady. There's some stuff in there that will roll around and I'm afraid the entire box will fall out halfway back to my place."

Krysta has one hand on her hip, but her expression shows nothing.

We leave Krysta behind, and once we're well on our way, I peer into the box. "What is all of this stuff?"

"Vegetables. From my garden." He wears a big smile and is obviously very pleased with himself.

"Oh yeah? Are any of your famous carrots in here?"

"There are. Dig around, you'll see."

I already am. Sure enough, there they are. They look like Earth carrots, more or less, but they're each only about an inch long. They might be a little more yellow than orange, but I'd definitely call them carrots. I hold one up and squint at it as if it's too small to see. "Wow, you weren't kidding in your E-Mail."

"Pitiful, eh?"

"I doubt any self-respecting snowman would want this for a nose."

"They're getting cooked."

"You'd eat this little guy?"

"That's where tonight comes in. You want to see my kitchen?"

"You mean, do I want to come to your place?"

"Something like that."

"I could eat."

~

It turns out that his quarters are only a couple of minutes from mine. Now that I know he cooks, I'm curious if the baking smell came from here. I'll be on the lookout for goodies when we go in.

"You'll have to pardon the mess," he says as his door slides open.

Wow. All I can say is that if I'd had a little brother, his bedroom would look like this. The first thing I notice is a steering wheel on a plastic base on the coffee table. Beside it sits a race car helmet. There are six NASCAR posters on the walls. Five of them are of cars. The sixth is a female driver. She stands in a relaxed pose with her helmet in the crook of her elbow. Celeres takes the box of vegetables out of my arms and hustles out of the room to where I can only imagine is the kitchen. When he comes back in, he dashes around the room, picking laundry up off the floor. "Just one second."

"You weren't planning on a visitor tonight?"

He looks at me with a comically guilty expression and grabs more clothing from the floor. "Almost done."

"I gotta give you credit, Celeres. You're very brave to bring a woman here."

"I didn't think you'd mind."

I grin. "I don't. Listen, while you finish in here, can I use the bathroom?"

He grunts and points to a door.

I let myself inside, and when I'm alone, I give a quick inspection. It's clean. That's a big plus for me. But for now, what I really want to do is take a look at whatever I put into my pocket at the zoo.

I slide it out and turn it around in my hand. I already knew it was sort of pencil-shaped, but now that I can see it, it's a dark, cold metal, with ribbons of green and gold within. One end is flat, and the other tapers, but not to a point. The tip is a shape, sort of like a starburst.

I return it to my pocket and wash my hands before returning to the main room.

He's busy with a last armload of clothes. He takes them through a different door and returns a couple of seconds later, closing it behind him. Clearly, he just dumped them on the other side. I shake my head but can't keep the grin off of my face.

I peer at the coffee table. "What's with the steering wheel?"

"Oh, I play racing games at night."

"I guess you could do a lot worse. You don't, um, wear that helmet while you play, do you?"

He looks over at his coffee table for a moment, and then back at me. "Hey, I'll give you a tour. The kitchen is over here..."

He heads in the same direction he took with the box of vegetables, ushering us into a brightly lit kitchen area. "This is where the magic happens."

On one wall is a display panel showing a woman preparing a curry. The volume is so low that I can barely hear it. He grabs the remote and turns it off.

I sit down at his kitchen bar. "You watch cooking shows?"

He puts the remote back down. "Busted."

I laugh.

"Stop, I know I'm weird."

"It's not that, it's just—it's not like you can run to the store to buy some cardamom or coconut milk."

"You'd be surprised. I have a great spice collection, plus there are plenty of veggies from the planet that are close enough. Here, look."

He takes the box of produce and turns it upside down on the bar. I have to be quick to stop a tomato-looking thing from rolling off.

"See?" he says, "Roots, leaves, flowers, stems—just like back home. I try to get as close to the recipes as I can."

"And meat?" I ask.

"You've already had some. With the right seasonings, it's also close to what you're used to, wouldn't you say? I consider it a fun challenge to make Earth recipes with this stuff. As time goes on, we'll discover and harvest indigenous spices, and I won't even have to bring them from Earth anymore. Tell you what, how about I make a stir-fry with all these vegetables? You can try them all at once. I'll throw some of that kabob meat while I'm at it."

"Sounds good."

I hope he makes it fast because I could easily take a chomp of that unwashed tomato right now.

"Leigh, don't think any less of me, but I should confess something before you get to know me better."

"Oh?" I brace myself for the skeleton.

"I miss fast food. I love it, can't get enough. Whenever I go to Earth, I go nuts."

I breathe a sigh of relief. "You had me worried for a minute. But when I met you, you had a salad with me."

"Yeah, I know. Last Burger wasn't open yet."

I smile and shake my head.

He grabs a vegetable to wash. "So tell me, what do you think you'll miss most from Earth?"

"Now that you mention it, cheeseburgers."

He flings a small carrot at me. "We have something in common. What else do you miss?"

"Drive-ins. On summer nights, my friends and I would grab some food and head to the local drive-in movie. There's just something special about it, you know?"

"Yeah, my parents used to take me, so all I ever saw were cartoons."

"That's it?"

"I never went with friends, and by the time I was old enough to date, I lived on the ACETEF Navy base in Patuxent River, Maryland. There wasn't a drive-in for miles."

I raise my eyebrows. "You were a sailor?"

"Aviator, though it wouldn't insult me if you called me a sailor."

"And that's where you got your wings."

"Yes, Ma'am."

He takes one vegetable and sets about it with a wicked-looking knife. "So, where did Krysta drag you today?"

"The zoo."

He's quiet for a few moments as he continues to work the knife. "Back when Krysta and I were friendly, we would go down there on our days off."

"And you're telling me this, why?"

He chops down on a carrot, and a piece of it flies off the island. "Because things got weird. It started one day when we had a picnic lunch, and she asked me to stay put while she went into the woods."

I lean forward. "She did the same to me today, but I followed her anyway."

"Well, I never did, and it got to where I'd take her down there, and we'd just go off in different directions. We had some conversations about it, and she stopped asking me to go. Next thing you know, she's flying down there with McClure, doing who-knows-what with him."

I grab one of the leaves out of the box and tear strips off it. "And so you got jealous."

He stops cutting and stares at me. "I don't even know what I did wrong. I felt like I was being used, and when I wanted to talk about it, she cut me out of her life."

"I was wondering why you had such a weird expression on your face when you picked us up today. Was it because I got the hike you never had?"

"I guess so. So besides the zoo, what *does* Krysta do down there?"

Why does he want to know? Is he merely curious, or genuinely still interested in her? Should I tell him about the wasp in that weird dark room? The plant she harvested in the forest, the one she looked so hard for? Maybe I should tell him everything, but I don't want to tell him about any of that stuff right now. Not yet. There's something else.

Celeres stopped cutting a few moments ago and watches me while I sort my thoughts.

I rub my temples. "This is going to sound really weird."

He nods for me to continue.

"I think, I mean, I'm pretty sure...that Krysta likes girls."

Celeres sets the knife down very deliberately on his cutting board, but doesn't actually say anything. I continue, "It's little things, like how she bumps into me, stands very close when we talk, or touches me in offhanded ways. The other night when she slept over, she got under the covers naked."

Celeres gawks at me. Is it shock or even deeper jealousy?

I put my hand on his. "I slept on top of the covers."

His mouth still hangs open.

We're both yanked out of the moment by a knock at the door. He looks in that direction, blinking. "Uh, hello?"

"It's Ashlan. Can I come in?"

He looks at me, and I nod.

He shakes his head as if shaking off what I said about Krysta. "Mi casa es su casa."

There are a few tones from the other room, along with the sound of the door opening and shutting. Ashlan enters the kitchen, looking like she's ready to go on a date—she has replaced her customary ponytail with flowing curls and is wearing a black skirt and a dark blue form-fitting sweater. Her eyes widen when she sees me sitting there. "I'm sorry, Should I—"

"No, no, sit down," I say before Celeres can respond. Of course I want her to stay. You know, so I can find out why she's here in Celeres's quarters, dressed to slay.

She pulls out a bar stool and joins me. "Thanks."

Celeres raises an eyebrow to her. "Why are you all dolled-up?"

"I just like to look nice sometimes."

She sure looks like she wants to impress someone. I maneuver my head so that I block her view of Celeres.

She focuses back on me with a mischievous smile. "Baxter's really settling in at Beastarium. You should come by tomorrow."

I immediately relax at the mention of his name. "I will. I miss him so much."

"He has a girlfriend."

"What? I didn't think there were any other dogs here."

"It's not exactly a dog."

"Oh?"

"It'll remind you of a gray fox."

"Hmm."

"Oh, don't worry. Different species can't mate."

Now I'm really curious, but before I can ask another question, Ashlan looks around me to address Celeres.

"Have you seen Brose? I was going to see if he wanted to grab something to eat."

Celeres doesn't look up while he continues prepping dinner. "Not lately. He's been working a lot of overtime. He hasn't even been by for gaming."

"Oh, okay, thanks." She frowns.

"How are things going with you two?" asks Celeres.

"They aren't. We hang out, but he isn't getting the hint that I want more than that. I thought it might help if I wore this outfit."

Celeres puts the vegetable peeler down and looks Ashlan square in the eyes. "You're going to need a stronger hint than that. He's an engineer. He'll probably think it's just too hot for pants."

Ashlan laughs. We all do.

"You are welcome to eat with us. Maybe he'll come by later...?" he says in that tone of voice that wants her to say no.

"That's okay," she says as she gets off the stool and tugs her skirt straight. "I'll talk to you later. It was nice seeing you, Leigh. She looks hungry, Cel. You'd better hurry it up with that stir-fry."

"You sure you're good?" he asks.

"Oh, yes, thanks. If you don't mind, I'll just grab some

appetizer." She opens one of the cupboards and stands on her tiptoes to pull down a plastic container. She pops the lid open and takes a blueberry muffin from inside before putting the container back where she got it. "Thanks," she says over her shoulder with a devastating smile, leaving the kitchen.

Aha, muffins! So it *was* Celeres doing yesterday's baking.

"Goodnight guys, see you soon," Ashlan calls from the living room, her mouth full. The door opens and closes, and I'm alone with him again.

"Ashlan and Brose?" I ask.

"Yeah, if Ashlan gets her way. Surprised?"

I shrug. "I guess not. She loves animals, and he *could* pass for Sasquatch."

He chuckles. "True. So what were you saying about Krysta?"

"I don't know. Maybe I'm just being paranoid or overly sensitive, but..." This is really uncomfortable.

"Yes?" he prompts.

"I think she might be interested in me."

He holds a good poker face while he continues to chop vegetables into a colorful medley and tosses them into a hot pan. "That might explain some things."

"Like?"

"Well, this is a little awkward telling you."

"You can tell me."

"Let's just say that she and I were never physical...back then."

I sit on a nearby stool and rest my hands on the kitchen island top. Now I'm really wondering what's going on. I feel like Krysta is actually *trying* to be physical with me.

Celeres turns away from me to work at the stove.

Once he adds the meat to the sizzling vegetables, the aroma wafts over, and my stomach makes a rip-roaring growl.

He looks over his shoulder and chuckles. "So, what are you going to do?"

I cross my arms over my belly so it doesn't do that again. "I think I'll keep working with her in the lab for now."

"And if she keeps coming on to you?"

"I haven't exactly been encouraging her, if that's what you mean."

He exhales, and his shoulders relax. I want to get to know Celeres better, and I need to keep my distance from Krysta until I can figure out why I'm even tempted. I don't think of her in the same way I think of Celeres, but when we're together, there's some kind of chemistry. I can't deny or explain it.

Once he finishes cooking, he surveys the kitchen island. It's covered with specks of soil and vegetable peelings. "Let's eat in the other room," he says with a sheepish grin. He hands me a steaming plate, and we go into the living room to eat at the coffee table. He puts the steering wheel and the helmet on the floor, then hands me a wine glass filled with IridiDew Brew.

I hoist my glass in his direction. "To a new life, and new friends."

He clinks his glass with mine. "Cheers."

We sit on the couch together, our knees touching while we bend forward to eat. "This is delicious," I say.

He grins. "Thanks. Those cooking shows are paying off."

After dinner, I gather up our dishes and take them to the kitchen. He tries to stop me, but I want to help with at least something. He appears behind me with a dish towel. "I'm glad you're here."

"Me too. This is nice."

"No, I mean *here*. On Sumerian. I'm glad you found your way after I tried to keep you out."

"I haven't forgiven you for that yet, you know."

"I'll keep cooking for you until you do."

"That might work. Tomorrow's Friday and I'm not planning on working the weekend. Let's go back down to your campsite?"

"You like being on the planet, don't you?"

"I do."

He grabs his tablet from the counter. "Tell you what, you can be here anytime you want, too. I'm giving you access to my quarters, so the palm pad will let you in."

I look over his shoulder to see how he's doing it. "Thanks, I'll do the same for you, but I think I could get in anyway. Krysta said I have universal clearance or something like that."

He taps his tablet with his fingers. "That's right. There's a *feature* in the code that gives your clearance level access to every palm pad on the station. We should get engineering to fix that."

I reach forward and close my hand around his tapping fingers. "Thanks for setting me up with access, anyway. It still means something."

He smiles. "I know it does. Does this make us official?"

I stand on my tiptoes and kiss him. "I guess so, Captain."

He cracks a wide smile and wraps his arms around me. "Okay, for tomorrow then, I'll stop by the lab after your shift, and we'll leave."

I raise my chin. "I want to bring Baxter."

He looks taken aback. "Let me double check with Ashlan about that. I don't want to put him at risk."

Back on Earth, McClure told me that Baxter could be more of a danger to the planet than the planet would be to him, but I agree with Celeres; let's let Ashlan decide. I trust her decision.

He leads me to the couch, and I lay my head on his shoulder while he plays with my unruly hair. It spills around my shoulders and onto his chest. He seems to like this, and it feels good to me, so I relax even more.

"Leigh?"

My eyes flutter open.

"You're taking long blinks," he says with a smile.

"Did I drift off? Sorry. Long day."

"Should I take you back to your place now?"

"That's probably a good idea. Tomorrow will be another long day, but it will be fun."

He lifts an eyebrow. "I have one request," he says.

Anything. Just look at those eyes, that 5 o'clock shadow.

"What's that?" I murmur.

"If you want to go hiking, can I come?"

I laugh, and then he touches my cheek with his hand, turning my face so that we stare at each other. I could get lost in those dark brown eyes. People say that eyes are the windows to the soul. His are soft and kind. I wonder what he sees in mine? Can he see my history, my damage? I want to heal, I want—.

His lips brush against mine. I open my mouth slightly and he latches on. I put my arms around his neck and push him backwards on the couch. His arms wrap around me and his hands creep under my shirt, up my bare back beneath. He kisses me and lightly scratches my back with his fingernails, sending chills down my spine. I kiss him with a renewed passion as I let my full weight drop onto his chest, pinning him to the couch. His arms are all the way up the backside of my shirt and now his hands hold my shoulders, pulling me into him even more. I break the kiss and I'm breathing so hard that a few of his hairs bend in the wind of my exhalation. We could go further. There's nobody else here, nothing to stop us. It would be as easy as tracing my hand down his body and undoing his belt buckle. Everything would flow from there. I could do it. Right here, right now.

I'm going to do it.

When I pull my hand out from under his body, he frees one of his own from my shirt and entwines his fingers with mine.

"Not yet," he says, "I want to, but we've had Brew. I want the first time to be something we will remember."

"Oh, I'll remember."

"I just don't want to take advantage of you. I couldn't."

I drop my head to his chest to catch my breath and we lay that way for a long time, my body pressed into his, his hands on the move again, lightly scratching my back. I close my eyes and enjoy the moment while my heart rate slows down and I fall into a deep state of relaxation. My body is warm from the tips of my toes to the edges of my ears. Maybe there's more to Brew than I thought.

I open my eyes again to him tracing circles on my cheek. "Ready to go home?" he asks.

"What time is it?"

"About 1:00 AM."

"No."

"No?"

"No, I'm not ready to go home."

In a swift motion, I pull his shirt off and try to stifle a gasp when I see his chest. He's got it all: the pecs, the six-pack, all of it. I want his skin on mine.

He kisses me passionately, and we roll off the couch, me on top of him. I sit up straight and grab my own shirt as I straddle him, but he stops me.

"Next time," he says in his soft, bedroom voice.

I put my hands on his bare chest and curl my fingers.

"Celeres, you're driving me crazy—"

"While I should be driving you back to your place. I'll always be an officer and gentleman to you."

I make a noise deep in my throat.

His eyes widen, and his head shrinks back. "Did you just *growl* at me?"

"Maybe."

After he drops me off, I stand outside until he disappears around a corner. I slap the palm pad to open my door, and I'm alone in my quarters.

I am so unbelievably horny right now. I leave a trail of clothes behind as I approach the bed, with my wet panties hitting the floor last. I crawl under the sheets, my skin tingling with anticipation. My hands find their way to the places I long for Celeres to touch, and I finish the job.

Chapter Twenty-One

Zero Days Since the Last Lab Injury

When I open my eyes, I realize I smell as ripe as the locker room at a dance competition. I flush with embarrassment when I realize I subjected Celeres to the full force of it last night. Then again, he didn't seem to mind... My thoughts drift from him to Krysta and how she always has such a pleasant scent. This is one thing that definitely sets her and me apart.

I daydream about Celeres for a bit longer and remember to give him access to my place. I go through the motions on my tablet, and now he's all set.

We're official. I wouldn't have thought that I could be this happy with a man again.

A blinking light on my speakerphone catches my eye. I scramble across the bed, kneeling on the mattress to reach the top of the dresser, and pull the speaker down. Four messages are waiting there, all from Krysta. I must have missed them when I got back last night.

I press Play.

Message 1: *Hi Leigh, it's me. Call me back.*

Message 2: *Leigh, sorry I thought you'd be back by now. Just call me when you get this.*

Message 3: *Leigh, I want to talk about some of the stuff from the zoo trip today. It's getting late. I'll just swing by your place tomorrow before work.*

Message 4: *Hi Leigh, I was just at your place, but you didn't answer the door. I hope you're okay. Just come to work later today when you can.*

I'm late for work. I flop down on my back and close my eyes again. I could use a little more sleep, but I should get moving.

This shower is so high-tech. I've mastered the soap and spray cycles, and I'm out of there in just a couple of minutes. The only thing I don't use is the dry cycle; my hair doesn't take too well to that, so I dry myself the old-fashioned way and then comb leave-in conditioner into my unruly red mop. I should jokingly suggest a waxing cycle, so I don't have to shave anymore.

I pull out a fresh Genomica outfit, grab a cereal bar from my fridge (they stocked it), and I'm on my way. The nice thing about the route to work is that I pass Celeres's place on the way. A smile creeps onto my face and I take a bite of my cereal bar as I walk. Occasionally, someone recognizes me and waves, but even though their faces look familiar, I'm not good with their names yet.

Celeres's moon buggy isn't outside his door, so he's already started his day. I make my way through the rest of the station until I get to the heavy door with the Genomica logo on it. Krysta's moon buggy sits outside. I've never tried to unlock this, so I hold my breath when I put my palm on the copper plate. The logo changes from red to green, some internal mechanism clicks, and the door slides open. Voila. I try to think of a good excuse for my lateness while I descend. The window/door must be open at the bottom because the sounds of the aquarium are clearly audible. I walk right in when I get to the bottom.

I scan the room. "Knock, knock."

Krysta's hunched over one of her machines. She looks up with her eyes narrowed. "Everything okay?"

"Sorry, I overslept," is the best I can do.

She snickers and looks back at what she's working on.

I cross my arms and lean against a lab table. "Hey Krysta, question."

"Yes?"

"I know it isn't my business, but if you don't mind my asking, why is it you've shown me the zoo, taken me on hikes, and showed me alien artifacts, but none of that with Celeres? You two were close, weren't you?"

She bites her lip for a moment. "In a way, yes, but I have my reasons. Remember that everything you hear and see with me is classified, and you can't talk about it. Not with him. Not with anyone."

I bite my own lip. "Okay."

She gives me a strange look, and I feel like she knows I already told him everything. "You look tired. I guess things are going pretty well for you two, huh?"

"You never told me he's such a great kisser."

Her hands work the dials of the machine, and she exhales loudly. "Because I wouldn't know."

Maybe I shouldn't have said that.

She pulls a bag from under the counter. "I got you something."

I take a step back. "For me? Why?"

She pulls a lab coat from the bag and sets it on the table. "I washed it for you."

"Thanks."

She looks back in the bag. "But wait, there's more."

I take it and look inside. There's a phone sitting on the bottom of the bag. It's in a pink case.

She smiles. Her charisma is inescapable.

I pull it out of the bag and look it over.

She leans in to watch. "I charged it for you last night. I programmed your same number into it. When you're visiting Earth, it'll work just like any other smart phone. When you're on *Sumerian,* it'll reach people here and on Apocrita."

"This is great, thank you." The address book only has one number programmed into it: hers.

She still has that beaming smile. "You're welcome."

I turn the phone over in my hand. "So I can't call Earth from here?"

"No, it's too far, and the signal is too weak."

"So I can get rid of that old speakerphone in my room?"

"If you want."

"Speaking of, I got your messages this morning. What were you calling about?"

She looks behind me to the lab door, then back to me. She walks over and shuts it. "What did you tell Celeres about our little outing yesterday?"

"Not very much. Just that we went for a hike and visited the zoo."

"That's all?"

"Yeah. He seemed a little jealous, though."

She looks taken aback. "Jealous? How?"

"According to him, you never took *him* along on your hikes."

"Oh, that. Yes, I was going through a phase back then.

Anyway, about our zoo trip. Remember, everything we do is—"

"Classified, I know."

She opens a drawer and pulls out a small black case. She opens it to reveal what looks like a large hypodermic needle and an empty blood bag.

I take a step back. "What's that for?"

"I need just a little more of your blood."

I put my new phone down on the bench. Is she trying to buy my cooperation? What's next? Jewelry?

She cocks her head. "What's wrong?"

"Didn't we just do this four days ago? I mean, is it safe? Shouldn't I wait awhile to recharge or something?"

She grimaces. "It won't be much. We'll do the other arm and then take a break for a few weeks. It's important for our research."

She stands before me, needle in hand, pointing at my vein. "I don't like it," I say.

"I really need it."

"Why?"

"Research." She pauses and looks past me to the planet floating outside the window, then returns her gaze to me.

I have to decide if I'm going to trust her, and right now I don't know how much choice I have. "This is all you need for a few weeks?"

"Yes. In fact, we might not need any more after this."

I extend my left arm. "Not a whole pint. If you *do* want more, I want to be involved in the research, learn how to do the experiments. I could use a break from taking voltage readings."

She nods as she swabs my arm and wraps the rubber band above my elbow. Soon, my lifeblood travels down a clear tube into the bag. She lets it flow for a few minutes, and then pulls the needle, letting me hold a cotton ball over my arm. I look over at the crease in my other arm. The bruise was almost completely gone, and now I have a new one.

She holds up the blood bag and nods to a door at the back of the lab. "I'm going to take this to the fridge."

Curious, I watch her go back and open the door. It opens into a short hallway with more doors to the right and left. On its ceiling are three different cameras, covering the doors and every inch of the space. She closes the door behind her.

When she returns, she hands me a cold bottle of orange juice, and I can't help but wonder if she got it from the same refrigerator where she put my blood. I can just picture it: drinks, packed lunches, blood... No big deal. Either way, I'm thirsty, so I unscrew the cap and take a long pull from the bottle.

"Let me know if you need anything else," she says.

I look down at the bandage on my arm and wonder if I should tell her the same thing.

She's patient while I finish the drink. "We have something different to do today."

Anything different would be great. "Yeah?"

"I have a different battery for the device. The other one's dead. Today, you'll be taking the readings with that."

I sigh. "Okay." I walk over to my workbench and pull on the lab coat. It looks like she already set everything out for me.

"Just do all the same measurements you did last time, and in the same order. I want to compare results."

"I thought you said I'd be doing something different today."

"Today, the power comes from a battery created by us."

"It's safe?"

"Should be."

All right, let's get this over with. I steel myself and grab the multimeter's probes. As soon as I touch the device with one, there's a popping sound and a wisp of smoke trails up from the battery compartment.

Krysta snatches the device away and stabs the eject button with her thumb. The battery drops to the table with a thud, smoke rising from it. It smells like burnt hair. It's gray and scratched with small strips of duct tape on each end. It's nowhere near as glassy and pretty like the alien ones with the purple glow inside.

She coughs while waving her hand at the cloud. "Awesome."

I pull my shirt up over my nose and take a few steps back, trying not to gag. "Now what?"

She pulls an alien battery from a drawer. "Back to Plan A, I guess."

The purple glow within is barely perceptible. She notices my look as she fits it into the device. "Yes, I know. You might only get one or two readings from this. It looks like this will be a short workday. Sorry for the smell." She hastens back to her own work area.

I blink at the device, wondering what it's doing and if this is all a colossal waste of time. Krysta is across the lab typing away on her laptop and not paying much attention to me, so I put my probes down and stretch while I stare at the thing. She didn't tell me not to move it, so I flip it over as quietly as possible. Now, the trigger points up at me. I lean my elbows onto the table and rest my chin in my hands. The gold/green color of this alien artifact reflects the light of the lab and is quite pleasant to look at. Beautiful, even. I sit straight again and caress the burnished metal with my gloved fingertips. It's smooth and vibrates faintly. There's power in there that wants to get out. I touch the battery. It's warm. I touch the trigger on the device, imagining what might happen if I pulled it.

But I won't. I pull my hand away for a moment. It's then that a small hole at the base of the trigger catches my attention. It's only a couple of millimeters in diameter, and it's only because of how it's catching the light that I'm able to see it at all. I pick up my probes and test the inner rim of the hole. Nothing, zero. This is the only place on the device where there is no reading. I push one probe into it, but don't get far. Only the smallest part of the tip goes in.

I clear my throat to get Krysta's attention. "Hey, have you seen this hole by the trigger?"

She walks over and bends over the device. "Yeah. Were you able to get any readings from it?"

"Nope. What do you think it is?"

She huffs. "No idea, but I'm glad you're having the same results. I feel like it's important, but how?"

"I don't know. I'll try leaving one probe in there while testing the other parts of the device."

She nods. "Good luck."

She returns to her desk and I pause for a moment to lift the device again and hold it at different angles, trying to catch enough light to get a better look at the hole. I strain my eyes, and I could almost swear that opening's perimeter is ever so slightly jagged instead of being a perfect circle.

Because it's fresh in my memory, and because I think *something* goes in there, I slip my hand in my pocket where I've been keeping the metal rod I got from the zoo. I make sure Krysta isn't watching and I pull it out.

I look it over, and the tip of the rod is jagged, yes, but it might be too big. It's hard to tell. I touch the hole with it, and it attaches with magnetic force.

I give it a twist, and there's an audible click. I try to get a look at Krysta out of my peripheral vision. She's still typing on her computer. I return my attention to the device, which has stopped vibrating.

The golden needle at its tip disappears into the body, and a metallic green needle emerges in its place.

I try to turn the key back in the other direction, but nothing happens; the battery compartment no longer glows. I think I just killed it.

I yank the rod from the device, then stuff it into my pocket as I lean back in my chair. The green needle feels sinister to me. Don't ask me why. Krysta is going to notice, and then what will I say? I have an alien key in my pocket?

I flip the device back over and sigh.

"Hmmm?" she says.

"I'm having some issues."

She pushes herself up from her desk and is beside me in a moment. "What's wrong?"

"It's dead."

She takes the device and ejects the battery. Sure enough, it's dark as night. She sets it down and lets out a deep breath.

The other battery on the table, the homemade one, stopped smoking, so I pick it up. "Where'd you get this?"

"Brose makes them in engineering."

"Oh? So he's in on the Genomica secret?"

"No. He doesn't know what it's for."

I nudge the alien device. "Well, I'm on the project and I don't even know what it's for. What *is* this thing? A weapon?"

"What? No. They, the aliens, call it a stinger," she says while pointing at the needle. "It's just their version of a hypodermic needle."

"A stinger? Why would wasplike aliens call it anything different? What's with the calipers?"

She shrugs.

She takes Brose's battery from me and puts it on a shelf. "They say Thomas Edison failed on the light bulb a thousand or more times before he got one to work. We don't have that kind of time."

She walks away to pack up her things, so I put my gear away, too.

She calls over her shoulder, "Leave the stinger out. I want to examine it a little more. You can head out if you're ready. I'll be up in a minute and give you a ride home."

"That's okay, I have plans."

"Celeres?"

"Yeah."

"Oh. I'll catch up with you later, then."

Sounds good to me. I grab my new phone and work my way out of the lab and up the stairs to the lounge, thinking of nothing but what she'll do if she notices the different color needle. I'm jostled from my thoughts when I reach the top by a steady knocking from the other side of the station door.

"Uh, hello?" I call out.

"Leigh? Is that you?" It sounds like Celeres, but the door is thick, muffling his voice. He must be borderline yelling.

I hustle up next to the door and put my cheek on it. "How long have you been out there?" I can't keep from smiling.

"Long enough! You off work now?"

"Yeah."

"Well, come on out!"

I open the door and face him with my hands on my hips. "You're not allowed in here."

He takes a few steps backward and covers his eyes. I saunter through the door and it whispers shut behind me. He spreads his fingers so I can see his eyes. "Is it safe now?"

He is only a few feet away, leaning against the opposite wall in a pair of jeans, a blue flannel shirt over a white T-shirt, cowboy boots, and a black baseball cap with "NASCAR" written on it in white stitching.

He winks. "Hi."

A thrill passes through my entire body as I drink in the sight of my space cowboy. "You're a sight for sore eyes," I say, trying not to sound as excited as I feel.

He leans down for a kiss, and I oblige. "You ready?" he asks.

"I have nothing back at my place except more of these same clothes. If it's just an overnight trip, I suppose there's no need to pack another outfit."

He takes a few steps to his moon buggy. "I bought some stuff for you." There's a shopping bag strapped to the seat where I usually sit.

A smile creeps onto my face. I hold my phone so he can see it. "This must be my lucky day,"

His eyebrows rise. "You have a phone now?"

"Yeah, Krysta bought it for me."

His brow furrows for a moment, but then he breaks back into a smile. "You haven't called me all day."

"That's not fair. I don't have your number."

He snatches the phone out of my hand and pushes the screen a few times. He looks up with a curious expression.

"Krysta's is the only number in here. I'll fix that right now." He taps the screen a few more times.

While he's tapping away, the door slides open behind me and Krysta bursts out, knocking me straight to the ground. I barely get my hands out fast enough to break my fall. She lands on me and we tumble to the floor together in a tangle. Her face is pale, and she pants as if she just sprinted the length of the stairs.

"What's wrong?" Celeres and I both say at the same time.

"Sorry," she says breathlessly before she swoons and goes limp. Celeres bends down to untangle her from me, and lowers her to the floor. I sit cross-legged and tell him to put her head on my lap. Once he does, he rises to his feet and makes a call to emergency medical services.

Nearby lab doors open and white-coated workers spill out into the hallway to see what's going on. These are the same people who wave when we drive by. I even recognize a few of them. One guy pushes ahead of the others and rushes over, yanking the piece of gum out of his mouth. "I know CPR."

She's breathing—her chest still rises and falls from exertion. I've seen some desperate attempts at a kiss in my time, but this guy is crossing the line. I shake my head and ignore him.

Another lab tech approaches and checks her pulse. "What happened?"

"I don't know. I had already left the lab and was out here talking with Celeres when she came barging out."

The sound of rapid footfalls approaches, and soon the scene is a lot more chaotic. A couple of medical technicians load Krysta onto a gurney. They ask us a few questions, but I can't tell them any more than I already told this other guy.

Once they leave, a man in a security uniform walks straight to me. He rests his hand on my shoulder. "Do you know what happened?" he asks me. He is soft-spoken, has a reassuring smile, and a kind of demeanor you just want to trust—which is exactly why I'm leery of him.

"I'm afraid not," I say, slipping my shoulder from underneath his hand and dust off my dirty knees. They still hurt from Krysta slamming me down.

The guy looks at me like he's waiting for a better answer.

I force myself to return his gaze. "Am I in some kind of trouble?"

Celeres moves to stand beside me, strong and silent.

The man looks at him for a second, then back at me. "Why would you ask that?"

"I don't know what's going on. I'm new."

"You're Dr. Collins's new assistant, right?"

"Right."

"Go on home. We'll reach out to you later."

He doesn't have to ask me twice. I go over to *Little Seven* and unstrap the shopping bag from the seat. Celeres hops in and starts it up. "You're not walking. I'll drive you."

Together, we leave the scene and the lab workers go back to what they were working on before all of this excitement.

Once we get out of earshot, Celeres tells me that once he makes sure that Krysta is stable and security doesn't pin him down with a bunch of questions, he'll pick me up within the hour to go on our camping trip.

"Are we in a hurry?" I ask.

"I don't know yet. Pack what you need for a weekend outside. We'll have plenty to eat, so don't worry about that."

Minutes later, he drops me off and speeds away. Once

I'm inside, I throw the clothing bag onto my bed and then add a few things from my bathroom to it. I'm ready in five minutes. I close my eyes and try to make sense of everything that just happened, but I'm not having much luck.

Now what? All I can do is wait. I can't call Celeres; he still has my new phone.

Chapter Twenty-Two

Hasty Departure

I really hope we can still go on this camping trip. It's not my fault what happened to Krysta.

I move to the window-side of the bed and perch my bare feet on the glass. Apocrita floats just outside. While I watch, a cluster of student pilots hovers in the distance, maybe halfway between me and the planet. That would be fun, flying one of those...

There's a knock on my door and my blood freezes. Please don't be security. I take a second to turn on my display to check, and I'm filled with relief. Just outside, Celeres paces back and forth. "Come in," I call.

He hurries into the room, nearly tripping. "Quick, we have to get going."

"Why the rush?"

"It's security. They want to talk to us. They want to know what's going on in that lab and what happened to Krysta."

"They know I can't tell them anything."

"I know how they operate. They'll say that if the station is in danger, then you have to talk."

"Do I?"

"Well, that's the thing. Here on *Sumerian*, who's going to stop them from detaining you if you don't cooperate?"

"Detain me how?"

"I don't know, and I don't want to find out. Where's your stuff?"

I point at the bag, and he looks inside to see what I packed. "I need to buy you a suitcase." He grabs it and heads for the door.

I hurry behind him. "Don't they have some sort of security override if they want to get into the lab?"

"No, but they'll still try to force Brose to break in."

"So, they can go bother him about it."

"Actually, no."

"Why?"

"Because he's coming with us. Sorry I didn't tell you. Ash, too."

Little Seven is just outside. We climb in and motor down the hall.

I settle in, the realization hitting me: this is going to be a double date. "How are things moving along with Ash and Brose?"

He looks into the rear-view mirror and steps harder on the accelerator, making me feel like we just robbed a bank or something. "What? Oh, pretty slow. You know Brose."

Celeres drives faster than I thought this thing could go. This mad rush is making my hands sweat as I grasp the clothing bag. We whip around a corner, and the bag flies open because I have to let go with one hand so that I can lunge at a grab handle. "Dude! I just about fell out."

"Sorry."

I roll my eyes and grit my teeth.

We hurtle through the halls and a few people who see

us raise a hand to wave before their eyes widen and they jump out of the way. We arrive at the hangar in record time. We park, and while he gathers a few other bags and a cooler out of the buggy's storage compartment, I steal a quick glance at my hair and face in his mirror. As usual lately, it's not my best look, but it's good enough for camping. He jumps out of the buggy and heads toward *Big Seven* at a fast walk. I have to hustle to catch up.

I take a few bags from his arms to even our load a little. "How's Krysta?"

"She is fine. For now."

"Huh?"

"She might be in trouble. You'll have to tell me what you've seen."

I look at him but say nothing.

He puts a hand on my shoulder. "I'll keep it between us, I promise. It might be good for you to confide in me. Maybe I can help."

"But help with what? I don't understand."

"I don't either. Yet."

Brose and Ashlan are just outside of *Big Seven*, pacing around. Brose wears jungle camouflage from hat to socks. His brown boots and bushy brown beard complete the outfit. Ashlan wears a khaki shirt dress with a safari hat and looks like she's ready to go glamping. She's even wearing makeup. I try not to compare myself to other women, but damn. I run a self-conscious hand through my hair as we approach, and she smiles at me like a kid who just won candy bar bingo.

She waves. "Hi Leigh!"

Brose is busy looking at his phone, but looks up in time to meet Celeres to take the cooler from him. "Got anything else?" he asks while shoving it into the cargo compartment. He also takes the bags from Celeres and I.

"Nope," says Celeres. "Let's get out of here."

Celeres reaches up and pushes a button on *Big Seven's* underside to open the hatch and lower the ladder. As soon as he does, a furry head appears in the hatch above and gives a loud bark.

"Baxter!" I say, jumping onto the ladder. I scuttle up to him as fast as I can.

Ashlan's cheesy smile turns into a laugh. "Surprise!"

If I was feeling a little crowded about sharing this trip with Brose and Ashlan, I'm not anymore. This is the best thing she could have done for me, and I *want* to spend time with them. Once I get to the top of the ladder, Bax licks my nose and gets out of the way so I can climb in. I drag him off to the side and love him up while the others join us.

Brose is the next one up the ladder. When his bushy head rises into the cabin, I get a funny flashback of whack-a-mole from the fairgrounds, and smile even more. He hustles over to the bench seat and buckles up. Ashlan is the next one up. I can't help but notice that below, Celeres looks away as she climbs in her skirt. She piles inside and buckles up beside Brose. Celeres bounds up the ladder, shuts the hatch, and hastens to the cockpit. His strides crunch on dried leaves from the plants that were here before.

Seconds later, we float out of the hangar and into space. We aren't even out for a moment when Brose's phone rings. He slides his finger on its face. "There. I'm officially off site on weekend leave. It'll just have to wait." He puts his phone back into his breast pocket and pats it.

"Hey Celeres," I call.

"Yeah?"

"Do you still have my phone?"

"Oh. Yes, I do. One second."

He points the ship toward Apocrita and pushes the throttle forward. As the planet grows in size, he unbuckles his harness and walks back to me.

"Is that safe?" I ask.

He pulls the phone out and extends it to me. "Is what safe?"

The planet looms ahead, and soon we'll be in its atmosphere. I grab the phone and point outside. He looks. "We have a good ten seconds." He turns around and returns to his seat in time to pull back on the throttle and flight stick. I swallow hard. He puts the *cowboy* in space cowboy, maybe with a dash of adrenaline junkie thrown in.

It's not ten seconds. In what seems closer to five, we're floating over treetops in a hilly, forested area. Up ahead, on top of a tall, tapered hill, is a cluster of lights. I point. "It's nice that they have lights on some of these, so you don't crash into them at night."

Celeres smiles.

"What?"

"Those aren't beacons. Here, watch."

He flies the ship closer to the hill so we can get a better look. It turns out that the light comes from plants growing at the peak. They are flowers. Some are green, some red, and some yellow. Each glows with an otherworldly light.

Ashlan holds a hand to her heart. "I love those. We call them star flowers. Legend has it that each blossom pairs with a star above, and takes its color. They mirror each other's light, hoping to be rejoined one day."

I smile. "I like that story."

"Me too. It's kind of romantic and sad at the same time."

I nod. "I guess the best stories twist you up a little."

"Mm-hmm. Problem with the darn things is they're hard to reach. They only grow in high places."

"Right," says Celeres, "I've never been close enough to touch one. As you can see, there's not enough room up here for me to land. Seen enough?"

"Wait a second," I say. "How about those lights over on the horizon? More star flowers?"

"That's the colony!"

"Wow. It's bigger than I expected. Can we fly over?"

He points the ship toward the sea of lights ahead. "Celeres Tours at your service."

I catch one last glimpse of the flowers as *Big Seven* races over the treetops.

"Looks like a soccer game tonight," says Brose, "We should get tickets sometime."

"We can do that?" I ask, "We can go? Even if we're not colonists?"

He shrugs. "Who's gonna stop us? Cel and I go all the time. In fact, I have some team shirts back in my quarters I can share with you guys."

"How many teams are there?"

"Two. I have shirts for both. I like to wear the one I think is gonna win."

"Oh do you, Brose?" says Ashlan, "When you take me to a game, I'll wear the other one."

"You want me to take you to a game?"

Celeres interrupts. "They are asking me to fly away. Apparently we're distracting the players."

Soon, we're flying back in the other direction and making a descent.

He lands *Big Seven* as expertly and softly as usual and opens the hatch. The fresh air of Apocrita fills the cabin and we all take a deep breath at once. It's a funny moment and we share a laugh. Spirits are high as we pile out of the ship and onto the soft grass of the planet. We're at the same campsite from the other night and Brose wastes no time in opening the cargo compartment to produce a small bottle of his home-brew mead. We enjoy the sounds of nature while we kick off the weekend by passing the bottle around. Baxter entertains himself by sniffing around the site and the fire pit.

Brose finishes the last swig. "This is my best batch yet."

"Got any more?" asks Celeres in a muffled voice while he stuffs his head into the cargo hatch to look around.

"Maybe," says Brose with a wink at us ladies. "I'll have to check my bag later."

Celeres climbs out of the hatch with a handful of paper and a lighter. He throws the paper and some nearby wood into the fire pit and lights it. "I like to get the fire going while I can still see what I'm doing."

It's early twilight, but the nearby forest is downright dark. Ashlan pulls some camp chairs out for us while Brose pulls his rifle case out of the compartment. He pauses when he notices me watching. "Might do a little huntin'."

While Ashlan pets Baxter, I approach Celeres. "I'm concerned about Krysta."

"Me too. They said they'd call me when they know something."

I nod, looking down.

He pulls me aside, out of earshot of the group. "Are you going to tell me what's going on?" I've never seen him quite this serious before.

"Where should I start?"

"The beginning? Let's walk."

Brose calls over to us, "Where you guys going? If you're

looking to stretch your legs, come with me. It's getting dark and I have the rifle."

"I think we'll be okay," says Celeres.

We go one way, and Brose heads in the opposite direction. Baxter watches Ashlan tend the fire for a moment, then bounds over to Celeres and I. As we walk, I tell him about Krysta's persistent requests for samples, our trip to the zoo, and the unsettling experience in the dark room with the wasplike alien and the backpacks filled with blood. Celeres's eyes widen at this revelation, but he remains silent, allowing me to continue. I finish by describing our hike and the peculiar plant Krysta harvested before we met him back at his ship.

After I'm done, he's quiet for a minute, and then looks through the trees to our campfire. Ashlan, tiny from here, sits beside it. "We should head back."

"That's it?"

He turns and heads back in the direction we came from. "I need to process all of this. Krysta's in the middle of a lot."

The sun is already below the horizon, and the crickets have begun their nightsong. It's at a low murmur now, but I know how loud it can get. Baxter cocks his head in different directions while he tries to make sense of the strange music.

Celeres scans the ground as we walk. "Do you think you could identify that plant again if we saw it?"

"From the hike? Yes, I think so."

"Good, keep an eye out. If she's been sneaking off to find it on all our excursions—if she left me behind because she didn't want me to see—there must be something to it. Maybe it'll help me understand what's going on."

We shuffle along as the nightsong gets louder. The campfire beckons with a shower of sparks as Ashlan throws a log onto it. Now I can smell the smoke. A few stars appear in the sky. Out of nowhere, a gunshot sounds in the distance and the crickets stop chirping. I grab Celeres's forearm, and Baxter presses himself against me; he doesn't like loud noises.

Celeres doesn't flinch. "Brose is an excellent hunter. The only way we could convince him to join Genomica and leave Earth was to promise regular hunting trips. Sometimes, he'll tranquilize various beasts for Ashlan, but he also likes to put food on his table the old-fashioned way."

My stomach rumbles at the thought of food. "We get to try his cooking, right?"

"Yep. Here, look at these bushes. You'll like the fruit."

He pulls my elbow and we walk a short distance to a clump of shrubs with red berries. They have a faint glow, and remind me of the lights on people's hedges during the holidays. These aren't as bright, but have the same effect. The sight takes my breath away, and I look up at Celeres in wonder.

"I know," he says, "you gotta try 'em."

He picks one and pops it into his mouth. "One for me..."

He chews for a second, then nods with delight. "Here, check this out." He opens wide. His whole mouth glows inside.

I stick out my bottom lip and nod with appreciation. "So, are you about to breathe fire?"

"...And one for you," he says, holding a berry in front of my face. I open my mouth and he places it on my tongue.

I bite down on it, and then his lips are on mine. A combined flavor of nectarines and strawberries floods my mouth while he kisses me. Wow. We pull each other to the ground and roll close to the cluster of bushes. The taste and fragrance of the berries dominates my senses.

We are a few minutes into swapping berry juice when he stops suddenly.

My eyes snap open. "Is something wrong?"

Now that we're still, I take a second to dislodge a rock that's been poking me in the back, but he stops me. "Shhh."

Celeres points his chin at Baxter, who huddles close, whining.

I turn my head to see what has Baxter worked up, and there it is at the edge of the bushes—an alien. Wasp. Apocritan. It's so close I could reach it in two strides. If they looked horrific in a telescope, this one looks ten times scarier in person. It's about four feet high. It's covered in a shiny dark carapace and, instead of a stinger on its butt, it has six-inch stingers on the tips of both hairy back legs. It fixates on Baxter for a few moments before turning to me. It leans forward, its antennas straining toward me, just like the wasp did at the zoo when I was with Krysta. Chills travel up and down my spine.

I open up to scream, and Celeres claps a hand over my mouth. Baxter growls and barks.

Celeres untangles himself from me and jumps to his feet, causing the wasp to melt into the bushes, out of sight. I grab Baxter's collar so he doesn't chase.

Celeres looks down, thrusts out his hand, and hauls me to my feet. "We have to get back."

I stop for a moment to pick a cluster of berries, but he isn't having any of that; he breaks into a jog toward our camp. I catch up to him, and we race through the dusk. It's hard to say if he's running to the camp as much as he's running away from the wasp. I know which one it is for me.

～

When the camp comes into view, Ashlan and Brose are both there. They have a rotisserie set up with some meat spinning. Brose is in the middle of cleaning his rifle, and bolts to his feet when we crash through the brush and into the site. "What's wrong?" he asks, squinting into the darkness while loading his gun.

Suddenly, the edges of my vision blur and become dark. The darkness expands over my entire view.

"Leigh!" screams Ashlan.

Chapter Twenty-Three

Debrief

Nightsong.

It's the first thing I hear. Someone fans my face and worried voices join the crickets.

Brose: "What's wrong with her?"

Ashlan: "We have to cool her down."

Celeres: "She's coming to."

Brose: "Is the dog too close to her face?"

With my eyes still shut, I moan. "Bax?"

Baxter's familiar licks lap at my forehead. My eyes flutter open. Everyone's hunched over me, their faces full of worry. Celeres reaches down and cradles my head in his hand. "Are you okay?"

Okay? How should I know? I've felt better. "Water," I rasp.

Ashlan scampers off to the cooler and runs back with a water bottle. She holds it to my lips and I take a small sip. I bring myself to a sitting position and drink some more.

Brose exhales loudly and rises back to his feet. He walks to the edge of the camp with his rifle in both hands. He glances back at me a couple of times.

I blink a few times and shake my head. "How long was I out?"

Celeres is still breathing hard from the run. "Just a few seconds. You just about fell in the fire. It's very lucky that Ashlan saw you wobble."

I touch the bandage on my inner elbow. "I should have known better. I shouldn't have let her take that blood."

Celeres's face grows dark. "She took blood *again*?"

"Not a whole pint, but still."

"What did you drink today besides mead?"

I give him a guilty look and take a long draw from the water bottle.

Celeres reaches down beside me and picks up the cluster of berries that I dropped when I passed out. "You should eat some of these. They'll help."

I reach out to take them, but stop when I see how bad my hand shakes.

He holds them closer to me. "It's okay. Take them."

I reach out again and take the cluster. I pop one in my mouth and am rewarded with that flavor mix between nectarine and strawberry, just like our kiss. "It's delicious. What are these called?"

"Uh, berries."

Of course. I smile and have a couple more. "These are filling."

He nods. "I bet you could live on them if you had to."

"Yeah, wow. I feel a little better already." I flick one to Baxter, who catches it out of the air, but then spits it out and sneezes a few times. Ashlan and Celeres laugh.

Brose is still at the edge of the camp, pacing around, one eye on me. He gestures to the rotisserie on the fire. "Don't ruin your appetite. I got something for us."

"Smells great," I say. It does, too. The meat hisses and pops on the spit.

I struggle to my feet and shuffle to an empty camp chair. I nibble on a few more berries and sip more water. Ashlan sits across from me and watches me through the flames. "Aren't you going to look at the clothes Celeres picked out for you?" She tosses the bag to me. Celeres grins in anticipation.

Meanwhile, Brose rejoins us and props his rifle against the tree by his chair. "There's nothing out there." He pokes the meat with a thick finger. "Almost done." He notices me rummaging through the bag. "What you got over there, Leigh?"

"Celeres bought me some clothes."

"Oh, yeah?" He looks over at Celeres. "I thought you were colorblind, Cel."

Celeres snorts. "I get by."

I let those two banter it out while I pull everything out. I find pairs of navy blue and green biker shorts, black leggings (all with pockets—yay!), dark green and black skirts, black, blue, and white blouses, a green crop top, a gray off-the-shoulder shirt, and a T-shirt with a giant *Sumerian* print on the front. I hold it up and look at him questioningly.

Celeres blushes. "I don't know. It's just a little something I found in the gift shop."

Brose leans over to get a look at everything. "What, no lingerie, Cel?"

Celeres holds a hand to his chest, looking shocked. "What do you mean? That's what the T-shirt is for."

Ashlan snorts. "You're so romantic."

Brose howls with laughter and rocks so much in his chair that it falls over sideways, spilling him onto the ground.

I watch Brose for a moment, then shake my head at Celeres. "This is your idea of lingerie? Are you actually *trying* to not get laid?"

Ashlan chortles.

I walk over to Celeres, swaying my hips as sexily as I can, and stand in front of him, looking down. He has a crooked grin. In a swift motion, I pull my Genomica shirt off and sit on his lap, my black bra at eye-level.

Suddenly, everyone around the campfire hushes and Celeres looks like a boy who just walked into the women's room by accident.

I angle my head down to force him to look me in the eyes. "What? You're bashful?"

I pull the new *Sumerian* T-shirt on.

His mouth drops open. "You..."

I lick my lips. "What, Cel? Too bad you didn't think to get me a new bra, too. It might have been a better show." I lean down and kiss him on the forehead.

That sets Brose off again, and he rolls around in the dirt as he lets out huge guffaws. Everyone else laughs, including me.

I return to my seat, and we all just take some time to enjoy the moment. Eventually, Brose walks over to the rotisserie and pulls it off with some tongs. "It's ready."

Celeres sets up a small folding table and hands him a knife. Brose sets about carving the meat while the rest of us watch him with our mouths watering.

Ashlan walks over to me. "Good one, Leigh. We needed a good laugh."

Baxter lopes over to her and sniffs her pocket. She gives him a little head rub. "Sorry, Bax. No treats today, but maybe you can try some of the meat?" She's talking to him, but looking at me.

"Go for it."

Brose must have overheard because a small chunk of the roast lands nearby. Bax sniffs it, but then looks at me.

"Go ahead," I say.

He wolfs it down.

Once we all have our own chunks of meat, we sit around the fire and we each get our own bottle of mead. Brose warns me to be careful with it, but I feel a lot better. A little mead is going to complement this meal perfectly. The camp is full of the sounds of chewing. Even Baxter gets another hunk.

Brose holds a piece of meat in the air with his fork. "You know what this is, Leigh?"

I grin. "Yep, Matlurf."

He leans back in surprise. "Whoa, Cel has taught you well. Do you like it?"

"Yeah, I do. Do they serve this on *Sumerian*?"

"Shhhh," he says. "No. They don't because I haven't delivered any to the kitchen. Once I found out how good these were, I wanted to keep them for me and my friends. If word got out, they'd have me hunting this instead of anything else. Not only that, there is a nice herd nearby where I hunt on camping trips. I don't want to thin it out just so people can eat it at the station."

I take another bite. "Do you keep some in your fridge?"

"Of course."

I wash it down with a swig of mead. "It's tasty, but it gets stuck in your teeth, doesn't it?"

He laughs and then picks at his teeth with a fingernail. "On another note, I don't want to upset you, but what were you two running from?"

Celeres looks up. "Wasp."

"Oh yeah? Why'd you run?"

"Baxter got excited. I didn't want any trouble."

I swallow a bite and look over at Baxter. "Krysta calls them Apocritans. She calls this planet Apocrita."

Ashlan looks at me. "That makes sense. It's a play on the scientific name for wasps."

Celeres nods in approval. "Apocrita has a nice ring to it. It's a lot better than New Mesopotamia."

I hold up a finger. "There's more. I'm not supposed to tell you this, but the wasps are trying to make human clones—"

Ashlan gives a sharp look. "How do you know?"

"I saw their cloning chambers."

"Where?"

"At the zoo. With Krysta." I look over at Celeres, and he nods for me to continue. "When she took me there, we went into a back entrance of a building. It was dark. The chambers were there. There was also a wasp. She gave it backpacks full of blood and it tried to touch me, but she held him back."

"What is going *on* with her?" says Celeres.

"It touched you?" asks Ashlan.

"No, no, it tried to, but it did something else I didn't like. Its antennas *reached* for me. The wasp we saw today did the same thing."

Ashlan's eyes narrow. "They were smelling you."

My mouth drops open and I take a sharp breath.

"Maybe we could go check it out," says Celeres.

Ashlan glances at him and then returns her attention to me. "Was it just the wasp? Did you see anybody else?"

"No, we crossed the room to a door that opened into the zoo. We left and slammed the door."

Celeres stands up. "Like I said, let's go have a look."

"What about Baxter?" I ask.

"He can stay on the ship. We'll leave him with some extra food and water. You can even open a window."

Ashlan looks around the camp. "If we're doing this, let's go."

Brose grabs his rifle, and both Celeres and Ashlan pull rifles of their own out of the cargo hatch. I take Baxter into the ship and open a window a few inches, then return to my friends after locking him in.

Celeres leads the way out of the camp. "We're only an hour's hike from the zoo."

"Don't I get a gun?" I ask.

Celeres stops and lifts an eyebrow at me. "You're a lab technician."

I fold my arms on my chest and give him *the look.* "So? Ashlan's a veterinarian, and Brose is an engineer."

Brose looks over. "I was paramilitary in a previous life, and Ash is a veterinarian, yes, but animal handlers occasionally need to know how to shoot, ya know?"

Celeres pulls a pistol from his belt and hands it to me. "Stay close to me, and be careful with that."

I've been skeet shooting with my dad, but this is my first time holding a pistol. It's heavier than I expect.

As we melt into the foliage and march into the darkening forest, I marvel at this situation. I think of home, my dance team, and that fateful morning when I met Celeres and had a salad for breakfast. It feels like those memories are light years away, in more ways than one.

Chapter Twenty-Four

The Cave

Celeres is first in line, and I'm right behind him. Ashlan follows me, and Brose is last. As we walk, he periodically scans our flanks and rear.

The multi-colored starlight casts a soft luminescence into the forest. That, combined with the nightsong, is a constant reminder that we aren't on Earth anymore.

My stomach twists at the thought of returning to the zoo, but being surrounded by my competent and armed friends is comforting. At least a little.

As promised, the hike takes about an hour before Celeres calls a halt. He crouches down and points straight ahead. "The landing pad is right over there," he whispers to me. "Where did Krysta take you?"

I point over to where I think the building is. He nods and stands back up, motioning for us to follow. We scamper across the landing pad, hunched over. Ten minutes later, we stand in front of the door with the alien letters stenciled onto it for the second time in as many days. The others gather around. Memories of the last time I was here come flooding back in a cold, dark wave, chilling me to the core.

Celeres traces the letters with his finger, then looks at me. "Any idea what these letters mean?"

"I don't know."

"What about these white pipes? Jeez, they must go up about fifty feet. Must be some kind of vent."

I follow his gaze up the pipes. "That's what they are—for compost."

Brose tilts his head. "Compost?"

"You know this is a zoo, right?" says Celeres.

"Makes sense, I guess."

"Now what?" I ask.

Celeres props his rifle against the building and motions for the others to do the same. I stuff the pistol into my pocket.

Brose nudges me with his elbow. "Hey Leigh, is that a pistol in your pocket or are you just happy to see m—"

Ashlan smacks him on the back of his head.

Celeres places his ear on the door and mutters, "It's quiet."

"They're dormant at night," Ashlan says in the same hushed voice.

He places his hand on the knob and gives it a slight twist. It gives. He looks at me with a surprised expression.

He twists the knob the rest of the way and pulls the door open.

As if in memory of last time, my hands sweat and I rub them on my leggings.

Celeres pulls a small flashlight out of his belt and turns a dial. He flicks it on, producing a dim cone of light. We peer within, and it's just as I remember it.

Brose picks a stick off the ground and puts it in the door to keep it from closing, and we all step into the room. It's how I remember it: several cylindrical tanks from floor to ceiling.

Celeres's light is very low and reveals nothing over ten feet from us. "Where was the wasp?" he whispers.

I nod to our right, and he points his flashlight in that direction. A small hallway extends about twenty feet to a dead-end. The top of a steel ladder protrudes from a hole in the floor at the end of the hall.

Celeres creeps over to the ladder. Brose makes a gun sign with his hand and goes back outside for a moment. He returns with the rifles and hands them out when we join Celeres at the ladder.

That hole ahead, its edges dark and jagged, triggers a visceral memory: the yellowjacket ground nests we used to have on the farm. I picture wasps pouring out of that hole to attack us, and if they do, these guns aren't going to do squat.

Celeres leans over the edge and points his flashlight inside. Shining dust motes float in the emptiness, and the ladder descends past the limits of our light. "You can wait outside if you want to."

I look toward the door and then back down into the depths. Which is worse? "I'm coming."

He nods. Brose claps me on the back.

The others put their rifles on their backs and we descend the ladder in the same order we used when marching through the forest. We're surrounded by a dank, earthy scent. After a few minutes, we see a floor below. It's bathed in a dim, purplish light, like some kind of haunted house.

Celeres is the first off the ladder. He looks around and gives us a thumbs-up. We file down the rest of the way to join him.

Now we're at another dead-end of a tunnel that extends

about fifty feet and then turns. The source of the creepy light appears to come from around that corner. The walls are rough hewn, and it's all dirt and rocks down here.

We walk to the turn and peek around. The tunnel continues another twenty feet before opening straight into a room without a door. The purple light spills out of there. Celeres creeps forward. "Maybe your blood wasp is in here."

We take a few tentative steps around the bend so that we get a clearer view into the room. It's just as rough-hewn as these tunnels and is little more than a cave. Shelves line one wall, but most are empty. One shelf holds about a dozen of the alien batteries, each glowing with a fierce purple light.

Brose gasps and walks straight to them.

Celeres bars him with his arm. "Whoa, not so fast."

"It's safe," says Brose, "they're just batteries. We have some on *Sumerian*. Except—"

"What?"

"Except these are much, much brighter than ours."

"What's it mean?"

Brose approaches them with reverence. "It means they have a lot of power, maybe full power. Krysta's been trying to get me to reverse-engineer them, but no luck so far. Just look at these."

I motion to all the empty shelves. "Looks like their stock is low."

He leans close to the full shelf of batteries, their purple glow reflecting off his face. "They have more than we do."

While Brose pores over the battery bounty, I look around the rest of the room. There are a few wooden tables lined against the walls. They look thrown together, something like you'd expect to see a seventh-grader make in a wood shop class. Each table has lab equipment on it, all made of greenish-gold metal. Besides that, there's what looks like a dorm refrigerator sitting in the far corner. I walk over for a closer look. Everyone but Brose joins me.

I tug the door, but it's locked.

Ashlan kicks at something soft on the ground. "What's this?"

Lying there are three backpacks with their flaps open. I run my hand through them, but come up empty. "These were Krysta's. The ones she gave to the wasp."

Celeres gives a tug at the refrigerator door, then shakes it like it's an errant vending machine.

Brose appears beside us and puts his hand on Celeres's shoulder. "Whoa, big guy, see the lock on the side? Let me try."

Brose pulls a device from one of his pockets. It's about the size of a harmonica with a straight, ribbon-thin piece of metal sticking out of the long end. He presses a button on its side, and the ribbon vibrates. "Watch this."

He inserts the metal into the lock, and several lights on the device flash. After about ten seconds, the lock clicks and about half of the lights on the device go out. "Yeesh. This one took almost every CPU to unlock."

Celeres gives a low whistle. "You're handy to have around, Brose."

"Thanks. I can unlock almost anything with this. It's one of my finest inventions."

"Stop bragging," says Ashlan, but the look she gives him is unmistakable admiration.

He opens the box's door, motioning for us to look inside.

Three racks of test tubes rest on a shelf. They each contain blood, and a label with a name. I saw these before, on *Ice Arrow*.

Celeres turns a test tube so he can read the label. "Who the hell is Jason Bank?"

I lean in a little closer. "A colonist, I think."

He puts it back. "Okay, then, *why* the hell is Jason Bank's blood in a refrigerator at the zoo?"

They're all looking at me. I shift my feet uneasily. "Don't you think I'm wondering the same thing?"

Ashlan pulls a vial. "Nerina Herbert. This makes no sense."

"Should we take it back with us?" asks Brose.

I shake my head. "Our best bet is to leave it. Don't let them know we've been here. At least until we learn more."

Ashlan puts Nerina's blood back on the rack and closes the door. "Makes sense."

It takes Brose a minute to re-lock it, and now we're ready to leave.

"Do you want to keep looking around?" asks Ashlan.

"Can we get out of here?" I ask.

"Good idea," says Celeres. "Everyone ready?"

We all nod.

Brose heads for the exit. "All right, then. I'll lead us out of this hole."

The sounds of his boots echo down the hall as he returns to the ladder and begins his climb. Ashlan files out of the room to join him.

I go next, and Celeres follows.

We hustle to join the other two and work our way up the rungs as fast as we can. I figure it's about two hundred feet of climbing. I just put one hand in front of the other until Brose clears the top of the ladder and disappears. When I emerge, he and Ashlan lean against a nearby wall to catch their breath. Celeres joins them, but I'm not terribly winded. I'd feel much better though if I hadn't given so much blood lately. I put my hands on my knees with my head bowed while my heart slows down a little.

Once everyone catches their breath, the bubbling cylinders in the room once again become the dominant sound.

I need to conquer my fears. "Give me your flashlight," I say to Celeres, my hand outstretched.

He tosses it to me. I grab it out of the air and walk out of this dead-end hallway into the main room, turning the brightness knob all the way to the max.

"Leigh, they'll see us!" hisses Celeres.

I sweep the room with the light. "Who? If they were paying any attention, they would have been here by now."

It's just rows and rows of cylinders, each with something floating inside. I approach the closest one to get a good look.

Inside floats a furry being, some animal, with tubes attached to several places on its body.

My three friends have caught up with me. I look back and see them all carrying their rifles at the ready. Brose has his raised with one eye on his scope.

Ashlan moves from cylinder to cylinder, then stops to point out a body that appears to have scales and wings.

"Don't tell me they're growing freaking dragons," Celeres mutters.

They look at me for a second as if I have all the answers, but then go back to examining the bodies. One chamber stands apart from the rest, so I approach that one. Inside is a girl, and her face looks very familiar. She's in her early twenties, pretty bone structure, and yellow hair. There's something about her, but I can't put my finger on it.

Ashlan notices me and hustles over. "What's she doing in there?"

I put my hand on the glass. "I'm not sure."

They look back and forth at each other, wide-eyed.

Ashlan pries her eyes from the tank and turns to me. "Leigh, why are you...do you recognize her?"

"Yes, from...somewhere."

"You do? How?"

Then I remember. "Earth, at the launch site. Her face was on a sign."

Ashlan scrunches her forehead. "Do you think this could be her? Or is it a clone?"

I shake my head because I absolutely don't know.

Brose pulls a dark object from his belt. It looks like a grenade. My eyes widen.

"It's a flash-bang," he says. "If I tell you to hold your ears, do it. Look the other way and close your eyes, too."

"Calm down, Brose," says Celeres. "I think Leigh is right. If they knew we were here, they'd be here already."

Brose looks dubious.

Celeres looks at his watch. "Either way, we should get out of here." He turns on his heel to lead us out.

Ashlan nods. "Yeah, no reason to push our luck. Brose, put that grenade away."

"No way. I've got my gun in one hand and my flasher in the other, and it stays that way until we're safely back at camp."

Brose, Ash, and I catch up to Celeres, and it only takes us a few seconds to get outside and shut the door behind us. We trade glances and heave a collective sigh.

We stealthily move across the landing pad and into the woods. Nobody talks, but as the adrenaline wears off, I feel terribly drained. This has been the longest day of my life.

The walk back is uneventful until the last stretch. There's a sound—Baxter's barks pierce the night. My first impulse is to guess that it's his separation anxiety, but it's not; I know that bark. Even though he's far away, he barks like a stranger has him backed into a corner. A nearby bush has a cluster of berries on it. I pop a few in my mouth and take a deep breath. Here we go again. Even though my body screams for rest, the berries help, and without a word to the others, I take off at a run toward the sounds.

Chapter Twenty-Five

Fear and Love

Celeres, Brose, and Ashlan try to keep up, and do for a time, but they don't have a chance; I'm running full-out. They call for me to slow down, but I won't. I can't keep this up for long, even with the berries, but I don't need to. I'll be there in a couple of minutes.

I run through the trees and bushes, the leaves slapping my face. Lights from the ship appear between spaces in the foliage. What do I do? Will I have to fight? I pull my pistol out of my pants. I look behind one more time, but I can't see or hear my friends yet. I'm not normally a super brave person, but it's Baxter.

I slow down when I'm close and creep to the edge of the campsite so I can see. The ship is close; I could probably hit it if I threw a stick. On the other side of the window, Baxter alternates between jumping up at the glass to bark through the crack, and hopping back down to spin in circles and bark in the ship. His barks are more frantic than ever, and I can see why.

Two giant wasps, tall as me, fly around the window,

occasionally getting close enough to push their face into the crack in the window. One has a nasty dog bite on its face.

I put my pistol back in my pants. If I shoot at them, I could hit the window. Although he's freaking out about the Apocritans, Bax is safe enough. Behind, my friends get closer, making a racket as they crash through the brush.

Brose is the first to get to me. Before I have time to register what he's doing, he yells "flash-bang" and throws it right at the ship. I barely remember to clamp my eyes shut and hold my ears before it detonates. Even with my eyes closed, I see vivid red. Even with my hands over my ears, my ears ring. I snap my eyes open to see what happened. The wasps fly away in woozy circles toward the tree line.

Ashlan and Celeres burst through the bushes to join us.

Bax is safely inside with his front paws up against the window. His barks turn to whines when he sees me.

As I approach, it's plain to see that they made a great effort to get in; scratches and gouges cover the trim around the window.

"It's okay, boy. Celeres will get you out in a minute."

I grab a water bottle from the cooler and stumble over to my camp chair. I have to take a moment before twisting off the lid because if I opened it now, I'd spill half of it on the ground with my shaking hands.

Celeres goes straight to the window and glides his hand over the damage with a scowl. "This is a first."

Brose collapses into a camp chair, trying to catch his breath. "Don't worry," he says in between wheezes. "We can fix that damage easy."

Ashlan stumbles over to the cooler for a couple of water bottles. She throws one to Brose and then flops down onto her own chair with her rifle across her lap.

Celeres reaches up and opens the hatch. Baxter jumps

out, landing on Celeres's shoulders, and bowls him over. As soon as they land, Baxter bounds over to me and jumps into my lap. He presses his quivering body against me.

Ashlan looks in the directions the wasps went. "You think that the wasp you saw on your walk with Celeres earlier could be one of those?"

"I don't know. Not sure how I'd be able to tell."

Brose takes a swig of water and then eases himself down and lies on his back with the bottle propped on his chest. "I'm an out-of-shape mess," he declares with a wry grin.

Ashlan looks over at him, a concerned look on her face, and murmurs to me, "He's exhausted, been working all kinds of crazy hours."

I nod, and we're quiet for a minute.

"Why didn't he shoot them?" I ask.

She scrunches her nose. "He probably—"

"Brose? Nah, he's actually a peaceful guy," Celeres says.

In response, Brose whistles a cheerful tune, which has to be the most out-of-place thing that could happen right now.

"You said they never did anything like this before?" I ask Celeres.

"No, never. I wonder what has them so riled up."

"You think they know we were at the zoo? Maybe we're in trouble."

"No, there would have been more of 'em."

"What if they come back?" I ask, smoothing Baxter's coat with long, comforting strokes.

"Would you?"

"No, but do they know they're outgunned? Are they oblivious to danger, like moths to a flame?"

"Maybe some, but just like humans, some are smarter than others."

I jerk my thumb in the direction they flew off. "Not those."

"No."

Ashlan speaks up, "It's safe, Leigh. We know how to handle ourselves."

Celeres nods. "Trust us."

I say nothing as I scratch Baxter's rump. He seems to be a little calmer, but I'm not.

~

We sit and reflect on the day's events, the batteries at the zoo, the woman in the cloning chamber, the attack on Bax. Enough time passes for Bax to calm down and fall asleep at my feet.

Celeres gives me a fresh water bottle before putting the cooler back in the hold. After that, he pulls a soft, thick bundle from inside. "I'll get your sleeping bag ready."

"You're completely sure we're safe?" My voice is an octave higher than normal.

"I've activated the ship's radar. We'll get plenty of warning if anything comes knocking." He drops the bundle to the fern-covered ground.

Hmm. I have a policy where I never go camping in a bad neck of the woods. I'll see what he has in mind, but I'm this close to demanding that we go back to *Sumerian* tonight.

Brose pulls a long canvas bag full of clinking metal out of the same compartment that my sleeping bag was in. Ashlan takes several shiny poles from it and works them into the ground, about six feet apart. Brose does the same thing in the other direction, and the two of them form a rough circle around our camp and the ship. Once done,

Brose gets a rake and clears the area of leaves and twigs between all the poles.

"What are you doing? Is that a fence?" I ask.

"Sort of. Watch this." He pulls a little remote from his belt and presses a button. Little red lights flash on the top of each pole. I kneel to keep a firm hold on Baxter.

Celeres puts a hand on my shoulder and gives it a soft squeeze. "Good idea."

I look back at him, and for a second I get lost in his soft gaze. It's been a long time since anyone's looked at me like *that*.

Brose throws a stick through two of the poles where it passes through and lands with a thud on the other side.

I look at the stick, and then at Brose. "Watch what?"

"Look."

I have to squint, but there it is—a wisp of smoke rising from the wood.

"You cooked the wood? Just like that, in the split second it passed through the fence?"

"Yeah. If anyone gets close, they're going to get real uncomfortable, real quick."

"I'll say."

He pulls some rubber wristbands out of a bag. He tosses one to each of us. "We'll wear these so the field doesn't hurt us."

We all take a wristband, and I attach one to Bax's collar. After everything that's happened, I wish we'd never brought him to begin with.

Brose seems to notice my displeasure. "Sorry. Now watch this."

He hops to the other side of the invisible fence. "See? No burny. You try."

I fasten a short leash to Baxter's collar. He might be safe

with that wristband, but I will not take that chance. "I'll just take your word for it."

Bax's tail wags because normally the leash means a jog. I feel bad, but once he realizes we aren't going anywhere, he curls up at my feet.

Ashlan places a couple of sleeping bags in strategic positions, spaced along the electric fence. Celeres follows her pattern and puts his bag down, and then another one near his. "For you."

It's been a long day for all of us, and it only takes a couple of minutes for everyone to settle in. Soon, Brose is over there snoring almost as loud as the crickets' nightsong.

Ashlan rolls her eyes at him, then turns so that she's facing outward with her back to us. It looks like she has an e-reader. The soft light from its display spills over her cheek and hair.

Celeres pulls his shirt off and hangs it on a nearby branch. I cast a sidelong look at his ripped chest while he settles into his sleeping bag and zips it shut.

"What a day," he mutters.

"Yeah."

"Crazy, too."

I smile. "Yeah, it was. Some of it was pretty nice, though. At least until we got interrupted." A blush creeps onto my cheeks as I recall the way he'd pinned me, his body warm and heavy against mine, his kiss stealing my breath.

"Yeah, that was terrible timing."

"I never thanked you for the new clothes."

"You're welcome."

We stare at each other in the dim silence and my mind drifts.

How mature is he? He's got that racing helmet by his game system. What about that childish moon buggy of his?

But I like that buggy, it shows pizazz. And the racing helmet? Boys will be boys.

He might be a little overprotective, but we can work with that.

If I'm being honest with myself, he's the reason I made this bazillion mile journey, even if I want to blame it on a cheating boyfriend and a life I wanted to run away from. I don't want to admit it, but it's true.

Baxter likes him.

I wish I knew how he really feels about me, how far he's willing to take this.

Am *I* ready?

What would Krysta think?

He stopped me the other night because he said he didn't want to take advantage of me after we'd had Brew. Was that the real reason?

What if we go supernova in a fiery ball of failure? Can I weather another heartbreak?

Is it okay not to know, to just take one step at a time?

Ashlan must have fallen asleep because the e-reader screen is dark and leaning on her face. I think we're alone now, Celeres and I.

My heart thuds in my chest because I know what I want to do next.

"What if we *hadn't* been interrupted?" I ask in a whisper, my mouth dry.

He shrugs and gives me a mysterious smile.

"I only know one thing," I say.

"What's that?"

"I'm cold."

I'm not really cold, but I *am* trembling.

"Oh."

"Yep."

He unzips his sleeping bag partway and I get another view of his chest and abs.

"I have the opposite problem. I'm too hot. Do you think maybe you could help cool me down?"

I point my toes in the air and extract myself from my leggings, then toss them aside. The pistol was still in the leggings pocket, and it falls onto the soft earth.

"Oops."

His smile disappears for a second. "Be careful with that. It might go off."

I reach inside my Genomica T-shirt and free myself of my bra, pulling it out of my sleeve.

He squints at it. "Well, I'll be. No Genomica logo on *that*?"

I tuck it under my leggings. "That's the only thing I have that doesn't have it."

I crawl in so that we're side by side, facing the sky. Baxter takes advantage of my free sleeping bag and curls up on it. I smile. As long as he's near me, he's content. It goes both ways, buddy.

Celeres stretches out an arm and I rest my head on it. His musky scent drives me a little wild.

We're quiet for a while, but then I turn my head to look at him. "I have an idea."

"Hmm?"

"Remember how you said you used to look up at these amazing stars and look for a constellation you could see from Earth?"

He looks up at the stars. "Do you see something?"

"Well, I was thinking we could discover a new constellation. Something we could call our own."

"Our own shape? How about something that looks like a race car?"

"How about something that reminds us of each other?"

"Right, sorry."

We both lie there, looking up at the colorful points of light.

He points toward the horizon. "I got it. See that group of red ones over there? Don't they sort of look like a heart if you connect them together?"

I smile. "Yeah, they do. I love it. What should we call it?"

"I want to call it Leigh."

My eyes get glassy. "Okay."

We're quiet for a while longer and I get another idea. "You know what else we need? A song."

He looks away from the sky and over to me. "I picked the constellation. You pick the song."

"I already have."

"Really? Okay, lay it on me."

"Nightsong."

"You mean like these crickets?"

"Exactly. This is our song, the first one we heard together."

"I like it," he says.

He turns toward me and pulls me close. We kiss until our breathing quickens.

"I thought you said I'd never get laid," he whispers through a devilish smile.

"Don't get too ahead of yourself, ace. I'm just cold, remember?"

"Oh, is that all?" he says, sliding his warm hand around my waist and then under my shirt to trace designs around the small of my back. It feels wonderful. He pulls me closer and I press myself into him.

Baxter lets out a loud snort in his early slumber. We both laugh.

I close my eyes and let out a shaky breath.

He scratches my back for a long time, covering every inch, along with my ribs, and a little higher than that, too. My entire body fills with good vibes. He leans in and kisses my neck and shoulder, then reaches past me to zip the sleeping bag closed to give us some privacy.

"You're getting me all hot and bothered, Captain," I whisper. "Maybe we should stop for now and pick this up in your quarters tomorrow."

"I can't wait," he whispers back.

I blow a puff of air onto his forehead, pushing his unruly hair to the side. "Well, you can't make love in a sleeping bag."

"Leigh, where there's a will, there's a way."

This isn't how I imagined our first time would be, but hey, I have the will if he has the way. He turns me so that we're spooning, and I can feel him down there. He's ready. Me? I've *been* ready.

He wrestles his boxers off, and then works my panties down to my knees, then pushes them to the bottom of the sleeping bag with his foot.

For a minute or so, it looks like I might be right. The sleeping bag is *just* constricting enough that we can't, well, you know. I'm not even kidding. I feel like we look like a giant inchworm, squirming on the ground.

"Come on, Celeres, dig deep."

"I want nothing more in the world."

"That's not *exactly* what I mean. Here, I'm going to help."

I bend my body enough that the sleeping bag is just about to rip wide open, but before it does, I'm able to reach down and guide him in, and...ohmygod. I close my eyes and sigh maybe a little too loudly as he finds his way. He gasps when I clench.

"See, we just had to get the angle right," I whisper breathlessly.

He chuckles and licks my earlobe. "Mm-hmm. It's all in the angle."

"I like to go slow," I say.

He reaches under my shirt to play with my breast. "I do too."

I don't really want to go slow, but I want this to last. And it does. Three times.

Afterwards, I'm finally able to fall blissfully asleep in his arms, surrounded by nightsong and contentment.

Chapter Twenty-Six

A Strange Discovery

I open my eyes before sunrise, and I'm way too warm in this bag with Celeres. It's a trend; I'm always getting sweaty around this guy. Baxter's still curled up in front of me on the sleeping bag.

Nightsong is over, and besides the rustling leaves, the forest is quiet. A couple of lights blink on *Big Seven*, and last night's crackling fire is now a glowing pile of ash. Brose continues to snore as he was before I drifted off. Maybe he's a *little* quieter.

I retrieve my panties from the bottom of the bag and wriggle myself out without waking Celeres, then walk around the ship with the rest of my clothes from last night. Baxter rouses and walks beside me until he veers off to find a landing strut to pee on. Then he sits, keeping an eye on me while I get dressed.

Once I'm all put-together again, I return to the sleeping area, intending to crawl into my own bag before anyone else wakes up. It's a brilliant plan until Ashlan's "sleeping" face breaks into a grin, still with her eyes closed. Busted. My whole body flushes with embarrassment. Instead of returning to my bedroll, I sit in my camping chair and study the ashes in the fire pit. I'm not ready for the others to know that we co-bagged it last night. I wonder how much she saw. Or heard.

A second later, Celeres's phone rings, waking us all.

"This is Celeres," he mutters.

"Yes? She is? That's a relief. Can we see her?"

There's more talking on the other end.

"I see. Thank you for letting me know."

He disconnects the call, and we're all giving him our undivided attention. Brose takes exaggerated blinks, trying to wake up.

"Krysta?" I ask.

He nods. "She's conscious."

"But?"

"But you know Krysta. She tried to leave the infirmary without the doc's permission. Now they're guarding her. They have questions."

"Questions? What do you think is going on?"

He lifts both hands, palms upward. "You'd know better than I would. I'm not privy to anything she does."

"What'd they say about seeing her?"

"Said they'd call me when they're done, whatever that means."

"Oh."

He shrugs. "Is there anything else you remember about what she was doing?"

"She was finishing up in the lab when I left to meet you. We know she hurt herself, but there has to be more to it than that."

I try to think back on those last few minutes in the lab for some idea, some clue, but the frosty morning air distracts me. I didn't notice at first because the sleeping bag was so warm.

"I'll think about it," I say, teeth chattering.

I rub my arms for warmth, then pull some kindling out of a nearby pile and arrange it on the coals.

Brose looks over at me and drags himself out of his bedroll. After a big stretch, he walks stiffly to the perimeter. "Nature calls. Thanks for getting fire going, Leigh," he says as he walks out of sight.

I puff on the smoking pile of sticks. "No problem."

Celeres takes a moment to have another look at the scratches on the window from last night.

Ashlan must have changed clothes through the night. She ditched the shirt dress for a plain khaki shirt and matching pants. She bustles around in the cargo hold and finds a metal pitcher. She removes the lid and fills it with water, then she puts a metal contraption inside that looks like a basket connected to the top of a tube. She loads the basket with coffee grinds and puts a lid on top. After that, she puts the pitcher on a nearby tray table. "Ready when you are, Leigh."

I eye the pitcher. "Isn't there an instant coffee maker on the ship?"

Ashlan chuckles and shakes her head. "That's not how we do it when we go camping."

Celeres winks at me.

The sound of a burp comes from Brose's general direction and soon the telltale rustling and jostling of the underbrush announces his arrival. He throws an armload of larger wood beside the fire pit, and I position a few of the logs around my pile of kindling.

We have a nice blaze going before too long, and Ashlan shoves the coffee pitcher right next to the flames.

While we wait for the fire to boil the water, Brose and Ashlan pack up the fence poles and put them away.

Celeres approaches me. "We should talk about yesterday."

Brose circles the fire and plunks down in his chair. "I'm worried we're getting into something over our heads."

I look back and forth between them both for a few moments. "Krysta has some explaining to do. What are they doing with all that blood?"

"Should we ask her yet?" asks Celeres. "Maybe we should spy on her first."

"What do you mean?" I ask.

"I say we just play dumb for a while. Don't mention the blood or our trip to the tunnels. You know, keep your friends close, but your enemies closer."

"You think she's an enemy?"

"Well, I don't know. She's giving human blood to these aliens. Until we know why she's doing it, I think we stay in a holding pattern," he says.

Now that my hands are warm, I lean back. "So when you say keep her 'closer,' what do you mean, exactly?"

"We each spend time with her alone, try to get her to betray what's going on."

I don't like the idea of Celeres spending time alone with her. "Do you think you can handle it? What if she tries to mess with your feelings?"

"What if she messes with yours?" he counters.

"Guys, I don't mean to interrupt," says Ashlan, "but I don't think you have anything to worry about, Leigh. Celeres and Krysta never got very far, and we can all see that he's been much happier since you've come into the picture."

"Actually," says Celeres, "that's not what I mean. Can I

tell them?" He looks at me, and it suddenly dawns on me what he's talking about. My mouth drops open.

"I guess so."

The coffee percolator has a little window in the top center of the lid. Little bubbles of boiling water pop against it as the pitcher transforms water into coffee. I watch it because I don't want to see their faces when Celeres tells them.

"Leigh thinks Krysta may be interested."

"I don't think so," Ashlan says.

"Not in me," Celeres says. "Her."

Ashlan gasps. "You think Krysta is interested in *you*?"

I continue to look at the percolator. "There are signs. Signals. But it's not just that. She has this magnetism. Sometimes I actually feel tempted in a way."

"I'm confused," she says. "Are you trying to say you might give her a chance? Who do you want to be with?"

"Celeres! But there's something there that I can't explain. I don't know if it's her, just me, or what. *That's* what Celeres is worried about. What if she gets in between us?"

What if she ruins everything?

What if Celeres ruins everything?

What if it's me? What if I'm the one who blows everything up? After last night, it's the last thing I want.

Silence covers the camp, and now we're *all* watching the little window on top of the pitcher. Bubbles dance to the soft popping music of the boiling liquid. Brose retrieves it from the fire and pours each of us a cup before regaining his seat. "There's something about Krysta,"

When no one responds, he looks at Celeres. "All the guys in engineering have a thing for her. When she comes in, they fall all over themselves to see to her needs. She always gets what she wants, but she never gets romantically involved with anyone. If anything, I thought you and she would work out."

Celeres kicks a small stick into the fire. "We were kind of close, I guess, but it never went to the next level."

Brose gives me a sidelong glance. "And now we know why."

Butterflies come unbidden to my stomach at the thought of Krysta having feelings for me. Celeres watches his little burning stick with a crooked smile. I bet he would love to know what I'm thinking right now. I sure would like to know what he's thinking.

Ashlan puts her hand on my arm and I'm startled out of my swirling thoughts and emotions. "Let's take a walk." She coaxes me up from my chair and toward a nearby forest path I didn't notice before.

Baxter's ears perk up at the mention of the "w" word (what Mom and I used to call it), and he runs a few tight circles around Ash and me. I pat his head a few times, and then get a harness from the ship because I want to be sure he doesn't get away from me down here. After yesterday, I'm not taking any chances.

I latch him up and Ashlan leads us away.

Baxter digs his paws into the ground and stops dead just before we set foot on the path.

"C'mon, boy. Make up your mind."

Celeres approaches. "He isn't having it."

I hand Celeres the leash. "Keep an eye on him for me."

"Sure. He can help while I fix some of this damage from the wasps. I might have some extra meat for him, too."

"If you do, he'll do every trick in the book to get it."

"Let's go, buddy," Celeres says as he guides Bax to the cooler.

I turn back to Ashlan. "They like each other."

"I know. It's cute. You ready?"

"Wait a minute," says Brose.

We both look back to see what he wants. He tosses a rifle to Ashlan, and she straps it to her back.

He holds a hand to his forehead to shield his eyes from the sun and looks into the trees. "Hey Cel, isn't your garden back there?"

Celeres nods.

Brose turns to address Ash and I. "Anyway, if you see anything that looks like a ripe tomato, bring it back. Dinner will be an authentic farm-to-table dining experience."

We turn to leave.

"Wait again," says Brose.

Ashlan turns and looks at him with eyebrows raised. "Yes?" she asks with humorous impatience.

He hands her a spare magazine for the rifle. "Just in case."

I look at him, wide-eyed.

"Better to have it and not need it than to need it and not have it," he says in the most reassuring voice he can manage.

Ashlan smirks and pockets the magazine. "We're leaving now, Brose. Stop scaring her. Let's get out of here before he hands you a bazooka, Leigh."

With one last look at the guys and my pup, I follow Ashlan further down the path, and soon we walk alone. After I get over the anxiety of possibly needing extra bullets, something else tugs at my anxiety. "Do you think Celeres is over her?"

"Krysta? It hasn't been long since their big falling out, but he seems a lot better. I wouldn't worry."

"Maybe I should back off."

"Isn't it a little late for that?"

"What do you mean?"

"I saw you this morning, remember?"

I blush.

"Hey, it's fine. It's only natural."

"I didn't say we had sex."

"I got up in the middle of the night and saw your pile of clothes."

"That doesn't mean anything. You ever try making love in a sleeping bag with a dude who practically fills it up just with himself?"

Her eyes unfocus for a second. "No."

"What's that goofy grin?"

"Not yet, at least."

I punch her on the arm, and we stop.

"I like him," I say.

"But?"

"Sometimes I can't get Krysta out of my head."

"So? Pick one and go with it."

"But I never felt that way about a girl."

Ashlan looks me right in the eyes. "I don't know if this makes any difference, but if things don't work out between Brose and I, and you and Krysta, don't, you know, *I* might give it a shot with her."

"Really? You're bi?"

"If she's willing and I'm willing, who cares?"

"I never thought it could be that simple."

"It really is that simple. You're attracted to who you're attracted to. That's it."

I pause for a moment as that sinks in. "You know, come to think of it, I don't think I've met anyone yet who doesn't want her."

"That's what I'm saying. She's more or less—"

"Perfect," I say.

"I was going to say irresistible, but yeah."

I rub my temples. "But I still don't know. These thoughts and feelings are all jumbled together."

She looks at me with compassion and then lets out a deep breath. "I think I can help you."

"How?"

She puts her arms around my neck and moves in close. Our heads are scarcely an inch apart. The breath from her nose tickles my upper lip. Her mouth approaches but stops just before making contact. "Do you think I'm pretty?"

"Of course, you're—"

She parts her lips and her warm breath bathes my face. "Kiss me now."

I push her away. "What are you doing?"

"I thought you liked girls."

"I don't. I mean, not normally."

"Well, there's your answer, then."

"You weren't really going to kiss me, were you?"

"Sure, if you wanted. I said I was helping you."

I take a step back and my eyes narrow. "Do you like me, Ash?"

She chuckles. "You're not exactly my type. No offense."

"Uh, thanks."

"Welcome."

I look back the way we came. "But what about Brose?"

"What about him?"

"You should try helping *him* like you just did me. I bet he takes the bait."

She smirks and resumes our trek through the woods. "I can't make it too easy for him, though I wish he would move a *little* faster."

The forest thickens as we delve deeper, forcing me to fall in behind her as the path narrows.

We get to a very dense section, and she stops. "Most of this was only knee-high last time I was here. I can't believe this stuff grows so fas—"

She stops talking and fixates her eyes on something high-up. I follow her stare to a fork in a tree trunk that has a thick spider web stretched across it. It's about the size of a tractor tire.

She pulls the rifle from her shoulder and looks through the scope. I put my hands over my ears—a habit I picked up when going hunting with my dad back in the day.

There are no spiders to be seen. Instead, a reptilian head protrudes from a dark hole in the webbing. It's deathly still. It considers us with its pale green eyes.

She holds her breath, her finger resting on the trigger. Her eyes are both open, with one eye focused on the scope. In the next instant, the reptilian head shifts and the creature —it looks like an alligator the size of a German Shepherd— jumps from the tree toward us and runs in our direction with remarkable speed.

Ashlan curses and points the rifle at the ground in front of us. It's impossible to see the creature under the vegetation. There's just a mass of boiling leaves where it runs, and it's getting closer. She fires one shot, then another. She squeezes off about fifteen more rounds before the leaves stop moving about ten feet ahead of us.

"That was too close," she says.

Trembling, I pull my hands from my ears. "What...just happened?"

She breathes hard and says in a breathless voice, "You don't want to mess with those. They're tree-dwellers, living in those weird web nests and have no fear. They're deadly."

"What are they?"

"They're called wisks."

"Wisks?"

"We named them after Marcus Wisk, the colonist who discovered them. He's dead now."

"What happened?"

She points to the wisk's blood-spattered trail. "A wisk happened. Keep an eye out for them."

She fits the spare magazine into her rifle, and we continue in silence. I spend much of the next half hour scanning the trees for more wisks, but don't see any. Finally, when I calm down, I decide to break the silence. "So, what do you think of Celeres?"

"Great guy. He can cook. What else do you need to know?"

"True, he can. I'm looking forward to seeing this garden that I've been hearing so much about."

"Oh, we aren't going to his garden."

I'm beginning to think I'm never going to see it. "Then where are we going?"

"We're here."

I look around, and sure enough, we are. A cabin stands amid a cluster of trees in a small clearing. It's quaint, with a screened window on each side.

Birds herald the morning with song, and a babbling brook winds its way past the building.

"What is this?" I ask.

"It's my cabin. Come on!"

She strides over and opens the door. A soft light illuminates the interior. I follow, trying to get at least a small look inside before I enter.

It turns out the inner light is from an entire wall of computer screens. They're all dark except for one. It seems to be showing aeriel forest footage, like from a drone. The door swings shut and clicks behind me.

"Have a seat," she says.

I do. "What is all of this?"

"Research. I stay down here sometimes to study the wildlife. See? There's my bunk, and a small refrigerator if you're thirsty."

"I'm okay, thanks. What do you study, exactly?"

"Lots of stuff, but right now it's strange migratory patterns. I call it the animal parade. Occasionally, animals will line up and march toward that zoo we visited last night. It doesn't happen real often, and it only lasts a few hours. Animals don't just do that, at least not on Earth. I'm trying to figure it out."

"Could the Apocritans be controlling them?"

"I don't know how. I bring batch after batch up to *Sumerian*, and they all seem perfectly natural. There are no implants, weird collars, or anything else foreign attached to them. At least as far as I can tell."

"Do you have any hypotheses?"

"Maybe some kind of electromagnetic effect? I don't know. I learned about migration in school, of course, but nothing like this."

I look at the screen, mesmerized by the trees rushing past below. "Where did you go to school?"

"Ohio State. They have a superb veterinarian program there."

"Really? I was thinking about going there."

"For what?"

"I hadn't decided. A friend joined their dance team and was trying to recruit me for it as well."

"They're good?"

"You could say that."

The screen with the aerial footage goes from showing a

forest canopy to a large section of cleared trees. I point at it. "What's that?"

Ashlan looks at the screen, and her eyes narrow. She stands and walks right up to it. "That wasn't there last week."

"Or last night," I say.

"How do you know?"

"Wouldn't we have seen this when we flew in?"

"I don't know, maybe. I mean, it was getting dark, and we had those distractions—the flowers, the soccer game."

"Is it close?"

"Yeah...it is."

She turns away from the screen and grabs the rifle. "Let's go."

Chapter Twenty-Seven

Death March

She keeps a brisk pace and doesn't talk. The day's been warming up, and sweat stains grow larger on our shirts. Eventually, we stop and she tells me to watch my step as she treads carefully ahead. The forest floor turns downhill until it's cliff-like. Below is what looks like a natural bowl in the topography. It's almost stadium-like, and we're in the nose-bleed section. What *isn't* natural is that the bottom of the bowl has been clear-cut and is devoid of trees.

While we both stare at the scene in confusion, a buzzing sound from behind interrupts the normal forest sounds. I spin around to see what's coming, expecting to see a gigantic wasp.

And I'm right. It's only twenty feet away and flying just above the ground. I grab Ashlan's arm. "What do we do?"

She looks over at it. "It isn't real. It's one of my drones. It's what was sending the video feed to the cabin."

"Why's it have to look so...frightening?"

"Sorry. We wanted it to blend in. Well hey, want to head down and take a look?"

"Getting back up this hill is going to be a serious pain."

"We don't have to if you don't want."

"Oh, I don't care. It'll be my workout for the day."

Bit by bit, we trek to the bottom of the bowl by grabbing branches and roots on the steeper parts, and by sidestepping where we can. It only takes about ten minutes, and we make it without falling, though at the bottom we take our shoes off to dump out the dirt and small rocks.

"What do you think this is?" she asks.

"It reminds me of my running track around the football field back home. It's about the same size."

In the middle of the cleared area are several tree stumps, but the outer rim, the running part, has been picked clean and maybe even graded.

I move ahead. "Let's do a lap."

She chuckles. "You never stop, do you?"

"I can't help it. Sometimes I jog twice a day at home."

"I'm sweating through my clothes as it is. I'm just walking."

"That's fine, I'll walk too."

I ran on high school tracks lots of times, but this track is almost impossible to describe. It goes beyond being in the middle of the forest, with no trace of civilization anywhere. I think it's the knowledge that I'm in an alien world, doing something familiar but in the most unfamiliar place imaginable, having a friend beside me with a gun to protect us from wisks and who knows what else. It's surreal.

Ashlan walks in silence. It's obvious that I'm enraptured by my surroundings. When I look up into the sky, though, I stop.

"What's wrong?" she asks.

"Is that...could that be...*Sumerian?*"

Up high in the sky is a metallic gleam. I knew *Sumerian* was big, but I never thought I'd be able to see it from the surface.

"It is."

I marvel for a second before something even more amazing catches my eye. They're faint, but I'm able to see several of the multi-color stars, even though it's a bright midmorning here.

"I know what you're looking at," she says. "The stars here are closer than what we're used to on Earth. They're bright enough to see in the daytime, if you really look."

"Not all of them."

"No, but some. Isn't it neat?"

"They're beautiful."

She lets me stand and stare for a minute before breaking the silence.

"So, Leigh, I have a question for *you*."

"Yeah?"

"What do you think of Brose?"

"You mean besides the fact that he needs a comb?"

She gives me a sidelong look and sighs. "I mean, you aren't wrong, but seriously, what do you think of him?"

"You didn't give me a serious answer about Celeres. There has to be more to an eligible guy than his cooking skills."

"Fine. Celeres is a great guy. I think you should give him a chance."

"What do you think Krysta will say?"

"Who cares? She snubbed him. He's free game."

I sigh. "Yeah, I guess so. It's just that I have to work with her."

"Maybe not for long."

"Huh?"

"Celeres said they have her under guard. Why do you think that is?"

"I don't know."

"You don't?"

"Not yet, but I'll try to find out. She has her secrets."

Ashlan nods, looking at the ground. "I know. She has Brose working for her on the side and he won't say much about it. I don't know how much I trust her."

"Around the guy you're thinking of dating?"

"Yes, but also in general. You should be happy she isn't hanging out with Celeres anymore."

"Oh, I am. Do you think he really likes me?"

She kicks a rock off the track, then gives me a teasing smile. "Don't you think it's kind of obvious?"

We continue to the far end, a little past the halfway point.

She waves a hand in front of my face to break me out of my trance. "So... Brose?"

"Oh, sorry. Let me see...he's smart, obviously. He's capable, has a great sense of humor, is good-looking in a mountain man kind of way, and likes long walks in the woods. Take him for a test drive, see how he corners."

"Funny, Leigh."

"Hey, it's all we can do, right?"

I pause and furrow my brow.

She raises an eyebrow. "What's wrong?"

"Not to change the subject or anything, but do you smell something weird? It's almost...minty?"

Ashlan pauses and inhales deeply. "Maybe, I don't know. Sometimes the forest just smells...like this."

Remembering the times I walked through onion grass

back home, I look down at my feet to see if I just trampled some herbs. Nope, it's just dirt right here.

She continues, "I think it's just the indigenous flowers and such. There's a lot we don't know about Apocrita yet."

On the far end of the "track," a six-legged orange and green lizard about the size of an enormous pig with two wriggling tentacles coming out of its neck crashes through the foliage. It isn't looking in our direction yet. I give Ashlan a wide-eyed stare. "What the hell is that now?"

She grabs my shoulder and pushes me down to kneel. "Drossler. They're generally peaceful, but let's not take any chances."

"It looks like it could rip us apart without a second thought."

"Let's wait and see what it does."

We crouch and try to become as small as possible.

It never sees us. It cuts straight across the track and disappears into the trees on that side.

As if a floodgate opened, animals burst into the clearing, making a beeline in the same direction as the drossler. They're moving fast; some roll by like out-of-control boulders, some fly, and some even ride on the backs of bigger creatures.

"It's happening," she hisses.

I stare at her blankly.

"The animal parade. This is it!"

I have a burning desire to follow them. "You want to check it out?"

"Definitely."

We stand together and approach the same opening that the animals are using. Behind us, more and more creatures emerge from the forest, following the path at a mindless sprint.

Ashlan clenches and unclenches her fingers. "I want to know what's going on."

"What do you think it is?"

"Leigh, all I know is that I want to follow this route more than I've ever wanted anything. I need to learn more about this place, the animals, why they do this."

"I feel the same way, but I don't know why. It's like raw desire."

She looks at me, and her eyes narrow. "Animal attraction," she whispers, and then continues along the path.

We can turn around and go back. I just don't want to—yet. I look behind me, then at Ashlan's back disappearing into the brush. I catch up to her in a few long strides. "Have you ever gone this way?"

"Not exactly, but near here. So have you, actually. The zoo is real close. We'll see it soon."

The more we walk, the more animals we see coming from every direction.

"You know what's weird, Ash? I think I've seen every life form on this planet today except for one—the wasps."

She doesn't respond. She's busy trying not to step on a family of rodents scurrying around our feet. When she gets a second to look up, she fixes a distracted glance at me and bids me to follow with a jerk of her head. She walks off of the path and into the trees another twenty feet. She stops and gets down on her belly.

I do the same. "What are we doing? Shouldn't we go see where all this leads?"

"Look, you can see from here."

I crane and twist my neck, searching for a gap in the foliage, and finally spot the main zoo building. A sea of animals swarm around the outside. Some wasps mill around within the mass of creatures, slipping nooses around their necks and leading them inside. So this is how they stock the zoo?

But then I notice something else, something sinister. Some wasps have stinger devices like what we have at the lab. They open the calipers at the tip and affix them around the necks of the animals. In fact, one is fastening the device to the drossler. There's a bright flash of purple and the drossler crumples to the ground. The wasp ejects the battery and drops it into one of several piles. It gleams purple, just as bright as the ones in the underground cavern that amazed Brose so much. It appears there's a battery pile for each different type of creature.

This whole parade, this carnage, is all to recharge batteries with zero regard to life. They're stocking up on them. There's a cart nearby with darkened batteries. Now the wasp takes one of those and fits it into the stinger and repeats the process on an animal that looks like a blue teddy bear. It melts into death just as quickly as the drossler did and the wasp ejects another brightly glowing purple battery.

I gulp in horror. "They're charging the batteries by *killing* things."

Ashlan points down at the kill zone. "Oh, no."

I look down to see a knee-high foxlike animal fall next. Ashlan's chin trembles and she clears her throat before adding, "That looked just like Baxter's fox girlfriend." Now her eyes are narrow and she's breathing hard.

I look back at the zoo. I have to go down there. I pull myself to my feet and start back toward the same path the animals are taking. Behind me, Ashlan lets out a sob. "No." She's already taken a few steps in the opposite direction, back from where we just came.

I grab at her arm, my nails biting into her flesh. "We

have to go down there. We can find out what is really going on!"

"No! They're slaughtering them! We need to get out of here."

I tug on her arm with all of my might, and she hauls back and slaps me hard across the face with her free hand. Tears spring to my own eyes.

She screams, "Leigh!" much like she did when I passed out last night. I release her arm and focus on her, the tears running down her cheeks. Something is very wrong here.

Her eyes are dark pools of fear and shock. "Think of Baxter."

Baxter. The word cuts through the fog and bounces around in my brain. For a moment, my lust to continue wanes.

"Come on!" she urges.

She's right—if Baxter gets sucked into this death march, I'll never see him again. We need to get back. It takes enormous effort at first, but with each step further away from the zoo, the fatal attraction to the slaughter lessens. Soon, we're jogging through the brush with easier and easier progress. Blood streams down Ashlan's arm where I gripped her. I look down at my hand, at the bloody fingernails I used to impale her flesh.

No time for that now; self preservation first, then I'm sure we'll talk about this.

"Do you think Baxter is okay?" I ask, almost crying myself.

"God, I hope so. Did you see...did you see?"

"I saw. We have to get back to the ship. Is this the fastest way?"

She looks down at her arm. Drops of blood fall onto the

verdant leaves on the forest floor. "The cabin's closer. I need first aid. I smell like a wounded animal."

I'm filled with instant regret. I hope she can see it on my face. "Please hurry."

"I know."

We pick up our pace and plunge ahead.

Chapter Twenty-Eight

Hasty Return

I lose all sense of time as we make our way. I focus on the rifle bobbing on Ashlan's back and follow where she leads. We eventually get to the cabin where she enters without even holding the door for me. When I join her, she's already running water over her arm at the sink. A first aid kit lies open on the table.

I take a roll of gauze from the kit and hold it at the ready. She dries her wound with some paper towels and then sprays something on it. She holds her arm out at me, and I wrap it for her. It's self-adherent, and I give her a few layers.

"I'm terribly sorry about this," I mutter.

She looks at my cheek. "I'm sorry about your face."

I look in the mirror. The whole side of my face is red from that epic slap.

"It's okay"—I puff my cheek and turn my head a few different angles to get a better look—"I think. Were you a boxer in a previous life?"

"It was pure adrenaline."

"I don't doubt it. You know, there's one thing that doesn't add up."

She leans back against the sink. "Just one?"

"Yes. We were attracted to the zoo just like the animals. What about everyone else? You know, the colonists?"

"The zoo was closed today," she says, her voice trailing off.

I'm so out of sorts that it takes several moments to notice the buzzing in my pocket. I dig it out, and my breath catches. I turn the phone so Ashlan can see the caller ID. It's Krysta.

Ash's eyes narrow. "Why is she calling you?"

"I don't know. Should I answer it?"

"Yes!"

I swipe the answer slider and put her on speakerphone. "Hello?"

"Where are you?" she asks, her voice raspy.

"I'm...on Apocrita. Are you okay? Celeres said they were interrogating you or something. What's it about?"

"I'm okay. Mostly. Listen, I need you to do something. Can you get somewhere private?"

I put my finger to my lips and Ashlan nods.

"Yes. I'm on a hike."

"Good. It's the stinger. I left it out in the open. Can you go to the lab and put it away?"

"Yeah, of course, as soon as I get back."

"It might be on the floor, I don't know. I think I dropped it. It's hopefully in one piece. I got out of there fast. I knew I was fading and didn't want to pass out down there." As she speaks, her voice sounds weaker and weaker.

"No problem, I'll take care of it."

She's quiet, but I can hear her breathing. She says in a shaky voice, "Can you do it soon?"

"Probably. When I get back to camp, I'll ask if we can leave."

She coughs for a few seconds. "Leigh, there's one more thing."

"Okay?"

"They're pressuring me to let them into the lab. Don't let them get to you."

"They?"

"Station security."

"Why do they want to get in?"

"I'll explain later. Come see me at the infirmary as soon as you take care of it."

"I won't get arrested or anything, will I?"

"Come as soon as you can."

She disconnects.

Ashlan, who was quiet during the call, narrows her eyes. "What's a stinger?"

I shouldn't say more, at least not yet. What would she think of me if she knew I have one of those same things that she just watched take the life of so many animals? What would she do? Who would she tell?

"An artifact from...here. I've been doing experiments on it."

"And?"

"Nothing. It doesn't actually *do* anything that we've found. It's Apocritan technology, like the subspace radios. I've just been taking energy readings."

"Stinger, though? Sounds a little sketchy to me."

"Yeah, I know it does."

We're quiet for a minute, then she leads me out of the cabin. "Lets get back."

She's pushes through the underbrush and holds the occasional branch so that it doesn't snap back and hit me.

Now that I've seen the aliens use the stinger, I wonder if it had something to do with Krysta's injury. She doesn't know that she has everything she needs to recharge batteries right under her nose. If she did, I doubt she'd hesitate to take the lives of animals. It's only a matter of time before she figures it out and heads to Beastarium.

The hair stands up on my arms. This isn't good. Baxter lives there. Should I get him out? She wouldn't actually kill my dog. She couldn't. Right?

Something on the ground catches my eye and I stoop down. Ashlan stops and turns around. "What do you see?"

I reach out to a small plant with triangular green leaves. Red dots decorate each leaf. "This is what Krysta picked the last time I was here."

"Wow, that'd be easy to miss if you weren't looking for it. What do you think it's for?"

"No idea. She told me it was decorative, but I don't know. She was looking awfully hard for it."

"Let's take it back and show it to the guys."

"Right," I say as I pull it out by the roots.

As we approach camp, Baxter hears us and barks. I can't see him yet because the vegetation is so thick, but I already know the difference between this bark and the bark when we returned from the zoo. This time, he's just being a good watchdog.

As Ash and I step out of the woods, Celeres unclips Baxter's leash, freeing him to race towards me with a happy bark. I stoop down to greet him, but he stops short when he's a few feet away, and approaches me tentatively. I reach out to scratch his neck, and he closes the rest of the distance, softly touching my puffy cheek with his nose and tongue.

Celeres also walks over to join us, but when he sees what Baxter is doing and the bandage on Ashlan's arm, his face fills with concern. "What happened?"

I give Baxter a quick ruffle and stand up. "We're okay."

He doesn't look convinced. "Who did this?"

Brose is also by our side, inspecting Ash's bandage. "There's blood."

She looks down to where Brose's fingers trace the red stain. "I know. We did this to each other."

Judging by the look on the men's faces, they must think we just escaped from the asylum. After a second, Celeres looks past us. "Did this happen at my garden?"

I look at Ashlan, and she takes the cue. "We didn't go. I took her to my cabin, and then we went to investigate a new forest clearing that was in the drone footage."

"And?" asks Brose.

"I witnessed the animal parade first hand. It went straight past us. In fact, we almost got sucked into it as well. I should warn you guys that if you see animals all walking in the same direction, paying almost no attention to you at all, run the other way. It's like being stuck in a rip current at the ocean. The only reason we're both standing here right now is because we beat the snot out of each other to snap out of the trance."

Brose looks in the forest from where we just emerged. "We felt nothing here."

Ashlan sits down heavily in a camp chair. "Whatever it is, it must be highly localized. Now I'm wondering if that's why they built the zoo so far away from the colony; so they don't get caught in it."

Celeres looks at Baxter, and I can guess what he's thinking. "I should leave Baxter on *Sumerian* next time."

He nods. "I need to get us out of here. It's not safe until we know what we're dealing with."

I scratch Bax under his collar. "Especially for you, buddy."

Celeres notices that the plant that I brought back. "Whatcha got there, Leigh?"

"This is what I told you about, what Krysta picked when I went hiking with her." I hold it out to him.

He takes it. "It's a pretty little thing. Do you mind if I plunk it in a flowerpot and keep it for a little while? I want to see how it looks when it grows up. It's the gardener in me."

"Be my guest."

This is as good a time as any to tell them about the phone call. "Guess who called me while we were gone? I assumed it *was* you until I looked at the screen."

Celeres motions to our little group. "Isn't everyone you know right here with us?"

"All except for one."

"*Krysta?* Did Krysta call you?"

"Yes, and you will not believe this. She wants me to go up to the lab and clean up the mess she left behind when she hurt herself."

Brose is already breaking camp, collecting his fence posts and folding chairs. Ashlan takes Bax from me and helps him back into the ship. Celeres comes over to me while they work. "Is everything okay?"

"Maybe I'm beginning to understand why you blocked me from leaving Earth."

He puts an arm around me, and I lean my head into his shoulder. "I'm glad you're here," he says, kissing my hair.

"Good."

Because I think there's a chance I'm stuck here.

"Let's finish packing up, and we'll go see what Krysta left us," he says softly, and maybe with a little trepidation.

He walks away to lift the cooler into the ship's hold and I'm left standing by myself wondering if I should show them the lab. How angry would Krysta be if I got some help? Especially if I need to get past some guards or nosy scientists? It sounds like Celeres already assumes that we're doing this together, but I just don't know—I've always been one for following the rules.

~

Once we pack away the camp and extinguish the fire, we pile into *Big Seven*. I'm the second one in, right behind Celeres, and I follow him to the cockpit to sit where Krysta sat when he brought the two of us down last time. He looks over at me.

I clip myself in. "This is my seat from now on."

He smiles and looks behind us as Ash and Brose enter the back of the ship. In a low voice that they can't hear, he says, "And those lovebirds can have the back seat."

I look back and make sure they're still not close enough to hear. "I don't know...Ash wishes he'd move a little faster."

He laughs, then nods, motioning to a red switch on the console. "Fire up the engines for me."

Just like on McClure's *Ice Arrow*, there are identical controls in front of both of us. I flip the red switch and the familiar soft hum permeates the cabin.

Ashlan and Brose take the seat behind us.

Celeres thumbs a control on the flight stick, and we float

straight up. I watch his every move. The more I witness piloting in action, the more fascinated I become.

He suddenly rolls the ship to the right and back again, causing some commotion behind us. When I look back, Ashlan and Brose are tangled up in each other.

"Hey!" says Ashlan, "I didn't get buckled in yet!"

"Sorry, I slipped," says Celeres, looking straight ahead. He's fighting a smile and is absolutely not looking at me.

I look back at the two of them again, and she regains her seat with Brose helping her. He grabs the strap and reaches across her waist to clip it in. She starts to take it from him, but changes her mind and sits back, allowing him to fasten her in.

Celeres looks over his shoulder to make sure they're all set. "Away we go."

He pushes the throttle forward and we rocket back to *Sumerian* and whatever adventure Krysta may have in store for us.

So much for lunch.

Chapter Twenty-Nine

Secrets and Suspicions

I'll probably never get used to how *fast* we can go from the surface of this strange new world, into space, and aboard the space station. The whole thing is like taking a quick trip to the corner store. We're barely docked, and Celeres is already up and bolting for the hatch. "I'll catch up with you. I want to get this plant into some soil before it wilts."

He's gone before the rest of us even unbuckle.

Ashlan watches him go. "Guy sure likes his plants."

I crane my neck to see the last of him disappear. "I'm learning more about him every day."

Ashlan puts Bax on his leash. "Do you want me to take him? I need to check in at Beastarium, anyway."

"That would be great, thank you. I'll make my way to the infirmary to see Krysta. Are you guys coming?"

"Absolutely," says Brose. "We'll take care of Bax, then grab Cel. We'll meet you there."

I only have to ask a few people until I find myself in a section of hallway with a glowing blue line on the floor. They say it leads straight to the Infirmary, and that it'll be obvious when I see it. It isn't long before the *smell* is obvious. You know...hospital smell.

That's not the only obvious thing; it's easy to see where they're "keeping" Krysta. A uniformed guard stands outside one room. Oh, I remember this guy. He's the same guard who questioned me at the scene of the incident. I try to look like I know what I'm doing, so he'll leave me alone. I'm wishing I had stopped for a lab coat first. How official do I look with my camping clothes and shoes caked with dirt? We're going to find out.

He looks directly at me as I approach. "Leigh Shires?" Just like that. He knows my name now. He doesn't offer his hand, doesn't smile. My heart rate picks up. They were expecting me.

"Yes? I'm here to visit Krysta."

"One second," he says, then takes a step into the room. "She's here, Cap."

I steal a glance into Krysta's room. The bed is a disheveled mess, and she isn't in it. There's the sound of a flushing toilet, and then she stumbles out of a door like she's three sheets to the wind drunk. She grabs the railing on the bed before falling over. She sees me and her eyes go wide. I can see from here that she's breathing hard by the rise and fall of her chest in that flimsy hospital gown.

I give her an almost-equally wide stare back. What happened to her? Why is she so wobbly? Pain killers?

Soon, another guy in uniform steps out of her room from just around the corner, blocking my view. "I'm Captain Richards. Let's walk."

Richards and I walk in silence, then enter a nearby

room containing only a conference table and four chairs. Once the door slides shut, he looks me up and down with his lips pursed. He gives my chest a second look before making eye contact. "I need to ask you some questions."

"I have a choice?"

He doesn't answer, but takes a seat on the other side of the table.

I sit down. I shouldn't have come here alone. I can't believe I'm sitting in a room with this perv while Celeres is potting a plant at his quarters.

Richards slaps a notepad onto the table and pulls a pen from his breast pocket. "Where were you?"

"Planetside."

"Why?"

"Camping trip."

"With?"

"Friends. Wait, should I have a lawyer or something? What's going on? Who the hell are you?"

"Head of station security. The nurses called us when your friend scared them with some of her delirious ramblings."

"I'm new. I don't know anything. I barely know her."

"We need to know if there is any danger to the station in that lab of yours. Is there?"

"No, of course not." (I hope not).

"What can you tell us about Vorefuser?"

"Vorefuser? Nothing. Never heard of him, or her, or whatever."

"What about power?"

"Power?" Is he wondering about batteries? C'mon Celeres, pot that frikkin' plant and come rescue me. "Power for what?"

"She kept going on about Vorefuser and power. Said

'Vorefuser is out' about a hundred times. And that there is too much power, then not enough power. I'm telling you she's making no sense, but she seemed crazy enough that she scared the staff."

I'm not telling this guy anything. I shrug my shoulders and give him the most vapid expression I can manage.

"Nothing?"

I shrug again.

He puts the pen down on his blank pad. "Alright then. We weren't able to get into her—your—lab to check anything out. Because you weren't around and she wasn't reliable, we cut power to that part of the station out of an abundance of caution. I hope that didn't cause you any problems."

"When can you turn it back on?"

"When you get there and put your hand on the pad to open the door, the power will reactivate. Come back here and let me know if everything is safe as soon as you know. I'll be monitoring her."

"Can I see her?"

"After you check the lab. It's important that we know the station is safe."

I have a sudden feeling of dread. If Krysta left the stinger on the floor, I should put it away before my friends see it, just in case the very knowledge of its existence might put them at some kind of risk. I stand up and open the door. "Which way to the lab?"

He looks at me like I just asked him which way is up. He points down the hall and I head in that direction without thanking him. I hope things look familiar after a little while.

As soon as I turn the next corner, I practically run head-first into Celeres, Brose, and Ashlan.

"Hey!" says Celeres, "You're going the wrong way."

"I have to check the lab."

"Did you see Krysta?"

"Only for a second across the room. I didn't get to talk to her. The security guy told me I have to check the lab first."

"What security guy?" asks Ashlan.

"Captain Richards."

Celeres raises his eyebrows. "*Him?* Wow, this escalated quickly."

I look behind me for a second, half-expecting him to be following me. "If he's so high-up, then why couldn't he just let himself into the lab?"

"He could, but it's so classified that there would have to be an actual fire, explosion, hole into space, or some other disaster first. If he went in there on just a hunch, he'd probably go to jail."

I give him a skeptical look. "Isn't that a little extreme?"

"They'd lock him up to keep him from betraying any secrets he finds, or from spreading false ones."

"It's bad enough that they cut the lab's power," I say.

"They *what?*" asks Brose, his mouth falling open. "They can't cut power to a working lab. What's wrong with those idiots? I'm coming with you."

I hold my hands up. "It's okay, I got it. You know we can't take that chance. I'll just check everything out and meet you in Krysta's room. Richards is waiting for me there."

"Sorry, but no," Brose continues, "Last time I checked, I'm the Chief Engineer at this station, and if there *are* any power related problems, I need to be there. I'll disable security cameras in that area for a brief time, then blame the power outage when they ask me about it."

"I'm coming too," says Ashlan.

What will happen to me if Krysta finds out I let them into the lab? What will happen to *them*? I look at Celeres to measure his intentions, but he's looking down the hall toward Krysta's room. I know he wants to check on her.

Ashlan gives a quick two-tone whistle. "Celeres?"

"What? Yes, of course I'm coming with you. Let's get going."

He turns and heads back the way he came without waiting to see if we follow. He leads at a brisk walk, his cowboy boots clacking down the hall. I have to hurry to keep up.

For better or worse, my friends are going to see the lab and it's anyone's guess of what to expect when we get there. The last person there was Krysta—as far as I know.

Chapter Thirty

Heroes in the Lab

There's a weird vibe in the station as we hurry to the lab. People fill the hallways, but are strangely quiet. They step out of our way and avert their gaze as we pass. The usual hellos to Celeres are absent. Could they think they're in danger, that Krysta and I could be the cause? Rumors travel fast on a space station.

I only know two things. One: Whatever hurt Krysta could still be in there. Two: I shouldn't bring my friends to the lab, but I'm glad they insisted. If there is danger, and there very well could be, I'm going to need their help.

In no time, we stand outside of the very door that Krysta careened out of before we left for the camping trip.

Brose taps on his phone for a few seconds and then clicks his tongue. "Go ahead, open it. The cameras are off."

Celeres and Ashlan nod, and I extend my hand to the pad. The Genomica logo changes from red to green, and the door slides open.

We're hit by a gust of hot air that smells like a back alley dumpster.

Brose gags. "Oh god. What is that?"

I have a mini coughing fit myself before I can answer. "I don't know. It wasn't like this before."

He scrunches his nose and looks at the ceiling. "Ugh! They had the air handlers turned off with everything else. This lab is so close to the station reactors that the handlers are essential for cooling."

Ashlan gestures to a handful of onlookers clustered down the hall from us. "We have company."

They keep a respectable distance but make no effort to hide the fact that they're watching us with great interest.

I force back the bile rising in my throat. "I don't know if I can go in there." I pull my shirt up over my nose in a vain attempt to block the foulness.

Brose licks a finger and holds it in the air as he steps inside. "The handlers are blowing again. We should be okay soon."

The small crowd is becoming a medium crowd, so we have to move along. The rest of us file into the lab's lounge and the door closes behind us. A pack of mini chocolate-iced donuts with the icing all melted away sits inside the vending machine.

The secret door to the invisible passage is wide open, just as Krysta left it. The awful, rotting smell wafts up from below.

Celeres's hand shoots up to cover his mouth.

"Keep it down, Celeres," I say. "If you lose your cookies in here, I guarantee you we're going to have a chain reaction."

He swallows and nods. Sweat covers his forehead. We're all sweating. That, combined with the ill expressions on our faces, makes us look like we have a severe case of the flu.

Celeres grabs Brose by the sleeve, and they walk into the invisible corridor together. "We'll take the lead."

Brose runs his hand along the unseen wall. "I wonder how they built this. I can't even see a seam."

When Ashlan and I follow them out, she gasps in awe at the beauty surrounding us.

And she's right. The multicolored Apocritan stars surround us. In the planet's atmosphere, bright sparks of chain lighting dance within a storm over an ocean. She reaches her arms out to touch either side of the invisible stairway for support, and makes a grasping motion, as if she's capturing a star in her grip.

The men are already far ahead, and we pick up our pace. Below, Celeres retches.

"Come on, man. Do *not* throw up," says Brose, "it smelled bad enough in here *before*."

Ashlan and I turn the bend at the bottom and join the guys in the lab. The air handling system is catching up, and even though it's possible that my nose is just becoming accustomed to the stench, I think the smell is abating somewhat.

Before I can assess the situation, Ashlan darts into the room—straight to the source of the smell—the aquarium. All of Krysta's fish float lifelessly in the stale, hot water. As she approaches the tank, the aeration system kicks on and millions of tiny bubbles fill the water, but it's too little, too late.

"This is awful," she says, fishing the bodies out of the tank with a little green net. "Stay back. It smells even worse over here."

I shake my head in sympathy for Krysta. Nobody likes to lose pets, even fish. Nearby, the stinger rests on the floor between a couple of lab benches. I need to put it away with no one seeing. Ashlan focuses on dealing with the dead fish, while Brose and Celeres occupy themselves with something a few tables away. As long as they are over there, I have a chance. The little battery window in the stinger's grip shows a soft purple glow. I squint at it. That battery was dark and dead when I left the lab.

The green needle is still showing, so I use my key to retract it and show the golden one. So that's it, the secret of the stinger. We know what the green needle does. We've seen it kill innocent creatures, and it nearly took out Krysta. So what does the gold needle do?

Before I can decide where to hide the device, Celeres and Brose appear next to me.

Ashlan disposes of the fish in the incinerator, and joins us.

Brose reaches for the stinger, but I pull it away.

He raises an eyebrow. "Leigh?"

I shake my head no. "You shouldn't touch it, it's...it's sharp."

He reaches again, and this time I don't stop him. He turns it around and examines it from every angle. He looks at the needle at the base of the calipers and grunts.

Recognition dawns on Ashlan's face, and her eyes become very round. Her breath catches in her throat. "Is that...?"

She remembers it from the animal parade. I nod slowly.

Her eyes narrow, almost as if to say, *we'll talk about this later*.

Celeres fixates on the device. "I saw this once before. It was the same day that I saw Sharon for the last time."

We all look at him and wait for him to continue.

He lets out a deep sigh. "I respect classified information, but I'm going to tell you this because I think it might be very important. It wasn't unusual for me to take Krysta to the surface, so when she asked one afternoon, we fired up *Big Seven* and headed down. What *was* unusual was that she brought Sharon along."

Ashlan cocks her head. "How could that be classified?"

Celeres rolls his eyes. "*Everything* Krysta does is classified. Anyway, the two of them went into the zoo compound. Only Krysta returned, and she carried this."

I take a sharp breath. "So, what do you think happened?"

"I don't know, and if anything happened to her, I will never forgive myself."

I put my hand on his shoulder. "You didn't know Krysta's intentions. For all we know, Sharon is alive and well."

He's quiet for a long time, and then nods. "So what *is* it?"

"We call it the stinger. I take readings on it all day, every day."

"And?"

"And nothing. I don't know what I'm doing. I just write the numbers down."

Ashlan returns her attention to a nearby desk and rifles through a pile of papers. "What's this underneath?"

I look over. "What?"

She pushes the pile aside to reveal a scratched and dented laptop. "It looks like someone ran it over with a moon buggy."

She sits it on the table and opens the warped lid. Several keys are missing, and of the remaining ones, only a few are still attached.

I touch it, and another key pops off. "Krysta told me she'd get me a new laptop because the old one was broken. I thought she just meant that the battery wouldn't charge or something."

A soft scent of cigarette smoke wafts from the device. I've smelled it before, on the lab coat Krysta tried to give me.

Ashlan touches my wrist. "Do you know what I'm thinking?"

"What?"

"That this was Sharon Hone's laptop."

And that would mean the coat was Sharon's, that she *did* work in this lab.

I settle into a stool, because frankly, I need to sit down. "How can we know for sure?"

"Maybe we can get it to turn on. What do you think, Brose?"

Brose puts the stinger down beside the laptop and traces his hand along the side of the broken keyboard and presses a silver button. The screen flashes for a second, then goes dark.

He grimaces. "It doesn't look good. We should keep this shut for now, so nothing important falls out."

Ashlan closes it up and hands it to him. "Do you think you could fix it?"

Brose grabs a nearby laptop bag and puts the computer inside. "Probably, but I'll have to take it to engineering."

Brose returns his attention to the stinger. "Show me your readings."

I take the device from him and we walk to my workbench while Ashlan and Celeres explore more of the lab. I pull my notebook from my drawer and hand it over. He flips it open and scans the rows of numbers like a doctor looking at a patient's chart. He flips pages and makes engineer noises. "So this is what my battery project is for."

"Yes."

He flips through more pages. "I wonder if Krysta was ever going to share this with me. You say you've only been at this for two days?"

"Yes."

He pulls his personal meter from one of his many pockets. "I want to poke at this stinger thing a little myself."

"Be careful, this is what hurt Krysta."

He spends the next five minutes taking measurements, and then comparing them to what I have in the notebook.

"At least it's consistent. These values are similar to measurements I get when taking readings on the alien communication device aboard *Ice Arrow*. I have to admit, this tech is still puzzling to me."

He turns a knob on the meter. "I want to check the impedance between this and this." He puts one probe on the needle and jams the other one into the battery compartment. There's a brilliant purple flash, brighter than his flash-bang.

All of us gasp at once. I'm blind. All I can see is a massive purple afterimage of the flash. Then there's the sound of Brose collapsing to the floor.

"Brose!" I shout.

In two heartbeats, Celeres and Ashlan feel their way back to us.

Brose groans. "I'm okay. I just feel...weird. I need a minute."

Our vision slowly returns. When it does, Brose laughs in a high-pitched voice. The others look at me, but I only shrug. I'm as confused as anyone.

Celeres rubs Brose's shoulder. "Talk to me, buddy."

"Yeah. Yeah, I'm okay, Cel. Wow, that thing has some kick."

Celeres pulls him to his feet and Brose points to the battery compartment on the stinger. "It's dark. It's dead. I must have discharged it. Oh jeez, I need to sit down again."

He fumbles around for a moment and almost falls, but Ashlan catches him and guides him to the nearest stool.

He exhales so hard that he nearly forces one of my notebook pages to turn. "I want to go lie down."

"Brose?" says Celeres.

"Huh?"

"Why are you smiling like that? You look drunk."

"I feel...strange."

He stands, then stumbles again, almost falling on me. Celeres catches him. "Can you make it?"

Ashlan takes Brose's hand, looking worried. "I'll take him back."

She drapes one of his arms around her neck and holds it with one hand while holding his waist with her other arm. As the two of them stagger out of the lab, Brose doesn't look weak as much as he looks dizzy. I know I've helped a dizzy friend once or twice in my life, and Ashlan looks like she knows what to do, too. The lab smell is just about back to normal.

Whatever Brose did took power *out* of the stinger, which is probably a good thing. I'd be more worried if the light were brighter.

I put the stinger back in its drawer.

Celeres looks in the direction that Brose and Ashlan went. "Brose isn't going to end up like Krysta, is he?"

"This is different. With her, I think the stinger took something out of her. It looks like Brose took something out of the stinger."

He clears his throat and looks away. Did his eyes look a little wet?

"I hope he's okay. There's no Max to fix him, not without more batteries," he says thickly, while walking over to the telescope. In an effort to change the subject, he says in an uplifting voice, "I wonder if I can find our campsite with this."

"Oh, I'm sure you can."

I walk up behind him and put my arms around his waist. I lean in. "What do you see?"

He looks up from the eyepiece. "You're trembling." He turns around to hug me back. And it's a genuine hug, the kind you give to someone you really care about.

I melt into him. "There's too much going on right now. More than I want to handle."

We hold one another for a long time and the tension in my shoulders and back fades.

He gives me a squeeze. "Why don't you come back to my place for a little while? I'll make you some hot chocolate and we'll try to relax."

"That sounds nice, but—"

"But?"

"Why don't we relax right here?"

"What did you have in mind?" he asks playfully.

I push him away slightly and loosen his belt buckle. "I think this workbench will do."

He releases me and pulls his shirt off. I thought he looked great in the dim light at our campsite. He looks even better than I remember.

I take my top and sports bra off in one motion, and his breath catches in his throat. He stares for a second and then bends down to remove my bottoms. When he stands back up, I do the same to him.

He hoists me onto the bench, and I lie back while his hands explore my body. He stands between my legs and inches closer. I put my head back, closing my eyes.

As he slides in, a gasp escapes my lips and I arch my back. Even amid all of our chaos, we steal this moment for ourselves, a moment of respite, a brief escape.

Chapter Thirty-One

Infirmary Visit

We're only a few steps out of the security door and into the public corridor when a small cluster of technicians from neighboring labs approach us, jabbering about how they saw Brose leave a little while ago, with Ashlan supporting him. They want confirmation of his well-being, the lab's integrity, and the station's safety.

I hold my hands out in an attempt to calm them. "The lab is fine, power restored, and there's no danger. Brose is fine, too. He just needed to lie down."

They look skeptical.

Celeres says, "It's true. Everything's going to be fine. There's no danger. We're on our way to visit with Dr. Collins now. We saw her an hour ago, and she's conscious. She's going to be okay."

They part to let us through and whisper amongst themselves once we've passed.

Celeres leads us to the infirmary, and I think about the stinger. Now that I've seen it drain *and* fill batteries, I try to reason why the Apocritans would give us the very tool we'd need to charge our own batteries when the batteries are their major source of trade to begin with. Something doesn't add up. Did Krysta steal it? If she did, what are her plans for it?

Celeres talks to me while we walk, but I only half-hear what he's saying. Something about dinner. I think of the parade, the pile of the dead animals, the pile of batteries. The stinger seems like a dangerous thing to have on a space station. It kills almost instantly to charge the very batteries that Krysta is desperate to synthesize.

Now the question is, why did that wasp give the key to me? So we'd kill ourselves? Or was it committing treason to his own species by giving us the means of filling our own batteries?

"Well?" says a voice.

I snap out of my musings and realize that we're already at the infirmary. Celeres is a few steps away and Captain Richards stares me down. He looks at me as if I'm the reason for all of his problems. That might not be too far from the truth if all of his problems have to do with the top secret lab he's not allowed to enter.

"We've restored power," I say. "Krysta will be fine. There's nothing to worry about."

"You're sure?"

"Yes. Can we see her now?"

He steps aside, grumbling while pulling out his phone. "Go ahead. I need to make a call. She doesn't look very fine to me." He gives a parting glare to Celeres and me, and then to Krysta on the bed before he stomps away, pushing on his phone hard enough to make his fingertip bend.

Krysta's absorbed in her tablet, and doesn't see us come in.

"Very good," she says to the screen, "the sooner the

better." Her translator sits beside her, turning her words into clicks and buzzing sounds.

I shuffle my feet to announce our presence, and she folds the tablet's case closed. Whoever she was talking to was in mid-sentence. She places the tablet on her sheet-covered legs, settles back on a pile of pillows, and gives us a weak smile. "Hi. You guys smell like campfire."

I stay on the nearside of the bed while Celeres walks around to the other side.

Celeres says, "We were down at—"

"I know," she says, "it's a nice getaway. Did you like it, Leigh?"

I nod.

She holds out a hand for each of us. "My two favorite people." Celeres's fingers close around hers. I hold the other one.

I point my chin at her tablet. "Working?"

She closes her eyes and is quiet for a few seconds before mumbling, "Just a side project."

Celeres gives me a questioning glance. I shake my head.

He looks back down at her. "The entire station is worried about you. What happened?"

She looks down at the hand that I'm holding. "Things are still a little mixed up in my brain. I was putting a few things away, and then..."

After her voice trails off, I say, "You worried security so much that they turned the power off to the lab."

"Oh."

"Your fish died."

She leans her head back and closes her eyes. Her jaws clench.

"I disposed of them," I say. I hate to steal the credit from Ashlan, but she wasn't supposed to be in the lab.

"Thanks."

"How are you feeling?"

"Weak. I can't walk straight. My sense of balance is shot. The doctors say that my central nervous system isn't working right."

Celeres looks genuinely concerned. "That's not good. What can we do to help?"

"I don't know. I have an idea, but I need to do a little more research."

He nods, and then squeezes her hand. My own hands turn cold and I tell myself he's just giving her support.

I still don't like it.

Krysta squeezes *my* hand.

I let go because now my cold palms also glisten with sweat. She turns her head to look at me. I can't read that expression. What is she thinking? What's behind those eyes?

I say, "Is there anything you want me to do in the lab? Any work? Anything?" I dry my palms off on my legs as I talk.

"Just do a walk-through and see if the power interruption screwed anything else up. Once I'm back on my feet, we'll get back to work. They tell me that as long as I can get around with a walker, I can go back to my quarters. Will you two visit me while I convalesce?"

"Of course. When will you be getting around on that walker?" asks Celeres. He's still holding her hand.

"This afternoon, in the next couple of hours. What are you doing tonight?"

"We have dinner plans with Ashlan and Brose at my place. Do you need any help to get home? Would you like us to check on you tonight?"

"No, no, you go ahead. I'll manage, and I wouldn't be good company, anyway. I'm still very woozy."

"We'll swing by tomorrow to look in on you, okay?"

"Okay."

I hold my new phone up. "We'll let you rest. Let me know if you need anything. You have my number."

"I will. Thank you."

I look across her body at Celeres. He breaks eye contact with her and looks back at me.

"Ready?"

"Mm-hmm."

I look down at her tablet with suspicion and then turn to leave. I'm back in the hall after a few quick strides with Celeres close behind.

"I need to get back to my place," I say.

"Okay, I'll walk you."

The infirmary wing isn't very large, and we're soon away from its sights and sounds. I turn on my heel and face Celeres. "So, what was that about?"

He looks at me quizzically. "What was *what* about?"

"The tablet? I saw how she looked at you when she shut it. What is she up to?"

"I have no clue, but I got a quick look at her screen. She was talking to a wasp. Just before she shut the lid, he said, 'almost ready.'"

"Ready for what?"

"Exactly."

He grabs my hand, and we walk in silence for the rest of the way to my quarters.

I stand on my tiptoes for a kiss goodbye. "Thanks for the camping trip."

He embraces me for the kiss and then smiles dreamily. "I like the smoke smell in your hair."

"It reminds you of your favorite spot?"

"Yep, my favorite spot, my favorite woman."

I smile and look down modestly. "And don't you forget it."

"I won't. See you later, then?"

"What?"

"Yeah, remember? Dinner?"

"Sorry, there was a lot going on back there."

"Just be at my place at 7:00, okay?"

That gives me all day. I could use a little me-time. "You got it."

He gives me another kiss, then leaves.

As soon as the door slides shut behind me, I walk straight to my bed and flop down on my back. It's *so* soft. Don't get me wrong, I *certainly* enjoyed my sleeping accommodation last night, but I also woke up with a kink in my back.

I turn my head to look through the window at Apocrita below and imagine that I pinpoint our campsite location. I also pretend that I know where the zoo is.

As I view the vast forests below, I go back to thinking of my walk with Ashlan and the memories of the animal parade. I think she should call it something else. Parades are supposed to be filled with happiness and cheer. What happened down there was a massacre. I shiver to think that it almost got me. If it hadn't been for the carnage that snapped Ashlan out of her stupor, we would have marched right in there with the rest of the fodder.

I try to put it out of my mind as I drag myself out of bed and head to the shower. It's where I do my best thinking, and I have some thinking to do. Soon, I'm covered in suds and the campfire smell melts away. More than anything, the smell of those dead fish is still in my nose. That was terrible.

All of my friends saw the stinger. Ashlan recognized it. She saw wasps kill with it. What is this device, and why is it on our station? I know one thing for sure—I'm going to be more careful around it the next time I'm at work.

I tame my hair and apply a little makeup. I wear the black top and dark green skirt from the bag that Celeres gave me. I'll give him one thing, he knows my style. Or maybe it's beginner's luck. Either way, he's winning so far. I give a twirl and a practice smile to the mirror. This works.

I wander over to my display and turn it on. As before, I'm treated to the view outside of my room. Krysta told me that there should be a keyboard in one of my drawers, so I open them all and dig around. I finally find it under some socks in the bottom drawer. Why are things always in the last place you look?

It's not a classic keyboard, though; it's a rectangular slab with an LCD screen that shows images of the keys. There's also a game controller, so I grab that too.

I hit the Enter button on the digital keypad and the display switches from my hallway camera to a login screen:

Leigh Shires
Sumerian, 300
<Authenticate>

Authenticate?

"Hello?" I say to the screen. Nothing happens.

I pick up the game controller and press every button. Nothing.

I press various keys on the keyboard. Nothing. There's nowhere on the screen to even enter a password.

I gather the damn things up and return them to the sock

drawer. Then I turn off my screen. There's not much else to do except look out my window until it's time to go to dinner, so that's what I do.

Chapter Thirty-Two

Games People Play

I knew I was going to drift off. Luckily, I had set the alarm on my phone to give me fifteen minutes to get to Celeres's place. After a few touch-ups in the mirror, I pull on some sandals and head out of my quarters.

I had hoped that I might wake up with a little time to spare so I could check on Baxter, but my body still craves sleep from the exertion and blood loss.

Some faces in the halls and shops are beginning to look familiar. Granted, I don't know anyone's name yet, but the waves and smiles border more on familiarity than wondering who I am. People seem a little more relaxed now than they did earlier this afternoon. News must be out that Krysta is okay, and the lab poses no threat.

Everyone knows how annoying a jealous partner is. I don't want to be that person, but I can't get the image of Krysta's perfect little hand squeezing Celeres's. Or the image of him squeezing hers. An involuntary growl escapes from deep within my throat. I know how this goes; it happened when Mom found mile-high-guy, and when Joe talked to Erica more than me at dance competitions. Everything seems innocent at first, and then BAM.

I need to put this out of my mind. I close my eyes for a moment and let out a deep breath.

Celeres mentioned that Brose and Ashlan would be at dinner tonight as well. Hopefully Brose is feeling up to it. I quicken my pace because now I want to see Brose, make sure he's okay. I only have a few friends here on *Sumerian*. I have to see to their well-being.

When I get to Celeres's door, I let myself in with my awesome palm pad powers.

He looks up in surprise when I walk in, and then grins. "The gang's all here."

Brose and Ashlan are on the couch, sitting close together. They look up at me with sly smiles.

Ashlan nods toward the door. "You gave her a key to your place."

Celeres glares playfully at Brose. "Yeah, but you know she can open any door anyway because of that bug in the security code."

Brose rolls his eyes. "We need to fix that. It's on the list."

"What bug?" says Ashlan.

Brose looks down and smooths his hair back. "Not too many people know about it. Technically, high clearance means access to sensitive information. But on *Sumerian*, it also means Leigh can unlock any palm pad she wants."

Ashlan tries to mimic the glare that Celeres just used. "You get that fixed, Brose. What if she opens an airlock by accident?"

Brose looks over at me with concern. "You won't do that...right?"

If I was worried about Brose during my walk here, I'm not worried anymore. His face is bright, and his speech is clear. He has a fresh set of jeans and an official work jersey with a logo on the breast pocket that looks like a pair of gears and lightning bolts. He also got a hair and beard cut.

I rub my chin to acknowledge the trim. "You clean up nice, Brose."

"She made me do it. The guys in engineering think they took a little too much off the top and that my beard looks like a fancy hedge trimming job."

"It's nice! I like it. Besides, it'll grow back."

Now, if we're being honest, his beard does look a little too round, a little too perfect. He looks more like a groomed poodle than a hedge to me, but I'll keep that to myself.

I can tell by Ashlan's face that she knows what I'm thinking and hopes I stay quiet. She also freshened up. She wears a pair of worn jeans and a cute yellow camisole that shows off her tan shoulders.

Celeres wears an untucked Hawaiian shirt and khaki shorts. I can't take my eyes off his legs.

"So what's for dinner?" I ask, forcing myself to look up.

"You're never going to believe this," he says, "but tonight we are having pizza all the way from Pittsburgh, Pennsylvania. I picked it up before we left and kept it frozen in *Big Seven*."

"Oh yeah? From where?"

"Some people recommended Fiori's, so that's what I got."

My mouth waters. "I *love* Fiori's pizza."

"Come and get it. Plenty of drinks in the fridge. Grab some chips, too," he says, gesturing to an open bag on the counter.

Once we all have our food, we find seats at Celeres's little dining table. There's nothing but chomping sounds as we devour the pizza and chips. This has got to be a long distance takeout record for an Earth restaurant.

When I feel full, I wait for Brose to finish his bite, and then I ask him how he's feeling.

"Great. I felt a little woozy at first, but it went away almost immediately after leaving the lab. Now I feel like a million bucks."

"I'm so happy to hear it."

He puts his slice of pizza down and rubs his hands together. "Leigh, there's something I have to tell you. I know what's going on."

Ashlan rests her hand on his wrist. "I'll tell her."

"Tell me what?"

Celeres looks back and forth between me and the other two, not in on the joke.

"I told him about the stinger, about what we saw on the parade," Ashlan says.

"Oh."

Celeres reaches over and takes my hand. "Now tell me what's going on."

I take a sip of my drink and clear my throat. "Remember when Ash and I took that walk this morning? We saw wasps use the stinger on animals at the zoo."

"Use? What did it do?"

"Killed them—"

"Instantly," adds Ashlan.

"So it *is* like a gun. I knew it."

I shake my head. "No, not exactly. It's more like a life sucker. It just sucks the life force or the spirit, or I don't know, the essence, right out of a person."

"Or animal," says Ashlan, spitting the words out.

"What's the point of that?" Celeres asks. "Isn't that what a gun is for?"

I sigh. "This is different. You saw the battery compartment in the stinger here at the lab."

"The purple?"

"Yeah. Anyway, that's how they recharge the batteries. We saw them kill animals to fill up dozens of batteries."

"You're kidding."

"I wish I were."

His hand is warm and his touch calms me down somewhat. I look at him, willing him to squeeze my hand like he squeezed Krysta's at the infirmary.

"So let me get this straight," he says. "Krysta has a battery charger right here on the station. The only catch is that you have to kill something to make it work?"

"That's what it looks like."

"So the batteries she gets from the aliens are all filled by taking lives."

"Yeah."

He takes a bite of pizza and his brow furrows while he thinks and eats at the same time. "Why would the aliens give us one of those? They know we could fill our own batteries and then what would they trade us?"

I shrug. "That's what I want to know."

"So then Krysta tried to kill herself? That makes no sense."

"Unless she truly doesn't know what it does."

"So the aliens want her dead? It almost worked."

I throw my free hand up in the air. "I'm as confused as you."

"Wait a minute," says Brose, "She has me working all kinds of overtime for her battery project—"

This causes Ashlan to frown. He notices and takes a deep breath before continuing. "Maybe she does know, but wants to find a better way."

"Maybe," I say, "but that still doesn't explain why she hurt herself. You should have seen her. She can't walk straight. She needs a walker. There's no way she would have inflicted that on herself on purpose."

As if on cue, Celeres's phone vibrates. He has it sitting beside him on the table. Before he picks it up, I can see who's calling. It's her. He lets go of my hand to pick it up. I stare down at my empty hand while he answers.

"Hello?"

...

"Yeah, we're all here, having dinner."

...

"Great. Sleeping in your own bed tonight will help. Get some rest."

...

"That's good. Right, turn in early. We'll check on you tomorrow, okay?"

...

"Me too. Take care, and we'll see you soon."

He thumbs the disconnect button and returns his phone to the table.

Ashlan dabs her face with her napkin. "Nice to hear she's home now."

"Yeah," says Celeres.

We finish our pizza in relative silence. I wish I could have heard what she was saying on the other side.

Ashlan pushes her plate away. "So guys, I'm going planetside in a couple of days to work from my cabin."

Brose snaps to attention. "Yeah? How long will you be down there?"

"As long as it takes. I need to figure out what's attracting those animals. When I began this research, it was 'just a weird migration.' Now, we know it's more. And we *also* know that our very own Krysta is involved."

I shake my head. "You don't know that. She doesn't even know what she has."

Her eyes are wet. "You saw what happened down there. You saw the stinger in action. *You* have one in your lab."

My stomach flips. "Ash, are you saying that *I'm* involved?"

"Of course you are. You and Krysta are in the middle of something, even if you don't know what it is yet."

"I didn't know. I just wanted to leave Earth, I just wanted—"

Celeres takes my hand again. I look at him, feeling as if I've just been backed into a corner. I'm shaking.

"We'll figure this out," he says.

"Sorry, I didn't mean to kill the mood," Ashlan says, her eyes down and face flushed.

"Maybe I can come with you," I say. "Krysta is out of commission for a while. I have nothing else to do."

She shakes her head. "No, you stay here. I don't want to put you in danger of that unseen force again. We were lucky last time. I think I can handle it. I was able to break from its pull."

"But—"

"And somebody has to keep an eye on Krysta. At least now that we've been in the lab and saw the stinger, and we also know what it does, you can talk to us about it. Keeping something like that a secret would have torn you up from the inside-out."

I nod slowly. "I'm looking forward to seeing her tomorrow, to see if she's improving at all. I might get an idea of how long this little furlough from work is going to be."

Celeres pushes his chair back from the table. "Not to

change the subject or anything, but what kind of host would I be if I didn't have some entertainment lined up for tonight?"

Brose, who's been studying the floor this whole time, looks up eagerly. "Yeah?" He grabs another slice of pizza and takes a huge bite, spilling a drop of sauce into his freshly groomed beard. Ashlan attacks him with a napkin, but he shrinks back. "What kind of entertainment?" he asks between chomps. Ashlan loses her balance, and he catches her with his free hand.

"I got a new game," says Celeres.

"Awesome, what is it?"

"It's not another racing game, is it?" asks Ashlan.

"Yeah, and it has some fun tracks. Wait until you see the water one."

Ashlan looks at me with a hopeless expression. "I always lose."

Brose looks at me. "Today might be your lucky day. We have fresh blood."

I give him a taunting smirk. "Hey, don't count me out. I am a beast at Mario Kart."

Brose lets Ashlan clean the sauce from his beard, but he makes a show of not liking it by making all kinds of unhappy faces.

"Let's go," Celeres says. "We can leave the pizza out if anyone wants seconds."

We file into the living room and find places on the couch. Ashlan and I sit in the middle with the guys on our opposite sides. Celeres hands everyone a controller and presses a button on his remote to turn his entertainment center on. He moves his steering wheel and helmet to the floor. "These are for when I play solo."

The screen flickers, and soon it displays a couple of

crossed checkered flags. The flags burst into flames, and the flames rearrange themselves to spell "Formula Fire." A yellow Lamborghini sails from the left side of the screen, through the fiery letters, and then off the right side.

Celeres looks at us with unbridled excitement. "Cool, huh?"

Just then, his phone, which he had placed on the coffee table, vibrates and lights up. A text message from Krysta. I wouldn't be able to read it without being obvious, so I try to play it cool, even though I'm annoyed.

Celeres reads it and shakes his head. "She wants to know if we're all still hanging out."

He taps on his phone. "I told her yes. Do you think we should check on her?"

Together, Ash and I say, "No."

I clench and unclench my sweaty hands. Why is she texting him like this? I let out a long breath.

Celeres picks up his controller. "First, we have to design our cars."

Ashlan throws her head back against the couch with her eyes closed. I'm beginning to think she's not much of a gamer.

"It won't take long," he adds.

Celeres picks a car, a paint job, the tires, and some big chrome pipes coming out of the hood. Next, it prompts him for a name. "I already have *Big Seven*, my ship, and *Little Seven*, my buggy. I dub thee, *Seven Speed*."

"*Seven Speed*? Like a bicycle?" I ask, "I have a ten speed at home that goes faster than that bag of bolts."

He huffs. "We'll see about that. Your turn."

One difference between Ashlan and me is that I *am* a gamer. I wasn't kidding when I said I'm good at Mario Kart, and this controller feels natural in my hands. I put

Krysta out of my mind and pick out a pink car and use the logo designer to make my best rendition of the red star heart constellation that Celeres and I found. We smile at each other. I pick the same ridiculous chrome pipes for my hood, and when I get to the naming screen, I call it *Heartspeed*.

"I like it," says Celeres. "I have *Seven Speed*, and you have *Heartspeed*."

Brose picks a tractor trailer, which he names *Broski*. Ashlan picks a motorcycle and calls it *Sally*. I look at her and she shrugs. "Bring it."

The game is fun, and Ashlan is about as bad as she said. The race track sits just above an ocean, with the occasional wave flooding over it. When you fall into the ocean, a crane trundles up and fishes you out. I fall off here and there, but Ashlan falls off every thirty seconds. She comes in last every time, and that's with me trying to throw a couple of races.

At one point, *Broski* takes a turn too fast and flips sideways right off the track. At that moment, Krysta texts Celeres again, and steals my attention away. *Heartspeed* follows *Broski* into the murky depths.

Celeres flips his phone over without reading the message. I'm annoyed.

I put my controller down and stand up. "I'm getting tired, plus this looks like a good stopping point." Bubbles rise from the area of the ocean where my car sank.

Ashlan climbs off the couch. "I could also use a break. I'll head out with you."

Celeres holds up a hand. "Don't leave yet! Your crane is coming to get you out. There's also more pizza."

"Next time," I say. What I don't say is, why the hell is Krysta texting you so much?

"You okay, Ash?" asks Brose.

She shakes her hand in the air. "My thumbs hurt, plus I have to prep for my trip to the cabin."

Celeres pauses the game and walks me to the door. Brose cracks his knuckles and stands up. "I should get going, too. I have to work early. Maybe with Krysta out of the action for a while, I can get a break from the battery work."

Celeres kisses me goodnight, and we leave. Before the door slides shut behind us, his phone vibrates again, and I catch him staring at it as he heads to the pizza box.

Maybe I stare a second too long because Ashlan puts her hand on my shoulder. "They're friends."

"I know, it's fine."

But I think Krysta should just leave him alone. She had her chance. She knows I'm with him tonight, knows I might see all of those texts.

Brose starts down the corridor. "Come on, Leigh, we'll walk you back to your place."

Chapter Thirty-Three

Wing

It's 10:00 PM, and the station is quiet. A little robot vacuum cleaner glides past us as we make our way from Celeres's place. Someone slapped a sticker on the back that says, "This job sucks."

The corridors are only about half as bright as they are during daytime, and as the little robot slides away, the silence is palpable. I feel like I should keep my voice down. "It's not *that* late. Isn't there a nightclub or something to do?"

Brose says, "Yeah, there's a bar. There's also a late-night snack menu at Solar."

Ashlan gives him a wry grin. "Your favorite place, huh? Let's show her night school. She might like that."

She has to be kidding. "I'll pass. I just graduated, and I'm all schooled out."

"Come on Leigh, this is different. Let's show her, Brose."

At that, Brose changes direction and heads down a different corridor. "Sounds good to me. Speaking of Solar, it's not too far from there. Maybe I'll grab a little something."

We're only walking for a few minutes when a room up ahead casts red light into the hallway. Beyond its open door come the sounds of explosions and the dull roar of several excited voices.

I break away from the two of them and rush over to look inside.

It's like a big gaming party, except the "game" is a flight combat simulation. A giant scoreboard and a screen of battling spaceships dominate the front wall of the room. Of the twenty pilots, I'd say there's an even mix of men and women. Pizza and donut boxes sit on almost every surface. Two-liter bottles of soda dot the room. An electronic marquee above each pilot's desk displays their call sign.

One group of pilots stands out, partly because they wear matching light blue flight jackets, but also because they are obviously friends, all sitting near each other, bantering back and forth. They fly in a loose formation, sort of in a mini swarm.

First, there's Pyro. Her hair is redder than mine, and she wears it in a tight pony. She turns and regards me for a moment before returning to battle. How'd she know I was here? In the simulation, her situational awareness is just as exceptional. She looks a little like Leeloo from *The 5th Element*.

Misadventure's aim is uncanny. It's comical how much effort her opponents spend to hide from her. Every kill from her is accompanied by, "Boom, headshot."

Queenie is everywhere. If you blink, you'll lose her. She takes out so many opponents from behind that you'd think they'd learn. And her makeup? It is on-*point*. She looks...ka-pow.

Then there's Brisk. He's so laid back he's the only one with his chair reclined. You'd never know how relaxed he is by watching his flying. He's got a gift.

Neidaram is the opposite. He sits bolt upright and bounces his knee. He harnesses this extra energy by shouting out encouragement just like your favorite coach. When things get loose, he says things like, "Stay together! Don't go in onesy twosy!" The back of his jacket features an embroidered depiction of a blond-haired woman wearing lacy lingerie and holding two pistols crossed at her chest. Above the image are the words, "No Mercy."

Amaiya doesn't wear a jacket, but she fits in with her support ship, supplying shield energy and extra fuel to whoever needs it. She's adept at staying out of harm's way while being the safety net for the team.

Finally, there's Moon. She doesn't wear a jacket either, but she flies with the others in perfect formation. Her intensity burns so brightly that it feels as if life or death hangs in the balance. They all rally around her, and together, they make music. I would not want to play against this gang. It wouldn't be a fair fight.

Across the room, a guy named Razor cries out in mock pain and falls from his chair, revealing an enormous image of a fireball on his screen with pieces of metal flying out of it. Queenie smirks.

From behind, Brose mumbles into my ear, "Razor's the guy who clipped the hangar door just before you arrived."

I giggle.

The giant scoreboard shows every call sign, grouped by team. Most names are green, but a new explosion turns another one red. Pyro lets out a woop and gives Brisk a high-five.

I turn to see Brose and Ashlan holding hands and

watching me with bated breath for my reaction. "Well?" Brose asks.

I nod excitedly. "Can I play?"

Brose looks in the room for a second. "Um, let's see what we can do. It's not really a game. It's training, you know."

The sound of rapid footfalls comes from a bend up ahead. We all turn to look as a white-haired youth whips around the corner and heads straight toward us. We barely get out of his way as he zooms into the room, to the only empty desk left.

He sits at his computer, and the screen prompts him to authenticate. He flips the keyboard over and places his palm on the back while he huffs and puffs. After a second, the screen turns green, and he's able to join the contest.

So *that's* how you login to the computer. How would I have ever guessed there's a palm reader under the keyboard?

I turn on my heel, my eyes bright. "Guys, I'm heading back to my place. Thank you for the tour."

"See you tomorrow?" Ashlan asks.

"I hope so. I need to get a Baxter visit in."

Brose winks at me, and I smile back.

Armed with my new knowledge, I spin around and head back to my place. Soon, I'm in the lit corridors again and walking fast. When I get to my door, I palm-punch it and the door whips open twice as fast as normal. Nice feature.

Once inside, I head straight to my dresser where my keyboard and controller are. I don't even bother to turn on my light. Moments later, the room lit only by the glow from my display panel, I'm once again prompted to authenticate. I flip my keyboard over, place my hand on the back, and hold my breath. The screen goes green, and I am...IN.

I bite my lip as I scan through my menu choices. Let's see, there's: *Food, Scheduled Activities, Movies, Music, Games,* and **Restricted**. I want to play the same "game" as those pilots in the lab, so I select Games. On the next screen, I'm presented with: *Disaster Derby, Lobster Crossing, Chess,* and *Haze Maze.* I'm disappointed, but not surprised—the simulator isn't a game, after all.

I go back and check out the Food menu. Looks like they have delivery on the station. There's a wide variety, including the same pizza, donuts, and sodas that the pilots had in their training room. I'd order something, but I'm still full from Celeres's pizza (I had four slices—shut up), so I back out of that screen as well.

I'm about to select Music when I hover my cursor over the Restricted option instead. Not expecting it to work, I click it. The screen freezes. Uh oh.

Channeling Dad when something stops working, I whack the side of my keyboard.

Well, that didn't help.

I wait another twenty seconds before the screen changes to show a new menu against a black screen. I breathe a sigh of relief and set the keyboard back on my bed.

The first option is *Genomica Labs,* and it's written in orange letters.

Below that is *Wing,* written in red letters.

Last is *Engineering* in blue letters.

I select the Genomica Labs option and I'm presented with a dark desktop with an orange border. The only icon on it looks like a folder. When I click it, it's empty. Nothing to see here. I return to the menu. Let's see what Wing is. Once again, I get a dark desktop, but this one has a red border and is bright enough to cast some red into my room, just like the red in the training room. As I look around at the red tint on everything around me, I get an ominous feeling—or is it guilt? I feel like a kid who just broke into the candy store. I know I shouldn't be here, but I can't resist the allure. I know what I'm looking for.

There's more on this desktop than on the Genomica Labs one. First, there's a folder called *Class*. Below that is an icon of a spaceship. I click it. It asks me to pick a room. The choices are *New*, and *Group1* (18/20). While I consider my choices, the 18 turns into a 19. I think we'll avoid the group stuff for now. I select New, then name it *Practice*. A (1/20) appears next to the name.

Now it shows me three different spaceships to pick from. One is cargo-style like McClure's, the one that brought me here from Earth. Then, there's a fighter-class like Celeres's. The last one has a lot of rounded edges and is tiny. Just by comparing it to the others on the screen, it only has room for one person inside. I don't remember seeing anything like that in the hangar. If I'm going to learn to fly, it will not be in that tin can.

I select the fighter ship, and my keypad replaces the keyboard image with a set of controls and instruments, like those in the cockpit of *Big Seven*. The image on my display panel changes to look like I'm inside the cockpit of a fighter in *Sumerian's* hangar. Ships are docked to my left and right. Various engineers scurry back and forth throughout the hangar, and I can almost swear that one of them is Brose. The beard looks right, but he's a little too far away for me to tell. But it *can't* be him; this is a simulation. Besides, he was going home to get some sleep. Ashlan was with him, so maybe even more than sleep if he's lucky.

I take a deep breath and hit the ignition. My keypad vibrates at a low level, similar to the vibration in *Big Seven* when the engines idle. A smile creeps onto my face as I feel the thrill. Ever since I sat in the cockpit of *Ice Arrow* on my trip from Earth, the idea of piloting has fascinated me. I don't know if I'm allowed to be doing this, and I don't even care. It's worth the risk; something deep inside of me knows I should learn how to fly no matter how long it takes—just in case the day comes that I need to grab Baxter and make a run for it. I'll feel more at peace when I know I have a way out. Like I said—just in case.

I stare at the screen for a while, and a message shows on the HUD. *Would you like to open the tutorial?* It can tell that I'm lost. Actually, I think I could take off; I've seen Celeres do it, and it seems simple enough. Problem is, he used a flight stick, which I don't have.

The tutorial tires of waiting for me to respond and instructs me to pick up the controller and push the "up" button. I do, and my ship rises into the air. All the men in the hangar back off until I don't see anyone else. I'm free to fly.

But I don't.

I can't. I won't let myself.

A major part of controlling anything—a car, a tractor, a video game, and probably a spaceship—is muscle memory. Once I teach myself how to run something, I train my movements at the same time. I can't let myself get competent at flying with a game controller, and that's all there is to it. There's another way, and I know what it is.

I need to get my hands on a real throttle and stick for this thing. There were plenty of them in the training room where the pilots were playing, and I need to get a set for myself. I pace around my quarters, deep in thought. Maybe I could borrow a set each night and return them before the training room opens again in the morning.

I do my best thinking when I'm moving around. I know

I told Ashlan that I'd swing by tomorrow to visit Baxter, but why not visit him now? I'll pass the training room on my route, and see if I can get any kind of feel for when things wind down for the night in there.

I strip off my skirt outfit and replace it with my usual Genomica black leggings and long sleeve shirt. I smirk in the mirror because I look like a cat burglar. It's fitting, I suppose. I put my hair up in case I want—or need—to do some running while I'm out.

With a last look at my display and the view from my simulated floating ship, I head out of my quarters to visit Bax at Beastarium.

❧

I breeze by the training room and peer inside. The crowd has thinned, and I think I see why; most of the names on the display are red now. There are only three green names left: *Misadventure*, *Moon*, and *Brisk*. Now that their opposition is gone, they dogfight with each other. About a dozen other pilots crowd around the survivors, cheering them on. I'm filled with a strange excitement. All I need to do is get a set of controls, and I can play this thing every night in my room. Who needs sleep, anyway? I turn away and continue my journey.

On my way to Beastarium, I come across a few people in the halls and decide to take a turn down a passageway where music echoes from farther down. I come upon the bar that Brose told me about. Thumping bass fills the room. Colored lights pulse within, and then switch to black light, making everyone glow according to the colors and whites that they wear. Just as suddenly, the lights go back to pulsing color. The music and lights seem to accompany each other, and the crowd goes wild. Razor is in there talking to a girl. Good luck, buddy. May your girl exploits fare better than your piloting. I turn and continue on my way. I'll have to come back here some night. Looks fun, and now I even have some clothes to go out in.

The rest of the walk to Beastarium is uneventful, and I head over to the building where Bax is staying. Simulated stars fill the sky above, and as usual, the place feels, smells, and seems like I'm on the surface of the planet. The only thing missing is the nightsong. I wonder why? Maybe those suckers are hard to catch.

Once inside Baxter's house, I walk down to room 3. He's inside, curled up on his bed. I get down on my knees. "Hey boy."

He rolls onto his back in response, but doesn't open his eyes. I scratch his belly until he drifts back to sleep. Poor fella must be exhausted. I've never seen him this wiped out. I'll bet it's that girlfriend of his. I'll have to get Ash to introduce us.

Bax lets out his characteristic loud snore, and I rise to my feet to leave.

~

When I return to the training room, it's empty and dark. The screen still displays the scores, and it looks like Moon won. I raise my hand to the palm pad, and the door slides open as expected. Now I *really* feel like a cat burglar.

Without thinking twice, I jump into the room to the nearest desk and take the throttle and stick controllers. I'm back out before the door even slides shut.

I must look ridiculous as I tiptoe-run through the corridors with my quarry. As soon as I get to my place, I lay everything out on my bed. As the throttle and stick approach the keyboard, little lights on all three blink to signal a connection is established. The text in the tutorial changes to reflect the new controls instead of the game controller. My smile widens as I cast the old controller aside, remembering the games we played in Celeres's quarters. *This* is the game I want to play.

I laugh out loud while my hand closes around the stick and I follow the tutorial's directions to place my thumb on the "hat" switch and push it forward to go straight up. I take a deep breath and dive in. I'll just have to return this stuff before anyone wakes up and notices that it's gone. It's midnight. I'll give myself four hours.

After some practice and a lot of reading, I'm able to maneuver my ship out of the station, fly at low speeds, and then go back inside. I've learned that the ship has sensors on it just like my car back home that provide proximity alerts and even emergency thrust (it hits the brakes) to avoid obstacles. How in the world Razor smashed his ship into the side of the hangar door, I don't understand.

I'm in the middle of the emergency thruster tutorial when the number beside my virtual room changes from a 1 to a 2. I freeze when I see *Moon has entered the room.*

A chat box appears, and inside:

Moon: Hey, Birdie.

Leigh: Birdie?

Moon: Yeah, that's what we call newbies. Who are you?

I don't know what to say. I'm a deer in the headlights, that's who.

Moon: Never mind, I see your name. This is your first time?

Leigh: Yes.

Moon: Cool. I wasn't expecting to see a new face tonight. You're going to need a call sign, you know. You can't go flying around with your real name.

Leigh: I'll think about it.

Moon: You do that.

There's a long pause, so I move the chat box off to the side and resume my tutorial. It wants me to try crashing into an asteroid to demonstrate the safety thrusters. I'm well on my way to slamming into it when the chat box dings again.

Moon: Where are you?

Leigh: I'm in my room for the night.

Moon: I'll be right there.

Chapter Thirty-Four

The Operation

Moon is coming to my quarters? At this hour? I want to say no, but the chat box is closed. I hastily turn my throttle and stick off and throw them into a drawer. There is a knock at my door.

I open it to face a young woman. I recognize her from the training room. She's in her early twenties, thin, with long, curly, dirty blond hair, wearing blue tights and a loose-fitting T-shirt with a picture of a velociraptor on it. Above the picture, it says, *Clever Girl*.

"Hi, I'm Moon," she says, handing me a Pepsi. "In case you need a boost."

I set it on my dresser. "Thanks."

She walks over to the bed, looking at my setup. "You're going to need a throttle and stick."

"That'd be nice."

"I have extra. I'll send you a set."

"Are you serious?"

"Sure!"

She just became my new favorite person.

"I looked you up," she says, "you're not a pilot."

"Yeah, I know, I—"

"Don't worry about it. Neither was I when I started. I used to be a software engineer, but I learned how to hack into the flight simulator. I was smitten right away. I was a little better at hiding it than you, but they found me when I joined one of their war sims and won a match. It's *so* much better than writing code. How did you get in?"

"I don't know. I just found it in the restricted section of the network."

"Oh, that's right. You work with Dr. Collins, and that means high clearance. You have free rein on the network. I'll bet you can access just about any program you want."

"Maybe, but I'm probably not supposed to."

She stares back at me, and there's an awkward silence.

"Congratulations on winning the game tonight," I say.

She smiles. "Yeah, I smoked them all. They spend way too much time on their work/life balance. Me, I practice all the time. That's what it takes, you know, if you want to be the best."

"Oh, I don't want to be the best."

She laughs.

"What?"

"That's good, because you'd have to beat me, and trust me, that won't happen. When you're working, I'm flying. When you're playing, I'm flying. If I'm not out there," she says, thumbing my window, "I'm in the sim."

"So you know Celeres?"

"Who? Oh, you mean Captain Nightingale. Yeah, he leads my wing. Why?"

"I'm dating him."

"Oh, you just got a lot more interesting. Do you think if

I get you those flight controls, you can get me a promotion? Quid pro quo, you know?"

"I—"

"I'm just kidding. You know, speaking of Dr. Collins, you know she and the captain used to have a thing?"

I grind my teeth. "I'm aware."

She stands and heads back toward the door. "Sorry. I know you've had a long day. I just wanted to meet you. I'm sure I'll see you around."

She grabs the Pepsi off the dresser, cracks it open, and takes a swig. Then she turns back to me. "Do you know why I work so hard to be the best, Birdie? Where I get the drive?"

"Because you like to win? To beat all those guys?"

"No, Birdie, that's not it. I do it *for* those guys. I work so hard because one day we're going to be in the shit, and it's going to be life or death. Somebody has to be there to pull our asses out of the fire. That somebody is going to be me."

I nod. "And that's why you do it."

"That's the price."

"I admire that. Can ask you what your real name is?"

"Let's stick with Moon. That's what everyone calls me," she says with a brilliant smile before slipping out into the hallway.

I am so tired, but I have one more chore before turning in. I retrieve the borrowed controls and make my way back to the training room. The station is still asleep, and the only thing in the corridors besides me are the cleaning robots. I let myself inside, and after I put everything back, I return to my room. The display panel still shows the simulation, and part of me wants to keep going, even if I have to use the game controller to play.

But I know I can't. Even though I don't have work tomorrow, we promised Krysta that we'd visit her. I should at least grab a few hours of sleep. I turn off my equipment and crawl into bed. Before I drift off, I look outside my big window to identify some parts of the station that I just flew past in the tutorials. I fall asleep with a smile on my face.

My phone pulls me out of a hot and sweaty dream about Celeres and me in his sleeping bag. "Uh, hello?" I say in a voice thick with sleep.

"Good morning, Sunshine." It's Celeres. "You up?"

"Does it sound like I'm up?"

"Sorry. Hey, when you're ready, swing over to my place and we'll go see her."

"Didn't you get enough of her last night with all of that texting?"

"Wait, what? Is that bothering you?"

"No, don't worry about it."

He pauses for a few moments before saying, "I'm sorry about that. She seemed so interested in what we were doing. Must have been lonely."

"Yeah."

"I told her I'd check on her. If you don't want to come, I can stop by after I visit her real quick."

"No, I'll come."

I disconnect the call, then stare at my display panel and think about last night. I enjoyed my first flying lesson and that quick visit with Moon. And then I think about earlier in the night: the pizza, the racing game, Krysta being obnoxious. I try not to read anything into it, but it's hard. It hasn't even been two weeks since I caught Joe and Erica together. I know Celeres isn't Joe, and it's not fair for me to suspect anything, but the wound is still fresh. The scar hasn't even finished forming yet. I hate that she has to be so *perfect*. She's exactly the kind of woman that you don't want your boyfriend anywhere near.

I get cleaned up and put on another cute outfit Celeres bought for me. It's a pair of navy blue biker shorts with an off-the-shoulder gray shirt. I love how it looks on me, and spend a little extra time teasing my red curls to fall around my shoulders. I never considered myself beautiful or anything—not like Krysta, or even Ashlan, for that matter— but I know when I look nice. I cock my hips and give the mirror my famous smile. Not bad at all.

I decide to pass the training room on my way to Celeres's place. I'm not prepared for what I find, however. Instead of a room full of young adults taunting one another and cheering at explosions in a raging space combat simulation, the room is full of middle-aged men and women slugging coffee, squinting at charts, graphs, and diagrams. Apparently, the boxes of donuts I saw last night were for these guys. One of them takes a big bite right over his keypad, showering it with crumbs. By day, this room must be the engineering room instead of the training room, and I've seen enough. On the big display is a periodic table of the elements instead of the leaderboard with Moon's high score. I can see why these people are drinking so much coffee, and I hurry along before I fall asleep myself.

~

I let myself in to Celeres's place and find him on the couch reading his tablet. He looks up and smiles. "Hi. Nice outfit." He's wearing the same khaki shorts and Hawaiian shirt from last night.

I yawn and grin. "Thanks, you too."

"You, uh, get enough sleep?"

"Not nearly. It's okay. Do you think she's up?"

He puts his tablet down and stretches. "Beats me."

All the text on the tablet catches my eye. "What are you reading?"

"Training manual. I wrote it. It's for the new guys."

"Oh yeah? Send me a copy. I'll proofread it for you."

"Really? Okay, but I warn you. It's pretty dry."

"No problem. I could use some reading material. I left my EZ-Read 3000 at home by accident."

"Alright, but you asked for it."

I lean back onto the cushion with my arms crossed. "Sock it to me."

He raises an eyebrow and gives me a mischievous grin, then taps his tablet. The "sent E-Mail" sound plays, then he puts it on the coffee table and stands. "Enjoy. Let's go see how our nosy friend is today."

I extend my hand, and he pulls me to my feet. Instead of stopping myself, I let myself smash into him.

He leans his head down and kisses my bare shoulder, and then my neck. "I've been wanting to do that ever since I bought this shirt," he murmurs.

I clear my throat. "I *said*, sock it to me."

His arms snake around my waist, and he pulls me into him. "Like this?" he asks, clamping his lips on mine. I pull him back down to the couch on top of me. I have one leg hanging off the side.

Just as our breathing quickens and his hands explore my new shirt, his phone vibrates on the coffee table.

"Ignore it," I tell him.

"I have to see who it is."

"You know it's her. The woman has no respect for boundaries."

He twists so he can see the phone. "It's Brose. I have to take it."

I flop my head backwards onto the cushion and stare at the ceiling while he takes his phone and goes into the kitchen. He wedges it between his ear and shoulder while digging around in the fridge. He keeps his voice low, so I can't make out what he's saying. He turns toward me, holding a box of frozen waffles, and gives me a questioning expression. I nod, and he puts two pairs in the toaster oven for us, then puts his phone down and asks if I want some coffee.

"That would be great. Is Brose feeling okay?"

"Oh no, I mean yes, Brose is fine. He wants us to come to the hangar."

"Us? Why me?"

"It's Krysta. She'll be there in a little while. She's got this crazy idea that Max can fix her screwed-up nervous system."

"Max? That spider robot from the Apocritans?"

"Yep, same Max. Let's eat first. It won't take long."

I walk over to sit at the kitchen bar while he plates our waffles. "This is different."

"Breakfast?"

"No, you serving frozen food from a box."

He chuckles. "Eggs Benedict next time?"

"Please."

We eat our food and drink the coffee in silence. We're still chewing when we get up to go to the hangar. He heads to the door while I have a couple last of sips of coffee.

I rush to catch up with him. "So originally, Max was a medical robot, right?"

"Excellent memory."

I purse my lips.

He looks at me with a confused expression. "What?"

"I can't wait to see this."

"Me neither. Let's go."

On our way, we pass a large group of junior pilots. I recognize some of them from the training room last night, especially the group with light blue flight jackets. The late guy who rushed into the room sees me and takes a double take. "You look familiar."

I give him a sweet smile. "Hi."

They all salute Celeres, and he returns it. "Hey guys, I finished up the new training manual. Look for it in your E-Mail."

"Will do, Cap."

There's a murmuring sea of low voices as Celeres and I walk away.

"You know that guy?" Celeres asks.

"I met him, sort of, last night."

He crinkles his brow. "You did? Where?"

"In the halls. He was on his way to a computer lab close to my quarters."

He nods.

I look behind us at the pilots. "What's with the light blue jackets that some of them have?"

He rolls his eyes. "The Blueberry Gang? Nobody knows why they call themselves that. It's their own thing. I can tell you one thing though—they're good. Really good."

∾

We get to the hangar, and Celeres stops me before we go in. "Try not to get too freaked out, okay?"

"What do you mean?"

"We're going to watch some alien variety surgery. You might see some weird things. If they don't conk her out for it, it'll help her anxiety if you have a good bedside manner."

"Oh, don't worry, blood doesn't bother me."

"One other thing—we have an Apocritan battery shortage."

"I'm aware."

He has a concerned frown. "Right, you know also that Krysta is crucial to the battery trade with Apocrita. With her feeling unwell like this, it might be a while before we see another delivery."

"So this has to work, or—"

"Or no more Max, no more subspace radio, no more lab experiments with that stinger that messed Krysta up."

I take a sharp breath. "I'll be as supportive as I can."

"Okay." He grabs my hand, and we walk in together. Krysta and Brose sit at one of the break tables. There's a backpack between them. A pair of crutches leans against the table.

It's a good thing that Celeres and I just had the conversation we did because my heart stops in my chest when she looks up at us. Her head rolls to the side, and she corrects it the best she can and gives a half-smile. Her left eye points at the far side of its socket. I wouldn't be surprised if she could see her own ear. She fixes her good eye at us and slurs, "Ish gotten worse."

I settle myself down in an empty chair beside her and take her hand. "What can I do to help?"

She exhales with a mournful sigh and foam trickles out of the side of her mouth. "I don't know."

She seems so vulnerable in this moment, so helpless, like she's falling backward into a void. I position myself a little closer, and I coax her head onto my shoulder. I smooth her hair, and without thinking, I kiss her head as if she were a child. She presses into me more, and the heat from our bodies touching is palpable. The guys watch, and Celeres furrows his brow.

I follow his gaze and realize that she has a hand on my thigh. In fact, a casual observer might mistake our position for something more than it is.

I point at the table. "What's in the bag?"

"Batteries," says Brose.

"Batteries? Why?"

"For Max. For the operation. This is the last of 'em. All we have. Hopefully, they're enough."

Celeres takes the bag and pulls three batteries out. None of them are very bright; they're about a third full, each. He holds one up and examines it as if it were a glass of fine wine.

"They'll be enough," Celeres says as if he has any idea what he's talking about.

Krysta tries to straighten and take some of her dead weight off of me. "This is going to work."

I scan the hangar. "Where's Max?"

"They're gearing him up," says Brose, "he'll be here in a minute."

Celeres lines up the batteries on the table, and Brose looks at his phone, tapping his foot. His foot-tapping is one of the few sounds in the entire hangar, besides some metallic clinks and squeaks.

"Are we the only ones in here?" I ask.

"Almost," says Brose, "Except for the skeleton crew, I cleared the place out. We don't need a bunch of onlookers. They were happy to get the day off. I already saw some of them at the diner with their Bloody Marys this morning."

I sigh and shake my head at the ceiling with a mocking smile.

"It's okay," he says. "They deserve a little fun. We'll get things humming again tomorrow."

Celeres cranes his neck to look through a long row of ships. "He's coming."

The clacking sounds of Max's mechanical footfalls grow in volume as he approaches. Today, he's not repairing a hangar or ship, but a person, and he looks the part. He still reminds me of a giant spider, but his frontmost legs are bent upward, like arms, each holding a medical instrument. He uses his other four legs to approach us.

Stomping boots also approach, and McClure appears from behind one of the ships. "What the hell is going on here?"

Brose puts a hand on Celeres's shoulder. "Let me."

McClure closes the distance between us and stares at Krysta. "Ew. What's wrong with *her*?"

Celeres's face turns red, and Brose steps in front of him. "I gave orders for the hangar to clear out, McClure. What are you doing here?"

"I'm in charge of hangar security and…what do you think you're doing with my repair robot?"

Brose draws himself to full height and moves so that he's toe to toe with McClure. He looks down, straight into his eyes. "We're doing repairs, McClure, which I'm allowed to do with Max, seeing as I'm Chief Engineer on this station."

McClure stares back for a couple of seconds, and then spins and walks away, muttering, "we'll see about that."

Once McClure is out of sight, Brose mutters, "McClure, McClure, you son of a whore."

Krysta coughs and a tiny stream of blood traces out of her nose. Brose looks at her and fits the batteries into Max.

It only takes a second to realize why people didn't like to be doctored by this robot. It looks scary, like it's here to do some torturing. Again, I try to maintain my bedside manner and not react with revulsion. Krysta passes out. Whether it's from the look of Max or because her illness is advancing is anyone's guess.

Krysta's breathing is shallow, her chest barely rises and falls with each breath.

Brose has a sheen of sweat on his forehead. "Fix her up, Max."

Max places his instruments around himself to free up his grips and then reaches toward Krysta. The rest of us spring out of the way. It's a good thing she's unconscious. Seeing spidery legs reaching toward you is enough to make anyone feel worse, not better.

He picks her up and lays her face-down on the table.

"Hurry," I whisper under my breath. Celeres takes my hand in his. Between the two of us, it's a judgment call whose hand is colder and sweatier.

Brose watches Max intently. Whether or not this operation works, Max is Brose's responsibility, and Max is an alien robot. Anything can happen, and Brose looks like he's ready to act if need be.

Max chooses a dark gray device shaped like a lemon. It makes a whining sound that gets louder as he holds it closer to Krysta. When it approaches her back, it gets very loud. I let go of Celeres's hand and hold my ears.

The noise stops, and Max extends an appendage to her spine. He doesn't hold any device in this one. Instead, when the tip of his leg gets close, a silver spike protrudes forth, which seems to follow the "stinger" theme of the Apocritans. I hold my breath. If he's going to jab her, I don't think I can keep my eyes open.

But I can't close them. The three of us stare in rapt bedazzlement as Max breaks the skin of Krysta's neck with the spike and then slides it in at least a whole inch. Her body convulses and Brose rushes behind the robot. "I'm turning him off."

I grab his wrist. "Wait. What chance does she have otherwise? We're past the point of no return."

Celeres nods, and Brose takes a step away from the spidery fiend, his face stricken.

Purple light erupts around the talon, and Krysta convulses again. She gags for a moment and then spews the contents of her stomach onto the floor where Brose stood just a moment ago. Celeres and I exchange queasy glances.

"Uh oh," says Brose, examining Max from behind.

"What?" asks Celeres.

"He's just about out of juice."

Krysta's eyes snap open and she screams as Max removes the talon, the purple light flickering out. Ignoring her feeble squirms, he swiftly applies a bandage, his movements precise and efficient. Gathering up his equipment, he says in a slow, echoey, metallic voice, "It's fortunate the injury was slight," before turning and stalking away from us.

"Wait a second," I say, "Max can talk?"

"Limited vocabulary, but yes," Brose says.

"Water," croaks Krysta. She rolls herself over so that now she's facing upward.

"Brose, can you?" I ask.

He nods and heads in the water cooler's direction.

I put a hand on her shoulder. "How are you feeling?"

"I think I'm going to be alright." She sounds weak, but color has returned to her cheeks and her eyes are both pointing straight ahead again.

We lift her off the table and onto a chair. When Brose comes back, he scrunches his face.

"What's up, man?" asks Celeres.

"Just like I said, it's Max. The batteries died."

Celeres gives a low whistle.

"That was close," I say.

"We're going to need more batteries," says Brose to no one in particular.

Krysta takes the water cup from him and takes a slurp. "I know. I'm trying."

She leans her head back to look at me. "What are you doing later?"

Celeres interrupts. "She has plans tonight, and you need some sleep. You can get back to the lab tomorrow."

Plans? What plans? I was going to fly the simulator all night. I look up at Celeres questioningly.

"It's a surprise."

Well, that could be fun, too.

Krysta looks to him, and then me. "You're right. I need to—"

She falls off the chair into a pile on the floor, snoring like a lumberjack.

Celeres scoops her up in his arms. "We'll get her home in *Little Seven*."

Brose nods. "Good. I need to figure out if I can move Max out of the way before McClure sees him. Of course, he runs out of batteries in the middle of the hangar."

He wanders off as Celeres and I load Krysta onto his moon buggy and putter off to put her to bed.

Chapter Thirty-Five

Mysteries, Gifts, and a Surprise Date

We arrive at Krysta's place in short order, and I have to admit I'm more than a little curious about what it looks like inside. As Krysta snores, Celeres lifts her from the buggy, picks her hand up by the wrist, and rests it on the pad to open the door. I chuckle in spite of myself. He raises an eyebrow.

I give him an innocent look. "Now that we know she's going to be okay, that just seemed funny."

We walk into her quarters together, and it's not what I expected. First, the place is a mess, exactly like *my* room on Earth. There are clothes on the floor, cups on the nightstand, makeup stains on the vanity, and an unmade bed. Hey, I get it; when you're living life, sometimes cleaning takes a back seat.

It's furnished with old-looking wooden furniture. I'll ask her later, but it's safe to assume that these pieces came from her Earth bedroom. Having my actual bedroom suite with me on *Sumerian* would be so comforting. Maybe someday.

Celeres eases Krysta onto her bed, her snores continuing.

An electronic tablet is among the clutter, leaning against the wall. Its protective case flipped open, and a crack extends from the top of the screen to the bottom. I pick it up. Was there a crack on the screen when I saw her using it in the infirmary? It was such a brief moment that I can't remember. I close the case and trace my finger along the embossed alien letters across its front.

"Hey Celeres, what do you think of this?"

"Krysta's tablet? What of it?"

"I found it over here at the base of the wall and the glass is cracked."

"Like she threw it?"

"Yeah. Why would she do that?"

He shrugs. "There's only one way to find out."

He walks over to Krysta and picks up her limp hand.

I hurry to his side. "What are you doing?"

"Unlocking this." He presses Krysta's thumb to the fingerprint scanner, and the screen comes to life.

There's a digital photo of Baxter on the screen, taken while he, Celeres, and I were on our walk and saw the wasp. My arm is even on the edge of the image. I grab the tablet out of his hands. I stare at it for a few seconds until I find my voice. "Why would she—"

"I don't know."

I close the image, and now we see that someone attached it to an E-Mail with an empty body. In the From: section, instead of a legible E-Mail address, there's: 8E847F35-A6FD-4025-A10E-6E2734E42B47.

I open the attachment again. "Look, you can see my arm. It's when we were on our walk. Who is sending photos of my dog to Krysta?"

He takes the tablet and squints. "It has to be the wasp we encountered, right?"

I nod.

Celeres touches my shoulder. "Maybe put it back for now?"

"You're right." I throw the tablet back against the section of wall where I found it.

He looks at me with wide eyes.

I stomp over to where Krysta sleeps and lean forward so that I'm only inches from her face. "What is going on?" I say in an even, ominous tone.

Celeres's hand on my shoulder pulls me back. "She can't hear you. We'll get to the bottom of this, I promise."

"What is she hiding?"

"I don't know, Leigh. She's the most confusing person I know—"

He pauses, staring across the room. I follow his gaze to a small, bushy plant on her oak dresser. "It's that plant from Apocrita, same as the one I have potted at my place."

Except this isn't just a potted plant. It's an entire planter full of it. A smaller one is on her nightstand in a little flower pot. It's the one she dug up while with me on the zoo field trip.

"It looks—glowy," I say.

"You're right, the red dots on the leaves seem to soak in some of the light from the stars."

"Like the star flowers we saw?"

"Yeah, don't you think?"

I walk over to her nightstand because it's closer to her window. "Celeres, turn off the lights."

When he does, it's clear that the dots are phosphorescent.

I lean in to get a better look. "No wonder she likes this. It's magical."

"It really is."

I give him an inquisitive look. "Wait, what about the one I gave you? Doesn't yours glow?"

"I don't know. It's not by the window."

"Why in the world not?"

"Hey, cut me some slack. I didn't know it was supposed to glow. At least I haven't killed it."

Call me crazy, but I would think most people would automatically put a plant near natural light.

"I want one in my room," I say.

"We'll find one for you the next time we're down there."

"Alright."

He puts a hand on my shoulder. "You okay?"

"I don't know."

He nods and strokes the glowing leaves, then glances at Krysta. "The most confusing person I know," he repeats quietly.

I sigh.

"Ready?" he asks.

"Yeah. Let's get out of here. Are we still on for tonight?"

He ushers me out. "Yep."

He boards *Little Seven*, but I take a step back and shake my head. "I'll jog back. I need to clear my head."

"Okay, be at the hangar at 18:00."

I groan. "The hangar? I hope someone cleans up the puke by then."

"It will be." He gives me a 'beep beep' and cruises away.

As he disappears down the hall, I think about tonight and how much I miss him already. I do a quick stretch and spring into a jog. The twists and turns in the station are familiar to me now. I think I could get to just about anywhere without too much trouble. I recognize more faces every day, and most of them wave as I jog by. After a few minutes, the knots in my mind loosen as the floor flows beneath my feet. Celeres enters my mind again and I fight the urge to turn around and go to his place for the day. He probably has to work, anyway.

Now that Krysta seems to be on the mend, I'll soon have to get back to work myself. Obviously, that stinger is dangerous, more than I could have guessed. If I prick my finger on that needle, what then? We have no more batteries for Max. Memories of the foam boiling out of Krysta's mouth send a chill through my body. It seems like a no-win situation that the stinger charges the very batteries that it runs on, and charging a battery takes a life. What are the chances that Brose will ever have any success replicating a battery like that? Slim to none? Krysta's going to have to do some fancy trading to get us some more batteries, if for no other reason than to power the subspace radios that the station depends on to stay in contact with Earth. That's a lot of pressure and means some overtime in my future.

That's going to be a problem. For "the new girl," I have too much going on. Besides the chunk of time that I spend in the lab, I want to spend time with Celeres. I also want to continue learning to fly. When am I supposed to sleep?

When I arrive at my quarters, Moon made good on her promise; a couple of cardboard boxes sit outside my door. I grab them and dash inside. The first box has the throttle and stick. The buttons are worn, and scratches cover both controls. There's an enclosed note:

I learned on these. They've seen a thousand battles and a hundred systems.

I took good care of them.

You do the same.

-Moon

So what's in the second box? As soon as I open the lid, I feel like I've just opened a treasure chest with glowing gold inside. It's a pair of haptic gloves and a virtual reality headset. It also comes with a note:

> *Use this. You'll never learn by playing on your TV.*
> *-Moon*

This is so great. I'm going to put them to good use, but first, I need to sleep. I put the controls away, overjoyed that I don't have to sneak them out of the training room anymore, then take three weary steps to my bed and flop face-first onto my pillow, shoes on and all. Despite my weariness, I take a long time to drift off to sleep. The image of Bax on Krysta's tablet haunts me.

When my phone awakens me, it shows 6:00, and that Celeres is calling.

"Hi," I say, trying to sound like he didn't just wake me up.

"You coming?"

I remember that 6:00 is 18:00 and I'm late. "Oh yeah, I'm sorry. I'll be right there."

I bolt out of my room and run to the hangar, where I find him staring at his wrist beside *Big Seven*.

He looks up at me and breaks into a grin. "Just wake up?"

"No, not at all. Why?"

"There are bed marks on the side of your face."

I raise my hands to my cheeks.

"It's okay," he says, "it's cute."

"I'm sorry, I fell asleep. I hope I didn't mess up your surprise."

"Nope, we're still good. I have some snacks. Jump up there and we'll get going."

As I climb the ladder, the telltale smell of hot, buttery popcorn wafts out. Holding onto a rung with one hand, I swing around to see him. He has his arms crossed and looks at me with a proud smile.

"What did you do?" I ask.

"Go see."

I finish climbing, and as soon as my head clears the floor of the cabin, I see it: two big tubs of popcorn up front, along with mega-size packs of chocolate-covered raisins and sugary sour candy. He's behind me in an instant and has his arms around my waist.

"Popcorn? That's different," I say.

He shrugs with a smile, then steps away to raise the ladder and close the hatch. "Yeah, there's a popcorn stand on the station. It's perfect for this occasion."

"Should I grab a seat, then?"

"Get comfortable. Let me take us out a bit for a change of scenery."

Once we get strapped in, he hits the hat switch on his stick to raise the ship. I hope it isn't too obvious that I'm watching his every move. So far, he's doing everything that I've learned on the simulator. After a quick radio exchange from the station controller, he pushes the throttle forward and we glide out of the station.

"I have a question," I say.

"Hmm?"

"I've heard that these ships have some sort of safety feature that keeps you from running into things."

"Yes, that's right. Thrusters will try to push you away from anything you're in danger of crashing into."

"Then how did Razor crash into the side of the hangar door?"

He looks at me, then nods. "Great question. We turn those features off during some training exercises. He forgot to turn his back on before landing, then got distracted on his way in."

"How can you turn them off?"

He points to a red switch on the console. "Do me a favor and don't press this, okay?"

"Sure, no problem."

But I'll make no such promises to my simulator. I play video games with the "hard" settings, and my personal pilot training will be no different. Besides, who cares if I blow up a few times in a video game? I lean back into my seat and try to envision the console in the simulation. I don't remember seeing that switch. I'll keep an eye out for it next time I'm playing.

I'm used to him heading straight to Apocrita from here, but this time, he doesn't. Instead, he flies straight out of the station for a fair distance, and then turns around so that we can see it through the cockpit glass. "Anything look familiar?"

"You mean the station? It looks neat from out here. It looks a lot bigger from the outside than it feels from the inside."

"No, not that. I mean, yeah, I know what you mean, but what else?"

I draw a blank and shrug.

"See that window?" He shines a laser dot on it. "That's your quarters."

It's impossible for me to tell, because it's reflective on this side. "How do you know?"

"I just do."

I nod, then motion to our popcorn. "Nice flying. Nothing spilled. You're a pro."

"Thanks. I wrote the manual, you know," he says, tossing a piece into his mouth. "Read it yet?"

"No, I've been a little busy. It looks like good bedtime reading. I'll get into it tonight. I'm sure it's riveting."

"You'll be asleep in no time."

"Then I'll use it as a pillow."

He snorts and looks away, toward the glass windows of my quarters, at the perfect reflection of our ship floating in space. When he looks back at me, he wears a mischievous grin. "So, are you wondering why I brought you out here? It wasn't to look at your quarters, you know."

"No? Why, then?"

In answer, he maneuvers us closer to the station until we're maybe fifty feet from a large section of gray hull.

"What's this?" I ask.

Again, instead of answering me, he types on the keypad in front of him. Finally, he looks at me. "You ready?"

"For what?"

"Do you remember what you told me down at the campsite? The thing you miss most, besides cheeseburgers?"

I look at the popcorn and candy, then burst into a wide grin. "Drive-in movies? Are we going to watch a movie?"

He presses a button on the keypad, and a projector on his ship lights an enormous rectangle on the side of *Sumerian*. "I hear this is an all-time classic." He's so excited about this that I can practically see the waves of thrill coming off of him.

The movie appears on the station hull, and I don't know if I'm more surprised about this date, or the film he picked: *Shawshank Redemption*. My mind instantly transports back to the plane ride between Pittsburgh and Phoenix when I watched this with Krysta and how she told me she gave him a copy for his birthday. I don't have the heart to tell him I just watched it, but I am a little annoyed that there has to be a little of Krysta in everything we do. I try to hide my stupefaction by fumbling with the box of chocolate-covered raisins.

"What do you think?" he asks.

I stay busy with the box of candy. "This is the most surprised I've ever been."

He puts his arm around me. "You'll love it. Just relax and enjoy your drive-in spectacular."

He grabs a handful of popcorn and stuffs all of it into his mouth at once, then takes a sip from his water bottle.

I rest my head on his shoulder as the movie gets underway. I'll have to remember to tell Krysta he enjoyed the gift.

Chapter Thirty-Six

The Track

My confusion turns to a new level of annoyance when his phone rings about halfway through the movie. When he pulls it out of his pocket, I can see that it's *her*. He pauses the movie and thumbs the *Accept* button. "Hey, what's up? You're on speaker."

"Hi," she says.

I dig around in my box of candy just to feign indifference while she continues. "Are you busy?"

"Yeah, I'm out with Leigh. Everything okay?"

"Hi Leigh, yeah, I'm better than okay. I feel completely fine."

"Already? Just this morning you were falling off of your chair."

"I know."

"Whatever you did, don't do it again, because I don't know what we'll do to save you next time. We'd probably have to take you down to see the bugs themselves, which is something I'd rather avoid."

"Oh trust me, I know. So listen, I want to show you something."

"Okay, I'll stop by tomorrow morning."

"Tonight. It's important, a surprise. A pleasant surprise. Bring Leigh."

I suddenly feel completely out of place. Can't he just tell her no?

"Hold on."

He puts the phone on mute. "You mind?"

What am I supposed to say? No matter what, the date is already over, at least for me. He had good intentions, and it started out wonderful. Unfortunately, the whole thing has been Krysta-flavored, including this unfortunate ending. I shake my head.

"Sure, why not?" I say, trying to keep the sadness out of my voice.

"See you in a bit," he says, then disconnects the call.

I toss a handful of chocolate into my mouth and chew it woodenly. Sometimes chocolate is the only thing that helps, if only a little.

He shuts off the movie. "To be continued," he says brightly, then guides the ship back to the hangar.

She's already at Celeres's berth, waiting for us. She wears a metallic sky blue unitard—which fits her amazingly well—and stands with her hip cocked. You would never know how ill she was just a few hours ago. She waves at Celeres, "Hey Peaches."

My eyes narrow.

In stark contrast to Krysta, Brose stands beside her in some greasy overalls. Farther down the hangar, Max lies in a heap between some ships. It looks like they accidentally knocked him over while moving him and couldn't stand him back up.

We land, and Celeres grabs the tub of popcorn before heading to the hatch. "Bring your candy," he says when he sees me chewing.

I was going to bring it, anyway.

I follow him to the hatch, and before it's even halfway open, Brose calls up to us, "Stay in there. We're coming up."

I know that Brose and Ashlan aren't an official couple yet, but I've gotten used to seeing them together. "Where's Ash?" I ask once we're all standing together in *Big Seven's* cabin.

"She's tied up at work. Hopefully she gets some free time tomorrow," Brose says.

"Everything okay?"

"Yeah, far as I know."

Celeres takes a bite of popcorn. "So what's going on?"

Like birds at a feeder, Brose and Krysta take some, too. She hands him a piece of paper. He squints at it and crinkles his brow. "Coordinates? Down on the surface?"

She nods excitedly. Brose fights a smile.

Celeres looks over at him. "You're in on this, too?"

Brose shrugs.

Celeres hands me the paper. "You want to go punch these in? I've noticed your interest in the controls."

"I'm not sure—"

"Chapter 3 in my manual. It won't take but a minute."

I take the piece of paper back to the cockpit, then pull out my phone to access his manual. I learn how to bring up the coordinate interface and enter the latitude and longitude. A map appears on the screen and zooms in on the location. It's Hoegaarden, Belgium. For a second, I'm utterly confused until I figure out how to switch the planet at the top of the interface. I'm so used to calling it Apocrita that I'm disoriented again until I find New Mesopotamia on the list.

Once I have the correct world selected, the map changes and zooms into the location.

I recognize this place. It's the dirt track that Ash and I discovered right before the animal parade started. Do they know the danger? Does Brose? Why would they want us to go there?

"You figure it out?" Celeres calls to me.

I twist in my seat so I can see him, then give a slight nod before returning to face the front of the ship.

He shuffles back to me and straps in while Brose and Krysta sit in the bench seat behind us. For the second time tonight, we leave *Sumerian* and return to space.

On our way to the planet, I consider voicing my concern about the parade and the irresistible force that compelled Ash and me toward the zoo. I decide to hold my tongue for now, because even if I'm leery of Krysta, I trust Brose. I know he'd never do anything to hurt anyone, especially his best friend. As long as I don't see a line of animals marching through it, I'll stay quiet—for now. I don't want to be a wet blanket.

As we approach, the track is easy to spot because it's surrounded by a ring of lights atop long poles. That's not the only new thing—beyond the ring of lights is a high chain-link fence. Now I feel a little more comfortable.

"You can land right in the middle," says Krysta.

He brings us to a soft landing and then looks over at Krysta. "What is this?"

"A surprise. I almost thought it was ruined when you came to see me in the hospital yesterday. I was in the middle of a call wrapping up the final details."

He looks confused. "A dirt track?"

"No, it's a racetrack," she says while spreading her arms wide in presentation. This is the best gift anyone could have given him.

"What did you do?" I ask her.

"I, with the help of our Apocritan friends, arranged some new entertainment."

"You know I love racing," Celeres says, "When does it start? Where do we sit?"

She puts her hand on his arm. "No, silly. We aren't *watching*, we're *racing*."

Celeres looks around. "Where are the cars?"

"Right outside," says Brose. "They're modified moon buggies, like *Little Seven*. I had the guys make a half dozen for down here."

Celeres jumps from his seat and out the hatch. Brose and Krysta chuckle and shake their heads. "Boys will be boys," says Krysta, climbing out of her seat.

Brose gets up to follow her out. "Think we surprised him?"

She turns around, wraps him in a huge, tight hug, and kisses his cheek. "We did! Thanks so much for your help."

Brose blushes and mutters something about, "No trouble at all."

They disappear down the ladder, leaving me alone in the cockpit. Outside are the sounds of rumbling car exhaust and good-natured laughter. This has got to be the strangest date I've ever been on. I pop a few more chocolate-covered raisins into my mouth and join the others outside. The nightsong is loud enough in this part of the deep forest that it's still audible behind the car noises.

The lights around the track remind me of streetlights back home. In fact, I wouldn't be surprised if they're actually *from* home. I have no way of knowing for sure, but I have the impression that the colony doesn't have any kind of manufacturing set up. I wonder what they would manufacture if they did? Do raw materials here act the same as the ones on Earth? What's new? What's the same? I feel like I'm rediscovering the sense of wonder that I must have had as a child.

I'm a lot less stressed now that I know we're fenced-in. Not only that, but I don't see any animals or feel any invisible force compelling me to walk to the zoo like last time. As soon as my feet touch the ground, Celeres motors past me on a buggy and down the track, pumping his fist in the air. Brose is right behind him.

It's a good thing Ashlan isn't here, based on her performance in the racing game the other night.

"Grab a buggy, Leigh!" yells Krysta as she blurs by.

Obviously, none of them remember that I've never driven one of these. The controls look pretty basic, though, like a go-kart.

I sit on a pink buggy with a painting of a daisy—my favorite flower—on the side. Everyone else is far enough away that I'm thankful they won't see me fumbling around back here. When I press the start button, the little "engine" roars to life, just like a real race car.

When I was young, my dad told me that race cars sound like this because when fossil fuels were banned on Earth more than a hundred years ago, everyone hated that the electric race cars didn't make enough noise. They wound up adding speakers inside the frames to simulate the old, loud mufflers, and they've been that way ever since. Most modern cars are nearly silent, just like the moon buggies on *Sumerian*.

I leave the gearshift in neutral and twist the accelerator a few times. The rumble and the roar give me a sense of genuine power as the vehicle shudders as if it's straining against an invisible leash. You'd never expect to hear or feel anything like this out of a pink daisy buggy. It's so badass. I grin in spite of myself, give it another rev, then put the car into gear...and almost fall off the back as the buggy jerks forward. I hit the brakes and look around. Good, nobody saw that. I cast about for some sort of seatbelt. It turns out I'm sitting on it. There's also a helmet in a little compartment behind me. I put that on and strap myself in.

They're coming around the track. I twist the handle and give Daisy a little gas. Just a little. I don't want this seatbelt to cut me in half. In fact, I'm going to the outside track so nobody runs me over.

While I creep in that direction, the sounds of their buggies, their hoots and whoops, become clearer. Celeres is the first to whip by me, giving a primordial holler of pure adrenaline as he tears by. After him comes Brose and Krysta, who appear to be jockeying for second place. They pay me no mind.

I twist the handle more and Daisy accelerates. Time for me to join this race. I let out a whoop of my own as I burst onto the track. Plenty of my red hair still shows under my helmet, and I pretend I'm some superhero on a foreign planet, hair on fire and tearing up the track. In moments, I'm behind Krysta. Looks like Brose pulled ahead of her, and now he's trying to get around Celeres.

I don't know if Krysta is being conservative or I'm being reckless, or maybe a combination of both, but I catch up to her and now we're side by side. She looks over with a crooked smile, then wets her lips with her tongue. Wait, is that a pucker? Did she just blow me a kiss? There is only one thing I'm sure about right now—she needs to be put in her place. What is she doing, setting up a gift like this for *my* boyfriend? I'm still annoyed about the movie, and that she interrupted it. Again, I'm reminded of how things started between Joe and Erica. It was an innocent gift here, a ride home there—clues that happened in plain sight. I came here to get *away* from all that.

With a little more gas and a low growl from me, I pull ahead of her. Up ahead, Brose and Celeres weave back and forth, each trying to get ahead. Celeres seems to have super human situational awareness, and Brose can't get around him no matter how much he tries. Celeres must be an artiste in ship-to-ship combat.

"Hey!" Krysta yells behind me. I can barely hear her over all the noise.

I laugh out loud and give it even more power. Now I'm next to Brose. He looks over at me, teeth barred. "No way, Leigh!" he says, then pulls ahead of me. Celeres is far ahead of us now, and Krysta falls more and more behind.

I get so caught up in the heat of the moment that I'm taken off guard thirty seconds later when Celeres leaves the track to cut through the middle, heading to the other side at top speed.

"Hey, no fair!" I say, "You're cheat—"

But I stop myself because I see what he sees; Krysta is on the other side, surrounded by three wasps. They stand on two legs, like us, and the stingers on each back leg glisten. Her buggy points at a haphazard angle as if she braked suddenly.

Brose sees them at the same time I do, and we both follow Celeres across the middle turf, pieces of mud and grass pelting us as we go. Brose unsnaps the leather pistol holster at his side.

We're there in a flash, and Celeres is off of his buggy before it even stops.

Krysta and the wasps watch us approach. She raises her hands to us. "Relax, it's okay. I work with these guys. They stopped by to see if we're satisfied with the track."

She holds her translator and speaks into it. "We're thrilled. You followed the specifications perfectly."

The closest wasp clicks and hisses, and the translator's weird voice emits, "Now give us the pattern."

She shakes her head. "It's not ready yet. Be patient."

Instead of answering her, the lead wasp pivots to look at the rest of us. My blood turns cold when its eyes lock onto mine, and its antennas stretch toward me, and just me. Why aren't they smelling the others? I'm filled with the same feelings of disgust and fear that I felt on every other encounter with these disgusting things.

After a few more seconds, all three of them jump into the air and buzz away.

Krysta puts the translator away and shrugs. "I'm sorry. I didn't know they were going to be here."

"What's a pattern?" I ask.

"It's part of the research we trade. I can explain more in the lab."

Brose snaps his holster closed. "I hate those things."

"You'll get used to them," says Krysta.

"No, I won't."

She looks him up and down. "Did you ever think that you look as scary to them as they do to you?"

His hand moves up to his beard while he watches them fly out of sight. "No."

Celeres gets back aboard his buggy and motors off without a word. The rest of us follow behind, but the mood is different now. We circle the track for another fifteen minutes before packing up and piling into *Big Seven*. I jump into the copilot seat before Krysta gets any ideas.

Chapter Thirty-Seven

A Strange Illness

On our way back to the station, I think about everything that just happened. Krysta interrupted our date and then forced her way into the evening with her...gift. Why?

Maybe I should just let it go. We all had a good time, and it's not like she made any moves on him, at least not outwardly. When she called, she even told him to bring me along. Could it be an innocent friendly gesture, no different from Brose making the racing buggies? I don't know, but calling him Peaches in front of me is pretty obnoxious.

Celeres guides *Big Seven* into the hangar. After landing, he stretches. "What an amazing day, all around."

I nod and smile. No need for me to kill the buzz.

He puts a hand on my knee. "Do you want to hang out?"

I want to spend time with him, but it's better that I get some rest and unwind from these emotions. Besides, there's something else I have to do right now. "See you tomorrow, okay? I'm exhausted."

His smile fades, but he recovers in an instant.

"See you tomorrow," he says in a voice I can barely hear because Brose is back there yawning the loudest yawn I've ever heard. We both roll our eyes at the back seat.

Krysta looks at her phone. "I guess it *is* late."

"Krysta, I'm no doctor, but I think you should get some rest after the day you had," says Celeres.

"Yeah, I know. I feel like I could sleep for a week. Still... Leigh, I'll call you when I get up. We're behind at the lab."

"Okay," I say as we all unstrap and head out of the ship.

Once we're out, Brose marches over to join some of his engineers tending to Max, who still lies in a heap in the hangar.

Krysta's knees wobble, and she thrusts out a hand, almost falling. Celeres grabs her wrist and puts his other hand under her arm for support. She closes her eyes and lets out a shallow breath.

"You okay?" he asks her.

"I think so. You might be right about me needing to rest."

"I'll walk you back."

"Thanks."

Celeres leans toward me, and we kiss. "See you tomorrow."

"Sounds good," I say, then head toward a door that I know leads in the general direction of Beastarium. As I'm walking out, I can't help but think I might have left a part of myself back there with the two of them—the part that wants to go along to make sure nothing fishy is going on, but I guess I just have to trust him. Trust and hope, I guess. I steal one last glance at them before heading out.

~

"Hey Leigh," Ashlan calls right after I walk into Beastarium. She must have been watching the door. She still wears the worn jeans and yellow camisole she wore at Celeres's place last night.

"Ash? It's 10:00 PM. What are you up to? Brose said you've been working a lot of extra hours."

"I have. Leigh, I didn't want to tell you until I was sure, but I think Baxter is sick, and I haven't figured out what's wrong with him yet."

My stomach drops to the floor. "He's sick? Can we see him?"

"Of course."

She leads me to his room and I burst through the door. He's curled up on his bed. I rush to his side and drop to my knees.

I stroke the top of his head. "Hey buddy." I can't tell for sure, but it looks like his eyes are open in the tiniest of a slit.

I run my hand down his neck and stroke his back. There's a strange mass under his skin, between his shoulder blades. Ashlan seems to notice my confusion.

"Subcutaneous fluid," she says. "It's like an IV for dogs. It'll absorb through the night, keeping him hydrated."

I look at Ashlan, my mouth quivering.

She kneels beside me. "He is very lethargic," she says in the voice a doctor would use next to a sleeping patient. "I've been running tests on every known pathogen and disease, but I've found nothing."

I scratch his rump. "Is this why you've been working so much?"

She nods. "I blame myself. I thought it would be safe to take him on that camping trip, but maybe I was wrong. I'll never forgive myself if anything happens to him. I'm so sorry, Leigh."

"I was here last night to see him, and he was in this same spot. I just thought his girlfriend wore him out... Hey, you don't think she got him sick, like some kind of viral host?"

"No, she's healthy, and spends a lot of time just outside. She's clearly missing him."

"What are you going to do?"

She looks at me with red-rimmed eyes. "I'll keep trying."

I put my hand on her shoulder. "I know. When was the last time you slept?"

She shakes her head, then looks down at Bax. She scratches him under the chin.

"Listen," I say, "Get some sleep. I'll stay with him tonight. If he looks like he's getting worse, I'll call you."

"Are you sure?"

"Yes, it's fine. I know you're only fifty steps away. Go."

She stands up and brushes herself off. "He should be okay for now. You could probably doze off, yourself."

"Maybe."

When she leaves, I lean back against the wall with my hand on Bax's paw. "Sorry for getting you into this, buddy. Please don't leave me."

How am I supposed to sleep? Yes, it's been a long day. Yes, I'm tired. But this is my best friend, my jogging buddy, and the only piece of my heart that I can depend on.

While I stroke his paw and stare at the opposite wall, a scratching, huffing sound comes from outside the building. I'm sure it's just some wild animal, and now I'm guaranteed not to sleep.

After about ten minutes of it, I decide to look. I scratch Bax behind the ear and climb to my feet.

When I get outside, It's quite dark. There's that noise

again—a quick huff, then a noise almost like a crow call. I look in that direction, and there are two sparkling eyes looking at me from within a nearby bush.

I keep the door propped open so I can disappear inside in a hurry if I need to. I squint at the eyes. "What are you?"

In answer, it emerges from the bush. It's a little fox-like animal with gray fur. It takes a few tentative steps toward me. I've seen one of these before. It was during the animal parade. Ash told me that Bax's girlfriend was one of these. This has to be her.

Blame it on tiredness, but against my better judgment, I open the door wider and beckon the little animal to enter the building. It darts past me and runs down the hall to Baxter's room, sniffing furiously.

I join her, then open Bax's door. She slips inside and goes straight to him, licking him until he opens his eyes. He snorts.

Well, that's a good sign. After a couple of minutes, she curls up beside him and soon they're both sleeping.

I return to my position on the floor and lean against the wall. I watch them for a while, wishing human love could be so simple. Eventually, their comfortable, quiet snores lull me into a slumber of my own.

I stir to the all-too-familiar touch of a wet dog nose on my face. Of course, my first thought is that it's Baxter, but then I gather my wits and remember the situation. It has to be his girlfriend, and since I don't know if she bites, I whip my eyes open and sit bolt upright.

Light from Beastarium's contrived "dawn" spills into the

room around the curtains, revealing them both sitting just inches from my face, mouths hanging open.

I throw my arms around Baxter and hug him close. He nuzzles my neck and licks the side of my face. I laugh and cry at the same time.

His girlfriend seems to have warmed up to me as well, because her tail wags furiously and she takes a step closer. I give her a tentative scratch on the neck. "You need a name."

"It's Milly," says Ashlan from the doorway. She's in pajamas and bare feet, leaning against the frame.

I start. "I didn't even see you there. Look at Bax! What do you think?"

She nods and smiles. "This is a step in the right direction."

"I'm so relieved. Thank you for everything you've done."

"You're very welcome," she says while settling down across from me on crossed legs. "They seem very happy."

I snort. "Yeah, maybe a little *too* happy."

"Maybe. Hey Leigh, would you be up for some girl talk?" she asks with a sheepish smile.

"Hell yeah, I'm always up for girl talk."

"Do you remember the other day when we were leaving the planet and Celeres tilted the ship so that I fell on top of Brose?"

"Oh, that was funny. When I looked at Celeres, he could barely keep a straight face."

"Well, in the instant I fell on him, I kissed him."

I lean forward with a huge smile. "You did?"

"Yeah. Obviously, I had to make the first move, and that was the perfect opportunity."

I laugh. "I'll tell Celeres you said thanks."

"You know what else?" she says, her face flushed. "We had sex."

"In a sleeping bag?"

She slaps my arm. "No, in my bed."

"And?"

"It was...okay."

"Oh yeah? Is that hairy beast too much for you in the sack?"

"Not exactly. This is a little awkward, but...I was his first."

I nod, smiling. "Good for him. Good for you. You'll have to teach him some things."

"Oh, don't worry, I've already started."

Tears spring to my eyes.

"What's wrong?" she asks, concerned.

"Nothing. I'm just happy for you. Maybe I'm just a little overemotional from Baxter."

"Oh good. I'm happy, too. I just don't get to see him much, between his job and all the crap he's doing for Krysta."

"I'll talk to her."

"Would you?"

"Of course."

She nods her head, then looks at Baxter. "We should put these love birds outside. Do you want to grab a coffee and relax on my sun porch while we observe them? I'll give you some hairy details."

I guffaw. "Good one Ash. I might have to take a rain check, though. What time is it?" I ask as I stand and brush the dog hair from my shorts.

"Nine-thirty."

"Krysta told me we're behind at the lab. I should get a shower and meet her."

Ashlan nods.

"I'll be back as soon as I can. In the meantime, I also have some things I need to discuss with Krysta besides Brose's working hours."

"About?"

"Last night—a lot of things. I'll catch you up, I promise. Call me if anything changes with Bax?"

"Of course."

I take a last glance at the pups, but they pay me no heed. Baxter looks like he's trying to jump on Milly for a piggyback ride. Ashlan said that different species couldn't breed, but from the looks of them, I have my doubts. Even if they don't have offspring, it won't be for lack of trying.

Despite Bax being sick, I had a good night of sleep, and the sudden rush of happiness this morning was just what I needed.

Now Ash has me thinking of coffee. There's a cafe on the way to work. I'll grab some there after I get cleaned up. I'm sure I'll need the energy to deal with Krysta.

Chapter Thirty-Eight

A Mysterious Delivery

I really do have a lot of questions for Krysta, and that's why I have two coffees when I get to the lab. If I can soften her up with a good mocha, maybe that'll help. Plus, I'm not sure if she's friend or foe, so I'm going to follow the "keep your friends close and your enemies closer" philosophy, like we discussed at the campsite.

In the grand scheme, there are more important questions, but I really want to know what her intentions are with Celeres, so I'm going to start with that.

"Hi," she grumbles as I enter the lab, her face a storm cloud.

Caught off-guard, I take a step back. "What's wrong?"

"I can't believe those morons shut the power off in here. Did they ask you for permission? Who authorized this?"

"I—I don't know. Someone in security. We were down on the planet."

She thrusts her index finger toward the aquarium. "Look at this."

Bubbles rise from the gravel bed and the external filter's

waterfall spills onto the surface of the water, but there are no fish.

"I know, I'm sorry. I told y—"

"I know you told me. I just can't believe it. Those fish were important to me. They think they can disconnect power to this lab, and that is *not the case.* They have no *right.*"

Those fish were her pets, and it makes me think of Baxter. "I'm very sorry about your fish."

"I know. You think I'm overreacting."

I put her coffee on the table. "No, I don't, not at all."

She nods in thanks and takes a small sip. "It's good."

"What can I do to help?"

She pulls the stinger out of a drawer. "I don't know. I'm at a loss."

She ejects the dead battery and gets another one out of her bag. It has a very dim purple glow. "This is my last one. I thought we had more time, but we had to use our reserve units to power Max so he could fix me. Brose hasn't been able to make a replacement, and none of your readings make any sense. We need more for the subspace radios, for Max, and for this stinger. Maybe we can live without Max and the stinger, but once the radios stop working, they're going to shut us down."

"Why?"

"Because we'd be alone out here. We're *light years* from Earth, Leigh. There's no human technology that can communicate at that distance."

"The jump points would still work, right? They can carry letters back and forth?"

"*Mail?* That will not be good enough. Not even close."

"I thought we traded research for batteries? Can't we just—"

"No, we can't just. I have almost nothing left to give them. Not right now."

"What are we going to do?"

We're interrupted by a chime and a gruff male voice on the intercom, "Dr. Collins, you have a delivery."

She jams the stinger back into the drawer and slams it shut. She then presses a button on her desk to unlock the main entrance above. "Okay, bring it in. You know where I want it."

Soon, two burly guys enter the room carrying a refrigerator-size box between them. They head to the back of the lab, through the door, then through the right-hand door beyond that. There's some thumping and bumping sounds from there, and then they leave, taking the empty box with them.

I look at the men, and then back at her. "What was that?"

"I can't tell you right now. Trust me, when I can, I will. We have other problems to worry about."

"That we have no more research to trade for batteries?"

She ignores my question and continues, "And the protests on Earth are getting worse. We have already canceled our next colonist recruitment event."

"Because they can't talk to their loved ones."

"Exactly. It's a Catch-22. We don't have the juice for civilian phone calls, and we can't get any more colonists."

"How is that a Catch-22?"

"It's complicated, a tangled mess. I need Brose to crack the code and replicate those batteries. Like I said, I'm at a loss. I don't know," she says in a far-away voice, looking like she's barely holding herself together.

Obviously, I don't know either, so I close the distance between us and wrap her in a hug. She buries her face in my shoulder, dampening my clean Genomica shirt with tears. After a minute, she breaks the hug to blow her nose. I know I promised Ashlan, but this isn't the best time to ask her to give Brose some time off.

"I'm sorry for breaking down," she says. "If I wouldn't have pricked my finger on the stinger, we would have more batteries, more time, and we wouldn't be in this situation."

"About the stinger." I say.

"Yes?"

"Tell me more about it. I deserve to know."

She blows her nose. "Why not? We're running out of time, anyway. Just remember what you signed. You can't share this information."

I nod.

"It's like a drug. For pleasure. I hoped that you and I could use it together sometime, that we could call it research."

So *that's* what the gold needle does. I don't want her to suspect that I know anything, so I play along. "*What?* It almost killed you!"

"Right, right, right, so I won't be touching that needle again anytime soon, but it never did that before. What's supposed to happen is that you put it on the back of your neck so the needle can touch you, and it makes you feel...good. It's a moot point anyway, after what it did to me. Besides, we're out of batteries."

My eyes narrow as I glance at the drawer holding the stinger. "What...*how* in the world did you ever learn how to use it? I'm sure you didn't just look at it and think, 'Gee, I'll put this needle on my neck.'"

"I won't share the details, but I saw it in action."

"Wow."

"That's it. Remember, it's classified."

I want to ask her how many batteries she drained for "pleasure," versus handing them over for radios, but I think the better of it. "I have something to confess."

She looks at me through red-rimmed eyes, her fingers forming a white fist. "Who else knows about the stinger?" she asks through clenched teeth.

"No, it's not that."

Her shoulders drop, and her fist loosens. She waits for me to continue.

"It's Baxter. I took him to the planet. I know I wasn't supposed to, but Ashlan thought it would be okay."

"And what happened?"

"He got sick. Ashlan wasn't sure if he was going to survive."

"He's better now?"

"Yes. For now. She's watching him."

"That's good. I remember when we were back on Earth, McClure warned you that Baxter could contaminate the planet, and here—"

"It was the other way around," I say.

She nods.

I sigh, then continue, "While there, we came across an Apocritan, and Baxter barked. After that, we locked him in the ship and went for a walk. When we returned, it looked like they tried to break in to get at him."

"I'm not surprised. The Apocritans have an interest in your dog," she says.

"What do you mean, *interest*? How do you know?"

"They sent me a picture. They've never seen a dog. They're curious."

"Curious? Well, they can stay that way because I'm never taking him down there again."

"Good. It's for the best. Now, is there anything else I should know?"

"No, but I need to ask you something. It's about Celeres."

"Oh?"

"You two have history."

"Yes."

"Is that all it is? History?"

"What do you mean?"

"What I mean, is…and I don't know how to say it, but… what are your intentions with him?"

She sits down and takes a sip of her coffee. "We're just friends. That's all we ever were."

"I feel like it's more than that, like you're leading him on."

She puts her coffee down so hard that some of it splashes out of the drink hole, burning her hand. She shakes it off, then looks back at me. "That's ridiculous. How would I do that?"

"Oh, I don't know. By building a racetrack on an alien planet for him, maybe? You know it's his favorite thing."

"Oh, so that's what this is about."

"It's not *just* that. We were on a date when you called him. It was shaping up to be a pretty good one, too."

She pushes her coffee a few more inches away, as if afraid to get burned again. She then leans forward, fixing me with her eyes. "Well, let me ask *you* something. Do you think he still has feelings for me?"

"I don't know, but if there's something going on between the three of us, maybe we should talk it out."

"I don't think that's a good idea, Leigh. Celeres still blames me for giving him the wrong idea, and now I feel like I'm giving you the wrong idea about my intentions."

"Then what *are* your intentions?"

"He's a friend. I feel responsible for what happened in our past. I have connections on Apocrita, and Brose was more than happy to modify some buggies for me. The racetrack is nothing more than an olive branch. I want our scars to heal."

"So you don't have feelings, then?"

"No."

I won't press the issue. I don't want this to turn into an argument, and she said she isn't interested in him romantically, but... can I trust *him*? This is Krysta we're talking about. The person on the station who everyone wants. Why wouldn't he redevelop feelings for her, especially after this gift? Part of me wants to trust him, but the other part of me —the part who has been burned too many times—is convinced that it's only a matter of time before he cracks and begins pining for her again.

Why does everything always have to get complicated? Why can't I just find a guy who ignores every other woman? Do they even exist?

"I'm sorry," I say.

"For what?"

"For putting you on the spot like that. I trust my intuition, but I get it wrong sometimes. I never should have accused—"

"Leigh?"

"What?"

"It's okay. Water under the bridge, bygones, spaceships through the jump gate, and all of that."

"Thanks," I say, looking down. "It must be hard sometimes when you're so irresistible."

Did I just say that out loud?

"What?" she asks, eyes glittering with mirth.

"Nothing. Sorry."

I take a long sip of my coffee and try to deflect her stare.

One corner of her mouth lifts to form a half-smile.

I want her to trust me, and I don't want things to be weird between us. She's answered my questions, and I have no reason to think she's lying. I feel like it's only fair to give her something. Something she wants. Plus, I need to change the subject. "I think I have the answer to our battery problem."

Her eyes widen. "You? What do you mean?"

"It could be dangerous."

"I don't care. What are you talking about?"

"I know where they—the Apocritans—keep them. When we were on the camping trip, we stumbled across a cave filled with racks of fresh batteries. There didn't seem to be any kind of security system."

"Cave? Where? Where were you?"

"We went to the zoo, inside that building."

"You shouldn't have done that. You shouldn't have taken our friends in there."

"Oh, don't worry, I have no plans of ever going in there again."

"It doesn't matter. It's bad enough that you followed me in there the first time. Were you seen?"

"No. It was at night. We didn't see one wasp."

She looks off into space for a few moments, then fixes her stare on me. "Leigh, do *not* go back there. Do you remember your first time there when that wasp reached out toward you?"

I nod.

"Well, let's just say it's not just Baxter they have an interest in. If it were up to them, they'd have you down in that lab, in some kind of cell."

"Like in jail? Just because I broke into the place after hours?"

She shakes her head. "Just listen to me, please. Keep your distance from there."

After seeing what happened during the animal parade, nobody could drag me back to that building. "I promise I won't go back. They just wanted to see it."

She shakes her head until I stop speaking. "So you found a cave with batteries?"

"Yes."

"And you remember where it is?"

"Not exactly. We went down a ladder. It wasn't far from there."

"All right, knowing about this stash could be huge. You've given me a lot to think about. Let's knock off for the day. I'll call you tomorrow and we'll go from there. Will you close up the lab and put the stinger away this time?"

"Sure."

"And please be careful with it. It bites," she says, spinning toward the stairs, her lab coat flaring. I haven't seen her move with such alacrity since before her injury.

After the clatter of footsteps disappears up the stairway, followed by the distant sound of the heavy latch on our security door, I look down at the stinger, and at the small battery charge we have left.

She said this thing can give pleasure.

I'm sure she's tried it.

I know more about it than she does; I should get to have a turn.

Chapter Thirty-Nine

Discharge

I stare at the stinger for a while, then walk over to the empty aquarium and study the clear water, devoid of fish. I lose myself in the dance of bubbles floating haphazardly to the surface.

Should I do it?

Or a better question—why shouldn't I?

I trace my finger along the aquarium, feeling the warmth of the water through its glass. It's normally the perfect temperature, except for the one time.

I could wind up as dead as these fish did.

But I don't think so. Maybe Krysta would lie to me and maybe she wouldn't, but I saw red dots on the back of her neck when she slept in my bed...

I walk back to the table and pick up the stinger, then make sure the golden needle is out. Let's call this Apocritan roulette. Here goes nothing.

I pull my hair over my shoulders, check the battery one more time to verify there's a charge, and I lift the stinger over my head to place the tip of the needle on the back of my neck.

I reach my hand back with my other hand, slip my finger onto the trigger, and pull.

I almost lose my nerve when the calipers close on my neck. When the needle pierces my skin, my anxiety spikes higher than it's ever been. What am I doing?.

Instantly, every care or concern I have vanishes and I'm at ease. I radiate calm, as if I'm lying on the beach after winning a dance competition. Krysta was right; this is wonderful.

But something else builds within. My entire body bristles with physical pleasure. I exhale with an involuntary whimper, even the breath leaving my mouth feels good. I place the stinger on the table, then sink to my knees.

Waves of pleasure course through my body with every heartbeat. I bend down until my forehead touches the floor, and then I fall sideways into a fetal position. I moan again and again.

The feeling builds. When I feel like it can't get any better, it does. Everything feels good—my fingers, my toes, all of me.

My senses cloud. All awareness of my surroundings evaporates while I float on this cloud of ecstasy.

Now my breath comes in ragged gasps, and I put my hand between my legs. The instant I do, I have an explosive, extended orgasm. Flashes of color fill my vision, even with my eyes closed.

I've had great orgasms before, but this is a whole new level. I ride the pulsing waves as long as possible.

Finally, the intensity recedes and I'm able to get back in control of my breathing, bit by bit. I am a limp noodle on the floor.

I lay there for a long time, maybe even an hour, coming down off of whatever high this was.

When I'm finally able to drag myself back to my feet, I feel lighter somehow, euphoric. I look at the stinger in wonder. Wow. It's no wonder there were so many red dots on the back of Krysta's neck.

I look at the stinger's battery compartment, already knowing what I'm going to find. The battery is darker than a black hole, with not even the tiniest hint of purple.

I know how to refill the battery, and it wouldn't be that hard to find some small animal in Beastarium, either. Of course, I would never do such a thing, but I know enough about illegal drugs on Earth to know that there are people out there who wouldn't think twice. Forget powering subspace radios or giant medical robots. They'd *kill* just for the high I just had.

But now I have a dead battery, and Krysta said it was our last one. I suppose I could tell her it discharged while I took a few extra measurements, but would she ever believe that?

I doubt it.

Krysta said that Brose was working on a battery. Maybe he could help. Of course, the last time he was in here, he was just as confused about them as me, which is a scary thought now that I think about it. But if the Chief Engineer of *Sumerian* can't help me, who can? I pull out my phone and call him.

He answers right away, sounding worried, like the person you only call when bad things happen. "Yes?"

"Can you come to the lab? I have a battery problem."

"Is Krysta with you?"

"No, she went home."

"I'll be right there."

～

I stand in the hall outside of the lab so I can let him in when he gets here. It only takes a few minutes, but when he comes into view, I'm taken aback. It looks like he's wearing the same greasy overalls that he wore at the racetrack, and he walks with the gait of someone who has already walked twenty miles. When he gets closer, it's easy to see his red-rimmed eyes. I open the door and hustle him inside.

There's a strange odor about him, something I've never smelled before. It's almost like sawdust, but not quite. Maybe wet sawdust. It's not repugnant or anything, but different.

"What's wrong with you?" I ask in a hushed voice, even though we're in a soundproof room.

He flops down on one of the couches. "I haven't slept. Been workin' ever since we got back. Between my regular job and trying to help Krysta, I've been burning the proverbial candle at both ends."

"What good are you to the station if you're a walking zombie?"

"Trying to make a replacement for Krysta's damn batteries is becoming the bane of my existence."

"Yeah, she's coming unglued about it. She thinks they'll shut the lab down, maybe even the colony itself."

"The colony? She said that?"

"Well, no, but she seems to think that if we don't have subspace radios to communicate with Earth, then they'll shut us down."

"She isn't wrong, but how far they'll go is anyone's guess. What if they pulled out and abandoned the colony to fend for itself?"

There's a long pause between us, and I want to change the subject. "Hey, that was really nice of you to make those race cars for Celeres. You even equipped them with the old-fashioned sound."

His weary face breaks into a slight smile and he nods. "It was fun, a nice side project. You know, the whole reason for the sound is because when they switched to electric vehicles, the spectators hated the silence."

"Yeah, my dad told me about that."

"But here's an interesting tidbit—when electric vehicles became more widespread, there was this vast supply and demand imbalance in lithium, the stuff they used in the batteries."

"Batteries?" I'm beginning to hate that word.

"Yep, batteries, and not just that, it's the search for lithium or a suitable replacement that became one of the top reasons we reached for the stars in earnest."

"Did we find enough?"

"Enough, yes, and some besides, but here we are, once again. It's all about the batteries."

"How is your research and development going on creating a replacement?"

"Terrible. The first problem is that the batteries don't store regular old electricity, at least in the way we know it. The second problem is that they only power alien artifacts. I don't have tools or equipment to take proper readings. I know Krysta has you down there with a multimeter, but that data is garbage."

"I'm wasting my time?"

"Maybe. Probably. See, here's the thing—you *might* find some pattern to it that makes sense."

"But I haven't."

"I know. Me neither. This might be more than you care to hear, but let me talk it out. Maybe it'll help me."

"Go ahead."

"The big problem is that they don't obey Ohm's law. Voltage doesn't equal current times resistance in this world."

He's right about this being more than I care to hear, but I let him continue.

"When I measure the current, it's all over the place, even if voltage and load remain the same."

"Load?"

"Er, sorry, resistance."

"So, what does that mean?"

"It means that I'm a caveman scrawling on walls, surrounded by Apocritan technology that'll I'll never understand."

"Wait. What do you mean, never?"

"Not in my lifetime. I'm only one engineer. I'm good at what I do, but this stuff is, well, *alien*. Every time I try to hook up a human-made battery to a subspace radio, it smokes. At least I haven't had one explode yet."

He closes his eyes and puts his head back.

"Stay safe, Brose. Let me know if there's anything I can do to help."

"Thanks, Leigh."

"I hate to ask you this, but I thought maybe you could help me with a problem of my own."

"Oh, that's right, that's why I'm here. What's up?"

"We're out of batteries. There was one in the stinger, but it...discharged."

He nods. "What do you expect me to do?"

"Do you have any spares?"

"Are you kidding? We have no spares whatsoever. I only have one left in my quarters. It's hooked up to a radio that I've been testing."

"How much juice is left in it?"

"Not much."

"Can I have it?"

He looks at me and blinks a few times, as if he's having trouble understanding. "You want my last battery?"

I nod.

He slaps his forehead with both hands and rubs his face for a few seconds. "Yeah, fine, you can have it. Why not? It's not doing me any good. Maybe I can finally get some sleep."

He grabs a candy bar from one of the vending machines, then turns to leave.

"Thank you, Brose."

"Welcome. I'll be right back." He exits the lab.

I grab a candy bar of my own and head back downstairs. I still feel the afterglow of the stinger and catch myself humming as I approach the telescope.

I spend the next fifteen minutes looking around the colony, the zoo, our campsite, and anything else that looks interesting. I see the racetrack and can't believe I hadn't noticed it before.

When another fifteen minutes goes by, I step away from the scope and pace around. Where is he? I walk back upstairs and poke my head outside to check the halls. No Brose. I text him, but he doesn't respond. I call him, but it goes straight to voice mail.

He wouldn't ghost me, not Brose. He's one of the most genuine guys I've met. Nothing bad could have happened to him, right? He was just grabbing a battery. There's nothing dangerous about that, *right*?

After another fifteen minutes, I try to reach him again, but with no luck. Maybe he *is* ghosting me, I don't know, but I want to get out of this lab. I'll just go back to my quarters and pace there instead.

On the way back, I pass a few people, and I think there's

something weird with their body odors. One guy smells of cut grass, and a woman walks by me smelling like hard-boiled eggs. Then I remember how Brose smelled like wet sawdust.

I touch the back of my neck. Is it possible the stinger did something with my sense of smell?

When I get to my quarters, I go inside, resisting the urge to go looking for other people to sniff.

I pull out my flight controls and VR helmet, but I can't concentrate on that right now. So much has happened. My sense of smell is screwed up, Brose is missing, I killed the battery in the lab. Krysta is going to find out what I did. There's no hiding that. The only thing I can hide is that red welt on the back of my neck, but I'll have to wear my hair down from now on. That's going to suck for running on the treadmill.

It's 7:00 PM already. That stinger really conked me out.

I sit on my bed, rehearsing the things I might say to Krysta tomorrow about how I used up the very last battery we had. If she was on the verge of a breakdown today, I'm afraid of what she will say, or worse, do to me tomorrow.

I sit for a long time.

There's a knock at my door.

Chapter Forty

Lover's Quarrels

That must be Brose.

"It's open!" I call.

The door slides open, and it's not Brose. It's Ashlan. My room immediately smells like a spring rain. She takes two steps inside, then turns around as my door slides shut. She curls her fingers into the air and lets out an anguished growl. Her face is red when she turns back toward me.

I stand bolt upright. "What's wrong? Is it Baxter?"

"Baxter's fine. Why can't we have regular doors? I *really* want to slam a door right now."

I don't know if it's my relief over Baxter or her door comment, but I have to try hard not to smile. "Why?"

"It's Brose. I want to know what the hell is going on."

"What happened to him?" I ask, my heart thudding in my chest.

"I cooked," she says, stomping toward my window. "We were supposed to have dinner at his place. I know he's been working, so I didn't want to call and interrupt him."

I nod, and she continues.

"Dinner at five, I told him. I had the table set and everything."

"Did he ever show up?" I ask, still panicked.

"Oh, he showed up all right. And do you know what he did? He ran right past me to his workshop to get one of those damn batteries. I don't think he even noticed the food."

Oh no.

"So what happened?" I ask in a small voice.

"I stopped him and gave him the business. He tried to apologize, but what's the use? Between his regular job and the stuff he does for Krysta, it's never-ending. There is no time for us."

"I'm so sorry."

"It isn't your fault."

I'm glad she's looking out the window, because I have guilt all over my face. It *was* my fault.

"So where is he now?"

"He's sitting at the table, waiting for me to come back. I'm going to let him stew for a while."

She turns around and gestures to the flight controls and VR headset on my bed. "What's all this stuff?"

"I've been playing with a flight simulator in my spare time."

She picks up the headset. "Yeah? You any good?"

"No."

She laughs and tosses the headset back to the bed. She sits beside it, then reclines until she's on her back looking at my ceiling. She closes her eyes and rubs her temples. "I'm starving."

"What did you make?"

"His favorite, spicy seafood gumbo. I caught the fish myself at Beastarium."

"Wait. You eat the animals there?"

"No, no, no. Just the fish. They multiply like crazy."

"Oh."

"Yeah. Okay, I should get back. He's waited long enough. He'd *better* be waiting. If he eats without me, then it's his ass in the stew pot."

I take a breath. "Before you go—I think there's something you should know."

She crosses her arms. "What?"

"Do you know the stinger we have back in the lab?"

Her face twists in anger. "You mean the weapon that murdered all of those creatures before our very eyes? How could I forget? Why do you ask?"

"I asked Krysta what it did. She swore me to secrecy and everything, and you will not believe this."

Ashlan raises an eyebrow and sits up, making a motion for me to continue.

"She said it gives pleasure."

"*What?*"

"Not only that, but that she wanted to use it with me sometime."

"First, you thought she was attracted to you, and now she wants to kill you?"

"I don't know, Ash. I don't think she knows it can fill batteries. I don't think she would be this twisted up about running out of them if she knew. I bet she'd be down on the planet, filling them up left and right."

"If I ever catch her in Beastarium—"

"You won't, at least not until she knows the truth."

"How does she not know the truth? She just about killed herself with it already."

"Exactly, but I found a secret switch on the stinger. It changes the needle."

"And?"

"And it changes the mode. Both needles are greenish-gold, but one is more green. That's the draining one. The golden one is for pleasure."

"How do you know for sure?"

I gulp, and realization appears on her face. "You idiot. You didn't dare."

I nod. "As she was leaving, she asked me to put it away because she didn't want to touch it."

"You could have been killed."

"I didn't think so. On my journey from Earth, she crawled into bed with me. She had red dots on the back of her neck. I didn't think much about it at the time, but when she told me you have to put the needle back there, it all made sense."

"So what happened?"

"She wasn't kidding. I felt almost every good feeling possible, all at once."

"Even..."

"Yes, even that. It was mind-blowing."

"Wow. I still can't believe you did that."

"I know, me neither. But there's a side effect. It screws up your sense of smell. Now everyone I come across has certain odors."

"Odors? Even me? What do I smell like?"

"Spring rain."

"Could be worse, I guess."

"Everyone smells different. I hate it. I want my old sense of smell back."

"What does Celeres smell like?"

"I don't know. I haven't seen him since."

"Leigh, that thing is evil. Please don't use it again."

"I won't."

"It doesn't add up, though," she says.

"What do you mean?"

"I mean Krysta. She wanted to share that pleasure with you? She obviously wants you. Why is she being so...*nice* to Celeres? She must have put a lot of work into getting that racetrack ready for him. She needs to make up her mind."

I throw up my hands. "I know. I don't know."

"Will we ever understand her?" she asks.

I shrug my shoulders.

"Well, keep an eye on her, I guess. Oh, hey, now that we're catching each other up, I have something to tell you. I almost forgot."

My hands instantly sweat because it has to be something about Baxter, but she already said he was fine...

She continues, "Since Baxter—"

I knew it.

"—is feeling better, there's something I need to do. Like I told you the other night, I'm going to take some time down in my cabin to study the parades more. I need to get to the bottom of them and figure out how and why everything is attracted to that zoo."

"What if Bax gets sick again?"

"Then call me and we'll go from there."

"How's Brose taking it?"

"He knew about the trip, but didn't know when. I plan to tell him tomorrow after an enjoyable night tonight."

"And he ruined it by being late for dinner. I'm sorry."

"It's fine, you know how men can be," she says, tracing her fingers along her thigh. "I shaved and everything."

I give her a contrite look.

She snorts and continues, "But I should get back to him. We'll start with dinner and go from there. Stay in touch and I'm sure I'll see you again soon." She heads for the door.

"Ashlan."

She turns.

"Be careful."

"Always."

As the door slides shut behind her, I'm filled with both relief and concern: relief because Brose is okay except for being in hot water with Ashlan, but concern for Ashlan's trip to the planet. If she's going by herself, who will have her back? It's not a safe city park down there. On the other hand, she was the one saving me during the animal parade. Maybe I'll try not to worry so much.

I'll try, but it won't work.

I return to my flight simulator equipment, eager to get back to it. I slip the haptic gloves and VR goggles on and am pleasantly surprised that I can still see my room through the lenses. After flexing my fingers, I ensure the throttle and flight stick are positioned correctly, and then I press the "link" button on the headset.

My keyboard flashes a "VR Detected" message and then my headset takes over. When I look down where my arms and hands should be, I see their digital equivalents. The gloves and sleeves are black, just like my haptics and my Genomica shirt.

It's like I'm in the actual cockpit of a spaceship, in the hangar of this very station. The hum of the ship is in my ears, and I'm filled with awe at the immersion.

As I lift from the landing pad, I wonder how long Moon must have practiced before jumping in on one of the training exercises. I think it would be a lot of fun if I could get good enough to go up against those guys, and who knows, maybe even spar with Moon herself. For now, I need to focus on controlling the ship. It'll be a while before I learn the weapons.

A message appears in front of me, asking if I want to continue the tutorial. I say yes, and then it picks up where I left off. I steer the ship out of the hangar bay and into space.

The multi-colored stars greet me like an old friend as I leave the station behind me. When I turn my head, it's like being in a real cockpit; the view is spectacular from every pane of glass, and an array of controls surrounds me. I dream of the day when I know what they all do.

The tutorial wants me to practice rolls. Just as I turn the stick, there's a female voice in my ears.

"Hey, Birdie."

"Moon?"

"That's me."

"What are you doing?"

"Look to your left," she says.

I do, and there she is, her ship right beside mine. She points accusingly from the cockpit. "You almost rolled right into me. Don't you know to look at your radar before moving around?"

I might not be an expert pilot, but the radar is pretty obvious, front and center in the panel before me. I feel stupid. "I didn't even think about it. I was just following the tutorial."

"Rookie mistake. Situational awareness is key to your survival."

"But it's just a simulator."

"Never think like that. Don't just practice, practice to perfection. That way, you'll always do it right."

We both float there in a sort of awkward silence, and then out of nowhere, I smell my grandma's special peach pie. It's only been a few hours, and I'm so tired of my nose misfiring since using that stinger. I hope and pray that my sense of smell gets back to normal.

"Leigh, you okay over there?"

I snap out of it. "Uh, I think I was going to sneeze."

"Oh, that sucks. There's nothing worse than sneezing in your cockpit, especially when your hands are full. Anyway, I just wanted to drop in and say hello. I'll let you get back to your rolls."

"Okay, thanks for stopping. Wait, I have an idea. Actually, it's a question."

"What's up, Birdie?"

"How closely does the simulator mirror the real world?"

"Real close. All the stuff in space is very accurate. Most of the planet is empty, though. You could fly down, but most of it's just rocks and grass. Why?"

"Could you show me how to fly to the jump gate?"

"The jump gate? The gate to Pluto? You planning on skipping town?"

"I just want to see how it works, that's all."

"Sure, okay, follow me."

She pivots away and flies off into space. It's everything I can do to keep up. She slows as she approaches a shiny metallic shape hanging in space.

The shape is more like an immense ring, a half-mile across. Lights blink along its surface.

"It's huge," I mutter.

She snickers.

I blink hard and try to take it all in. "So, what do you do? Just fly right through the middle?"

"Yep, that's it. See that button above you with the ring of stars on it? Press it."

When I do, every light on the jump gate turns into a brilliant spotlight, pointing right at my ship. It's blinding. "I can't see."

"I know. I don't know why they do that. Your ship will take it from here. You'll fly straight through and then—"

There is a tapping on my shoulder, in real life. I scream.

Moon gasps. "Leigh? What's—"

I rip the headset off and return to reality. Celeres is here, standing right next to me, looking down at me like, well, the way I look at trigonometry. He holds a bouquet of star flowers, each one still glowing from the light it captured from the stars. I think back to the time we flew close to them and he said how difficult they were to get.

The peach smell was him. Oh god, the peach smell. My eyes grow wide and I forget to breathe. The stinger makes him smell like this. This is why Krysta calls him Peaches. He doesn't even know.

"What's all this, Leigh?"

I blink a few times. I'm reeling from the shock of his presence, of his scent. All I can manage is, "I didn't steal it."

"Huh?"

I shake the headset and nod at the gloves, throttle, and stick. "This stuff."

"What? I don't care about that. I heard you say jump gate. Is there something I should know?"

I inhale deeply through my nose. "Do you smell a peach smell?"

"No. Leigh, what...are you okay?"

"No, I'm not. There's something wrong with my sense of smell, and Bax has been having weird health problems."

He sits down beside me and puts a hand on my knee. "Do you think something happened to either of you on the planet?"

"I don't know. It's just that flying the simulator helps me feel, I don't know, less trapped if that makes any sense."

He looks hurt. "You feel trapped here?"

I shrug.

"With me?"

"I don't know."

His whole body seems to deflate. "This is like déjà vu."

"What's that supposed to mean?"

He looks up at the ceiling, and when he speaks, his voice sounds a little weird. "I'd give anything to make a relationship stick."

"Well, that's funny."

He whips his heard toward me, eyes flashing. "How is that *funny*?"

I grab his hand and remove it from my knee. "I'd give anything to not feel like each day with my boyfriend is my last."

He places the bouquet on the bed. "Help me understand, Leigh. What have I done wrong?"

I stand. "I didn't appreciate it when Krysta kept texting you during our pizza party. I didn't find it romantic when she interrupted our date to go see the racetrack she commissioned just for you."

He closes his eyes. "Leigh—"

"Do you still have feelings for her?"

He looks down. "No. Not anymore."

"She sure seems to have them for you."

Now he stands. "Maybe I'll just never understand women."

"Maybe you should try harder."

He points at me. "Maybe you should try to understand men."

Oh no, he didn't. I feel blood rushing to my face. "Why would you say that to me?"

He rubs his forehead, and he takes a minute to find his

voice. "I don't know. I'm sorry. I thought this time could be different."

"So did I."

His beautiful eyes bore into mine for another moment before he turns and storms out of my quarters.

Moon's voice continues to sound from my headset. I tell her I'm okay, then turn it off.

I stare at the flowers he brought, and then back to my door, willing him to come back.

But he doesn't.

Chapter Forty-One

Making Up is Fun to Do

I barely slept last night. After Celeres left, I put the flowers in water and then stomped around my quarters for a good hour. He shouldn't have just let himself in like that. Did he even knock? Would I have been able to hear him if he did? Anyway, it doesn't matter; he stood there and listened to my private conversation with Moon. He has some nerve.

And now Ashlan is leaving.

And I never got that battery from Brose.

And I have to go to the lab and deal with Krysta.

And I'm really beginning to hate it here.

When I look in the mirror, there are circles under my eyes and my face just looks...saggy. I'm still wearing my Genomica clothes from yesterday, and my hair could use a touch-up. I don't care. Not today, not right now.

I grab a cereal bar from the fridge and gnaw at it woodenly as I leave my quarters. Crumbs fall to the ground as I walk.

I'm dreading this meeting with Krysta. By now, she already knows the last battery is dead, and now that I know about her dirty little *Peaches* secret, I don't even want to be around her.

But I have no choice. My best friend is down on the planet, my boyfriend is pissed at me, and all I have left is this job. Soon, I might not even have that.

~

If I thought I looked bad this morning, Krysta is worse. Her eyes are all red and she sniffs as I enter the lab. This is getting to be a trend with her.

Before I even take three steps into the room, she glares at me.

"Let me see the back of your neck," she snaps.

"Fine," I say, pulling my hair up and turning around, "I did it, okay? I had a right to know."

I stand like that for a half minute in silence before I let my hair drop and turn back to face her, not sure what to expect.

"We're done," she says, "but you knew this was coming. I hope your fun was worth it. When they find out..."

"Find out what? Don't even think of throwing me under the bus for this. I've seen the back of *your* neck. Unlike you, I've only used it one time."

For a second she looks like I just slapped her, but then her eyes narrow.

"You've seen? How? How long have you known?"

"Does it matter?"

"What else do you know?"

"I know why your nickname for Celeres is Peaches."

"It's pretty obvious, isn't it? You could start calling him that too, you know."

Ew, I'm not calling him any nickname that she came up

with. What I want to do is get a whiff of Krysta with this new nose of mine. I drift further into the room, approaching her. When I get within ten feet, I stop. This should be close enough.

"I talked to Brose," I say. "He doesn't think he can synthesize the batteries."

She rolls her eyes. "I have another job for Brose, now."

"What is it?"

"I'm not ready to talk about it."

"Well, whatever it is, now he can work as long as he wants. Ashlan went planetside."

Her eyes widen. "She *did*?"

"Yeah."

Krysta nods to herself. "This could work," she mutters.

"What could work?"

She ignores me and taps on her computer for a few moments, then nods. "You're right, she's not on the station."

This whole time, I'm inhaling through my nose, trying to determine Krysta's scent, but other than the undertones of the toothpaste from her constant brushing, I detect nothing.

"Can I ask you something?" I ask.

"Hmm?"

"What do *I* smell like?"

"You don't want to know."

"Why not? Is it dog poop or something?"

She snickers. "I'll tell you sometime. Not today."

This is ridiculous. It's like she's suddenly closed off from me.

"Look, I'm sorry about the stinger. I wanted to know what it was like. Can you blame me?"

"And risk your own death? I already told you we can't

power Max anymore. He can't fix you. You saw what it did to me."

"You said it gives pleasure. I wanted to learn the truth."

"But at what cost? I can't trust you anymore. You need to go."

"You're firing me?"

"There's no work, Leigh. Unless I can get some more batteries, this is the beginning of the end."

"What do I do? Where do I go?"

Her eyes are wet again and her voice wavers. "I don't know. If I can figure something out, I'll let you know."

"So that's it, then?"

"Yeah, that's it. I'll see you around, Leigh."

Although she's shutting me out and dismissing me, a part of me wants to close the distance between us and comfort her. I still have a soft spot for her I can't explain, but I don't think a hug is in the cards right now. I back away and head for the exit. She says nothing as I walk through the door and make my way upstairs.

It seems different now. The lab, I mean. When I first got here, there was the promise of a new career and a new life. Now, everything is in question.

I wander through the halls, past the other labs, the coffee shop, clothing store, and all the people busy at their day jobs. I don't know, maybe I could be a barista, make some tips, and even get free coffee.

I return to my quarters. My VR equipment sits at the foot of my bed. Since I have nothing else to do, I plunk myself down on the mattress and pull the stuff toward me. It'll at least pass the time until I get hungry or something.

The headset blinks to life as soon as I put it over my eyes. I'm still at the stargate, but Moon is gone, of course. As

I float here in simulated space, the stargate's lights dance around its circumference in a hypnotic circle.

I watch it for a while, wondering what it would be like to return home. This gate would take me to Pluto, and I'd have to get myself the rest of the way to Earth. Could I do it? I could always try. This is just a simulation, after all. What's the worst that could happen?

But I don't activate the gate. I continue to float in simulated space with my scattered thoughts. After a few minutes, my radio crackles to life.

"Who's there?" I ask.

"Permission to come aboard, Birdie?" comes Moon's voice.

"Huh? You can do that?"

"Sure! Watch."

Not knowing what she means, I look around the cockpit for some sort of hatch or door. In the next instant, she materializes in the copilot seat.

"Hi," she says with a sprightly grin.

"Uh, hi."

"Whatcha doing?"

"I don't know. I lost my job, and now I have all the free time in the world. I thought maybe I'd fly for a bit, but I don't really feel like doing much of anything."

"Oh."

"So, where are you?" I ask.

"In my room. I thought you might like a copilot."

"So you can actually use the controls in my ship from your own simulator? That's pretty cool."

"Yep. So what do you want to do?"

"Wait a second. How accurate are these simulators?"

"Very."

"And everything you can do on a ship, you can do here?"

"Yep. That's the only way to learn."

"Celeres took me on a date once and projected a movie onto the hull of the station. Could we even do that?"

"Probably. That's a pretty cool idea. Kudos to him for thinking of it. It's not really a movie projector, per se, but there's no reason it couldn't be programmed to do that."

"Can we try it?"

"You want to spend simulator time watching a movie?"

"Just humor me, please."

"Suit yourself," she says, punching some keys on the pad in front of her. "This is actually a beam weapon we've been working on."

"Like a laser gun?"

"Exactly, except it's still a work in progress. We still use kinetic weapons exclusively. There's nothing like putting high-velocity steel on target, baby. Oh, I see what he did. He must have put hours into this program. It's in the fleet's database."

She taps another key, and *Shawshank Redemption* continues playing where we left off. It's projected onto the stargate.

"Pause it," I say.

"Like I said, pretty cool," she says as she pauses the video. "He must really like you. There have to be two thousand lines of code here."

"Last time I saw him, we parted on a sour note. I want to surprise him with this, to pick him up and finish the date in the simulator."

Moon smiles. "That's romantic."

I hug myself and blush. "We'll have everything we need."

"Well, not everything. There's a lot you can do in the simulator, but there's a lot you can't do, if you know what I mean."

"That's okay. I just want to take things at least one small step in a better direction. Can you show me what to do?"

"It's easy. Just go into this menu, search for Project L, and press Start. I assume the L is for Leigh."

I smile. "At least it's not Project K."

"What?"

"Nothing."

"Okay, well, good luck on your virtual date. I guess I'll get back to training. The others are getting better. They almost took me out in the last exercise."

"Thanks, Moon."

"Don't mention it. Celeres is off work today, so this is meant to be. Go get him, girl."

Her image blinks out and I'm alone again in my virtual ship.

This is going to be great. I fly back to the space station, land, then pull my VR gear off just as my phone buzzes. It's a text from Krysta.

Hey, do you want to meet in the lab quick?

This isn't a good time. I'm getting ready to see Celeres. Can it wait?

Sure. Hit me later.

I strip my clothes off and head into the shower with a spring in my step.

I go over my plan while I wash my hair. This whole thing will be a surprise. I'll grab some popcorn on the way to his place so that he can have it in real life while we're in the simulation. After that, I'll tell him to put his VR gear on, then wait. I'll come back here, log in myself, invite him aboard, and we will finish the movie that was so rudely interrupted the other night. After that, I'll just go back to his place for the rest.

After the shower, I put some makeup on and fix my hair. I put on the green skirt he bought me and I wear the white blouse, untucked. I like the look. I think he will, too.

When I leave my quarters and head to the shopping zone where there are more people, I'm reminded that the stinger still dominates my sense of smell. It crosses my mind to refer to it as the stinker, but I'm too annoyed with my screwed-up nose to find any humor in this.

At least when I get to the popcorn vendor, the smells from the various flavors of popcorn dominate the air. I get a bag of caramel corn and munch on a few pieces while I walk to his place. I pass one guy who smells like a moldy basement, and I steer far clear of him. It's a shame, too, because he's decent-looking. I'm glad Celeres got peaches. I can live with that.

I'm in mid-crunch when I get to his door. I already ate a quarter of the bag. This stuff is amazing.

I place my palm on the pad and his door slides open. Celeres's display is on, showing his racing game. He sits on the couch with his back to me. Krysta is there, straddling him, looking in my direction, the top three buttons of her blouse undone. Her eyes meet mine, and she reaches up to pull her shirt closed with one hand.

Chapter Forty-Two

Forbidden Kiss

The blood drains from my face and I feel lightheaded. I slump against his door frame and lean my head against it as my eyes fill with tears. I drop the popcorn and it scatters across the floor.

No.

No, no, no, no, no, no.

This can't be happening. Not again. Not with him, oh please, not with him. And with *her,* of all people. But of course it's with her. It was always going to be with her.

She stands up from the couch, buttoning her shirt. She's fully clothed, so at least I didn't have to witness them screwing.

His head swivels back to see me.

"Leigh?" he says in a thick voice. Has he been drinking?

The bastard doesn't even stand up.

I slap the door-open panel so hard that a sharp pain blossoms in my wrist and races up my arm. Once the door opens and I'm back out in the hallway, I turn to get one last glimpse of them before the door slides shut. Krysta stands there, looking back at me. Celeres still sits on the couch.

Bile rises in my throat, I feel the jagged popcorn down there, begging to come up. I force it down and walk briskly, mindlessly away, wanting only to put distance between them and myself. Neither one of them tries to follow. My wrist hurts. My heart hurts.

❧

There is only one on this station I have left: Baxter. I walk to Beastarium in a fog. If people say hello to me, I don't hear them. If they smell good or bad, I don't notice.

I find my way soon enough and head to Baxter's place. I open the door to his room, and find him there on his bed, curled up with Milly. They look a little like Yin and Yang. I smile.

I crouch down to pet him. "Love is always so pure with you, buddy. Why can't I be so lucky?"

Milly is the first to stir. She opens her eyes and licks my sore wrist (could she know?), then she arches her neck and licks Bax.

I scratch him behind the ear, just the way he likes. He lets out a snore sound and opens his eyes. When he sees me, he rolls onto his back so I can scratch his belly.

A sneeze from behind interrupts our moment.

"Bless you," I say reflexively as I turn.

A young woman stands in the doorway. She's in her mid-twenties, and has shoulder-length, black hair. She wears a name tag that says ALLISON. "Thanks. You must be Leigh Shires."

"I am. Do you prefer Allison or Ally?"

She smiles and rolls her eyes. "I prefer Meri. Allison is my last name."

"Oops, sorry."

"No problem. It happens all the time. I let Baxter's girlfriend in. I hope you don't mind."

"Not at all. It's good for them both."

She kneels down and pets each one at the same time. "Ashlan told me all about him. I know his history. Don't worry, he's in excellent hands with me."

She exudes confidence, which puts me at ease. "Okay. Call me if anything comes up."

"I will."

She smells like anise.

I leave Beastarium and head back to my quarters to get out of this silly outfit and into some running clothes because I'm due for a serious run. I find a black sports bra and biker shorts combo, then put my hair up. I grab three bottles of water from my fridge and head to the gym.

It's 3:00 on a Tuesday, and the workout room is empty. I pick the same treadmill I used back when I outran Celeres. It's been a while since my last big run, so I start slow. I gotta shake the rust off. As the first hour passes, a few people come in and I do my best to ignore their smells in my deep breathing.

The only time I falter is when I cough at someone's balsamic vinegar scent. It belongs to an old lady who walks in wearing a one-piece swimming suit and has the hairiest legs I've ever seen on a woman. She saunters past me and leaves through the natatorium door across the room. After her, several other station dwellers follow her in.

Another hour passes and the hairy lady leaves. I try not to breathe through my nose as she walks by.

Another hour, and I'm in my groove. Every time I think

about Celeres, I temporarily increase the incline to blast those thoughts from my mind and focus on my breathing instead.

After the fourth hour, I'm getting close to the end of the workout—26.2 miles.

I let the treadmill slow to walking speed and I reach for my water bottle. I feel better, and I feel optimistic about Baxter. As for Celeres, I'm spending as much effort as possible to not think about him.

As I cool down, the breeze from the oscillating gym fans hits me. I close my eyes and inhale deeply through my nose, filling my lungs with...*her*. I know it's her without looking. I know the smell of the Dental Hygiene Queen by now. I open my eyes and stare toward the entrance.

Krysta stands there, wearing a blue bikini and holding a towel. She regards me with pursed lips. "I knew I'd find you here."

"What do you want?"

She approaches me. "Let's go for a swim. You look like you could use one."

I keep walking on the treadmill, looking straight ahead.

She stands in front of me. "You can't trust men, you know."

I look down, drops of sweat fall from my hair onto the moving belt. "You told me you were just friends, that you weren't interested."

She turns and walks toward the pool. "I guess he still has feelings."

Every shred of peace and calm that I worked for over the last four hours vaporizes. I stop the treadmill belt.

"Krysta?"

"I'll be in here," she says over her shoulder as she disappears into the natatorium.

I gather up my empty water bottles and phone, then step off of the treadmill and cross the room, following her in before the door slides shut. She's a few steps away, tossing her towel onto a chair. I put my belongings on a nearby table. She turns to me, eyebrows lifted.

"You remember," I say.

"Remember what?"

"Erica. You remember her, don't you?"

"Wasn't she the one—"

"—The one who cheated with Joe back on Earth, yes."

"And you had me kick her out of the program as revenge before her plane ever landed in Phoenix. Leigh, are you threatening me?"

I try not to clench my teeth. "But why Celeres? You could have anyone."

"I know," she says, slipping down the ladder into the pool. She takes a gulp of air and disappears beneath the surface, swimming away.

With my biker shorts and sports bra being soaked from sweat anyway, I kick off my shoes and jump in after her.

She pops up several feet away and then swims toward me, stopping when she's within punching distance. We stand facing each other, the water halfway up our chests.

"I already told you I don't have feelings for Celeres," she says, panting slightly from the exertion, her breath puffing against my face.

I snort. "You aren't making any sense. I know what I saw."

She reaches for my shoulder, but I flinch away.

"Leigh. He's a guy. He can't help himself."

I shake my head. "He's a grown man, and yes, he can."

"Maybe I could make it up to you."

"How?"

"Baxter."

"Leave him out of this."

"Listen, if he has any more problems, I know Apocritan scientists who can help him. If Baxter did contract some sort of disease or virus from the planet, they would know what to do. They would be happy to examine him if you wanted. Just say the word."

"I would have to talk to Ashlan about it first."

"I understand. Just know that my offer stands."

Somehow, during the conversation, she inched closer. She's just about at head-butting distance now.

For as angry as I am about recent events, I'm helpless to her magnetism, and I let her advance. I swear, the woman's a siren.

"I want you to be happy," she says.

I drag my brain back into focus. "Maybe you can make Ashlan happy, too. She's ready to break up with Brose because you're drowning him in battery work when he already has a full-time job. They never see each other."

"They both know that our mission comes first, plus if I don't get those subspace radios powered, it's my ass."

"At any cost?"

"I always get what I want, Leigh," she says, getting closer still.

I think I know what she wants right now.

"Krysta," I say, just above a whisper.

"Yes?"

"Tell me what I smell like."

She closes her eyes, inhales, then sighs, her breath once again washing over me. "Your scent is absolute intoxication, like a field of sensual flowers and fresh air. When you sweat, like when you're on that treadmill, it's amplified so much that it's maddening."

She reaches toward me and puts her hands around my hips. "You're trembling."

She's right. I'm melting right here in front of the woman who just tried to steal my man. It seems so wrong, so... what's wrong with me?

She pulls me in so we're touching. She isn't athletic like me. She's soft, and her shape fits against me like a silk pillow, her skin electric. She leans her head in, her breath tickling my nose.

She closes the rest of the distance, and her lips are on mine. And then her tongue, oh...oh. In that infinite moment, every ounce of my restraint shreds into a million pieces, and I kiss her back.

Her hand travels down my stomach and into my shorts. She keeps reaching until she finds that place between my legs. She presses on it and a lightning bolt of pleasure shoots through my body.

I move my hand up her torso and under her bikini cup, flipping it up. I cradle her breast in my hand, and then pinch her nipple. She moans, still kissing me.

We both moan and kiss and never hear when the door to the natatorium opens.

Chapter Forty-Three

Breaking Up is Hard to Do

"**E**xcuse me?"

When his voice rings out, it takes us both by surprise. I look in that direction and Krysta fixes her bikini top. Celeres stands at the edge of the pool, his arms crossed, his jaw clenched.

Krysta's eyes go wide and she looks like she wants to sink to the bottom of the pool.

I face him with defiance. "Jealous?"

Did I really just say that? I brace myself for whatever comes next.

He stares at me, ignoring Krysta. "What's going on?"

"You have no right to ask me that, not anymore."

He points a trembling finger at Krysta. "It was all her. *She* came to *me* looking for comfort because she had to shut the lab down."

"*Comfort?* You outdid yourself on that one, big guy."

"I didn't touch her, but I guess it doesn't matter to you. I mean, it *obviously* doesn't," he says, casting a glance at Krysta.

"That's bullshit. I know what I saw. Don't turn this around on me."

"Whatever. What's it matter now that you have each other? How could you even consider being with her? You see what she's like."

Krysta's mouth drops open. "Wait a second. What's that supposed to mean?"

"You know what I mean."

She straightens her straps. "Hey, I go with the flow. You didn't object when I unbuttoned my blouse."

While she talks, I wade to the ladder at the other side of the pool, putting distance between myself and the both of them. Unfortunately, I can't leave the natatorium without passing him, so I climb out and stand there with my arms crossed at my chest, water pooling at my feet.

His eyes burn at her, and he turns back to me.

Me, the woman who still has the taste of Krysta in her mouth. Should I be the one apologizing? Am I a hypocrite? Am I to blame?

"Leigh, I know what you saw, and I know how it looked. It all happened so fast and my mind is spinning over it. But it doesn't even matter, because now I know the truth, that I would never make it with either of you. It was all a lie. Have fun. You two deserve each other."

While he talks, I'm thinking that whatever just happened between Krysta and me came out of nowhere, just as he said it did for them, and probably just as fast.

He continues, "Leigh, this hurts, it does. It was bad enough when I saw you were trying to find a way back to Earth, but this? With her? It's going to take a long time to get over this one."

I huff through my nostrils. "I told you not to turn this around on me."

But he doesn't listen, and now I don't have to worry about passing him to escape the room because he turns on his heel and storms out.

Krysta is still in the pool and turns to face me. "Well?"

"What?"

"This is where you decide."

I take a few steps backward. "What did you do?"

"What do you mean?"

"How did you do it?"

"What are you talking about?"

"Celeres, me, and every other person on this station lusts after you. What's your game?"

"Look, I don't know what you're talking about. Yes, I'll admit I use my God-given assets to get what I want. Is that what you want to hear?"

"So what is it you *want*?"

"I told you I go with the flow. I live in the moment. If it feels good, I do it. Tell me you didn't enjoy what we just did."

I did enjoy it, but I will not give her the satisfaction. I clamp my mouth shut and several seconds pass.

Her face twists into a curious expression. "Hey, wait a minute. You said Ashlan was planetside."

I'm stunned for a moment by the change of subject, but force a reply, "Yeah, so?"

"Then who is taking care of Baxter?"

My stomach ties into knots just thinking of him. "Somebody else. She promised she knew what to do."

She nods thoughtfully. "Oh, okay."

I shake my head because this whole thing is so unreal. "I'm going to my quarters. I want to be alone."

She parts her lips and licks them playfully. "You sure?"

"I'm sure."

Without wasting one more second, I gather up the rest of my stuff and fast walk out of the natatorium and gym. I pull out my phone and block Celeres.

And then I block Krysta, too. I've had enough.

I barely make it to my quarters with a straight face. I flop onto my bed face-first onto the pillow and scream until the tears come.

Chapter Forty-Four

Relapse

When I finally stop sobbing, I dwell on Krysta's line of questioning before I left. Is she trying to cast doubt on Baxter's care? I pull out my phone and call Meri at Beastarium.

"Hello?"

"It's Leigh. How's he doing?"

"Oh, hi. I'm not there at the moment, but he was fine when I left. Do you want to come meet me at Solar? You could grab a bite, I'll catch you up, and we'll go visit him."

"Yes, that would be great. I'll be there in fifteen."

I disconnect the call.

Meri's waiting for me in a corner booth, and she ordered for me. It's the same as hers: some sort of meat and vegetable medley. Looks healthy.

As soon as I settle into my chair, I ask a nearby waitress for an IridiDew Brew.

I can only pick at this food. My stomach is in such knots that I don't think I can eat for a week.

I bury my face in my hands. "Thanks for ordering. So he's still fine?"

"Yes."

"Thank God."

When my drink arrives, I down it all at once.

Meri raises an eyebrow. "Thirsty?"

I wipe a trickle from my chin. "Yeah."

She shakes her water glass at me. "Be sure to stay hydrated."

The waitress motions to me, wondering if I want another, but I wave her away.

"One and done," I continue, making a show of picking up my glass of water.

I force myself into some small talk with her. I learn that she's one of the original *Sumerian* people, here even before Ashlan. She used to run Beastarium, but now only fills in when Ashlan needs help. It turns out she's allergic to many of the pollens and such from the planet, and asked to be reassigned. Now, when she's not filling in, she works in one of the research labs.

She finishes before me, and I push my plate away after eating only a quarter of the food. We've been here twenty minutes, and I'm eager to head to Beastarium.

I'm unprepared for what I see when I open the door to Baxter's room: he's sprawled on his bed, looking lifeless. Milly is in the far corner of the room, shaking the same way Bax would during a thunderstorm. Meri and I fall to our knees where

Baxter lies. I put my hand on his belly, afraid it might be cold, but it isn't. He's warm and his chest rises and falls with his shallow breathing. I'm filled with a mixture of relief and terror.

"You said he was doing better," I say in a tone that's more accusatory than I intend.

"He was! This makes no sense. He was fine before dinner, I swear."

Her voice trails off, and she looks over at Milly. If Milly could melt into the walls right now, I think she would.

"What is going on?" asks Meri, as if Milly could answer.

I bolt to my feet. "I'm calling Ashlan."

Meri nods her head and picks up Baxter. "I'm going to hook him up to some equipment, get a read on his vitals, and get him stable."

She exits the room with Baxter's floppy form in her arms, his head rolling back and forth with each step she takes toward the main building.

I shut the door and slump against the wall, pulling my phone out. I stab Ashlan's phone number with my thumb and wait while it rings. After about the third ring, I pace the room.

Finally, she answers.

"Leigh? Is everything okay?"

"It's Baxter. He's sick again, worse than last time."

"Meri hasn't called me."

"This is new. Meri is with him now, hooking him up to the machines. You told me to call you if he relapses. We need you."

"Leigh, I'm so sorry. I can't leave right now."

"Ashlan! I—"

"Listen, you can send him down to my cabin. Just take him to McClure and have him fly him down."

McClure. Shit.

"McClure won't do it. He hates Baxter, and he hates me, too."

"I'll call him and make the arrangements."

There's no sense in arguing. I'll just have to suck it up and do this. "Okay, I'll get Baxter right now and take him to the hangar."

"And Leigh—"

"What?"

"I've seen more of that stinger thing in action. We need to get that thing off the station before Krysta figures out what it's for. If she learns how to refill her own batteries, she'll do it. She won't be able to resist that temptation, and I know she's getting more desperate by the day."

"You want me to steal the stinger?"

"Yes, send it down with Baxter. Hide it in his bag of dog food."

I will get into a lot of trouble over this, but Ashlan is right. With unlimited batteries, Krysta could power all the radios she wants *and* have all the pleasure she can handle. Genomica would love her and she'd be set for life.

"Okay. I was with Krysta a bit ago at the pool. She must be home by now and nowhere near the lab."

"All right, I'll call McClure. He'll be waiting."

I disconnect and jog to the building where Meri took Bax. Milly follows me. Meri looks over at me with a worried expression. "He's stable, but—"

I brush past her, and disconnect the pads and an IV needle. A splash of blood squirts out when I do that, staining Meri's shirt. She wraps gauze tape around his leg where the needle was.

"What are you doing?" she asks, aghast.

"Ashlan said to send him down. I'm taking him to the hangar. Can I have a big bag of food for him?"

Meri steps away and returns with a cart holding a massive bag of kibble on the bottom shelf. "Here, I'll help you put him on."

We scoop up Baxter and put him on top. His eyes open a slit and I bend down so that we're nose-to-nose. "Hang in there, buddy. Please."

Concern fills Meri's eyes. "Do you want me to come?"

I shake my head. "No, I have to stop by my lab first. Thank you, Meri. For everything."

She nods, and I push the cart out of the room.

My legs are so worn out, but I press on. Milly lopes along just behind me. I almost forgot she was here.

First, we go to the lab and I get the stinger. I bury it deep within the food. Two minutes later, we're off again.

When we get to the hangar, McClure is in his normal spot, arms crossed at his chest. He has a smug look on his face. He smells like a dumpster. Why am I not surprised?

He sneers. "I told you this would happen."

I really want to punch him in his ugly face. "Let's go."

He steps aside. "Take him to the ship, put him in a stall."

I come conspicuously close to hitting him with the cart as I head to the ramp. Once inside, I do as he says. Milly hovers around us, sniffing and licking Bax. Apparently, she's going, too. McClure follows behind.

He looks at the dogs, and his eyes narrow. "I told you back on Earth. I said he could introduce any sort of illness to the planet, but looks like the planet got him first. He *should* die. He has it comin', and maybe it'll teach you to listen to your betters."

Okay, that does it. I slap him as hard as I can, and he takes a step back.

He rubs his jaw but has a nauseating grin. "I like a woman with spunk."

I fix him with a look of icy hatred. "I'm coming too."

He rubs his jaw again. "After that? I don't think so. You get off of my ship and I'll be your dog taxi, or maybe I should say hearse."

I lift my chin. "I *said*, I'm coming."

He shakes his head and looks down at Baxter. "I'm not taking you. Are you sure you want to waste time talking to me?"

"Fine. Whatever. Here's his food. See that Ashlan gets it."

He slams the stall door. "If you say so."

He smirks and I really want to hit him again, but that last slap exacerbated my arm injury from earlier, and now I'm in serious pain. I spin on my heel and fast-walk back down the ramp, not looking back. He's still in the midst of an evil chuckle as the ramp closes, sealing the back of the ship.

Seething, I stomp back to my quarters. As I pass one of the corridor windows, I get a good view of McClure's ship, *Ice Arrow*, leaving the station and thrusting down to the planet. I put my hand on the glass for a moment, and then continue my walk.

I'm beyond exhausted, but I know there will be no sleep for me tonight.

Chapter Forty-Five

Laptop

Surprisingly, I was wrong about that. When I open my eyes, I check my phone to see that it's 7:00 AM, Wednesday, July 27th, 2225.

Wednesday, humpday. There won't be any humping today.

I drop my phone to my sheets and stretch. I know I needed that sleep. I didn't even brush my teeth last night. I trace my tongue around my dirty teeth in disgust, then remember that just twelve hours ago, my tongue was in Krysta's mouth. I shake my head in wonder. That was a first for me.

Baxter.

I get my phone again and text Ashlan.

Good morning. How is he?

I wait, but she doesn't respond. My stomach twists into a pretzel and my hand grows ice cold. What if he's dead? He can't be dead. While I wait, I replay the scene from the hangar last night in my head and hope McClure just stays on the planet. I hate that he's always in the hangar, but I guess it doesn't matter as much since I don't have a reason to go there anymore.

There is a photo attached to her text message. It's of Baxter looking at the camera while doing his happy pant. Milly is in the background, eating out of a bowl on the floor. I'm filled with relief and joy.

This is good. As long as Baxter can stay healthy, maybe she can figure out what his weird problem is. If we can give him something to stop the relapses, or something to treat them while they're happening, maybe he can live out the rest of a normal doggy life. If anyone can help, I know it's Ash.

I don't know what I'm going to do today. We're still out of batteries, so there's no job. Things with Celeres are messed up, and Krysta tells me I have to decide.

When Krysta's in the room, all I want to do is touch her, but is she a good person? It seems pretty obvious that she wants me, but is it possible that she staged the whole thing with Celeres just to break us up?

I mean, he's to blame, too. He might not have had his hands on her when I walked in, but he still let her climb onto his lap. Then again, her breast was in my hand just a bit ago. A part of me feels guilty even if I was self-right-eously vindictive when it happened.

It would be smart just to punt on both of them and move on. But I can't. At least not yet. He's kind, funny, thoughtful, successful, and as Ashlan was quick to remind me during our hike, even knows how to cook. I think back to our night in the sleeping bag when we rolled around on the ground. I can still feel the thrill of when he slid inside of me for the first time. I get wet every time I think about it.

Excuse me for a second while I catch my breath...

...But for as amazing and perfect that Celeres is, when I'm together with Krysta, the attraction is unstoppable. Is it infatuation? Crush? The excitement of something different?

I don't know how I got myself into this.

I hop into the shower, and while I'm scrubbing my hair, I decide that it's a good idea to just let everything cool off for a day or two. I'll stay away from both of them and just focus on Baxter's condition. I could get some running in and maybe experiment with the simulator. I'll stay away from the pool for now.

I'm just rinsing off when my phone rings from my bed in the other room. I slip when I jump out of the shower and teeter for a second before slipping again and splatting on the floor. I dive across the room and grab my phone, thumbing the answer button.

It's Brose.

And it's a video call.

And he sees my breasts.

I toss the phone across the room and stand in horror while his booming laughter comes out of the speaker. I stand rigid with my eyes wide until he composes himself.

"Nice dogs, Leigh," he says, gasping for air.

"What? Shut up, Brose!"

He bursts into another fit of laughter. "You just made my wildest dreams come true."

"Okay, okay, Brose. Lucky you," I say, rubbing my sore knees. "Now, what do you want?"

"Uh, sorry. Can we meet up? I have something for you."

"Yeah, sure," I say, my heart rate returning to normal, "I have nothing going on today."

"Well, you're about to. Breakfast at Solar?"

"Yes, and it's *your* treat."

"It's the least I can do. See you there." It sounds like his voice is actually smiling.

I shake my head while I pull on a pair of loose-fitting black shorts and a modest gray/black plaid top. I can't believe that happened. I'm not bringing this up next time I talk to Ash, that's for sure.

I tame my hair and wear it down, but skip the makeup.

When I get to Solar Snax, a lot of the tables are full already. It's the breakfast crush. I don't see Brose, so I snag a table for two and sip some coffee while I peruse the menu. What does he have? A new battery? Did he crack the code?

I resist the urge to call Ashlan. I want to know how Baxter is doing, but I know she'd call me if there was a concern, plus she sounded busy.

My thoughts drift toward Celeres, but I'm brought back to the present when Brose shows up at the hostess stand. He's dressed all in black and has a backpack slung at one shoulder. He walks over when he sees me wave.

He sits across from me and lowers his backpack to the ground. "Hey."

"Hey."

The waitress is nearby and turns to us. "Hey," she says, very pleased with herself.

I smirk at her.

"What can I get ya?" she asks.

I point at the menu. "This looks good. I'll take the farm-stead breakfast."

Brose holds up two fingers. "Make that two."

We drink coffee over the next couple of minutes and he explains the engineering of putting a natatorium on a space station. It's mildly interesting, but I'm not paying too close attention. One thing about living in space is that you can't talk about the weather, so you have to be creative.

The food comes on two plates for each of us. One

has a giant pancake that takes up the whole thing, the other has eggs, sausage, bacon, home fries, and toast. Wow.

Brose looks at me. "I can help you with that if you need."

"Don't worry, I got it. I ran a marathon yesterday."

He smiles and nods while shaking ketchup all over his second plate. He puts it on everything except his toast. It looks like a murder scene.

"So have you talked to Ashlan since she's been down there?" I ask.

His face sags. "No."

"Are things okay with you two?"

"We're taking a break, spending time apart, thinking about the relationship. At least that what she says we're doing."

"Sorry to hear. I hope it all works out."

"It's my fault. It's my work hours. We almost never see each other."

I nod.

"What about you and Celeres? Are you guys done?"

"I don't know. I think so. I mean, for all intents and purposes, I guess we are."

His face droops. "Love sucks."

"Yeah."

After a quiet stretch of eating, he breaks the silence, his eyes still fixed on his food. "Do you think she's seeing someone else?"

"She isn't," I say in a soft, sympathetic tone.

When he looks up, his tired eyes glisten with unshed tears. Just seeing him like this makes me tear up, too.

"Just look at us, we're pathetic," I say, and we burst into a sad giggle, wiping our eyes with our sleeves.

We munch on our food for a couple more minutes before he reaches down and lifts his backpack off the floor.

"Like I said on the phone, I have something for you."

I stop chewing and stare while he unzips it.

He pulls a laptop computer out of the bag. "Sorry it took so long, but here it is. It's that one from your lab. I fixed it."

I reach over and take it with reverence. "You had time for this?"

"I made time."

I stroke the scratched and dented lid, then open it to reveal a brand new keyboard and screen. There's a prompt for me to authenticate. I close it for now and place it beside me.

"What's on it?" I ask in a hushed voice.

"I don't know, but the storage appears to be intact. Whoever broke it must have thought they did enough physical damage to render it useless."

"How can I use it? My authentication won't work on someone else's classified laptop."

"Oh, it will. Your hand works on everything, remember?"

"Even this?"

"Yep."

"Thank you Brose. Maybe this will give us some answers. Now that you've done this, and the battery project didn't work out, you might have time to just do your regular job."

He laughs, but it's not his normal, jovial laugh. It's more sardonic.

"What's so funny about that, Brose?"

"There's no rest for the weary. Krysta has another 'job' for me."

"Oh, she mentioned something about that."

"So you heard. Can you believe it?"

I shake my head, but not because I can't believe it. It's because Krysta refused to tell me what it was.

He leans forward and whispers. Trouble is, with Brose, even his whispers are loud. "How can I be sure those batteries are still in the cave?"

She couldn't. She wouldn't. Is she planning to get Brose to steal batteries from that cave at the zoo? Put him in that kind of danger? He would do it, too, out of a sense of duty and because he couldn't get his homemade prototypes to work. I've lost what little appetite I had. I never should have told her about it. I've doomed my friend. Ashlan would kill me if something happened to him.

He waves a hand in front of my stricken face. "Leigh?"

"You can't," I say.

"I can't be sure the batteries are there?"

"No, you can't go."

"It'll be fine. We've already been there once. I'll just do the same thing as last time. I'll slip in late at night when the bugs are dormant, throw as many batteries in my pack that'll fit, then get the hell out."

"You? By yourself? I'm coming."

"Sorry, no. I'm trained for this. You aren't. Not only that, but I already talked to her about bringing backup, but she wants to keep it quiet, doesn't want anyone else. A small, surgical strike, if you will. You know how convincing she can be."

I reach over and grip his wrist. "It's too dangerous."

He gives another grim chuckle. "Don't worry, I have my flash-bangs."

"Brose, I have to ask you something, and you need to be honest with me."

"Hmm?"

"Has she been seducing you?"

He shrugs his shoulders. "I don't know, maybe. Like I said, you know how convincing she can be. Besides, so what if she is? I'm single now."

"Well, she isn't. Besides, you're beginning to sound like a guy on the rebound."

"Huh? What do you mean she isn't?"

"I walked in on her and Celeres. She was sitting on him with her shirt open. If I had walked in a minute later, who knows what I would have seen?"

"Oh, yeah, that. He's distraught about it. She somehow tied him up with the wires from his race car game, of all things. He's still trying to figure out how it all got out of hand so fast."

"She tied him up? All I could see was his head because I was behind the sofa."

"Yeah, I know. Weird, right? I didn't think he was into that sort of thing, but hey, it's none of my business."

I look down at my plate and push a piece of meat around with my fork. "I just don't understand, though."

"Who could ever understand these things? They just happen."

"Yeah, but why? She could have had him before."

Brose shrugs. "Beats me. At least we know you were wrong about her being attracted to you."

I shake my head no. "Brose, we kissed. She had her hand in my pants."

He leans forward, wide-eyed. "Oh yeah? Tell me what happened."

"You should see your face right now. Relax, before I have to hose you down with the fire extinguisher."

He laughs, then leans back. "Fine, keep your secrets,

but I hope you and Celeres can work things out. I liked you as a couple."

I nod slowly. "Yeah."

We pause again, but then I sigh and shake my head. "Back to Krysta. Please be careful. Yes, I know she's convincing, and I know she's beautiful, but I don't think anyone knows what her agenda is."

"I know. I get that. I'll reach out to you as soon as I safely can."

"When are you leaving?"

"Right after you and I finish, here. What will you be doing?"

"Me? Until now, I've had absolutely nothing to do, but thanks to you, I'll be diving into this laptop. Call me when you can, and we'll catch each other up."

"Deal."

Chapter Forty-Six

Sharon's Story

We stand outside of Solar and say our goodbyes. I give Brose a big hug.

"Call me as soon as you're safe," I say once we separate.

"I will. It'll be quick, in-and-out. I'm traveling light."

"How light?"

"Like I said, I'll have my flash-bangs."

"And a gun?"

He doesn't answer right away, but then, "And a gun."

I can't explain it, but I'm choked-up and afraid my voice will crack if I say anything, so I just nod, then pat him on the shoulder and begin the trek back to my quarters. I thank my lucky stars that I have this laptop to distract me.

Once inside my place, I hustle over to my bed, flip the laptop open, and authenticate with my palm. The new display flickers to life, showing me a beach scene with two young girls playing in the sand with buckets and shovels. Surely Sharon wouldn't have left children behind on Earth?

I'm reminded she was a real person with real friends/family, and for all I know, she's really dead.

I reverently touch the side of the laptop. "I'm here, Sharon. Tell me your secrets," I whisper.

I open her File Explorer, and the folder structure looks like mine. There are folders for data, folders with instruction manuals, and a bunch of folders that make no sense, like *Registry*, *System256*, and *Perf Logs*.

I click *My Documents*, and am presented with...about 100 recipes.

I click *My Videos*, and there's only one there. I open it.

It's a video of her addressing her laptop camera. I see our lab in the background. She wears her (my) white lab coat, and has blond, shoulder-length hair. A phone in a pink case is on the table in front of her.

Like mine.

Her eyes are red-rimmed, and she smokes a cigarette as she speaks in a hushed voice.

Something has happened, and I might be in danger. If I disappear and anyone ever sees this, maybe you'll know what happened to me.

I am Sharon Hone, lab assistant to Krysta Collins aboard Sumerian. *My husband, Simon, is still on the planet, keeping the household running. We're colonists, and everything was fine for months. We had a nice little home and were thinking of starting a family until the weirdness started.*

It started with, you know, that feeling you get when you think someone's watching you. I'd turn around and catch a glimpse. And here's the creepy part—it was never human. *No, it was those big hairy wasps. The first time I could get a good look was when one stood outside of my bedroom window one Saturday morning. It was standing, yes, standing! It pressed its antennas into the screen so hard that they almost ripped right through. It was like they were reaching for me.*

I screamed bloody murder, and it flew off. To Simon's credit, he believed me. Nobody else did.

The bugs weren't supposed to come so close to our settlement. We had a treaty or something such.

After that, things settled down for a couple of weeks and I foolishly thought I'd scared my stalker off for good. Boy, was I wrong about that.

Sharon jams her cigarette butt into an ashtray and lights another, her lighter shaking in her grasp, the flame jittering at the tip. I don't think I've ever seen someone smoke so fast. She looks over her shoulder and then continues.

Life returned to normal, and Simon stopped asking if I saw "it" again. Just to be safe, I only went out at night. They're supposed to be dormant when it's dark. It turns out that if they want to do something at night, there's nothing stopping them.

For example, if they want to sneak up on me while I'm outside star gazing.

You don't like it when a wasp lands on you. Imagine when a wasp as tall as you comes up from behind and puts a sticky leg on your shoulder. Without looking, I thought it was Simon for a second. When I reached my hand back to rest on his, I felt the hard, I don't know, "foot" of the bug instead. In my utter panic, I whirled around and struck it on the head with a roundhouse punch. It was stunned long enough for me to run back inside. I didn't get an exact count, but when I went to the kitchen window, I think I saw at least twenty of them flying away. Simon saw them this time, too, and called the cops while I came unglued right there on the spot. I was carrying on so loudly that he had to go into the other room so he could hear the emergency operator on the other end.

To make a long story short, that's how I ended up with Krysta. Her goal was to figure out what it was about me that attracted the bugs. None of the other colonists had this problem. Mosquitoes never bothered me on Earth, but here, I'm a wasp magnet.

She believed that my DNA, or something related to it, was involved. Don't ask me what, I'm just a civil engineer. Look at the tracks on my arm. She's taken a quart of my blood in the last two weeks.

I was clueless about her until she left her laptop unlocked, and I did some snooping.

Another cigarette, another look over her shoulder. I look at the tracks on my arm and every hair is sticking straight up.

I expect her back soon, so listen, I have to tell someone. Hopefully, you understand the depth of Krysta's corruption and can stop her. I'm certain that possessing this knowledge is my death warrant. I'm not supposed to know what's going on, and she knows I know.

Ostensibly, Krysta is trading genetic research for alien tech. It's all bullshit. The bugs are so much more advanced than us, it's embarrassing. Krysta is humankind's foremost expert in cloning research and genomics, but she's a rank amateur compared to them. They have some sort of living goo that grows and matures rapidly into whatever life form they have the DNA for. And when I say rapidly, I mean adult size within a few days.

So, the subspace radios? The batteries? That big robot? What did Krysta trade for all of it? She trades ten people from every colonization ship straight to the bugs, never to be seen again. That's why they don't allow anyone to call home— because some people never reach the colony at all.

I don't know what the bugs do with the unlucky ten, but

whatever it is, I can't help but think they also want to do it to me, or with me. I'm extremely sought-after by them, and Krysta's plan is to keep me away from them until she finds out why. If she can find more like me, just think of all the batteries she could get.

But now I know her most hidden secret, and unfortunately for me, I know she'd kill to keep it that way. I think I have at least as much time as it will take her to crack the code in my blood. After that...

Not only that, but ever since she's been back, I feel like she's always looking for a way to stand close to me. It's a little unnerving and makes me feel the same way I did when the wasps stalked me. Something must have happened down there, but she won't talk about it. I glance at her sometimes, and she's staring back at me. It's like she's eating me with her eyes.

She puts out her latest cigarette and reaches forward. The recording stops. I unclench my fists, revealing deep fingernail marks in my palms.

At the bottom of the video, the view count displays "2." I run my hand along the chassis, feeling the scrapes and dents that are still there. What are the odds that whoever the first viewer was, decided that this laptop needed a good smashing?

I shut the lid.

Not gonna lie, one of those cigarettes sounds great right now. I would never smoke, being a long-distance runner and all, but still.

What I need is my Baxter.

Chapter Forty-Seven

Vorefuser

I want to call Ashlan for an update on my pup, but this isn't the time. Krysta and Brose are away from the station for who knows how long, and I need to take advantage of this opportunity to snoop around the lab. If what Sharon said is true, then I should be able to find some kind of proof, at least now that I see Krysta's operation through a different lens.

At least now I know why our "work" is so classified. If Sharon's revelations were made public, it'd mean prison for Krysta, and maybe even me. Could I claim plausible deniability? Who would believe me? Krysta would go down and take me with her. Maybe she has a crush on me, but she'd throw me under the bus if it meant any chance of saving herself or getting a lesser sentence.

I hustle out of my room and head straight to the lab. I try to ignore the smells of the folks in the corridors as best I can. I think of an acquaintance from high school who got pregnant and gagged on smells. I didn't feel bad for her at the time, but I do now.

I usher myself into the lounge and hurry down the stairs

to the lab. My stomach goes into knots in anticipation of what I might find. Problem is, I don't know what I'm looking for.

Sharon's old desk is a good place to start. I whip every drawer open and rifle through the contents.

There's nothing but basic office supplies, a photo of who must be Simon (who is strikingly handsome), a pack of cigarettes, and her lighter. Could this be the same pack she was smoking from in the video? There are only three left inside. I flick them out of my way and slam the drawers closed.

I move to where Krysta always sits, and I check those drawers. Empty. I check about fifty cabinets, and they're also empty, or have boring-looking instruments and supplies in them. Of course, she would be careful and not leave anything to be found.

The only thing left is the back room. I know it isn't locked, but I also know that there are cameras back there. If I go in, she'll know. Maybe not right away, but eventually. Even worse, I could find nothing, but she'll know that I was suspicious enough to snoop around.

If she asks me about it, I could say I was scouring the place for a battery so I could take more measurements. Would she have any reason not to believe me? She knows how bored I am right now. I could say I wanted to work so I could take my mind off Baxter and Celeres.

Okay, I'm going to do it. I'll just have to be careful not to *look* like I'm tearing the place apart for clues. I open the door and try not to stare at the camera at the end of the hall. I'd only glimpsed this area before, but it's pretty much how I remember it: a short hallway with a door on each side. I'll start with the one on my left. It opens into a small room with walls painted black. A red light bulb illuminates when I walk in. The only things in here are a small desk with a display panel, and what looks like a black plastic tennis ball with buttons and blinking lights—Krysta's translator. Strange that she and Brose didn't take it with them.

Wait a minute... My breath catches in my throat and I pull out my phone to text him.

Have you guys left yet?

I stare at my phone, waiting, hoping to see the three little "typing" dots. If they're still on this station, I could be discovered in here at any time, especially if she comes back for the translator.

Almost as if in answer, the display panel on the desk flashes to life and there's a ringing sound. It has to be Krysta; she's the only one who would have this number. My god, she already knows what I'm doing. I have to set my phone down before I drop it. I stare at the display panel on the desk and at the flashing red answer button.

There's no sense in delaying the inevitable. I'm caught, and I'm going to answer it. Before I do, I want to cover up the webcam on the small off-chance that it isn't her. The ringing continues while I cast about, looking for something, anything, to put over the camera. I finally just whip off my shirt and drape it over the lens before hitting the answer button.

And it's a good thing I did, because it isn't her.

It's a wasp.

It buzzes and clicks and I don't know how to use the translator. I grab it and press a green button. "What?"

More clicks and a long buzz.

I shake the translator like it's a Magic 8 Ball, then press a blue button and try again. "What?"

The ball vibrates in my hand and emits some buzzes and clicks.

The wasp buzzes again, and the ball translates.

"Why aren't you on camera?"

I take a shuddering breath. "It's broken."

"Fix it before we talk next. Where are they, Collins?"

"Uh, *they* are right where they're supposed to be. Why do you ask?"

It makes some angry buzzing sounds like you get when you throw rocks at a hornet nest. The translator dutifully translates: "Stop playing games. If you want batteries, you have to deliver. If we don't get a new set of patterns soon, you won't receive another shipment."

Patterns? As far as I know, Krysta only trades colonists for batteries. Is there something screwed up with this translator? I'll play it off. "They will arrive soon. You know they travel on a slower ship."

"Then get a faster ship. Our elite are becoming impatient. What about the dog? We haven't forgotten about it."

"Th—the dog? I'll have to get back to you on that."

"We're running out of patience, Collins."

"I'm sorry."

"So are we."

Silence for a few seconds, and then it continues. "We're still missing a Vorefuser."

"Um, I don't know what to tell you. If I come across it, I will let you know."

"You do that. You also get that camera fixed."

The screen goes dark and I'm left in this strange room with more questions than before. I pull my shirt back on and look down at my phone. It looks like Brose responded.

So they left without the translator on purpose. I guess when you're expecting to rob their warehouse, you travel light. Speaking of robbing, Celeres said something about Krysta coming back with the stinger. Could that be the Vorefuser? It would make sense, considering the reports of Krysta saying that "the Vorefuser is out" in her delirium after zapping herself with it. Vorefuser, stinger, I'm not sure which is the creepier name.

And it sounds like they still want Baxter, but for what? Part of me is relieved that he's safe with Ashlan, but another part of me is terrified. If the wasps find him down there...

I let out a tremendous sigh as I leave the room. There is one more door in the hallway, and I'm filled with the trepidation about what I might find after what I've discovered already. I'm curious, though, because this is where that big box delivery went.

Steeling myself, I open it. This room is three times larger than the last one. At least it has a normal white light fixture. The most obvious object in the room looks like a cloning chamber similar to the ones we saw at the zoo, except this one is empty. So they delivered a cloning chamber. Why?

Besides that, there's a desk and computer terminal, along with a few pieces of lab equipment. A biohazard waste bin sits on the floor near the cloning chamber.

Biohazard?

I walk over and step on the pedal to open the lid. It's just the normal stuff: test strips, some needles, gauze. It's so full that a couple of test strips stick to the lid. Outwardly,

Krysta is an immaculate person, but after seeing her quarters, and now this overflowing waste bin, there is obviously more than one side to her. By the time this thing ends, however it ends, I wouldn't be surprised if I find even more sides yet.

I kick the bin onto its side, spilling the contents to the floor. It's more of the same, except for one thing—a buried empty blood bag is in there. A few drops of thick, red blood dot the bag's insides.

Perplexed, I look at the empty cloning chamber, and then at the computer. I have a seat at the desk and wiggle the mouse. The computer unlocks without even asking for authentication. Is Krysta so sure of herself that she doesn't even lock it?

There's a spreadsheet on the screen that appears to be a comparison between two different blood samples. At the top of one column are the letters, SH. In the next column, LS. I'm going to go out on a limb here and guess that they mean Sharon Hone and Leigh Shires. She's comparing mine and Sharon's blood. Why?

Most of the data is marked nominal or unremarkable, but when I reach a block of data labeled "Immunity," Sharon's numbers and mine are not only the same, but at max value. Krysta said something about this back on Earth when I applied to this gig. Yes, there's a row of data labeled "Cytotoxic CD_4 T-cells." I remember she remarked on that.

So I'm here because I'm the new Sharon. Krysta needs me so she can finish her research. This must mean that she disposed of Sharon, protecting her secrets before she could complete her experiments, just like she's going to kill me when she finds out that I've been here. Is it possible that the whole recruiting mission on Earth was to find someone with this type of immunity? Was it all to find...me?

There's still an eight-hundred pound elephant in the room—that cloning chamber. What would she be cloning? What's the most twisted thing she could do?

I know the wasps want Baxter. What if she cloned him?

What if she cloned *me*? She could make all the Leighs she wanted for her research and get rid of me. I'd be nothing but a pattern...a *pattern*. But she would need a good DNA sample to make a clone, right?

I open the searchable index on her computer and type: *Does blood have DNA?*

After speed-reading a couple of scientific articles, I learn that blood does *not* have DNA.

Oh, wait a minute. *Red* cells don't.

But white cells do. You don't suppose... You don't think...

I'm so stricken with these revelations that I can't think straight. I almost feel like I'm having an out-of-body experience while I gather up the biohazard waste and return it to the bin.

I leave the lab and fast-walk back to my quarters. As soon as I sit down, I pull out my phone and call Ashlan.

Chapter Forty-Eight

Instant Replay

Ashlan answers on the first ring. "Leigh, look!" She points her camera to Baxter and Milly. They roll around on her floor, nipping at each other while making lots of doggy noises.

My focus shifts to my beloved Bax and my face breaks into a huge smile. "Hi, Bax!"

He looks around upon hearing my voice and Ash holds the phone so he can see me. He launches toward the screen and the entire thing fills with nose and tongue. After a moment of intense licking, Ash turns the camera so I can see her face.

I can hardly believe it. "He looks great! What did you do?"

"Nothing at all, but don't you worry. I'm going to get to the bottom of this weird illness."

"I know."

"Are *you* okay?" she asks. She must see something in my face.

"I found some things."

"That Krysta's a terrible kisser? You still need to tell me all about that, by the way."

"No."

"What do you mean?"

"Brose fixed that laptop we found in the lab."

"Sharon's?"

"Yeah, and she left a recording on it. Not only that, but I found more than just what's on the laptop. I don't even know where to begin. Actually, I do. First, please keep a close eye on Baxter because the wasps are serious about wanting him."

"How do you know?"

"I'll explain later if there's time. I have more to tell you."

Ashlan nods and I continue, "Apparently the wasps are far ahead of us, technology-wise, like, way ahead. Everything Krysta says about how we trade technology with them is a lie. You want to know why her operation is top secret? It's because if anyone found out what was really going on, she'd be in prison, or worse."

"What is she doing?" Ashlan asks in a small voice.

"She's trading ten people per colonization ship for technology and batteries."

"She's *what*? What are they doing with them?"

"I don't know, but I think whatever happens to them also happened to Sharon."

"Holy shit."

"I know."

For a moment, a doubtful look crosses Ashlan's face. "How could she be getting away with this? She's gotta be working with somebody, but who?"

I shrug. "McClure? He's in charge of the ferry between here and there."

She gives a low whistle. "Of course it's him. The guy has no friends...except her. It all makes sense."

"Ash, what should I do?"

"Stay away from McClure."

I roll my eyes. "I've done everything possible to stay away from him *before* all of this."

"We need to figure out a way to keep you safe."

"It might be too late for that. Listen, do you still have the stinger?"

She nods.

"Good, keep it hidden. The wasps want it back. They certainly don't want us recharging our own batteries."

"I'll hide it as soon as we get off the phone."

"Good. Ash, all this is really bad. I may never see you again."

"Why?"

"Everything I've learned...I had to sneak into the back room of the lab to find out."

"So?"

"So I'm not allowed back there. There are cameras. Krysta will find out. It's just a question of when, and then I'll be the next Sharon."

She shakes her head no, her face pale. "What are you going to do?"

"I don't know yet. I might be screwed no matter what I do. If anything happens to me, please take care of Baxter."

"Nothing is going to happen. Tell someone. Tell Celeres."

"I don't know, maybe," I say, my voice trailing off.

The tension in my shoulders is overwhelming. There's one more thing she needs to know, and I have to force myself to say it.

"Ash, I hate to say it, but there's more. Brose said you two are on a break?"

She heaves a sad sigh. "Yeah. He's just never around. It's better to break it off sooner than later."

"I'm sorry."

"Me too," she says, her eyes moist.

"I don't know how to tell you this."

"Tell me what? I can't take much more."

"I know, it's just, well, it's Brose."

She clutches her chest. "What's wrong?"

"He's on the planet with Krysta."

"Why the hell is he down here with *her*?"

"She found out about the battery cache beneath the zoo. She persuaded him to go down with her and steal some."

She turns white. "Oh, my god. He isn't safe."

I wait for her to regain her voice.

"Why didn't you stop him?" she asks.

"He convinced himself that he had to go, and I didn't know these things about Krysta yet. I'm so sorry."

"I'll call you later," she says, and ends the connection.

I stare at my phone, desperately hoping that she's still my friend. I feel terrible dumping so much on her at once.

I pray she doesn't do anything stupid. I told her about Brose because it was the right thing to do. On the other hand, she has my Baxter with her. I know this sounds selfish, but I want her to find out what's ailing him, and I just destroyed her focus.

No. I can't blame myself. It's Krysta.

Krysta. She's going to kill me. Whether or not she has a crush, she's going to kill me, anyway. I know too much. For all I know, she already has the camera footage on her phone. It's just a matter of time before she sees it.

I lie back on my bed and close my eyes while doing

deep breathing exercises. I need to calm down, but my racing thoughts aren't having it. I should be down on the planet with Bax and Ashlan. What am I even doing here? What good am I on this station?

I'd better find *something* to pass the time before I have a full-blown anxiety attack and flush myself out of the nearest airlock.

Come on, brain. I roll off the bed and stand beside my big window and look down on the planet. "What do I do?" I scream into the glass. I pull my foot back to give it a good kick, but then think the better of it. I'm not ready to flush myself out yet. Yet.

Sharon used to live in this very room. Did she stand here once, just as lost, just as afraid?

I walk over to my dresser where the beautiful carving of Baxter sits, the one that Celeres made. I scratch its little wooden neck with my fingernail, and then it's as if the universe (or Sharon's ghost?) answers my plea. I get an idea.

But I'm going to need Meri for this.

On my way to Beastarium, I take some less-used corridors to avoid the people smells. Once there, it seems deserted, save for the songbirds hidden in the trees.

"Meri, are you here?" I call with my hands cupped to my mouth.

"Leigh? Yes, I'm in my office," comes her voice from a second-story window in the main building.

I let myself in, and she looks up from her desk.

"Coffee?" she asks with a cup of her own in hand, steam rolling off the top.

"No thanks, I'm wired enough as it is."

"What's wrong? Ashlan told me that Baxter is feeling much better. I'm sure you miss him, though. So do I, if I'm being honest. He sort of filled a void left by my dog back home."

"Are there surveillance cameras here?"

Her brow furrows. "Huh? Cameras? Yes, why do you ask?"

"Outside cameras too?"

"Yes, inside and outside. We record everything in our research."

"I was just thinking. Back on Earth, Baxter used to eat dandelions. If I gave you the timeframes from when he fell ill, could we watch him? See if he did any grazing in your flowerbeds?"

She nods. "You know, dandelions are actually good for dogs, but what you're saying makes a lot of sense. If he's getting into an indigenous flower, who knows what havoc it could wreak on his system?"

She nods to herself as she sets her coffee mug down and pulls her keyboard close.

"Okay, when was the first time you saw him acting funky?"

"That's easy. It was four nights ago. I was at Celeres's place with my friends, and I went to visit Baxter right afterwards. I could tell something was off with him. At first, I wrote it off as exhaustion from playing with his new girlfriend. The next day, he was much worse."

Meri nods and taps a few keys.

"Here we go. Saturday morning. There he is, outside with Milly. He looks good so far. Let's skip ahead a few hours."

I lower myself into a chair and we stare at the screen together.

"Okay, here we are at quitting time. There's Ashlan, feeding him his dinner."

Ashlan pats his head, then leaves and dims the lights.

Baxter circles his room a few times, then stops to bark at his window. Finally, he curls up on his bed.

"What time did you go see him?" Meri asks.

"Like I said, it was after visiting with Celeres and my friends. It was late."

"Let's watch until you show up? Here, I'll play it at 10x."

We sit and watch Baxter sleep at high speed when the door to his room opens. Meri mashes the button to get us back to 1x and we watch Krysta walk in. I grab Meri's arm for emotional support. Baxter awakens and walks over to Krysta, who remains absorbed in her phone.

I cover my mouth with one hand.

Krysta closes the door and pulls something out of her lab coat. It's a hypodermic needle. I stop breathing.

She kneels down, and just as Baxter licks her face, she jabs the needle into his scruff.

Meri looks at me, then returns her attention to the screen. "She's drugging him."

I don't move. I still haven't taken a breath.

She continues, "What was so important on her phone? What was she doing just before—"

"Texting Celeres," I rasp.

It suddenly makes sense why she bothered the four of us so much that night at Celeres's pizza party. She wasn't trying to sweet talk him; she only wanted to be sure of where we were, that we were out of the way.

Baxter's legs wobble, and Krysta hoists him upright by his collar and drags him over to the bed. In the next instant, she's out of the room.

"I'm sorry," says Meri.

I nod, still watching the footage of Baxter.

"Do you want to watch the second time he got sick?" she asks.

I nod again and remind myself to breathe.

She taps a few keys and looks sidelong at me. "Okay. It was yesterday. You and I were getting food, and—"

"Ashlan was on the planet. Nobody was in Beastarium. Krysta somehow knew I was with you," I say.

We return our attention to the screen. Once again, Krysta enters the room. This time, Milly is also in there. Baxter runs up to Krysta, tail wagging with trust and admiration. Milly, on the other hand, barks madly at her. Every time Krysta tries to get close with the needle, Milly snaps, forcing her back.

"Good girl," I murmur.

Finally, Krysta winds up and kicks Milly across the room, slamming her against the opposite wall. Blood drains from my hands as I clench my fists. No wonder poor Milly was so shaken up when Meri and I saw her.

Meri pauses the video and puts her hand on my arm. I'm practically hyperventilating. Neither of us talks for a full minute. Meri motions for me to return my attention to the screen. She zooms in on the needle. "It's a single use tranquilizer."

After administering another shot to Bax, Krysta makes a hasty departure.

"She's keeping him sedated," I say in a whisper.

"Now we know," says Meri.

"Now we know. And this explains why he always bounces back."

Meri scrunches her face. "Why would Krysta do this?"

"She wants to take Baxter to the aliens."

"Why?"

"I don't know, and I don't want to. She's told me that their scientists can help him with this 'strange illness.' She wants me to let her take him under the guise of trying to help him, but that will never happen."

"Does she know Baxter is with Ash?"

"No."

"We'd better give Ash a head's up."

I nod.

Chapter Forty-Nine

Ashlan's Resolve

The call to Ashlan rings endlessly. I hang up.

"What do you think she's doing?" Meri asks.

"I'm worried that she might do something stupid. I told her Brose is down there with Krysta and now she's probably trying to be the hero."

Meri wrings her hands. "I don't like this. Try again and keep trying."

I hit redial. This time, she answers on the first ring. "*WHAT?*" she asks in a fierce whisper. She's audio-only.

"Ash! It's important."

"Dammit. Hold on, let me get to a safe place," she says, still whispering.

From the sounds of it, she's moving through thick vegetation. There's a muffled curse at one point.

"Okay, what is it?" she asks, slightly out of breath.

"Where's Bax?"

"He's safe. I locked him in the cabin with Milly."

"Where are *you?*"

"I'm sneaking around the zoo. If I can intercept Brose

and Krysta before they go in, maybe I can save his life. After what you told me about Krysta, I doubt she'd lose any sleep if she got him killed, especially if it means she can get her hands on the precious batteries."

"I don't like it, Ash. That zoo has secrets the wasps don't want us to uncover. If you get caught—"

"I'm doing this Leigh. By the way, I found something *very* interesting, but first tell me why you're calling."

"Meri and I figured out what's been making Baxter sick."

"Really?" she says a bit too loud, and then lowers her voice again. "Tell me."

"It's Krysta. We found her in the video footage. She's been snowing him with some sort of sedative."

"You're kidding."

"No, and during the last time, Milly was in there, snapping at her. At least until Krysta kicked her across the room."

"That unbelievable bitch. What *isn't* she capable of? Why would she do that?"

"She wants me to send Baxter to the wasps for 'treatment.' They want him. I don't know why, but they are pressuring her."

"I'm shaking, I'm so angry."

"Listen, she doesn't know that Baxter is with you. You must keep it that way."

"I'll protect him with my life."

"Thank you, Ash."

"Listen Leigh, can you and Meri comb through more footage? Chances are, Krysta is drugging Baxter with drugs stolen from my office. Will you try to find more evidence? We can build a case against her."

"Sure. It'll help take my mind off of worrying. You said you found something?"

"Yeah. You know that compost bin at the zoo? The one with the twin PVC pipes that goes way up high?"

"What about it?"

"I looked inside the bin. It's stuffed full of that herb that Krysta likes."

"But why would they compost *that*?"

"Hell if I know. Who knows anything anymore?"

Meri looks at me with a quizzical expression. "What's so dangerous about the zoo?"

I shake my head and look back at the phone. "Ash? Tell me what's happening now."

"Remember the animal parade? That smell, that minty smell? It's back. There's smoke. Hold on, I'm going to get closer."

"No, wait—"

"Shh, keep it down. I'll be there in a minute."

My hands break out in sweat and my heart rate picks up.

"Well, look at this," says Ashlan.

"What do you see?"

"I think we just solved another puzzle. That bin isn't for compost at all. They're burning the herb, sending smoke up the pipe like a giant diffuser. It's like when you're starving and smell someone cooking your favorite food from a mile away, except this isn't food, and it's irresistible. That's what's been causing the smell all along. It's getting stronger."

"You're sure Baxter and Milly are locked in your cabin?"

"Yes. Leigh, I really, *really* want to go down there."

"Ash, get the hell out of there. You might not break free this time."

"Me? What about Brose? I have to save him."

"And if Krysta gets in your way?"

She exhales, then her face turns to iron. "Then I'll shoot her."

She disconnects the call.

Chapter Fifty

Leigh's Resolve

We sit in stunned silence for a few minutes, but then spend the better part of the next hour reviewing camera footage and finding multiple occurrences of Krysta sneaking into Ashlan's office, stealing drugs. We write all the dates and times, and then lean back in our chairs. My back is so tight from stress.

"Do you want to tell me what's going on?" asks Meri.

"I don't think I can. Not right now. I'm barely beginning to piece it together myself."

"I want to help you."

"You can't. I can't. My friends are down there and we're up here."

"Ashlan's my friend, too."

"Ashlan was supposed to be at her cabin, doing research, taking care of Baxter. Now she's putting her life on the line to save Brose. If the wasps don't get her, Krysta might. And then what? She'll be dead, and Baxter's as good as dead."

Meri puts her hands in the air, palms up. "Does Ash have any choice?"

"What's that supposed to mean? Of course she does."

"I know she and Brose broke up, but—"

"She still cares about him, I know."

"Wouldn't you do it for Celeres?"

I'm completely taken off guard. "He hurt me."

She cocks her head.

I look down and study the ground for a moment. "I would."

She lifts my chin with a gentle finger. "Do you believe in love? I mean, really?"

"I want to."

She nods. "What happened to you two?"

"We had a fight, then I caught him messing around with Krysta."

She gasps. "That doesn't sound like him at all."

"I seem to have this curse with guys."

"Still..."

"I know. And get this—she had him tied up."

Meri snorts.

"And this is funny, why?"

"Because that *really* doesn't sound like him."

"I know, but she gets what she wants and who she wants, doesn't she?"

"Have you heard his side of the story?"

I shrug.

"So what will you do?" she presses.

"I already did it."

"Meaning?"

"I, uh, sort of messed around with her, too, after I caught them."

"*What?*"

"Yeah."

"Whoa, she gets around. Are you sure you know what you're doing?"

"It gets worse."

"How is that possible?"

"There's a decent chance I got farther with her than he did."

Meri's self control crumbles, and she spits out a laugh. "So that makes you even, then."

"*Even?* Because we both got a piece of Krysta? No. I can't believe it '*even*' happened."

She crosses her legs and leans forward. "So. Celeres."

"Yeah?"

"You'd still risk life and limb for him, just like Ashlan is doing for Brose. After everything?"

"Of course I would."

Meri stares at me as if we just unlocked a secret of the universe.

I put a hand in the air. "What are you getting at?"

"If you would even think about sacrificing yourself to save him, there's a piece of you that still loves him."

I look at her like she just slapped me across the face. Because she's right. Because that piece of me still burns in pain. "It's not that easy, Meri. I've been through this before. I know how it ends."

"Maybe, but then maybe there's a piece of him that still loves you. There might be something to save if you think it's worth saving."

I nod, looking down.

"Do you love Krysta?"

"No. Not even close."

"Does he?"

"I don't know."

"You should both work this out before you let something beautiful slip through your fingers. Plus, you know, maybe he could fly you to the planet and you can be with your dog."

I'm already on my feet. She told me what I already knew, but maybe I just had to hear it from someone else. "Thanks, Meri," I say, and then run out of the room.

"You're welcome," she calls to my back.

Chapter Fifty-One

Mint

I rush through the corridors, onlookers hastily stepping out of my way. As I approach the shops, the barista lifts her hand in greeting, but her face twists in confusion as I whiz by.

I burst into my quarters and run to the dresser. I change into the green crop top and black leggings that Celeres bought me, and then run to the bathroom for some quick makeup. I know he'll love this look. I'm out the door five minutes later.

I'm at his quarters in a few minutes and I stop at the door to run a few fingers through my hair and let my breathing slow down. Before I can talk myself out of this, I give three smart raps on the door while my mind races for the right words to say.

I'm going to tell him everything I know about Krysta. I'm also going to let him know she coerced Brose to go back down into that battery cave with her. He'll see her for what she is.

I'll tell him that I love him. I should have done that a long time ago.

I wait a minute and knock again, but he doesn't come to the door. After all that it took for me to come to my senses and gather up my courage to come, he has to be here. How dare he not be home?

I'm going in. I place my palm on the pad and the door slides open.

The thing that catches my attention first when I walk in is his couch. A mental picture of Krysta straddling him on it is still burned into my memory, like a bright afterimage. My stomach lurches at the thought. I turn to leave, but stop myself. I'm doing this.

"Celeres?" I call.

Nothing. He's not here.

It looks like he moved his plant over to the window, after all. Its leaves glow in surreal luminescence. I walk over and peer out into space, thinking I might catch his ship on patrol or something. Amazingly, I believe I see *Big Seven* speeding toward the planet, getting smaller and smaller as I watch.

I must have just missed him. It figures that when I finally want to patch things up, he flies away. Should I wait here for him? Maybe for a little while.

I look down again at the plant. So they're smoking the leaves of this thing to create the animal parade. I reach down and pluck a leaf. It still glows as I raise it to my face.

"What are you about?" I ask in a whisper, partially to the leaf, but also to Krysta.

At the thought of her, I crumple the leaf in my fist. The air fills with the unmistakable smell of mint, just like the scent at the parade. I stare at the plant and bite my lip in contemplation.

I catch myself inhaling deeply through my nose. The

scent of this thing is intoxicating. I almost want to bury my head in it.

My eyes narrow.

There has to be more to this plant. What does Krysta know that I don't? It's the key to Ashlan's parade puzzle.

...And maybe to mine.

I lower myself to the floor as realization dawns on me.

Mint.

Attraction.

Krysta.

All of that fresh breath isn't just toothpaste at all. Is she chewing this and using its properties to bend everyone to her will?

She is. Of course she is.

Everyone wants to know her secret, why she's so irresistible. Goosebumps cover my body.

My attraction to Krysta is a lie.

What happened between Krysta and Celeres wasn't real.

I stare blankly ahead while it all sinks in.

My phone rings three times before I even register the sound. It's Ashlan.

Chapter Fifty-Two

And Then There was Leigh

I almost cry with relief at seeing Ashlan's name show up on my phone. She must have broken free of the pull and is in a safe place. I hit the green button to connect the call.

"Ashlan! I—"

"Leigh," she sobs. Her eyes are red and tears line her cheeks.

"Brose? Is he—"

"No, it's Baxter," she says, crying hard.

Terror threatens to consume me. "Baxter? What do you mean? What happened? Tell me!"

"I locked him in. It was safe. I made sure."

"Ashlan, tell me what happened."

She stops crying for a moment and looks at me questioningly. "You don't know? You aren't with Celeres? *Where* are you?"

"You know where I am—at the station, by *myself*! Why would I be with Celeres?"

"He was going to call you."

"I blocked his number. Wait a second," I say, my voice

trailing off. I look at the blocked calls on my phone, and he *did* call, about six times.

"Okay Ashlan, tell me what's going on, and tell me now."

"I barely made it out of the zoo area. The pull was getting too strong, and I didn't think I could resist for much longer. It took me a long time to get back to the cabin because I kept turning around, thinking maybe I could beat it, could still save Brose. Somehow, I didn't give in to the allure, and made it back."

"Is Baxter alive?"

"I don't know. When I got back, I found that he and Milly both jumped through the window screen."

"He's done that before," I mutter.

"I called Celeres right away. I told him there was no time, that he had to get you and come down."

I sit down on the couch. "He's not here. I'm at his place right now. Ashlan, he can't. *You* barely made it back to your cabin. He won't stand a chance."

"How do you know? He might."

"He won't. I'm one hundred percent certain."

"How?"

"Because that Mint you found in the compost bin, er, the diffuser? The same thing that Krysta collects? She chews it. It's her secret to getting whatever and whoever she wants."

Her mouth drops open. "Of course. The toothpaste—"

"Yes!"

"It all makes sense now. And he's always been like putty in her hands."

"As soon as he gets a whiff, he'll jump out of *Big Seven* faster than Baxter jumped out of your window. He's going to wind up like Sharon, or even the colonists that Krysta trades for batteries."

"What will they do to him?"

"I'll never see him again. I'm sure of it."

Two new tears trace down Ashlan's cheeks. "I messed up. I shouldn't have called him, but it's Baxter. I didn't know what else to do. Please forgive me."

I take a few seconds to breathe. "And Brose?" I ask with a shaky sigh.

"He finally answered his phone. I was so stunned when the call went through that I almost lost my voice."

"He's still with Krysta?"

"Oh, he's still with her, all right. When I told him there was an emergency at the colony power station and that they needed him, she about lost it. You should have heard her."

"What emergency?"

"Nothing. I made it up. I don't want him anywhere near the zoo."

"So you bought him some time."

"He'll go to the colony to help. That's the kind of person he is. Once they realize it's a false alarm, Krysta will march him right back to the zoo. Maybe he will see Celeres. Maybe he can help."

There is no help. Between the Mint coming from the diffuser and from Krysta's mouth, what chance do our men have?

"Leigh," she continues, "I'm locked in my cabin for now, but I don't know how much longer I can resist. They must be using more herb than ever before. Will you stay on the phone with me?"

"Of course I will. You know, Ash, I just remembered something. When I first asked Krysta about the diffuser and she told me it was for compost, she told me she had something to do with the installation."

"So *she* is behind the parade? Why would she do that?"

I shrug. "Batteries? What else could it be?"

Ashlan nods.

We just stare at each other through our phone screens as I prop the phone across from me and wrap my arms around my knees. Her breathing becomes more labored and I know it's only a matter of time before she succumbs to the pull. My eyes become wet and I exhale, trying to fend off an ugly cry.

They're going to use the Vorefuser on Bax and Milly. It's what they've wanted since the beginning. If Celeres tries to intervene, *when* Celeres tries to intervene, they'll kill him, too.

I learned the truth too late—the truth about Krysta and the truth about Celeres. He was true to me all along, but I was so wrapped up in expecting him to be unfaithful that I didn't see it. Now, he's going to die because he's trying to save my dog.

Krysta played us all, and she did it right under my nose. Now my friends are going to pay the price.

I bend forward, my head touching the ground to weather the stabbing pains in my abdomen.

"Leigh?" Ashlan asks.

I shake my head.

In the midst of my grief, something scratches at the edge of my consciousness. Wait a minute. Wait a minute. I open my teary eyes and stare at the iridescent leaves of the other-worldly plant by the window.

"Ash, I have to go."

I disconnect the call and grab the plant.

He was true to me. As I think about it, my doubts about

him fade away in waves. I would be thrilled if it weren't for the abject panic of this situation, and for what I'm about to do.

I take off at a reckless run and trip on one of the throw rugs, causing half the dirt from the vase to fly across the room. I'm able to keep the vase from breaking, but not before I whack my chin on the floor.

I don't even register the pain as I return to my feet, hold the plant close like a running back, and dash out of his quarters.

Chapter Fifty-Three

Heartspeed

I must look like a lunatic as I run through the station, spilling small piles of soil out of the flowerpot. Not only that, but my eyes are red and puffy from all the crying.

I don't care, I just want to get to my place.

It only takes a few minutes and more than a few questioning glances from just about everyone I pass. It's almost a relief when I get through the door and lock the rest of the station behind me.

I put the Mint plant on my desk and grab the backpack I brought from Earth. I'm overcome with nostalgia when I unzip it and rediscover the blanket I brought from home. I pull it free and bury my nose deep within it for a few moments, remembering what home smelled like. I force myself to break away and set the items on my bed.

I take the wood carving of Baxter off my dresser, and an involuntary sob bursts from my lips at the thought of him and Celeres. I fight to regain control. This isn't the time to fall apart, Leigh. I wrap the carving in my blanket and return it to the backpack. I zip it shut and pat it a couple of times.

Next, I sit at my desk and look at the plant.

"Here goes nothing," I say aloud while tearing off about a dozen Mint leaves.

I stuff them into my mouth, one by one, chewing as I go. The minty flavor and scent fill my mouth and permeate my sinuses. It's exactly how Krysta's mouth tasted at the pool.

Should I swallow them? Would they poison me? I shrug and gulp them down. What difference does it make?

I stand and pull the backpack over my shoulders. I walk to my door, then turn, remembering everything that's happened since I got here. This was supposed to be my new life. I was so silly with joy back when I flashed the planet after my shower. Yeah, I had some rough patches, but I also had some good times and made some good friends.

I sigh and turn around, heading out into the hallway. Next stop: the hangar.

I zoom through the hangar doorway, causing McClure to rise from his desk. "Now, what do you want?"

"I left something on one of the ships. I need it right now."

He smirks. "What's so important?"

"My medication."

I shoulder past him, and he grabs my arm.

"You aren't going anywhere, Miss Shires. I'll have someone get it for you. Hold on."

I twist away. "Listen, I'll only be a minute. It can't wait," I say while exhaling with every word. This Mint had better work.

He inhales, but his eyes narrow. "It's nothing doing. I'd end up in the brig."

I give him another breath of Mint in the face with my sexiest pursed lips pose. "Please? We could grab a drink after your shift."

"That's in an hour. I'll come to your place. Maybe we can have a drink *before* we go out for a drink. Know what I mean?" As he's saying that, he hikes his kilt up an inch like it's some subliminal message. This has got to be a record for as not-turned-on as I've ever been in my life.

"Anything's possible," I say while cocking my hips and giving him my famous coy smile. I think the mint's helping, but let's be honest—I look super cute in this outfit.

My stomach turns as he looks me up and down.

"Make it fast," he says, sitting back down with a wolfish grin.

It's no wonder Krysta always got what she wanted. If *McClure* is putty in my hands, I could have my way with anyone.

This is it. There's no going back now. The only question is which ship I am going to take. There are several to choose from, but the one that draws me in has a painting of a disembodied hand holding four playing cards fanned out— all aces.

"Aces for luck," I mutter, and climb the steps.

Once inside, I close the hatch and the life support systems start, optimizing the temperature and oxygen levels.

I sit in the cockpit and strap in. The palm pad sits in front of me, daring me to touch it. This is do or die. Actually, it's probably die or die, so let's get on with it. I place my palm on the pad and wait.

And wait.

This can't be good. This definitely isn't good. I'm toast. Thirty seconds pass and my hands glisten with sweat.

The pad turns green and the familiar female computer voice says, "New pilot. Provide callsign."

I let out a shaky breath. "Heartspeed."

Her voice returns. "Heartspeed, you are cleared to depart. Egress hangar door four."

I take the controls and lift the ship into the air, nice and easy. I look for the large number four painted near an opening and fly toward it. This is scary and exhilarating all at the same time. I'm so caught up in the moment that I don't immediately see McClure down there, waving frantically. He points at me and it looks like he's shouting. Veins bulge in his neck and forehead.

"Heartspeed, return to your berth," from the radio.

A loud creaking sound forces my attention back to where I'm going. The large door on bay four has begun its descent.

Holding my breath, I push the throttle forward, breaking every intergalactic hangar speed limit there is. I race over the parked ships toward the narrowing gap, trying to align my ship so that I'll slip through.

The door closes faster, and I push the throttle forward even more. The station blurs around me as the ship accelerates. Less than a second later, I fly free of the hangar and into the black.

I'm doing breathing exercises in an attempt to calm down. Okay, what's next? The planet. I point the ship to it and pull the throttle back to a reasonable speed. Next, I look for the safety controls and turn them off.

There's a dinging sound as a green dot appears behind my ship on the three-dimensional hologram radar. I'm being followed. I knew this would be a short flight, but it's about to get a lot shorter. I can't let them blow me up. I reach behind me and squeeze my Baxter figurine through the backpack, then put my hand on the throttle because nothing is going to stop me. I got past McClure. I'll get past this.

As soon as I barely push the throttle forward, a human female voice comes over the intercom this time: "Heartspeed, what is your mission?"

I recognize that voice. It's Moon.

"Hi Moon," I breathe.

"Leigh? *Leigh?* What the fuck are you doing?"

"Zoo delivery."

"Yeah right. I never expected this from you. If anything, I thought maybe you'd head to a jump gate to Earth."

"Me too."

On radar, she is directly behind me.

I have a delivery, all right. I set my course on autopilot.

I burst through Apocrita's clouds. Moon also slices through and paces me on my starboard side. A raptor is stenciled on the side of her ship.

"The wasps don't like your course, Birdie. Look."

She's close enough that I can see where she's pointing through our cockpit glass.

A black ship races toward us from below.

"Uh oh," I say.

"Leigh, they're not expecting you. Let's get out of here before there's trouble."

"Moon, there's trouble already. Everyone I love is down there, and their lives are in grave danger. Remember how you said you'd be there to save your friends one day? Today it's my friends whose asses are in the fire. Celeres is down there too."

"The captain's in trouble? He's down there? How can I help?"

"Get that ship out of my way?"

"Roger that. Let's see how much I can piss them off."

She pulls ahead, heading straight for the interceptor. It's like they're playing spaceship chicken. At the last moment, she pulls up and blasts the ship with an incredible thrust from her exhaust, sending the alien vessel spinning toward the ground. It recovers in time and then races back toward her. For a moment, I lose myself in her art. She makes flight look effortless and beautiful, like a bird of prey. She lets the ship catch up to her and then flies off with her pursuer behind.

Her voice comes over the radio again, "Go, Heartspeed. I'll deal with this fool."

Chapter Fifty-Four

Rescue

I get my first glimpse of the zoo—the smoke from the diffuser gives it away. I disengage the autopilot now that I'm close. The animal parade is in full force down there, with at least triple the number of animals that Ash and I saw.

I ease the ship toward the line, follow it to the racetrack. Even with the track fenced off, they still stream around it like a column of ants.

I hold my breath as I fly closer and squint, trying to find a familiar face.

And my prayers are answered. There's my favorite fur-face, my precious Baxter. Milly lopes along beside him as they march along with the other hapless animals toward the Vorefuser at the end of the route. A smile creeps onto my face.

My smile grows wider when I see the man walking beside them. I could recognize that mop of a hair anywhere. Celeres. I fly close and dip a wing, but they pay no attention to me, fixated as they are on the siren scent of the Mint. Just look at him. It's no wonder Krysta had her way with him. I have a brief dirty thought of having my way with him myself.

Okay, this is it. I check my straps to make sure I'm securely attached to the seat. I move the flight stick until I'm pointed at the diffuser. I resist pushing the throttle forward because need to make this look like an accident.

An artificial female voice fills the cabin.

Pull up.

Altitude.

Altitude.

"I know! Shut up!"

Altitude.

Pull up.

The zoo is less than a mile away. This is it.

I give the Baxter figurine one last squeeze through my backpack and pull the ejection handles above me.

In the next instant, I'm surrounded by minor explosions breaking the canopy away from the ship and out of the way. A split second later, something underneath shoots me straight up and out into the Apocritan sky, seat and all, like a potato out of my dad's spud gun.

Up and up I go until I finally slow and begin my descent to the ground. A parachute deploys from my seat and I have a spectacular view as my ship slams into the diffuser in an immense ball of flames. Fortunately, the diffuser structure bears most of the damage from the impact, leaving the rest of the zoo complex unaffected.

Below me is complete disarray. The sudden interruption of Mint gas, combined with the explosion, has broken the parade trance. The creatures shake it off and scatter to the treeline.

The heat from the explosion is uncomfortably warm against my skin. To distract myself from it, I look for Celeres and Baxter. It takes a minute, but they sort of stick out amid a mass of other animals scrambling away. Celeres is on one knee, his hand on Bax's collar. He shakes his head as if he's still shaking off the Mint's spell. Milly sits nearby. I holler at them and they look, their faces filled with confusion. Then Celeres breaks into an enthusiastic wave.

I'm so caught up in the moment that I'm only ten feet above the ground before I realize I'm about to come to a sudden stop. I thrust my legs straight out so that the seat is the first thing that touches, and then oomph! The parachute falls over me as I rush to unclasp my straps.

Soon, I'm free of the harness and pulling the parachute away so I can get out from underneath. Once free, I spring to my feet and find them again. They're farther away than I thought, but the important thing is that they're safe. Tears of relief and joy fill my eyes.

Wait. Celeres waves his arms and then points at me. His face is full of concern...or is it fear?

"Behind you," he yells at the top of his lungs, his voice small from this distance.

I pivot to see what he's talking about, and I see the danger. A woman emerges from the tree line and runs straight toward me. Her hair is pulled in a tight pony and she wears a black Genomica jumpsuit. She's far enough away that I can't make out her details, but my first instinct is that it's Krysta. Why is she running? What does she think she's going to do to me? I look past her to see if I can get a glimpse of Brose, but don't see anyone else. She's fifty yards away and closing. Now I can make out her facial features.

It's not Krysta. It's me.

Me.

Celeres's voice continues behind me, but I'm fixated on the perfect replica of myself. How?

She slows to a walk when she's within ten feet, panting through her nose, nostrils flaring like a bull. Her eyes narrow and her fingers clench.

"Hello?" I say.

She growls and jumps at me. I barely raise my arms before she grasps my shoulders and plows into me with the full force of her bodyweight, bowling me to the ground.

She straddles me, fingers still gripping my shoulders, digging into my flesh. Yes, it hurts, yes I'm panicking, but I'm not thinking of those things. I'm thinking about her intoxicating *scent*. Could there be a hint of lilac? The smell of air in September? It's deeply pleasant, and well, wonderful. It's not like the Mint; with Mint, it's a pure, irresistible animal attraction. So that's what Krysta was talking about. It's what I smell like to someone with a sense of smell warped by the Vorefuser.

She knocks me out of my reverie with a painful slap across the face.

"I kill you, *pattern*," she mutters, moving her hands to my neck.

My fight-or-flight response kicks in and I twist away from her, jumping to my feet before she can get another hold. I don't *want* to hit her, but I feel like I must, to slow her down. Do I really want to punch myself?

She closes on me again, and I swing at her at hard as I can. My fist connects with her nose, and we both cry out in pain. My wrist was damaged to begin with.

I grab my wrist with my other hand. "*That's* for screwing up the switch leap in Toledo and making us lose the whole dance competition." (I've always hated myself for that).

Her eyes wet with fresh pain, she lunges again, and I kick her in the gut, sending her to the ground. I'm not sticking around for any more of this. I turn back toward Celeres and I run. I run as fast as I can. She won't catch me. She might have my body, but she doesn't have my conditioning.

Apparently, she's going to try. Her labored breathing is close behind me, but if it's a race she wants, she picked the wrong person. I dig deep and run faster. Ahead, Celeres pulls out a gun, and I almost trip in surprise.

What is he doing? I wave my arms and yell, "No!"

Behind me, my lookalike also yells it.

After all this, he's going to get me killed. I take ten more steps, and the following series of events unfold in an instant, but my brain tracks everything as if it's in slow motion.

He fires, but it isn't very loud. Silencer? I can actually see the bullet coming. It looks bigger than I'd expect and is red-colored.

It whistles past me and hits her. It sounds like he hit her with a stone.

Um, she's still running behind me.

I should get to them in about thirty seconds. Baxter doesn't recognize me yet, but is watching with great interest.

Celeres lifts the gun to take another shot, but she suddenly falls heavily to the ground behind me. I'm not stopping.

After a few more seconds, Baxter realizes it's me and launches himself in my direction. He's at me in a heartbeat and we're transformed into a mass of fur, sweat, laughs of relief, and a big, floppy tongue.

Celeres joins us and I stand up and melt into his arms. We kiss with Baxter still jumping at me, but I finally pull away.

"What did you hit her with?" I ask.

"I borrowed Ashlan's tranquilizer gun."

"You shot her with a tranquilizer dart? Made for *animals*?"

"I brought it to use it on Krysta. You know, just in case."

I snort.

"We have to get out of here," he says. "Fast."

I nod hurriedly. "Where are we going?"

"Racetrack. I have Ash's vet buggy. We'll book it back to her cabin."

"Ashlan to the rescue today, huh?"

He winks. "We've all been doing some rescuing today."

I turn toward the track. "Yeah, let's get going. I have so much to tell you."

"I'm looking forward to it."

"But before we leave," I say, stealing a glance at the clone of myself. "How did you know which one was me?"

He laughs in genuine amusement. "Come on, baby, I've seen you run."

I beam at him. "I love you."

His eyes shine, and he reaches for another hug. Our lips meet again, but we're interrupted by a fresh explosion back at the zoo.

"Let's go," he says, breaking the embrace and jogging away.

I run with him, with the dogs pacing alongside us. The warmth on my back from the flaming diffuser grows fainter as we go.

Chapter Fifty-Five

Confronting Krysta

We run.

We're dodging critters of all types for most of the way, but they thin out as we plunge deeper into the forest. Before long, the light poles of the racetrack creep into view above the treetops. In thirty more seconds, Ashlan's vet buggy is visible through the ground cover. With our bodies drenched in sweat, I worry about Baxter and Milly overheating. The buggy has a roomy crate in the rear that'll allow good airflow, so hopefully that'll cool them down.

Celeres jumps into the driver's seat and starts the buggy while I open the crate in back and usher the dogs inside.

"I know, Bax, I'll hose you down as soon as I can, just like back home."

I shut the crate and give it a tug to be sure it's latched before racing to the front of the buggy and jumping into the passenger's seat. I barely have my seat belt fastened before Celeres guns it.

"We should be at the cabin in a few minutes, if we're lucky," he says in between gulps of air.

I look behind. "Do you think they're following us?"

He responds by pushing on the accelerator even more, pinning me back into my seat while the dogs tumble into a mixed pile at the back of the crate. For a second, I'm reminded of how he did the same thing to Ashlan and Brose in the rear seats of his ship when we left our campsite.

"Nice driving, here," I say.

He gives me a sidelong glance. "Nice flying back there."

"Yep. My insurance rates are definitely going to skyrocket after this."

He laughs. "I love you too, Leigh."

Under normal circumstances, I would be climbing on top of him right now, maybe even before he could park. As it is, I crow internally for joy, but still grasp the buggy's roll bar for dear life.

We bounce along the uneven ground, and he maintains control. When Ashlan's cabin comes into view, it almost looks deserted. The door is shut, and the windows boarded up from the inside. The screen that the dogs jumped through flaps in the breeze.

I jump out of the buggy and dash to the cabin before Celeres even comes to a complete stop. I try to whip the door open, but it won't budge. I pound on it.

"Ashlan! Are you in there? Are you okay?"

"Leigh?" comes a timid voice from inside.

"Yes!" I say, my voice cracking with relief. "Let us in."

"I nailed it shut. I couldn't resist the pull for much longer."

"The diffuser is destroyed. It's safe," I say with my cheek pressed against the door.

"Is that what the explosion was?"

"Yes."

"Hold on."

Scratching sounds come from the other side as she

works the nails loose. After another minute, the door opens. I'm not prepared for what I see.

Ashlan stands before us, with angry red lines down both cheeks, as if she raked them with her fingernails.

"Ash! What—"

She turns away and sits down. "I just need a minute. I never imagined it could be so powerful."

"Tell me about it," Celeres says. "I had no chance of breaking free. I remember being in a casino once, in the grip of compulsion. This was worse. I knew what I was doing, but I felt like I was outside of myself, watching helplessly. All I could do, all I wanted to do, was get to the zoo. I kept telling myself I would snap out of it once we got there, and we'd hide. I'm surprised you had the wherewithal to barricade yourself."

"It was the hardest thing I've ever done. I doubt I could do it again."

I touch her trembling shoulder. "You won't have to."

"Thanks, but the wasps are going to be *pissed*."

"I know."

"What's your plan?"

I look back and forth between them. "I was hoping you two could help me with that."

Celeres begins to say something, but we're interrupted by the dogs as they scamper over to a cupboard, sniffing at the door.

Ashlan smiles and stands. "They want a treat."

She opens the cupboard to reveal several containers. When she grabs one, both dogs spin in circles, and we all chuckle. This small bit of cheer is just what we need right now. When she peels the lid open, a mouth-watering scent permeates the cabin.

"What *is* that?" I ask.

"Treats. Brose made them," she says, her voice trailing off.

She flicks one to each dog, and they gobble them right out of the air. She gives each one a head-pat and clears her throat. "I'm worried about him."

"Brose? What's going on?" asks Celeres.

"Remember that battery room underneath the zoo?" I say.

"Yeah, what of it?"

"Krysta coerced him into going back there to steal some."

His eyes go wide. "You're kidding. Wait, do you think he might have gotten hurt in that explosion?"

Ashlan shakes her head. "He wasn't there. I fabricated a lie about some emergency at the colony power station, just to keep him away from getting caught in the diffuser's lure."

Celeres nods. "We have to find him."

Ashlan sits again. "Yes. Problem is, his location services are off, and he hasn't answered his phone ever since my fake emergency call."

"Try again."

She shrugs. "Okay..."

She taps her phone, and it connects almost instantly. We all freeze with bated breath.

Before she can say a word, it's Krysta's face that shows up on the screen, not Brose's.

"He doesn't want to talk to you after your little stunt. Imagine his face when he realized you lied to him about the problem at the colony. Stop calling this number. We're trying to work."

Ashlan seems tongue-tied, so I interrupt. "Where are you?"

"Leigh? What are you doing? Who's with you?"

Ashlan places the phone so that Krysta can see all of us.

Krysta's eyes widen slightly. "Why am I not surprised? I was a fool to think I could break you and Celeres up."

"You'll never have him," I say.

"Oh, give me a break. I could have had him a thousand times before you came along if I wanted."

Celeres bites his lip and looks down.

Krysta continues, "He used to be a good friend. I was sorry he fell for me back before you came into the picture, but it turned out to be rather convenient."

Celeres looks up. "So you come to my place and tie me up. That makes total sense," he says, choking out a sarcastic laugh. "Just in time for Leigh to—"

"—Catch us," she says.

"Yeah, that. What are you playing at?"

Just listening to this is twisting my stomach.

"What do you think?" Krysta snaps. "Come on, you're smarter than that."

Celeres shakes his head in disbelief and throws up his hands.

I shake my head and look back at the screen. "Maybe he's smarter than that, but I'm not. I don't understand. Obviously, you want him. You built a whole racetrack for him, you text him when we're on dates, you molest him on his own couch."

"No, I *don't* want him, Leigh. He doesn't want me, either. He already told me in so many words when I had him on that couch."

I look at him, and he nods. I look back at Krysta, and I don't know what to say.

She continues after a second, "It's you, Leigh. You. Isn't it obvious? I want you. And I almost had you, too."

I shake my head. "Wait a second. Something isn't

adding up with this story. Why did you text me to come to the lab just before I caught you? What if I had gone to the lab instead of Celeres's place?"

"Then I would have had you in the lab instead of the pool. Breaking the two of you up was just a bonus."

I'm trying hard not to punch the screen. "No Krysta, it *never* would have worked out for us in the end."

She gives a mocking smile. "Oh? Why not?"

"Because now I know it wasn't real. You've been chewing Mint."

For the first time, Krysta looks shocked.

Now it's my turn for a mocking smile. "That's right, I know your secret."

Celeres looks at me with a look of puzzlement.

"I knew you were a smart one," Krysta says.

Now my smile is a scowl. "You might have gotten me, but it would have been a lie."

"So what if I used Mint? Anyone would do it if they could."

"Oh?" Now my voice is getting louder. "What else would they do to get what they want? I know you were drugging Baxter. You just wanted to convince me to let you take him to the wasps for 'treatment.' I'm so glad and thankful that Ashlan was here to help, or I might have fallen for it."

"So you've got me all figured out."

"Not even close. I know you cloned me. Why? Is that your idea of a sex doll?"

Krysta recoils. "How could you say that?"

"Is it?"

"Don't talk about things you don't understand, Leigh."

"Then explain it to me, because I'd like to know. It just tried to kill me."

"Where is she?" she says, leaning closer to the phone.

"Back near the zoo somewhere, I don't know."

Ashlan snatches the phone and holds it so she's face to face with Krysta. "I demand to talk to Brose right now."

"You can't."

"Where is he?"

"You know, back near the zoo somewhere. I don't know."

"Tell me where he is, you *cunt!*" Ashlan hollers, her face crimson.

Krysta ends the call.

Chapter Fifty-Six

Escape

We're all quiet, save for Ashlan's loud, deep breathing. With a strangled cry, she hurls her phone against the cabin wall, then slumps into a chair, burying her face in her hands. "I chased him away when he needed me most. This is all my fault."

I kneel and try to soothe her by rubbing her back. "We'll find him."

"Maybe not right away," says Celeres.

Ashlan snaps her head up. "Of course, right away! He's your *best* friend."

"I know, but things are boiling right now. For all we know, we might have sparked a war. If we have any chance at all of saving him, we need to survive ourselves. And that means I need to get to my ship and lift us out of here. You two stay here."

I grab Ashlan's rifle from where she has it propped in the corner. "No way. I'm coming with you."

"No, you aren't," he says. "I just got you back. I can't lose you again."

I fix him with a glare. "Yes, I am. I'm already committed."

He looks behind him through the window, to the pillar of smoke from the zoo, and nods while opening the door. "Let's go. Ash, be ready to go in ten minutes. We'll fly back and drop a litter for you and the pups."

"If you think you're going without me, you're crazy," she says, grabbing the leashes on both dogs. "We're all going. Head for the buggy."

"Let's go," he says.

This is the first time I've ever seen Celeres look nervous. He says nothing else as we hustle to the buggy and load the dogs into the rear crate. I clamber into the back seat with Ashlan.

A terrible wood-cracking noise approaches the cabin. We look, and to our horror, deeper into the forest, entire trees shake and crash to the ground by whatever is coming, and coming fast. A low mechanical hum accompanies the sounds.

Ashlan looks at me with a look of panic. "I left the stinger back at the cabin!"

Celeres regards the falling trees. "We're out of time, ladies."

I'm not about to argue with him. Ashlan and I buckle our seat belts with quivering hands. "Go!" I yell above the din.

Celeres pounces on the accelerator. We barely make it a hundred feet before the buggy heaves to the side and we get stuck in a ditch. "Sorry! I didn't see it. Hold on."

For a few seconds, I think we'll have to get out and push, but after rocking back and forth and a lot of tire spinning, we break free and continue through the woods.

We burst into a clearing. *Big Seven* is about fifty yards

away. Just when I think we can't go faster, we do. A ramp-like slab of stone looms ahead of us, and he heads straight toward it.

"Hold on!" he yells.

Ashlan and I are already holding on with both hands and with every ounce of strength. We just look at each other as we head toward the natural ramp.

I close my eyes.

Ashlan screams.

In the next second, we're riding up the incline, and then…air.

When we land, the jolt almost knocks the air out of me, but it isn't any worse than my parachute landing.

I open my eyes and check the dogs. They're panting hard, but seem otherwise okay. We lurch to a halt.

We're right next to *Big Seven,* and its ladder is already down.

"I'll get her started while you two get the pups," says Celeres. "Soon as you're on board, close the hatch and we'll get out of here. Hurry, before that…thing gets to us."

Whatever's crashing through the trees is catching up. Celeres is already halfway up the ladder while Ash and I crawl out of the back.

I let the dogs loose and they join us on our jog to the ladder. Once we haul the dogs up and we're all inside, I steal one last glance at the tree line. A glistening black robot shaped like a gargantuan beetle bursts from the trees. It's about the size of a single-story house. Massive pincers at the end of its front legs cast trees aside with reckless abandon. If it grabbed a human with one of those, you'd go from squished to half-height in the space of a second. The dogs bark furiously and I slap the button to close the hatch.

"Celeres, go!" I yell.

I barely get the word out and *Big Seven* rises straight into the air.

Celeres looks over his shoulder. "Get strapped in quick. Did you see that thing?"

Without answering, we buckle up and each hold a dog.

Up, up we go. Ashlan presses her forehead against the small window by her seat. "We'll come back for you," she says in a quiet, sad voice.

I put a hand on her knee. "We'll find him, Ash. We will."

She nods, and focuses her attention on Milly, running her hand down the little dog's soft coat. "Maybe Milly could be mine."

"I bet she'd love that," I say, rubbing her knee.

Ashlan looks at me with a crooked smile. "Good." A small tear runs down her cheek.

Seconds later, the view turns into the blackness of space and glorious, multicolored stars.

"Whoa," says Celeres.

Ash and I turn our attention to the front of the ship. Outside, there are about twenty spaceships from *Sumerian*.

"Orders, sir?" comes a woman's voice from the intercom.

"Hey Amaiya, what are you guys doing here?" asks Celeres.

"Moon. She told us there was trouble."

"Oh, there's trouble, all right, but for now, stand down and head back to the station. We don't want this to look like an invasion. I have Doctor Carter with me, but we have to go back. Brose is down there."

"You don't want any help?"

"Not yet. I'll stay in touch. We're headed back down now."

"Roger," says Amaiya as the ships disperse.

"Why didn't you tell them Leigh's with us?" asks Ashlan.

Celeres raises an eyebrow. "You mean the woman who stole a ship and crashed it into the zoo? We need to keep her off the radar for the time being."

Ashlan's eyes go wide. "Wait. *That's* what happened?"

"Yeah, I'll fill you in later," I say.

"Fill us both in," says Celeres as he points the ship back to the planet and begins a descent.

"Where are you taking us?" I ask.

"The colony. I have an apartment there for times when I want to come down for a holiday and sleep somewhere other than a sleeping bag in the woods. We'll stay there while we figure out a plan to get Brose."

"You can keep me off the radar at the colony?"

"I think so. The apartment will be a safe house while I handle the messy details. I'll say you were a new trainee and lost control of your ship. That's what I'll tell *Sumerian*, and that's what I'll tell the wasps. They have no reason to suspect that we know how they weaponized the zoo, and that you destroyed their smoke stack on purpose."

As we fly over the colony, I'm struck with how big it is after only a couple of years. The "city" is very much like cities on earth, with a mixture of small buildings and streets separating them into blocks. Beyond the city are what look like housing plans. Funny how similar it all is to Earth. I expected it to look like some cyberpunk city from the movies, but alas. After a minute of letting us take in the sights, Celeres says, "Home sweet home," and we drift down.

We land atop a square building and clamber out of the ship. The zoo is far away, but I can still make out the column of smoke in the distance if I squint. I follow the smoke upwards, high into the sky. *Sumerian's* up there, glinting in the sunlight. Another large object approaches it, glinting just as much.

I point it out to them and ask what it is.

Celeres shades his eyes with his hand and squints into the heavens. "Well, I'll be damned. It's the colony transport, fresh outta Phoenix. Remember them?"

"Oh wow, it feels like a million years ago since we were there."

"Tell me about it, but you're kind of right. It's been a million *light* years."

I nod thoughtfully, grateful that Krysta isn't up there to process the new colonists. "I wonder who the unlucky ten would have been."

"Huh?"

"I'll explain later."

Celeres shrugs and leads us through a hatch and down into the apartment building.

Chapter Fifty-Seven

The Garden

It's been two weeks at the apartment, and we're all getting more than a little claustrophobic. On a positive note, Celeres feeds us like queens, and things have been great in the bedroom (and the bathroom, and um, the closet), but enough is enough. The weather has been spectacular and we just need to get out.

Ashlan is practically climbing the walls. We all want to get Brose back, but she's especially forlorn because still blames herself for pushing him away and letting him fall into Krysta's clutches. For all we know, his phone is dead or lost; all our calls just go straight to voicemail.

We just finished breakfast, and Celeres returns from the other room after a call. "I think I smoothed things over with *Sumerian* concerning the ship you crashed. McClure is being McClure and making everything difficult, but I went over his head. Now it's up to them to convince the Apocritans that it was an accident."

"So we can get out of here for a while?" I ask.

"Sure. What do you want to do?"

"I need to get to my cabin," says Ashlan as she wipes the pancake syrup from her chin.

"We'll join you," says Celeres.

"That's okay. I'm just going to send some drones out to sweep for Brose. Once I get them going, I'll grab the Vorefuser and rejoin you two. Besides, you have to take good care of Milly for me."

"You don't want to take her?" I ask.

"I want her to be with you and Baxter for now. She's expecting, you know. She needs her man."

"She's *pregnant?*" Celeres and I exclaim together.

"Yep. Life finds a way."

I give Baxter the naughty stare, and we all burst into laughter.

"Well, okay then," I say. "In that case, you still owe me, Cel."

"Owe you what?"

"Can you believe that after all of this, I've still never seen that garden of yours?"

He laughs. "No, I can't believe it. Then let's go. Should we bring the sleeping bag?"

"Yes!"

I make my way to the garden while Celeres sets up camp. It's a nice little patch surrounded by a picket fence. The rows of vegetables are straight and their composition shows just how meticulous he is.

I lean against the fence and breathe a sigh of contentment. Things with Cel have been going so well, and I'm genuinely happy with a man for the first time in my life. It occurs to me it wasn't so long ago that I leaned against a fence like this at home, looking out over our fields, filled with angst over Joe. I wonder whatever happened with him and Erica. No, actually I don't care. Things are so different now, and so am I.

The soothing smell of campfire wafts by me, and Celeres approaches from behind. I don't smell peaches like I used to—the effect of the Vorefuser wore off, thank heavens.

"Done setting up?" I ask.

"Yep," he says, slipping his arms around me, hugging me close from behind.

It reminds me of our first camping trip in the sleeping bag, and I press my bum into him. He kisses my neck.

"I'm worried about Brose," I say.

Celeres smooths my hair. "We'll get him back. I truly believe it."

"Let's check in on Ashlan before we call it a night."

"Okay."

"Celeres..."

"Hmm?"

"Thank you for rescuing Baxter. You risked your life for him, even when we weren't speaking to each other. Why?"

"I already told you. I love you, Leigh Shires."

I rest my head back against his chest.

He gives me a squeeze. "And thank you for coming to save *me*. I thought I could resist the pull of the Mint, but I was wrong. What you did... Talk about risking your life."

"And I already told you, Captain Nightingale, I love you, too."

He pulls me closer, and the dogs suddenly bound out of bushes to join us.

I can't help but to chuckle at the pair. "Party crashers."

His eyes sparkle at the sight. "I wonder how they pulled it off."

"Huh?"

"Bax and Milly. Ashlan said different species couldn't breed."

Thinking again about the sleeping bag, I say, "It's all in the angle, you know."

We both laugh, and I close my eyes and smile.

He turns me around, and then his lips are on mine.

A Note from Dan

Dear readers,

Thank you so much for joining Leigh and her friends on this adventure! I truly hope you enjoyed reading *Heartspeed* as much as I enjoyed writing it.

As a special thank you, I'd love to offer you a free copy of my short story, *Long Distance*. This story offers a glimpse into the colony and features some exciting tie-ins to the world of *Heartspeed*. To grab your copy, simply head over to my website and find it in the Short Stories tab:

www.danieljstutzman.com/short-stories

If you loved *Heartspeed*, I would be incredibly grateful if you could leave a review. Your feedback not only helps others discover the book, but also lets them know what to expect.

Thank you again for reading! I hope you'll stay in touch and continue to explore the worlds I create.

Warmly,
Daniel J. Stutzman

Acknowledgments

I have so many people to thank for helping bring *Heartspeed* to life.

First and foremost, my amazing wife, Pam. Her unwavering belief in me kept me going through the long hours and countless revisions. I truly couldn't have done it without her.

I am eternally grateful to my incredible developmental editing team—Rachel V. Knox, James Michael Starr, and Lissa Johnston. Their insightful feedback and unwavering support throughout the past five years have been invaluable. They saw the potential in this story from the very first chapter and helped me shape it into the book it is today.

To my Mom and Dad, thank you for always believing in me and supporting my, shall we say, *unconventional* path. Your love and encouragement mean the world to me.

And a special thanks to George E. Ambroe Jr., the first person who ever suggested that someone might actually pay for my words one day. You planted a seed of possibility into a high school kid's dreams that has finally blossomed.

About the Author

Daniel J. Stutzman hails from Pittsburgh, Pennsylvania, not too far from where Leigh grew up.

He enjoys spending time with his family, writing, trading, and gaming. He's a proper geek from the 80's.

facebook.com/WriteFright

x.com/WriteFright

instagram.com/writefright